ENGULFING EMMA

samantha christy

Saint Augustine, FL 32259

Cover designed by Letitia Hasser | RBA Designs

Cover model photo by Reggie Deanching | RplusMphoto.com

Cover model – Blake Sevani

ISBN: 9781706386346

For everyone who has been touched by 9/11.

ENGULFING EMMA

CHAPTER ONE

BRETT

"Mommy," Leo exclaims, carrying a picture of Amanda over to the table where I'm enjoying my morning coffee.

I pull him up on my lap, briefly looking at the smiling face of the woman who is now technically my ex-wife. I glance at the thick packet of legal papers that was delivered yesterday. I'm torn between wanting to think of the first six blissful years we spent together, and the two miserable ones that came after. The two that started the day our son was born—the day she checked out. Checked out of our marriage. Checked out as Leo's mom. Just checked out.

Our marriage might have just legally ended, but it's been over since the day Leo came into our lives twenty-five months ago.

Leo puts down the picture of Amanda and picks a crayon up off the table. He begins to color in the book I place in front of him. I watch him as he colors, thinking how much he looks like her, with his blond, slightly wavy hair, green eyes, and pouty lips. Sometimes I wonder if he really understands that Amanda is his mother or if he's just repeating what I say. Or what Bonnie, his nanny, tells him.

He hasn't even seen Amanda since his birthday six weeks ago. She comes around every once in a while for what seems more like an obligatory visit than a wanted one.

I rest my chin on top of his head, inhaling the fresh scent of his clean hair. "We're good, aren't we? I mean, it's pretty much been us for a long time now. Nothing's different. Those papers haven't really changed anything."

"Pony," Leo says, showing me the picture he colored.

I laugh, looking at the haphazard way he tried to stay inside the lines of the drawing using his purple crayon. "That's right. Pony. Good job, son." I ruffle his hair.

The floorboard behind me creaks as Bonnie comes into the room. "How are my two favorite boys?" She walks over to give us each a kiss.

Over the past two years, Bonnie has become like a grandmother to Leo and a mother to me. When Leo was only a few months old, Amanda decided that not only did Leo need a nanny, but a live-in one. I thought we were perfectly capable of raising a child without full-time help. I was more than willing to parent him when I wasn't working my two weekly twenty-four-hour shifts. Amanda basically had a nine-to-five job at the department store. Between the two of us, we only needed help a few days a week.

It became evident early on, however, even before we brought Leo home from the hospital, that Amanda didn't want to be a mother. She thought she did. For years before she got pregnant, we fantasized about how we'd be a perfect family. But when it happened, every dream I had about us being the family in the Norman Rockwell paintings went right out the window. We thought it was post-partum depression at first. But it soon became clear that Amanda didn't want Leo. And since Leo and I are a package deal, she didn't want me either.

"Oh, that's a lovely pony," Bonnie says in a grandmotherly tone. "What've you boys got planned today?"

"I thought I'd take him to the park," I say.

"Swing! Swing! Swing!" Leo says excitedly.

I laugh. "Yes. You can go on the swing and the slide and the horsey."

He wiggles off my lap and runs around the table, pretending to gallop.

"Should we play with Joey today?" I ask.

He doesn't answer but nods gleefully.

Joey is a few months younger than Leo. I work with Joey's dad, Denver, at the firehouse. Well, Denver is not technically Joey's dad yet, but he will be soon.

"Do you have any big plans today, Bonnie?" I ask.

"You know me. I'll take my usual walk to the market, stopping to feed the birds along the way. I think I'll help out at the soup kitchen tonight before I make our dinner."

"Why don't you let me cook for once?" I ask.

"Brett, sweetie, you know how much I like to cook. Any requests for dinner?"

"We'll eat whatever you want to prepare, Bonnie. You really are too good to us."

She waves off my comment. "Taking care of the two of you gives my life purpose."

Bonnie lost her husband five years ago, having never had children of her own. It was awkward at first, a stranger living in our house. Someone who heard every fight. Every squeak of our bed when we occasionally made love. Every silent dinner when

Amanda stayed late at work. But now, I can't imagine life without her. She truly has become like family.

I get up and put my coffee cup in the sink. Then I tuck the thick envelope, signifying the end of an era, behind my laptop on the counter. I'll deal with it later.

"Come on, buddy." I scoop Leo into my arms. "Let's go."

On our way to the park, we duck into the corner market for a few bottles of water. While I'm paying, I hear sirens and then a fire truck goes past us. Leo bounces in my arms. "Daddy truck. Daddy truck."

"That's just like Daddy's truck, isn't it?"

I like to think he's proud of me, or at least that he will be someday. It took a lot of training to get where I am, the lieutenant of Squad 13. I've taken every single course and gotten every certification, being both a trained paramedic and a hazmat responder. I made the decision years ago, on the fateful day I lost my mother, that I would become someone who would make a difference, just as she did.

"He's soooooo cute," someone says behind us.

I turn around and see a young girl staring at Leo. "Thanks. I think so too."

The girl places a bottle of iced cappuccino and a Pop-Tart on the counter. I raise my eyebrows at her. "Aren't you a little young to be drinking coffee?"

"I'm twelve," she says, like that explains everything.

I laugh. "Okay then. Have a nice day, uh…" I wait for her to offer her name.

"Evie." She extends her hand confidently, like we're in a business meeting.

"Evie—that's an unusual name. But it's great."

"I have an unusual but great mom."

"Well, Evie, I'm Brett, and this is Leo, and it's been nice meeting you."

"You too," she says, swiping a debit card through the machine like she's done it a thousand times.

I look at her as we leave the store. This twelve-year-old acts more like she's twenty-five. I glance around, hoping she's not alone. Although I've always considered our neighborhood safe, we are in Brooklyn, and unfortunately, I've seen more than once what can happen to kids who are left unattended.

When I look back through the window, I see a woman join her, an older sister perhaps, and feel a sense of relief. Evie hands the lady the cappuccino and then she takes a big bite of her Pop-Tart. I chuckle at my thought that the coffee was for her.

The lady with Evie gazes out the window and looks at the passersby, her eyes stopping on Leo as she smiles at him. Then her attention returns to Evie and she gestures toward the door.

"Come on, buddy, let's go find those swings." I put Leo down and grab his hand as we turn the corner and go to his favorite place.

CHAPTER TWO

EMMA

"I'm going to miss you." Lisa pulls me in for a hug.

I laugh as she squeezes me hard. "It's not like we're never going to see each other. We're still doing Taco Tuesday's this summer."

"I know. But not seeing you every day will take the wind out of my sails."

"You're crazy," I tell her. "Go enjoy your ten weeks off. Stay out late. Sleep in. Rejuvenate."

She gives me a sideways look. "Oh, like you won't long to be back here in a matter of weeks. I'll bet you've already cried because you're missing your students."

I shrug. I don't need her to know I've shed tears more than once. I miss every single one of them. Even little Bobby Riggs, who was a thorn in my side all year.

I love my job more than anything. A lot of teachers can't wait for the last day of school. In fact, they are worse than the students, counting down those last few weeks before summer. Not me. I wish we had year-round school. I dread the last days of school, and I look forward to the first day like an excited kid on Christmas Eve.

Lisa picks up the rest of her bags and looks around my classroom. "As usual you're dragging this out. How come you're always one of the last to leave?"

I take a moment to admire the drawings made by my students that are still pinned on the wall. I can't bear to get rid of them. I swear I'll soon need to rent a storage unit large enough to hold everything I take home.

I unpin some of the drawings and start a pile. "I'll bet Becca and Kelly are still here."

"You're probably right. Maybe I'll stop by the fifth-grade hallway and say goodbye."

"You'd better," I say sarcastically. "It's not like you won't be seeing them every Tuesday this summer."

"I know. I'm just going to miss you guys so much. And I'm not going to see you *every* Tuesday."

"That's right. You'll be busy traveling the world with that hot husband of yours. Where is he taking you this time? Paris? Rome? Morocco?"

She looks embarrassed. "Yeah."

My jaw drops. "All three?"

"And Dubai."

I push her toward the door. "What are you waiting for, girl? Start packing."

She leans in for one more hug. "Have a great summer, Emma."

"I plan on it."

After watching Lisa walk down the first-grade hallway, I duck back into my classroom and pack up the rest of my stuff. We're not allowed to leave anything. The school provides us with boxes, and they have people to haul them down to the basement for storage.

The school is leased out for other purposes during the summer, and they don't want our belongings cluttering up the classrooms.

I think about the coming summer. I don't travel much, like some of the other teachers. I don't like to fly. My summers are flexible, as I teach an online English class for high school students, so I could travel if I wanted to. I even got my passport a few years ago, intending to take a vacation to Bermuda. But I chickened out at the last minute, refusing to get on the plane. My daughter, Evelyn, doesn't seem to mind that we don't travel, however. She hates leaving her friends for too long, and she loves her summer camps—both the sleep-away and the one here in the city. And then there's Mom, who probably has a thousand vacation days saved up, but she never takes them except at Thanksgiving and Christmas. So, when we do travel, it's usually limited to long weekends.

Last summer we spent a few days at Niagara Falls. The summer before that, we rented a little cottage in Vermont for five days. The one before that, we took Evelyn to a few amusement parks along the East Coast so she could ride roller coasters.

Not exactly world travelers. But I like my life. I like the way the three of us support each other. Evelyn and my mother have always been my best friends.

I hold back more tears as I tuck the last of the drawings into my bag. My first-graders colored pictures of what they will miss the most about school. Bobby Riggs drew the jungle gym in the courtyard behind the school. Of course he did. He hates school.

Karly Hilliard drew a picture of Bobby Riggs. Poor girl has a thing for bad boys, and she's only six years old.

Most of the other students drew pictures of a woman with long brown hair and hazel eyes. *Me.* They drew pictures of me when I asked them to draw what they would miss the most.

I scan the room once more before I turn off the light and shuffle slowly down the hallway.

The school is almost deserted, most of the other teachers having already cleared out their things over the past few days. I think about heading around the corner to see if Becca and Kelly are still in their classrooms, but I know that would just be prolonging the inevitable. I have to leave my favorite place on earth eventually. I might as well do it now.

When I reach the front, I look back at the long empty hallway. "Goodbye," I say loudly, my voice echoing off the cement floor and walls. Nobody says it back, and that makes me sad.

I struggle to get my rolling cart through the front door, being careful nothing falls off inside because the doors will lock behind me and there's nobody left to open them. It gets hung up on the floor mat. I'm leaning down to free it when I hear a commotion in the street.

Sirens are coming from both directions, and people are yelling and running. I leave the rolling cart where it is and walk down the front steps.

That turns out to be the worst decision of my life.

A guy wielding a gun walks around the corner. A few people surround him. People who look terrified.

"Do what I say, motherfucker, or I'll shoot you," the gunman says.

The thin man on the other end of his words holds up his hands in surrender.

The sirens get closer and the guy with the gun panics. I turn to run back up the stairs into the safety of the school. But it's too late.

"Stop right there, lady!" he shouts.

I turn around to see him dragging his entourage of hostages closer to me. I say a silent prayer, hoping my daughter will not have to go through what I did when I was a child.

I hold my hands up, showing him I have no intention of fighting. "W-what do you w-want?"

He waves his gun at the door that's still propped open by my cart. "Is there anyone in there?"

"Uh … uh …" I'm trying to think clearly, but all I see are the faces of Evelyn and Mom.

"Answer me, lady!" he shouts. "Is there anyone in the fucking building?"

I don't know what to say. If I tell him it's almost empty, will I be endangering the lives of the few people still inside? If I lie and say there are a lot of people in there, will he hurt me?

"Maybe a few," I say. "The school year is over."

"Hold the door open!" he screams. "Do it now!"

My legs almost fail me as I climb the last steps to the front door and attempt to nudge my cart aside and hold the door open like he told me. The whole time I'm thanking God that school is out and there are no kids inside.

I can't get the cart fully out of the way, and the gunman isn't happy about it. "Are you completely useless?" he asks, violently pushing it inside.

Then the loudest noise I've ever heard echoes off the walls, hurting my ears. A young man—a hostage—drops to the floor, yelling in agony.

The gunman looks stunned that his weapon went off. "Shit," he says, looking nervously out at the street. Then he tries to open the door that leads behind the front counter, but it's locked. He kicks it in, breaking the doorframe. He points to me and the guy standing next to me. "You two, pull the kid over behind that counter."

I look down at the injured man, who is barely more than a boy. He can't be over eighteen. His hands are covered in blood, and I cringe.

"My leg," he cries.

As we drag him behind the front desk, we leave a trail of bright-red blood. It runs all the way from the front door, around the corner, and over the threshold of the admin door. We settle him against the wall, and blood pools under his leg. The kid's face is going ashen, and I'm not sure if it's from blood loss or because he's terrified.

My eyes dart to the door that leads back into the classroom hallways and I wonder if Becca and Kelly are still here. If so, did they hear the gunshot? Will they come investigate?

The gunman paces around as if trying to figure out what to do. I take a moment to study him, wondering if I'll need to describe him to the police if he escapes. His complexion is dark, Hispanic perhaps, though he doesn't speak with an accent. He's young, maybe the same age as the kid he shot, and he's got black hair. He's tall and lanky. He doesn't seem high, just mad. And a little scared.

While he's distracted, I pull out my phone to text my friends and warn them to stay put or exit out the back, but the phone is slapped out of my hand. It cracks as it hits the floor ten feet away.

"Everyone gimmie your phones," our captor says.

The three other people in the room—a woman and two men—show varying degrees of compliance.

The thin man looks like he wants to jump the guy with the gun. The black-haired woman puts a hand on his arm. "Do what he says. He's already shot one of us."

The gunman runs his hands through his hair, pounding the weapon repeatedly against his head. "I didn't do it on purpose."

"Doesn't matter," the thin man says, handing over his cell phone. "You're going to get charged with a lot more than robbing that store."

"What store?" I ask.

"Shettleman's Grocery."

My hand covers my mouth, stifling my gasp as I picture the nice old couple who run the small corner store next to the school. "Oh my gosh, are they okay?"

"Will the two of you shut up?" the gunman says. He looks down at the man he shot, who is screaming in pain. "And shut him up too. I need to think." He points to me. "You were coming out of the school. How many ways in and out of here are there?"

I gesture to the door at the rear of the administration office. "There are several emergency exits beyond that door, but they are locked from the outside."

Red and blue lights flash in front of the building. We are corralled into the back corner of the office, out of sight of the windows.

The gun is pointed at the thin man. "You, go around the counter and barricade the front doors with that couch and chairs. Try anything, and I'll shoot you too."

The man pales and does what he's told.

The kid with the gunshot wound is still screaming.

"I told you to shut him the fuck up," the gunman says to no one in particular.

I look at all the blood on the floor. The woman with black hair is pressing her hands against the wound, trying to stop the bleeding, but it's not doing much good.

I ask, "Does anyone here have medical training?" I get blank stares. "The blood is bright red. I think that's bad. The bullet must have hit an artery."

"How do you know that shit?" the guy with the gun asks.

"I, uh … watch a lot of TV."

The kid cries out again.

"I can't think with him screaming like that." He walks over and kicks the kid's leg, making him bellow even louder.

I position myself between the gun and the injured kid. I feel the need to protect him. It wasn't so long ago that he was a student. Maybe even in a school like this one.

I take a deep breath and confront our assailant. "Did you kill anyone at Shettleman's?"

The guy looks pissed off. "I didn't kill no one," he says, patting a pocket in his coat. "I was just there for the cash. I ain't no murderer."

I gesture to the kid on the floor. "Not yet, but if he dies, you will be."

He looks at the screaming kid and then at me. "Well why don't you make it your job to make sure he don't die?"

"My job?"

He points his gun to the door on my right. "What's in there?"

"It's a storage room."

"Open it."

I step over and open the door. He keeps me in his peripheral vision as he pops his head in and looks around. "Perfect. No windows. Take him in there. That way I don't have to hear him."

"Take him in *there?*" I ask.

"Yeah, and you damn well better make sure he don't die. If he does, there won't be no reason to keep you or anyone else around. Got it?"

"You want me to put him in a closet and try to help him? I'm not a doctor. I teach first grade."

"You knew about the blood," he says. "You're the best chance he's got. Now get the fuck in the closet." He turns to the thin man. "Move the kid inside."

The door to the back hallway opens, and Becca and Kelly walk in.

"Run!" I scream.

Horror crosses their faces as they see the blood on the floor, the barricade at the front door, and the man with the gun.

Kelly, who is behind Becca, manages to turn around and run back into the hallway. She tries to grab Becca, but Becca is frozen in place and doesn't move. The gunman hustles over and pulls her inside.

"Becca!" Kelly screams from down the hall.

"Sit your pretty ass down over there with the rest of them," he says. He turns to the man who just put the kid in the storage room. "Find some shit to block off that door."

"Like what?" the man asks.

"Teacher," the gunman says to me. "Suggestions?"

"Um … there are some desks in the storage closet. And boxes of paper—those are pretty heavy."

He waves the gun at the man doing all his heavy lifting. "Do it."

Becca tries to ask what's going on, but he shuts her up. I stare at Becca. Becca stares at me. We're both wondering how this is going to play out.

When the gunman is busy making sure the door is securely blocked, the man who moved the stuff whispers to me, "I saw a box of phones in that room."

The kid moans in pain, drawing our assailant's attention back to us. "What are you waiting for, teacher? Get in there."

I step inside the room, already feeling claustrophobic and wondering if this storage room will become my tomb.

I look at Becca. Tears roll down her cheeks as the door closes. And then it's quiet. The large storage room door muffles the sounds on the other side.

The kid cries out again, reminding me I have an important job to do. I grab a few shirts from the lost and found box, drop to my knees, and press them to his wound. When he screams, I try to calm him. "I'm Emma. What's your name?"

"C-carter. Goddamn, it hurts."

"I know, and I'm sorry. But we have to control the bleeding. How old are you, Carter?"

"Nineteen."

"You look strong," I tell him. "That's good. Can you hold these on your leg while I look around for anything that can help us?"

He puts a shaky hand on the blood-soaked shirts, not able to keep much pressure on it. "I don't feel so good."

"Hang in there, Carter."

I riffle through the boxes, looking for anything I can use, when I remember the man said he saw phones. If I can call 911, surely they will tell me how to help Carter. Maybe they can help *all* of us. But there may not be anywhere to plug a phone in, and even if there is, we're stuck in a storage room. It's not like I can stitch up his leg or remove a bullet with hole punches and staplers.

"Here they are," I say, finding the box.

I move other boxes out of the way, examining the lower walls in my search for a phone jack. I find one behind the leg of a shelf. "Thank God," I say.

I pull out one of the phones, watching the door the entire time. What if the gunman opens the door and sees me with the phone? Will he shoot me?

Knowing I don't have a choice, I plug it in and pull out another shirt from the lost and found, figuring I can use it to camouflage the phone on the floor. Then I pick up the handset, never happier to hear a dial tone in all my twenty-seven years.

CHAPTER THREE

BRETT

My heart sinks as I listen to the voice over the loudspeaker, dispatching us to the elementary school for a shooting and hostage situation. I can't help but think about Leo and how he will be going to that school in a few more years.

Captain Dickerson, or J.D., as we call him, sees my concern as we race to our respective trucks. "School's been out for a week, so more than likely there aren't any kids involved."

I shake my head. "We can only hope."

I hop in the passenger seat of Squad 13. Justin Neal takes the wheel, and Cameron and Miles sit in the rear. We follow Engine 319 out of the firehouse and head down a few blocks and around the corner.

Justin pulls up and waits for the police to direct him where to park. In situations like this, our rigs are often used to block traffic, create a perimeter, or get in the way of a potential escape route for the perps. Justin parks where they tell him, and we exit from the "safe" side of the truck, standing by to get our orders from the chief.

On calls like this, it's a lot of wait and see. Sometimes they are false alarms. But judging from the onslaught of NYPD vehicles and S.W.A.T. team trucks, I'm guessing this is the real deal.

We stand behind our rigs, everyone from my company gathering together.

"Anyone know what's up?" Sebastian Briggs, the driver of 319, asks.

Denver Andrews, who's also on Engine 319, shouts to a policeman. "Jake. Hey, man. What's going on?"

Jake walks over. "Here's what I know so far. We think the perp robbed the grocery store on the corner. Someone inside the store called the police, and before he could get away, we had two units en route. The robber must have heard the sirens and panicked, grabbing bystanders to give him cover, and then he ducked into the school, taking several people with him. A teacher ran out one of the fire exits. She said two of her friends are still inside, along with a few other people. She said there was a lot of blood on the floor. A gunshot was heard right before they disappeared into the school. We still aren't sure if he's working alone or if there is another perp with them."

"Shit," Denver says. "So this is a real live hostage situation."

"I'm afraid so," Jake says. His radio goes off. "My sergeant is calling. I'll try to keep you updated."

Justin waves at our surroundings. "All this because some addict was probably seeking drug money."

J.D. looks more than a little concerned. "That's the scary part. If this guy is whacked out on drugs, you never know what he might do."

We stand around and speculate about what could be happening, but whatever it is, it's happening slowly. NYPD and the S.W.A.T. team have their protocols to follow. I suppose they are trying to get in touch with the gunman to see if they can get him to surrender.

Chief Mitzell is being briefed by the police. He gets a call and heads over to our rig. He holds up his phone and motions to it. "Nine-one-one is being bombarded with calls right now, as you can imagine. Someone claiming to be inside the building needs immediate medical help. I'd like a paramedic to get on the line."

I step forward. "I'll do it, Chief."

He hands me the phone. "I'll have them transfer the call to your cell if you give them your number. After you handle the crisis, the police will need to talk to whoever is on the other end of the line."

"Understood," I say before reciting my cell number into his phone.

A few seconds later, my phone rings. It's a 911 operator. She patches me through to the caller. I find a quieter place to talk. "This is Lt. Cash. I'm a paramedic. Someone needs medical attention?"

"Oh, thank God," a woman says in a hushed voice. "He's been shot and has been losing blood. I'm putting pressure on the wound, but it won't stop bleeding. He says he feels sick. The two of us have been locked in a storage closet. I don't know why that guy is doing this, but he says he'll kill me or the others if I don't save Carter. He doesn't know I have a phone. I found it in a box. I—"

"Ma'am, slow down." I motion for Denver to bring me something to write on and then I jot down the information I think is pertinent for the police. "What's your name?"

"Emma. Emma Lockhart."

"Okay, Emma. I'm Brett, and I'm going to do my best to help you and the gunshot victim. Is he awake and alert?"

"Yes."

"Where has he been shot?"

"In the leg."

"Above or below the knee?"

"Above. There's a lot of blood."

"Damn. The bullet might have nicked an artery. If it had torn right through, he might not still be alive. But since he's still conscious, he might be bleeding out slowly. Can you take a picture of the wound and text it to me?"

"Uh, no. I'm not on a cell phone. This is a landline. Like I said, we're stuck in a storage room and everyone else is in the main office."

I jot down some notes as uniformed NYPD officers look over my shoulder.

"How many perps?" one of them asks.

I mute the phone. "Do you mind if I try to save this guy's life first? The woman is already panicking. I can hear it in her voice." I unmute. "Emma? If the gunman opens the door, put the phone down—wait, does it have a speaker?"

"I, um, hold on. I don't think so."

"Okay, listen to me, Emma. You have to stop the bleeding, or your patient is going to lose consciousness and bleed out."

"Oh, God. He's going to kill us all if that happens. He said if Carter dies, it won't matter if anyone else does too."

"We're not going to let that happen. First, I need you to elevate the leg to slow the flow of blood. Can you do that?"

"I did that already," she says.

"Good. That's good thinking. Are you or Carter wearing a belt?"

I hear her shuffling around. "No. No belt."

"Do you have rope or something else that can be used as a tourniquet to stop the bleeding?"

It sounds like she's riffling through boxes. "No, there's nothing." The panic in her voice is getting worse.

"Emma, I know this is an impossible situation, but try to stay calm. We're going to help Carter. You and me, okay?"

"Okay."

"Can you ask one of the people on the other side of the door for a belt?"

"You want me to go out there?" she asks, her quiet voice rising in horror.

"It may be the only way to save Carter."

"All right." She takes a few deep breaths. "I keep thinking that Carter is someone's son. He's only nineteen. What if this had happened to Evelyn? I'd want someone to do everything they could to help her."

"Evelyn?"

"My daughter."

"I think Evelyn has a very brave mother. I can tell that about you. Do you have a pen? I'd like you to write down my number in case we get cut off."

She laughs quietly. But it's not a genuine laugh. How could it be? "Pens I have. About five boxes of them. Go ahead with your number."

After I give it to her, I ask, "Are you ready to open the door? You'll need to put the phone down and cover it. But leave the line open so I can hear what's going on."

"I'm putting it down now. Please don't go anywhere."

"I'll be here, Emma. Go ahead."

I hear her put the phone down and then I hear another voice. "You're going out there? Are you crazy?"

That must be Carter. At least he's still talking.

"I have to," Emma says. "You're losing too much blood."

"Be careful," Carter tells her.

I hear a knocking sound. "Hello?" Emma shouts. "Can you hear me? I need a few things in here."

She bangs on the door a few more times, and then I hear an angry voice. "I thought I told you to stay in here, you stupid bitch."

My heart sinks. What have I done to her?

CHAPTER FOUR

EMMA

Face to face with the gunman, my heart is beating out of my chest. He's so close I can smell the rankness of his breath.

"I know you told me to stay in here," I say, "but you also told me to keep him alive. I need a few things to do that. He's bleeding very badly."

He looks over his shoulder, presumably to make sure nobody is going to jump him from behind, but from what I can see, everyone is sitting in a corner, huddled together. Becca's mascara is running down her face, and she's holding hands with the other woman.

Our annoyed captor glances at Carter, who's still moaning. He pauses before giving me an answer. I wonder if he's weighing his options. "What do you need?" he asks.

"A belt," I say. "A bottle of water, and some hand sanitizer."

He looks down at his own belt, but then shouts behind him, "You, Skeletor, take off your belt and slide it over here." His attention turns to Becca. "You go through those bags and shit over there. Chicks always keep water and hand sanitizer in their purses."

Becca crawls across the floor to where he's thrown our things. She scavenges them, holding up her bounty.

The gunman looks at me impatiently. "Don't just stand there, teacher. Go get them."

I walk over to Becca and grab a small bottle of sanitizer and two full water bottles.

"Are you okay?" she whispers.

"Hey, Goldilocks!" the guy shouts at her. "No fucking talking."

I nod at her, pick the belt up off the ground, and return to the storage room. But not before I look at the faces of the other hostages. I wish I knew their names so I could tell Brett. Then again, it's probably better if their families don't know what's going on. They can remain blissfully unaware that their loved ones are sitting ducks, ten feet from the wrong end of a gun.

My mother would be worried sick. I hope this isn't all over the news. If they mention the name of the school, I'm sure twenty of her friends will call her to find out if I'm okay. And when she tries to call me and I don't answer, she'll know I'm not. *Oh, God.* To put her through this twice in one lifetime is more than any woman should have to face.

I've never been happier that Evelyn is far away at camp. I'm usually sad when she's gone. And she's gone for two whole weeks this time. She left just yesterday. I cried, of course. But now, my eyes well up with tears of relief. She's not going to hear about this. And maybe if I can save Carter and we get out of this, she'll be none the wiser.

Carter. I try to clear my head and focus on what I need to do. Everything hinges on my being able to save him.

I walk back into the storage room but turn around before the gunman can close the door. "Thank you," I say.

His brows draw down. He's confused as to why I'm thanking the guy pointing a gun at me.

"I'm Emma, by the way." I gesture at the kid on the floor. "That's Carter." Maybe if he sees us as people, he'll be less likely to hurt us. "I know this was an accident."

I almost think he's going to tell me his name, but instead, his icy demeanor returns. "You don't know dick, teacher."

He slams the door in my face.

I sink to the floor, bile rising in my throat. I breathe deeply and then crawl over to Carter, who doesn't look as good as he did a few minutes ago. I touch his hand. It feels clammy. "Carter, are you still with me?"

He moans.

I glance back at the door, confirming it's still shut before I pick up the phone. "Brett, are you there?"

"I'm here," he says. "Good thinking with the water and hand sanitizer. And telling him your names—that was brilliant. He's beginning to see you as more than just hostages."

"I was terrified."

"I know. You're doing great. Do you have a belt?"

"Yes."

"Good. Find the bullet wound. There may be two, an entrance and an exit wound. He won't like it when you move his leg. He may even scream. But it's important you do it."

"Okay. Hold on."

I sanitize my hands. Then I grab another shirt from lost and found and show it to Carter. "I'm going to put this in your mouth. I have to look at your leg and it might hurt. Bite down on the shirt. Scream into it if you have to. But we don't want to give the guy out there a reason to come in here and see me on the phone. Do you understand?"

He nods.

"Here we go then."

I push up his shorts. Blood trickles out of a hole two or three inches above his knee. I roll him onto his side and look for an exit wound. There is so much blood caked on the back of his leg, I can't see much. I open a bottle of water and spill some on his leg, then carefully wipe the back of his thigh. This makes him scream into the shirt.

I quickly cover the receiver in case the gunman opens the door.

I roll Carter onto his back again and wait to make sure our captor doesn't come in the room. When I'm convinced he won't, I pick up the phone. "I only see one bullet hole just above his knee."

"Good job. Now wrap the belt around his upper thigh a few inches above the wound. You're going to have to pull it tight, tighter than you think it needs to be. If you can't poke a notch in the belt to secure it, you'll have to use something to tighten it. A metal ruler maybe. Slip the belt around it and turn it around and around like a corkscrew, tightening the belt to the leg."

"Hold on."

I do what he says, but it's hard. Carter fights when I try to tighten the belt. Then he goes limp.

"Oh, God. Carter? Carter wake up." I shake him gently.

I pick up the phone. "I think I did it wrong. He passed out."

"Emma, listen to me. You didn't do it wrong. Look at the wound. Do you see blood coming out? Wipe it clean and watch for a second."

I do what he says. "There's no more blood."

"You're doing great. How's Carter's breathing?"

"A little fast, but he's not hyperventilating or anything."

"Can you check his pulse?"

"I know how to do that, but I don't have a clock to count how fast it is."

"I've got one. I'll tell you when to start counting. Just tell me when you're ready."

I pick up his arm and lay his wrist on my lap. "Ready."

"Start now."

I close my eyes and count the pulsations in my head until Brett tells me to stop. "I counted seventy-two. Is that bad?"

"Normal is between sixty and one hundred beats per minute. I had you count for thirty seconds so his pulse is one hundred and forty-four. He's lost blood and may be in the early stages of hypovolemic shock. But it's not high enough to panic, okay?"

"What's high enough to panic?" I ask.

"Let's not worry about that yet. There is a man here who wants to talk to you. A police officer. You are our only contact inside the building. He wants to ask you a few questions."

I shake my head vehemently even though I know he can't see me. But I really don't want him to give the phone to someone else. Brett's voice is calm and soothing, and he's my only tie to the outside. "No. I don't want to talk to anyone else. Brett, please."

"Okay, okay," he says, assuringly.

His words become muffled. He must be cupping a hand over his phone. Then he's back. "How about if the police officer tells me what to ask you, would that be all right?"

I slump against the wall next to Carter. "I guess that would be okay."

"Good. They want to know how many gunmen are inside."

"Just the one," I say.

"Are you sure? There wasn't anyone else who came in the school with you who could be working with him?"

"I'm pretty sure. I mean, he kept making this one skinny guy do everything, but he was just caught up in it, like I was. He looked as scared as everyone else. It even looked like he might jump him at one point."

"Did the gunman tell you his name?"

"Yeah, we're BFFs now, in case you hadn't noticed." I laugh weakly. "Of course not."

"I didn't think so. They want to know exactly where you are in the building and where the other hostages are being held. Are any of them tied up?"

I watch Carter's chest rise and fall as I give Brett as many details as I can. I've worked here for three years, and I could find my way around the place blindfolded.

"You're being very helpful, Emma. They are asking how many hostages there are."

"Aside from Carter and me, three others, but I don't know their names except for the teacher. Her name is Becca Jamison, but don't call her family. They would be devastated. You can't let them call, okay, Brett? I know all too well what that feels like. Please don't let them call."

My pulse races as I remember when my mother got the call that the World Trade Center was attacked, and my father's company had gone to help.

"How do you know what it feels like?" he asks.

I close my eyes. I've thought about my dad a lot today. I've also thought about my mom and Evelyn, and what losing me would do to them. "I lost my father on 9/11."

"You—"

He stops talking, and I think maybe we lost the connection. "Brett, are you there?"

"I'm here," he says. "I lost my mother that day."

"Oh, no. Really?"

"She was a nurse who ran in to help. How about your dad?"

"A firefighter. A lieutenant here in Brooklyn."

"Damn. I'm sorry," he says, emotion bleeding from his voice.

"I'm sorry for your loss too."

"This is going to turn out differently. Evelyn is not losing her mother today. How old is she?"

"Twelve."

"I have a child too. A son. He's two."

"What's his name?" I ask.

"Leo."

"I like that name."

"Is there anyone you'd like me to call for you, Emma?"

My heart pounds, and I feel the walls closing in on me. "I don't want you to hang up."

"I won't. I promise. I can use someone else's phone. Can I call your husband for you? Maybe even patch you through?"

"I'm not married. It's just Evelyn and me. And my mom. It's always just been the three of us."

"Your mom never remarried?" he asks.

"No."

"Neither did my dad. He moved to Florida when my younger sister graduated high school four years ago."

"Florida's nice."

"You've been?"

"No. I just assume it's nice. And I think maybe I'm rambling to keep you on the phone, because I'm feeling claustrophobic in this closet. How long do you think he'll keep us in here?"

"You don't have to worry about keeping me on the phone. I'm not going anywhere. Even if you don't want to talk, I'm here.

The police are still trying to contact the gunman, but he won't answer the phone in the office. They don't know what he wants."

"I don't know either," I say. "I mean, except that he wanted money. That's why he robbed Shettleman's. I assume he wants this finished as much as we do, but he's probably scared. He didn't mean to shoot Carter. But the fact that he hasn't let us go is very upsetting."

"It is. I'm sorry you have to go through this."

"Can you just talk to me?" I ask. "Tell me something about yourself. About Leo. Or your wife. Anything to get my mind off this."

"Well, let's see. Leo is great. He recently became this little chatter box. He's so curious about everything. He loves the park. And dogs. He loves dogs. But his nanny is allergic so we can't have one. Sometimes I'll take him to the dog park or the pet store so he can play with them."

"I love dogs, too. But I don't think it's fair to leave them alone all day. It's why I've never gotten one. So, Leo has a nanny? That must mean your wife works as well."

"It's just Leo and me," he says.

"Oh, I'm sorry. I didn't mean to assume anything."

"It's fine. I did the same thing with you. We recently divorced."

"That sucks."

"Yeah, well, we didn't really have a marriage for the last two years."

"Two years? Isn't that how old Leo is?"

"Yes. That's when Amanda completely shut down and pulled away. She never really wanted to be a mom."

"I love being a mom. I don't know what I'd do without Evelyn. She's away at camp for two weeks, and it's killing me."

"I love being a dad. I can't imagine life without Leo."

Carter moans, and I lean over to check on him, feeling his pulse and determining it's about the same as before.

"How's he doing?" Brett asks.

"Okay, I think."

"Is the tourniquet still tight?"

I look and see very little new blood around the wound. "Yes. Listen, how long can this thing stay on him? I know we need it to stop the bleeding, but isn't it stopping all blood circulation to his leg? That can't be good."

"It's not good. We shouldn't keep it on him longer than an hour, or we'll risk ischemia."

"Does that mean his leg could *die*?" I whisper so Carter can't hear me.

"It's possible. We'll assess him closer to the hour mark. If he's regained consciousness, we may try to remove the tourniquet for a few minutes to feed fresh blood to the lower leg. But let's hope this doesn't go on that long."

I sigh. I can't believe this is happening. It's like a nightmare. "How did I get here?"

"Wrong place, wrong time," he says. "That's really what it boils down to."

"I'd rather be anywhere else in the world."

"I know you would. If you could be—where would you be? It can be anywhere."

I close my eyes and think for a minute. "Myrtle Beach."

He laughs. "Emma, I said *anywhere,* and you pick a place you can get to in less than a day?"

"My aunt lives there. She has a house on the beach just north of the city. We would go there every summer for vacation. My mom and I haven't visited since my dad died. We just couldn't bring ourselves to return to a place that reminded us so much of him."

"Tell me about him," he says. "I mean, if it's not too difficult."

I settle against the wall and think of all the best parts of my dad—which was pretty much *every* part. "He was amazing. He only worked a few twenty-four-hour shifts a week, and when he was home, he spent every minute of the day with me when my mom was at work. He took me ice skating in the winter, boating in the summer, and when I went to school, he walked me there, and he'd be waiting for me when I got out. I know it's been a long time, and I'm probably only remembering the good parts, but he really was the best dad."

"It sounds like it. That's how I want it to be for Leo and me. Bonnie—that's Leo's nanny—lives with us because that's what Amanda wanted when he first came home. She's more like family than his nanny. She's there when I'm on shift, and she watches him when I go out with my friends, but for the most part, I'm Leo's primary caregiver whenever I can be."

"I think you must be a lot like my dad."

"I hope so."

"Brett?"

"Yeah."

"I'm really worried about Carter. His pulse is racing, and he's breathing like he's running a marathon."

"What does his skin feel like?"

I put a hand on his head and then his arm. "Cool and clammy."

"Can you open his eyes and look at his pupils? I'm not sure how much light you have in there, but I need to know if they are enlarged."

"Hold on."

I cradle the phone with my shoulder and open his eyelids with my fingers. "They could be enlarged, but I don't have a flashlight in here to tell for sure."

"Damn it."

"What is it?"

He blows a breath into the phone. "I think he's going into hypovolemic shock."

"What does that mean exactly?"

"It means …" He hesitates, and I know the next words out of his mouth won't be good. "It means he'll die if he doesn't get a blood transfusion."

My eyes well up with tears that quickly spill over. I'm already crying for Evelyn and my mom. I'm crying because I know the phone call they'll get will devastate them.

"Emma, are you listening?"

"I'm here. What can I do?"

"You can get the gunman to let me in."

CHAPTER FIVE

BRETT

"Let you in? Are you crazy?" she yells in my ear.

"Emma, be quiet. You don't want him to catch you on the phone."

"Are you crazy?" she whispers loudly.

"It's the only way to save him. Knock on the door again. Don't tell him you're on the phone. Tell him Carter will die in a matter of minutes if he doesn't get blood. Lie and say you've had some kind of emergency training because you're a teacher. Tell him you're sure of the situation. Make up whatever you can to get me in there. Either that or maybe he'll understand the severity of things and let Carter out. Either way we need to help Carter."

There is a long pause.

"Emma?"

"Brett, I think I'm having a heart attack."

My adrenaline spikes. "I really doubt that. You're probably having a panic attack. I need you to sit down. Or better yet, lie down and put your head back in case you pass out."

I hear movement and then she says, "I'm lying down next to Carter."

I can hear the quickness in her breath. She needs to calm down. "Listen to me, Emma. You have to breathe. Take in a deep breath for five seconds, hold it briefly, then breathe out for five seconds. I'll count for you. Ready? Breathe in. One, two, three …" I count in a soothing voice until she's completed the cycle three times. "Talk to me. What do you do when things get bad? Do you pray? Meditate?"

"I listen to music."

"Do you have a favorite band?"

"Not really, but I have a favorite song. Have you heard of 'Bennie and the Jets?'"

"You like Elton John?"

"Just the one song."

"Why just that one?"

"The doctor had music on in the operating room when Evelyn was born. The first time I saw her, when they placed her by my head and let me kiss her, that song was being played. When I hear it, I remember that moment."

I can hear in her voice that she's getting calmer just talking about it.

"I'd sing it to you myself," I say. "But I don't know the words. Plus, I'm not sure you'd want me to sing. I can't hold a tune to save my life. Can you sing it in your head?"

She goes quiet. Time seems to stand still, yet we're in a rush to save a man's life.

"Did that help? Are you feeling better now?"

"Yes, thank you."

"How's Carter doing?"

"Not well."

"He needs you, Emma. You are the only person who can help him right now. Can you knock on the door and do what we talked about?" I hear her counting as she exhales. *Good girl.*

"Okay. I'll do it."

"Don't hang up the phone," I tell her.

"I won't. But what do I tell him to do? I can't call your number from the administrative phone. He'll know we were talking."

"Tell him to put the office phone back on the hook and answer it when it rings. We'll take care of the rest."

"But he'll wonder how you know someone in here is dying. How will you explain that?"

"We'll tell him we saw blood on the front steps and anyone who's lost that much blood won't be able to live long without intervention."

I can hear her take a few deep breaths. "I guess that could work. But what if it doesn't?"

"It will. You've got this, Emma."

"All right, here I go."

I hear the phone being put down and then the knock on the door. She has to knock several times before she gets a response.

While I'm waiting to see what happens, I tell the guys to get some O-negative blood and a transfusion kit in case the gunman won't let Carter go and I have to go inside.

"What the fuck is it now, teacher?" an angry voice in the background shouts.

"Mr. … uh, listen, Carter is going to die," Emma tells him. "Look at him. He's pale. He's lost too much blood. His pulse is racing, and he's going into shock."

"How do you know this shit? You a teacher, right?"

"I am, but I've gone through special training in case a student gets injured. Please believe me when I tell you he'll die if you don't let him out of here."

"Hell no. I ain't lettin' nobody outta here until I figure out what to do. My homie Jeremy's working on the outside. He'll come up with something. He always do."

"You won't let him out?" she asks. "Then he'll die."

"No he won't. You bullshittin' me, teacher."

"Look at me," she says. "I'm not lying. He will die, and you'll be charged with murder. You don't want that. I can tell you don't want that. If you won't let him out, will you at least let in a paramedic? Someone who can bring in blood and help Carter stay alive?"

"You want me to let someone else inside?" the gunman says. "Are you crazy, bitch? That's just a way for the pigs to get in and take me down. No way I'm fallin' for that shit."

"That's not what will happen. Please put the phone back on the hook, and when it rings, I'll answer it. I'll talk to them if you don't want to. But please help Carter. It will help your case when this whole thing gets resolved. I'm sure they will do whatever you ask to make this happen."

There is a long pause and I wonder if he's looking at Carter to see if she's being truthful.

"Do it," he says. "But put the speaker on. I ain't talkin', but I don't want nobody pulling no shit."

"Thank you," Emma says.

They must walk away, because their voices recede. I nod to the police behind me. "Try to call now. And get me that kit and the blood. I'm going in."

The officer in charge shakes his head. "You can't do that. One of us will go in and pretend to be you, then we'll disarm the perp, and this will all be over."

"Carter is going to die if he doesn't get blood in the next few minutes. We need to deal with that first and then work on a plan. Remember, the gunman doesn't know there's a phone in the storeroom. I'll call you as soon as he's stable."

"We have a live line!" someone shouts.

As the police call and then negotiate the terms of my entrance, I work with the other paramedics on scene to gather what I need.

An officer shows me a zip tie. "The woman said he insists you go in with your hands tied."

The woman. So Emma did end up speaking to the police on his behalf.

"How in the hell am I supposed to carry everything?"

"She said to put everything in a bag and wear it around your neck. No knives, just the needles to do the infusion. She said—" He stops talking and a look of grave concern comes over his face.

"She said what?"

"She said he'll hurt her if we don't follow his exact instructions."

I nod, terrified that if I screw this up, Emma will pay the ultimate price. "Let's do this. Carter doesn't have much time." I remove my FDNY shirt. "Someone get me a different T-shirt. I don't want to intimidate him with this one."

After I put on a plain nondescript shirt, someone hangs a bag of supplies around my neck and then zip-ties my hands together in front of me. I walk around the trucks with my hands in the air and approach the school. Debbe or Ryan or J.D. could have done this. We're all trained paramedics. But I could hardly ask one of them to go. We all have families to think about, not just me, and I already know what's going on with Carter. I can treat him more quickly than the others. It has to be me.

There is movement by the front door. Things are being cleared away to allow access. A woman steps out, a gun to the back of her head. She's young, maybe mid-twenties, with long brown hair pulled back into a ponytail. She looks oddly familiar.

Before I climb the steps, the gunman yells, "Turn around!"

I turn slowly, keeping my arms above my head and showing him I don't have any tricks up my sleeve. In fact, I don't even have sleeves. He wanted me only in a T-shirt and pants. Not even a belt. He's worried I might attack him. Then again, he's the one with the gun. He holds all the power right now. It's my job to keep him thinking that.

"Walk up slowly," he says.

I climb the steps in a non-aggressive manner. When I get close to the door, he tells me to stop and directs the woman to take the bag from around my neck.

They back up, and he aims his gun at me as I come through the doors. A slender man moves the barricades back into place behind me. He marches us into what I assume is the administrative office.

"Over there," he says to me, gesturing to the back corner. "You a big fucking dude. But you ain't bigger than my piece so you best not try nothin'. Got it?"

I nod.

"Goldilocks, lift up his shirt to see if he's packing."

A different woman stands and does what he asks.

"Now let me see his ankles," the guy says.

She lifts each of my pant legs.

"Now drop his pants."

She looks at him in horror. "You want me to remove his pants?"

"Do it, bitch," he says, holding the gun to the brunette's temple.

"I'm sorry," she whispers to me as she unbuttons and then unzips my pants, letting them fall to my ankles.

"Turn around, Ace," he says to me.

I'm momentarily relieved that I chose to wear boxer briefs today. It'll be clear that I don't have any weapons. I'm almost positive the guy would have made me strip naked if I were wearing regular boxers.

Once he's convinced I don't have a weapon, he allows me to pull up my pants with the woman's help.

"Teacher," he says to the woman still holding my bag. "Show me everything he brought."

She carefully unpacks the bag, showing him three units of blood, a bag of saline, the tubing, a needle, bandages, and a few other supplies. She picks up a box of candy I didn't know was in the bag. He must have asked for it as part of the deal.

"Here you go," she says and hands it to him.

My eyes snap to hers. That's her voice. I'd know it anywhere. That's Emma. But she looks younger than I thought she was.

"You take a bite," he says to her. "Make sure they ain't tryin' to poison me."

She hesitantly opens the package of candy bars and takes one out, eyeing me the entire time. I wonder if she knows it's me. I haven't spoken yet. Maybe she thinks I'm a cop posing as a paramedic. I honestly have no idea if they are trying to poison him, so I can't even nod encouragement.

She bites off the end of the candy bar and chews it. Once the gunman is satisfied she's not going to die, he pushes her away.

"Take the shit, and you and Ace make sure he don't die. Got it?" He threatens me with the gun. "Don't try anything, Ace."

I hold up my hands. "I won't. I'm only here to help."

Emma gives me a sharp look after hearing my voice. She knows it's me. And for some reason she looks incredibly relieved. Maybe she thought I was here to jump the gunman.

"I'll need my hands to administer the blood," I say. "Can someone cut the ties off me?"

"Do it, Goldilocks," he says, holding out a pocketknife. "Any funny stuff, and the teacher gets it."

My eyes are glued to the gun pointed at Emma's head as the blonde woman cuts the zip ties and then hands the pocketknife back to the gunman.

He gestures to the door. "What the fuck you waitin' for? Go."

We walk into the storage room, and he shuts the door behind us. I hear something heavy being moved in front of it.

"Emma," I say.

"Brett?" she asks, even though I'm sure she knows the answer.

I nod, and she falls into my arms.

CHAPTER SIX

EMMA

I quickly remove myself from his arms, remembering why he's here. "Can you help him?"

"Let's take a look."

Brett goes into action, taking Carter's blood pressure and pulse before swiftly laying out all the supplies and then hooking Carter up to the blood. He hands me the bag. "Hook this over that shelf please."

"Then what?"

"Then we wait and hope we did this in time."

I look at the other bags of blood. "How many will he need?"

"We'll take it one at a time and see how he does." He nods to the unit of blood I hung up. "Squeeze that gently for me. We need it to infuse quickly. I'll watch him closely for the first fifteen minutes or so to make sure he doesn't have an allergic reaction."

"As in, he could be allergic to the blood?"

"It's possible," Brett says. "We're giving him O-neg. It's the universal blood type. He shouldn't have a reaction, but you never know."

"Do you think he's going to be okay?"

He looks at Carter's leg and all the blood staining the floor. "I hope so."

Brett gives nothing away as he assesses our situation. He seems calm and collected—two things that are barely in my vocabulary at this point. I'm trying to read his face, but I can't tell if he thinks Carter will live or die.

"What are we going to do? I mean, assuming he gets better and that maniac doesn't kill us, what are we going to do?"

"As soon as he's stable, I'll get on the phone with the police, and we'll come up with something. But for now, let's concentrate on what we can control, which is helping Carter."

I pull a chair over and sit down while I continue to squeeze the bag of blood.

Brett keeps his fingers on Carter's wrist. He looks at me. "Have we met before? You look familiar."

"I don't think so."

"How is it you have a twelve-year-old?" he asks. "You barely look twenty-five."

"I'm twenty-seven. And it's a long story. But it starts with a slutty fifteen-year-old and a foreign exchange student."

His eyebrows shoot up. "That sounds interesting. And we've got nothing but time right now, Emma."

We may be hostages in a robbery gone bad, but oh, how I like the way he says my name. "You really want to hear about it?"

"If you're willing to tell me."

"Okay, well, as you know, I lost my dad. I was eight when he died. The therapist my mom took me to when I got pregnant would tell you that because I lacked a father figure in my formative years, I craved attention from boys and used any means to get it."

"I think I would have liked you when I was in high school," he jokes with a wink.

I snicker. "Yeah, but nobody seemed to like me for very long. As soon as they got what they wanted, they moved on to the ones who were girlfriend material."

"You didn't fit in that category?" he asks.

"I wanted to, but I went about it the wrong way. When I was a sophomore, I met Stefan in my pre-calculus class. He was from Germany. He was a year older than me. Like most girls, I was enamored with his accent. He was the first boy who wanted to keep me around longer than a week or two. But then I got careless and ended up pregnant. He bolted soon after I told him. He went home to Germany for Christmas and never came back, even though he was supposed to go to school here for the entire year."

Brett looks upset. "And he hasn't contacted you since?"

I narrow my eyes. "How did you know?"

"You said on the phone it had always just been you, Evelyn, and your mom."

"I tried to look him up once the baby came, figuring he'd fall in love with her instantly, as I had. But he had a very common name, and there was just no way to find him."

"Do you have a picture of your daughter?"

"I have about a thousand." I gesture to the door. "But they're all on my phone, and he broke it."

"He broke your phone? Why'd he do that?"

I sigh. "I tried to text my friends, Becca and Kelly. I knew they were still in the building, and I wanted to warn them. But he saw me and knocked it out of my hand. Then he confiscated everyone's phone."

Brett takes my hand in his and examines it. "Did he hurt you?" he asks, concern evident in his expression.

I clear my throat. "I'm okay." Heat from his hand warms mine. "Everyone says Evelyn looks like me. We're often mistaken for sisters."

"She must be beautiful if she takes after you," he says, tracing the curves of my face with his green eyes.

I feel warmth spread across my face. "Thanks." I bite my lip and look away wondering what the hell I'm doing blushing. How can I react to him like this when we're being held hostage by a whacko with a gun?

"Your mom was a nurse?" I ask, changing the subject.

"She was," he says, looking proud.

"And you said you have a little sister?"

"Bria. That's short for Brianna. She's twenty-two. She's a singer."

"She is? What kinds of songs does she sing?"

"Pop mainly. She's never been on the radio, although she's cut an album. But she can't get picked up by a label, even though she's fantastic—and that's not just her big brother talking, she really is good. She mainly works as a backup singer while she's trying to get her career off the ground."

"So she was little when your mom died."

"Bria was three. I was eleven."

"That would make you … thirty?"

I have a hard time tearing my eyes away from his face. He's really attractive. Rugged too, with his hair on the longish side of what would be acceptable for a firefighter. He's clean shaven, but I can see the hint of a five o'clock shadow even though it's not nearly five o'clock. And his tattoos. Oh, don't get me started on those. He has a string of them that go up his left arm and disappear under the sleeve of his shirt. This guy is probably on the cover of FDNY's firefighter calendar.

"Yup. I'm an old man," he says, laughing.

He's laughing. We're locked in a storage room at gunpoint, and he's laughing.

And I'm swooning. I roll my eyes at the whole ridiculous situation.

He takes Carter's blood pressure again.

"How is it?"

"His BP is improving, but he's not out of the woods. We'll have to give him more blood when this bag is empty."

"How long do you think we'll be here?"

"Hopefully not too long. I have a plan for when Carter is stable." He sets the BP cuff aside. "I'm going to put those folding tables between the two of you and the door to protect you from, well, whatever. Then I'll lure the gunman over and rile him up so he doesn't hear the police break through the front entrance."

"*Rile* him up?" I say in horror. "Brett, the man has a gun."

"Yeah, but there are five—uh, six hostages here, one of them clinging to life. We need to end this."

"But what about Leo?" I ask. "You can't risk your life like that."

"Emma, I'm a firefighter. I became one to help people."

Tears well up in my eyes. "So did my dad."

He exhales a deep breath. "I'm really sorry you lost him."

I nod and swallow. "Not a day goes by that I don't remember Mom getting the phone call telling her my dad was inside the south tower when it collapsed." I press my lips together and look at the ceiling, trying to keep more tears at bay. "I was home sick that day. We watched it on TV, along with other women who were married to firefighters in my dad's company. For an eight-year-old like me, it was like watching a movie. I didn't understand that it was real.

Not until Mom dropped the phone, and she and some of the others fell to the floor in hysterics."

He puts a comforting hand on mine.

"Brett," I say, my tears having won the battle. "You can't put Leo through that. He'll never forgive you."

His hand comes to my face and a finger wipes away my tears. "You never forgave your father?"

"I … I can't." I shake my head sadly. "He knew what he was doing when he ran into that tower. He knew what he was doing when he risked his life then and so many other times. He was willing to leave my mother and me. How can I forgive him for that?"

"Emma, it wasn't his choice to leave you. You must know that."

I try to control my breathing, but suddenly everything is sinking in. Carter barely hanging on to life. Us trapped here with God knows what happening on the other side of the door. "I'm s-sorry. I guess this is all getting to me."

He looks at his watch. "I have to release the tourniquet for a few minutes or he could lose the leg."

"But won't he start bleeding again?"

"He will, but hopefully the blood he's getting will keep him from getting worse. I have to try. I'd want someone to do it for me."

"What can I do?"

"Keep squeezing the bag. I need blood going in as fast as it's coming out."

I watch in terror as blood runs out of Carter's wound. Brett looks more than a little concerned, and after only a minute, he tightens the belt around Carter's leg. Then he stands and squeezes the bag of blood harder than I could have.

He scrubs a hand across his face. "Damn. I hope I didn't make it worse."

"He's young," I tell him. "I'm sure he would want you to try and save his leg."

He runs his hands through his hair. "His leg won't mean much if he loses his life."

When the blood from the first bag is all gone, he hangs a second. "I have to get him out of here. Where's the phone?"

I point to a shirt on the floor. "It's under there."

Before he moves toward it, I put my hand on his arm. "Please be careful."

He looks into my eyes. I don't even know this guy. I'm not sure why I'm having this visceral reaction to him. Maybe because he reminds me of my dad.

"I'm getting you out of here, Emma," he says, touching my hand. "Nobody is dying today, I promise."

CHAPTER SEVEN

BRETT

"Ready?" I ask Emma after I barricade her and Carter behind several overturned tables.

"Yes. No."

"Keep your head down and stay behind the table no matter what. I don't want you getting hurt."

"What about you?"

"It's my job," I tell her.

"Confronting gunmen is not your job, Brett. You're not trained for this."

"Well, it's my job today."

She nods, knowing I speak the truth. They've been locked in the school for hours, and as far as I can tell, no one has tried anything. I'm not even sure the gunman is trying to negotiate with the police. Whoever this Jeremy is, that Emma told me he mentioned, he obviously isn't doing much to help his friend. I'm grateful, because I can only imagine what kind of 'help' another criminal would provide.

"Brett," she says, looking terrified.

"I'll be careful. Don't forget to give them the signal over the phone when you hear me yelling."

"Got it."

"Get down now."

Her eyes lock with mine, and I hope I'm doing the right thing. I pray Leo will not have to grow up without a father. I pray Evelyn doesn't have to be raised by her grandmother. I close my eyes and see my son laughing as I push him on the swing at the park.

I breathe deeply and shake my head. Nobody will be lying on the floor in hysterics today. That's not going to be how this goes down.

I shove a heavy hole-punch in my back pocket. It's not much, but if it came down to it, and I hit him in the side of the head just right, it might subdue him.

I knock on the heavy door. I get no response.

I make sure Emma is still behind the tables and knock again. "Come on!" I shout. "I know you can hear me. A man is dying in here."

The door is ripped open. "I told you not to fucking bother me." Then he sees all the blood on my face and clothes.

I did that for effect, hoping to keep his attention on me and not on the overturned tables at the back of the room. It seems to be working.

"I don't know what your agenda is," I say angrily, "but this kid is dying, so quit being an asshole and let us out of here."

"Asshole? Did you just call me an asshole? Maybe you're forgettin' who's got the fuckin' piece, motherfucker."

We're yelling at each other, and the hostages are screaming because they're afraid. There's even more noise than I anticipated. I hope Emma has given the police the signal.

"Motherfucker? Oh, that's original," I say. "What a limited vocabulary you have."

"Stop it!" one of the hostages says. "You're provoking him."

The others chime in, and there is so much chatter in the room, it's turning into chaos.

The gunman puts the gun to my temple. "Have you always been this much of a troublemaker, Ace? Now shut the fuck up so your homies will calm the fuck down."

The hostages are on edge, and now that I've riled up the gunman, they are crying and yelling. I'm yelling. The gunman is yelling. I hope this doesn't have to go on too much longer, because he just might pull the trigger.

There's a loud noise behind the counter, and the police break through the office door. The gunman's focus wavers, and I grab his arm and slam it against the wall. The gun falls to the floor. I push him down, grinding my knee into his back to keep him there.

"It's clear!" I yell.

Twenty cops and S.W.A.T. team funnel through the door with their guns drawn. They're not taking any chances that a second perp could be among the hostages. The gunman is hauled away, and each hostage is checked for weapons before being directed outside.

"I need a gurney back here," I tell them.

I run to the overturned tables and move them out of the way. Emma stands quickly. "You did it," she says, right before her body goes limp and she faints into my arms.

"Make that two gurneys," I say.

Emma and Carter are wheeled out. Emma will be okay. The stress of the situation overwhelmed her, and as soon as her body felt it was safe to shut down, it did. I've seen that happen many times. I'm more worried about Carter.

Paramedics Debbe and Ryan take Carter out first and then paramedics from another company wheel out Emma.

When I emerge, my entire company stands at attention, clapping for me. I shake a bunch of hands and then I'm whisked away to give my statement, like every other hostage.

Several hours later, when I'm done at the police station, I head back to the firehouse, wondering how Emma is. She hadn't arrived to give her statement by the time I left. But I won't check on her. I never do. I learned early on not to get caught up in the aftermath of our rescues. There are too many emotions. Too much drama. Besides, it's better to think that everyone lives happily ever after.

But that doesn't keep me from thinking about her.

J.D. sees me walking into the garage at the firehouse. "Go home, Cash. You've earned the rest of the shift off. I already called in someone to cover you."

"You know, for once I think I might take you up on that, Captain. I could really use a hug from my son."

The moment the words leave my mouth, I hear the pitter-patter of small feet. Then little arms wrap around my legs. Leo grabs onto me like he always does after a shift. I pick him up and hold him tightly.

"Somebody told me you might need to see him," Bonnie says.

I smile my thanks. "Somebody was right."

I sit on the couch with Leo on my lap.

"Truck," he says, pointing into the garage. "Daddy truck."

I look at the rig. "Yes, that's daddy's truck."

"Your pop was a hero today," Justin says, ruffling Leo's hair.

Leo looks at me with pride, almost like he understood what Justin said, even though I know he couldn't have.

Bonnie leans down behind me and wraps her arms around my neck. “Oh, my boy. Must you make everything so exciting? I damn near keeled over when your captain called and told me what had happened.”

“I’m fine, Bonnie.”

“You saved that boy,” she says.

“Carter is going to make it,” Captain Dickerson says. “He’d be six feet under if you hadn’t been there.”

“Emma’s the real hero,” I say quietly. If she hadn’t stood up for Carter, found the phone, and had the courage to call for help, he would have died.

“What’s that?” J.D. asks.

“Nothing,” I say, standing and hauling Leo onto my shoulders. “Come on, buddy. Let’s go home.”

CHAPTER EIGHT

EMMA

My blanket is ripped off me, subjecting my eyes to the bright light of midday.

"Mo-om, stop it," I say, pulling the covers back over my head.

"Honey, it's been three days. Don't you think it's time to get out of bed?"

"I got out of bed yesterday."

"Only because I refused to bring you food anymore. Come on, you can't just lie here."

I point to my laptop on the nightstand. "I'm not just lying here. I've started working on my online class."

"You know what I mean. You have to get out of this funk."

I throw the covers off my face. "You stayed in bed for an entire month after Dad died."

She gives me a stern look, and I immediately feel guilty. "It's not the same, and you know it. Nobody died three days ago, Emma. You should be celebrating the fact that you're alive. Have you even talked to Evelyn?"

I turn over and hug my pillow. "She doesn't want to talk to her mom when she's got better things to do at camp. I texted her goodnight, see?"

I shove my new phone at her—the phone *she* went out and got me—so she can read the last few texts I sent Evelyn and the ones she sent back. They're all the same.

Me: Goodnight, baby. I love you and miss you.

Evelyn: Night, Mom. Love you back.

"You haven't told her yet?" she asks.

"Of course not. She would freak out. I will tell her, because I'm sure her friends at home will talk about it when she gets back. But I'm not saying anything when she's a hundred miles away and I'm not there to show her I'm okay."

"But you're *not* okay. You don't give her enough credit. My granddaughter is stronger than you think. She's just like her mother—which is why you need to set a good example and get out of bed."

"Set a good example for whom? She's not here."

She turns her back on me and walks out. "I'm not bringing you anything today, honey. If you can't get out of bed, maybe you should call a therapist."

"I'm not calling a therapist."

"Right," she says from the top of the stairs. "Because clearly you've got this."

I hear her gather her things and walk out the front door.

After a moment, I sit up and look at the window, the curtains barely shading the afternoon light. I stand and pad my way over, approaching slowly. Stepping to one side, I push the curtain back.

"I can do this."

Taking a deep breath, I stand in front of the window, proving to myself that nothing bad will happen.

I have ten days until Evelyn comes home. Mom's right. She can't see me like this—scared to go outside. Scared of the world.

Everything turned out okay. Carter lived. Although despite Brett's best attempts, I heard he ended up losing his leg. But he's alive and he has his whole life ahead of him.

Brett Cash.

His name rolls around in my head.

I'll bet he's not holed up in his room, hiding under his covers. He saved Carter. Heck, he may have saved all of us. He's a hero. I should thank him. Maybe one day I will. I look out the window again, then shut the curtains and crawl back into bed.

But not today.

~ ~ ~

I stand at the front door, frozen. It's just a door, I tell myself. I've gone through it a thousand times. But not once in the last four days.

Just do it, Emma. Walk up to it. Open it. Walk through. Close it. Easy peasy.

I wrap my fingers around the door handle.

I let go and back up, falling into the chair in the foyer.

Not today either.

~ ~ ~

I sit on the bottom step in front of my house, where I've been holed up for six days, watching people stroll by. Wondering which of them could be potential threats. I can't seem to go any farther. My goal is to make it to the school.

School. It was my favorite place on earth. But I'm afraid I'll never be able to go inside that building again. Maybe I could work at a different school. Would that help? No. I have to go back. I love it there. My students. My coworkers.

As if Becca heard me thinking of her, my phone rings.

"Hey," I answer, in a more melancholy tone than I meant to.

"Did you leave the house yet?"

"Yes."

"That's great, Emma. I'm so proud of you."

"I'm sitting on the front steps."

"Oh." There is a long pause. "I guess that's progress."

Becca seemed to be equally traumatized by the incident, yet she was not only able to leave her apartment the next day, she went back to school and picked up her things. She picked up mine, too, delivering them to me here. Like Mom and Lisa, she's tried every day to get me to leave the house.

"It's *not* progress," I say. "What the hell is wrong with me?"

"Nothing is wrong with you. People deal with traumatic events differently, that's all. I'm sure you'll be back to your regular self in no time. I mean, what is Taco Tuesday without Emma Lockhart?"

I laugh. "I could use a margarita."

"So why don't you make it your goal to come to the next one? That gives you five days to work up the courage to get back on the subway. I'll come by beforehand, and we'll do it together."

"That sounds good, actually."

"It's a date then. You know you can call me anytime. I'm here for you, Emma."

"I know. Thank you."

I end the call and walk back up the steps to my house.

~ ~ ~

My heart pounds as I sit on the bench next to the park on the corner. I used to bring Evelyn here when she was little. What if the gunman had robbed the store next to the park and taken kids hostage? What if a young child had been shot? I go crazy, thinking of all the things that can go wrong. I feel myself panicking. Then I start to breathe and count like Brett taught me. I've had to do that more than a few times over the past eight days.

I think of him and how calm he seemed in the face of danger. He confronted the maniac with the gun—a man who'd already shot one person. He did that to save Carter. How can someone like that face those kinds of odds and come out unscathed, and someone like me can't even walk to the school four blocks away?

I pick up the bag full of banana nut muffins I made for the guys at the firehouse. The station is only one block away—halfway to the school. But I know they won't be getting the muffins today.

I walk back to my house, feeling like a failure for the umpteenth time in the past week.

Maybe tomorrow.

CHAPTER NINE

BRETT

This week at work hasn't been nearly as exciting as last week. No hostage situations. Just run-of-the-mill traffic accidents, a few dumpster fires, and a woman threatening to jump off the bridge.

We're killing time doing inventory on the rigs this morning as we wait for the next shift to come in.

"You ever hear from Amanda?" Bass asks.

I shrug. "I have a closer relationship with her lawyer at this point."

He pats me on the back. "It'll get easier."

"You have the wrong idea, brother. I'm over her. I think I've been over her for a long time. It's Leo who's getting the shaft. He's basically growing up without a mother. Hell, sometimes I think he believes Bonnie is his mother. Although he recognizes her picture, Amanda is practically a stranger to him. He's not comfortable around her. She hasn't come to see him in months."

"Maybe it's time to get back out there," Denver says. "Sara has some friends I could introduce you to. Even some nice single moms from the playgroup she goes to with Joey."

Denver mentioning single moms has me thinking of Emma Lockhart. And not for the first time. I've thought about her often over the past week. She's been through a lot—losing her dad, being dumped by her baby daddy, and then what happened last week. I've never wanted to reach out to someone I've helped as much as I have the last few days. But the truth is, she may not want to be reminded of that day.

"Or, if you're not ready for dating, but you're ready for … you know"—Bass makes an obscene gesture with his hands—"I could always hook you up with Ivy's sister."

Justin Neal pokes his head out of the rig. "Yeah-ah-ah," he says with a smirk. "I can vouch for that one."

I laugh. "I don't want your sloppy seconds, Neal."

"There's nothing sloppy about Holly Greene."

"Think I'll pass. I'm good, guys."

I've been hit on by more than a few women in the past several months. Once word got out about my impending divorce, I became known as a catch. I don't think it's me, however. It's Leo. He mesmerizes women everywhere. He never met a woman who isn't crazy about him. Correction—he never met a woman besides his mother who isn't crazy about him.

Since when did being a single dad become so sexy? Changing diapers, wiping snot, digging in the dirt, running errands—what's so great about all of that? A lot of guys I know lead much more interesting lives. The most exciting thing I do is get together with my friends and watch baseball.

"Lieutenant, we have a visitor," Cameron calls from the front of the garage.

I circle the truck and see Emma Lockhart carrying a large basket. She holds it out to me. "I just wanted to say thank you for everything you did last week." She looks around at the guys. "All of you."

They take a step back, none of them wanting praise.

I try to take the basket from her, but I forget to put down the tool I'm holding first and almost drop it on her foot. *Way to be awkward, Cash.* "Uh, sorry." I put down the halligan bar so I can take the basket.

"That's an interesting looking … hammer," she says.

"It's a halligan bar."

"It looks dangerous. What's it used for?"

"It's mostly used for quickly breeching locked doors."

I peek under the covering on the basket, and the smell of freshly baked blueberry muffins wafts out. "These smell great." I motion to the guys. "Who wants one?"

Justin comes over and takes the basket from me. "Thank you," he tells Emma.

She shrugs her bare, tanned shoulders. "It's the least I can do after … well, you know."

I get the idea she doesn't want to talk about what happened.

As the guys gush over the muffins, and her attention is on them, I can't stop staring at her shoulders. Last week, in the storage room, she had on a T-shirt and pants. She was pretty even with her hair up in a ponytail and wearing no makeup. But today, in a halter top and a pair of shorts, with her hair flowing halfway down her back, she's gorgeous. But when she smiles, it doesn't touch her eyes. Is she still upset about last week?

Men from the next shift walk into the garage.

Emma takes that as her cue to leave. "Well, I just wanted to say thank you," she says.

I don't want her to leave. But I can't think of a reason to get her to stay. "No need. It's our job."

"I doubt that single-handedly taking on a gunman is part of your job description, Lieutenant."

I almost correct her and have her call me Brett. But damn, I like the way she called me Lieutenant. I never thought that word could be sexy until she said it. "I guess it's not, but we do what we have to."

Cameron takes a huge bite from a muffin and mumbles around his food, "Emma, if you ever need to unload more baked goods, bring 'em over."

Her lips crack into a half-smile. "I'll remember that." She turns and heads for the exit. "Thanks again," she says, her eyes locking with mine.

I nod. For some reason, all words leave my brain when she's looking at me like this. She maintains the connection another few seconds … until she almost trips over the bushes lining the driveway. She blushes and hurries away.

"Daaaaaaamn," Denver drawls. "Correct me if I'm wrong, but I felt some serious heat between the two of you."

The others nod in agreement.

"You're full of it," I tell them.

"I think *you're* full of it," Justin says. "Full of luuuuuuve." He puckers his lips and blows air kisses.

"Cash is most definitely hot for teacher," Cameron says.

"Get back to work." I'm annoyed at their joking around. "We have to pack this shit up before next shift."

Twenty minutes later, I leave the firehouse with my duffle bag over my shoulder and see Emma standing next to a bench across the street. She's not looking at me. She's looking down the street in the direction of the school.

I watch her for a minute. She takes a step, then stops and looks at the sky. Then she shakes her head in frustration and sits on the bench, putting her head in her hands.

I cross the street, drop my bag, and sit next to her. "Everything okay?"

She looks up, shocked that I'm sitting by her side. "Brett … uh…" Her gaze shifts to the sidewalk, and with her eyes, she follows it to the end of the street.

"You still haven't gone back to the school, have you?"

She shakes her head. "The firehouse is as far as I've gotten."

I look into her beautiful, tired eyes. "This last week has been hard on you, hasn't it?"

"Yes." She stares at the firehouse. "I'm sorry. You must think I'm the biggest wimp. You probably deal with traumatic situations all the time, but what happened—it was the first time since my dad died that I was up-close and personal with something horrible."

"I hardly think you're a wimp, Emma. The man held a gun to your head. Of course you've been traumatized."

"So how come *you* aren't?"

I shrug. "I don't know. As first responders, we're trained to handle stressful situations. It's not that I wasn't scared—I was—but I put that aside to do my job."

"You were really scared?"

"Hell yes, I was. I might have had to change my shorts when I got home."

She laughs.

God, I love her laugh. It makes me want to reach out and touch her.

"I did *not* need to know that about you," she says.

"I'm kidding. But in all seriousness, I was scared shitless."

"Somehow that makes me feel better," she says.

"I'm glad. I guess I've done my good deed for the day."

She smiles and this time her lips curve even higher.

I nod in the direction of the school. "What do you say I walk with you?"

Her eyes close briefly. "No. I'm not ready."

"Can I walk you somewhere else then?"

She leans forward, planting her hands on the bench on either side of her as she rocks back and forth. "I'm going to sit here for a while."

I stand and sling my bag over my shoulder. "Well, if you think you might be ready on Friday, I get off shift at this same time."

She looks back in the direction of the school. "I don't know. Maybe."

"Either way, I still get off at this time." I stare at her, hoping she gets the meaning behind my words. I want to see her again. I want to see her again so badly, it's hard to find the words.

"Okay," she says.

"See you around, Emma Lockhart," I say.

"See you around, Lieutenant."

I can't help smiling the entire way home.

CHAPTER TEN

EMMA

I'm not a nervous person by nature, the past eleven days notwithstanding. So as I put freshly baked croissants into a bag to drop them by the firehouse, I wonder if it's the daunting possibility of making it all the way to school this morning that has me on edge, or is it the thought of seeing Lt. Brett Cash again?

He specifically told me to come back this morning. *Didn't he?* Then again, he's a firefighter. A civil servant. He probably thinks it's his duty to help me make it to the school. He's being nice.

But when we looked at each other …

No, Emma. Don't go there.

It's not that I haven't thought about a serious relationship with a man. I have. I've often wondered what kind of man it would take to make me want to consider someone as a father for Evelyn. Once I got over the fact that Stefan didn't want her—or me—I tried many times to put a face on the fantasy that would be our happily ever after.

But I've never been able to. Not until my dream last night.

Even if the gorgeous lieutenant was interested, I could never allow it to happen. I mean, he's a firefighter.

I finish filling the bag with croissants as Mom comes into the kitchen, ready for work.

She raises an eyebrow. "Baking for the third time this week. Are you feeling better?"

I shrug. "Maybe."

"You've been back to school then?"

"I'm trying, Mom."

She wraps her arms around me from behind, giving me that supportive hug she's so good at. "You'll get there. Maybe Evelyn coming home Sunday will be just the thing you need to turn everything around."

I've missed my daughter so much. Although I dread telling her what happened, I've never been more excited to see her.

"Want me to go with you today?" she asks. "I don't have to be at work for another hour."

"This is something I have to do myself."

It's a lie. Deep down, I hope it's something I get to do with the gorgeous lieutenant. But I can't tell her that. She'd get all excited and want to know every detail. Then she'd be the meddling matchmaker mom, pushing me to do things I don't want to do. Hell, she'd probably plan our wedding before I even found out if he likes me.

Which he probably doesn't. And even if he does, it wouldn't matter.

It's not that I don't bring men home. I do. But I don't ever introduce them to my mother or Evelyn. The rule is strict: in after my daughter's bedtime and out immediately … well … *after.*

Mom knows I have them here. Our townhouse is old, and the floorboards creak. I'm just glad Evelyn is a heavy sleeper.

I pick up the bag and move toward the door when Mom's words stop me. "Something's different," she says, eyeing me up and down.

"What are you talking about?"

She studies my face. "Is that mascara?"

I roll my eyes. "Yes, Mom. Women have been wearing it for a hundred years."

"Hmm," she mumbles. "And that's the shirt I got you for your birthday. You said you were saving it for a special occasion." She glances at the bag. "Who are you taking those to?"

"I'm hoping it *is* a special occasion today. These are for the summer staff at the front office … if I get there."

"You wore your new shirt for the summer staff at school?"

"I guess I did." I look at the clock over her shoulder, not wanting to be late. Brett's shift ends in ten minutes.

She follows the direction of my eyes. "In a hurry?" she asks suspiciously.

"I want to get this over with, Mom."

She finally drops the third degree. "Good luck, honey."

"Thanks. Have a nice day at work."

I get to the firehouse as the trucks are backing into the garage. They're busy. Maybe I should come back another time.

"Emma!" a familiar voice shouts as I walk away.

I turn around to see a dirty, sweaty Brett talking to me from the passenger seat of one of the trucks. Our eyes meet and that same feeling I had the other day—the one where butterflies are doing somersaults in my stomach—is back in full force.

I watch his truck retreat into the garage and then he opens the door and jumps down. I can't look away as he removes his heavy coat, pants, and boots. I have to keep myself from ogling him.

Because apparently sweaty, dirty Brett is even more gorgeous than regular Brett.

"Yes!" one of his buddies says, eyeing my bag. "More goodies?"

I hand it to him. "I hope you like croissants."

"Sweet," he says. Then he kisses my cheek and takes them inside.

"Sorry about that," Brett says, approaching me. "Justin has always been a ladies' man."

"It's okay," I say, laughing. "I'm glad he's enjoying the food."

"Everyone raved about the muffins. Did you really make them yourself, or did you stop at a bakery?"

"I made them. I do a lot of baking."

He looks over my slim figure. "You obviously don't eat what you bake."

My face heats up under his perusal. "I didn't mean to bother you while you were working."

"Shift's over. Give me fifteen minutes to clean up. Why don't you wait for me on our bench?"

Our bench. I'm not sure why those two words affect me so much, but they do. "Okay."

He goes around the corner, but there are windows that separate the hallway from the garage, and I can still see him. He runs down the hall. That puts a huge smile on my face.

Nine minutes later—but who's counting?—Brett joins me on the bench, popping the last bite of a croissant into his mouth. "This is really good. If you ever wanted to moonlight as a baker, you'd make a fortune."

"Nah, they have to be up at like four in the morning. I'm not really a morning person."

He eyes me speculatively. "What kind of person are you, Emma Lockhart?"

I blush at his seductive use of my full name. "I don't know. A regular one, I guess."

He laughs. "Somehow I doubt that."

"Were you at a fire this morning?"

"No. Why do you ask?"

"You were dirty when you came back."

"A dump truck full of dirt overturned in a ditch, and the driver was pinned underneath it."

"Oh, gosh. That's horrible."

"He's fine. We got him out. But Mrs. Petrucha's flowerbed may never be the same."

"Mrs. Petrucha?"

"Her house is on the corner and her yard literally has a ton of dirt on it."

"Oh, no." I giggle.

"I've been wanting to ask you something."

My heart pounds. *Please don't ask me out.*

"The other day—did you know I was going to be on shift? I mean, did you specifically come to the firehouse to see me, or was it to give a general thank you to everyone?"

"I may have called ahead to see if you were there," I admit. "I wanted to thank you for saving Carter. He's alive because of you."

"He's alive because of you, too." He frowns. "I heard he lost his leg though."

"I heard that too. But he's young. He'll adapt."

"The department is putting together a fundraiser to help pay for a prosthetic leg."

My eyes light up. "They are? Please let me know how I can donate."

"Sure. I think it will be a picnic later this summer with games and auctions and stuff."

"I'd love to help. Maybe I could sell some of my baked goods. Between Evelyn, and my mom, and me, we could make enough to set up an entire booth."

"That's a great idea. I'll let the organizer know." He stands up and gestures down the street. "What do you say? Are you ready?"

I look at the ground and then at him. Then I nod.

He holds his hand out. When I put my hand in his, I feel I can do anything. It's as if holding his hand gives me some kind of superpower. But once I'm standing, he lets go.

Brett leads, walking slowly, letting me take this one step at a time. The closer we get to the school, the faster my heart beats.

He tries to make conversation with me, but I'm too busy thwarting a panic attack to hear him.

When we turn the final corner, and I see Shettleman's Grocery and the school, my legs buckle. Brett holds onto me and helps me to a nearby bench. "Put your head down near your knees. Remember the breathing we did last week, when I had you count to five? Let's do that now."

As I calm down, my heart rate slows. Especially when he runs a soothing hand up and down my back. But then it beats faster for an entirely different reason.

"I'm proud of you for making it this far. We'll sit here and look at the school today. Maybe next time we'll cross the street. You don't have to do everything at once."

I let out a sigh of relief. He gets me. This big, tough fireman who saves dump truck drivers and confronts lunatic gunmen, thinks it's okay that I can't walk into the school yet. "Next time?"

"My next shift is on Monday. I have Tuesday off. I mean, if you're free."

"Tuesday sounds great. I'll bring scones."

He laughs. "You're going to spoil us."

Then we just sit. We don't even talk. We gaze at the school across the street.

So many things could have happened differently that day. What if I'd been quicker about cleaning up my classroom? I'd never have gotten caught up in everything. What if I'd moved the cart fully out the door? Then maybe Carter wouldn't have gotten shot.

What if the gunman had never robbed that store? His name, I read in the paper, is Kenny Lutwig.

What if none of it had happened? I'd never have met the man sitting next to me.

Maybe everything happens for a reason, my father says in my head. He was a huge believer in fate, or destiny, or whatever. Maybe the way he met my mom had something to do with that attitude. They met when a dispatcher sent his company to the wrong address when he was a probationary firefighter.

Every time something bad happened to me, he would try to find the good in it. I fell off my bike and sprained my wrist when I was five, and I met Julie Kirkland at the emergency room. She had fallen off her bike too. It turned out she lived just a block away, and we became fast friends. Dad always reminded me that if I hadn't fallen off the bike, I never would have met her.

When I was seven, Mom lost her job. She was devastated. She was a sales rep for a pharmaceutical company. When she couldn't find a similar job, she volunteered at local charities. Twenty years later she is the chairperson for one of the largest charities in the city. I can almost hear Dad saying, "*I told you so, sweet pea.*"

"What is it?" Brett asks. "You look like you want to say something."

I shake my head. "Nothing. It's just that … life is strange."

He laughs again, and I realize how much I like hearing him laugh. "That it is," he says, smiling at me.

And as he looks at me, I'm left wondering if he, like my dad, believes in destiny.

CHAPTER ELEVEN

BRETT

I've never looked forward to being on a shift as much as this one. Specifically, getting *off* the shift, because Emma will be here. With scones.

But it's the not the scones I'm excited about.

For the first time in a long time, I'm interested in a woman. I find it hard to sleep in my cot just thinking about her.

Amanda and I were together for eight years. We dated for three, were married for five, and were separated for the better part of this last year before our divorce became final. I have to go back to when I was twenty-one to remember what it was like to be with someone other than my ex-wife.

The last girl I dated was named Kristin. She was the daughter of my captain at the time. I had fun with her at first, but she became needy and clingy. I wanted to ditch her, but she was the captain's daughter. In hindsight, I never should have dated someone related to one of my superiors. It took months to get rid of her. I tried to become a boring person that no girl would want to hang out with. It was torture. I never went out. I watched mindless television. I took her to the same cheap, Italian restaurant when we went out to eat. Eventually she broke up with me as planned. The next week, a friend introduced me to Amanda, and I thought I'd hit the jackpot.

Oh, how wrong I was.

I try not to be too bitter. I did get Leo out of the deal. If I'd never met Amanda, he wouldn't exist. So I can't begrudge that relationship.

I smile, thinking of the tiny person who is the best part of my life. I love how curious he is. I love his passion. His wit.

Would he like Emma? He tends not to like most women. Apart from Bonnie, he's around men most of the time. My friends. My coworkers. Leo is at the firehouse so much, he's our unofficial mascot. I wouldn't be surprised if he followed in my footsteps and became a firefighter.

I think about what it would be like to have a woman in my life. In Leo's life. Emma has a child, so I know she likes kids. And she seems compassionate. She fought hard to save Carter.

I should ask her out.

I stare at the dark ceiling, planning a date with Emma. We'd go to dinner, maybe a club after, so we could dance. Anything to get her in my arms again. The few times I held her, it felt right—even when she was passed out or having a panic attack. Something stirs inside me, and I turn on my side to hide my growing erection. It's dark in the bunkroom, but not so dark that someone walking by wouldn't see the tented covers.

Before I can fully immerse myself in an Emma fantasy, Dispatch comes over the loudspeaker, waking up the entire room and summoning us to a residential structural fire. Lights come on, and we race downstairs to our rigs.

Cameron laughs at me as we're pulling on our gear. "Damn," he says, noticing the bulge in my pants. "Don't you hate it when a good dream gets interrupted?"

"Fuck off, Curtis." I climb into the front cab, a smile cracking my face.

We arrive at the house to see smoke coming out of several windows.

"It's a live one," Justin says from the driver's seat.

He parks the rig, and we help Engine 319 hook up their hose.

J.D. shouts orders. "Briggs and I will take Nelson and Curtis and attack from the back. August and Andrews will man the hose and be ready to go on my command. Cash and Neal, go through the front and take the second floor."

We grab our gear and disperse.

Justin and I put on our tanks and masks and head to the front door. It's locked, but the house is old and a swift kick to the door does the trick. The smoke is thick, and the glow from the fire is at the back of the house. Kitchen or family room maybe. The other team will handle that.

Once we're up the stairs, I hear a woman screaming and banging on the wall, but I can't see through the smoke, it's so thick. "Fire department, call out!"

"Here. I'm here," she says, coughing.

We feel our way down the hall until we run into her. "Ma'am, we're going to get you out. Is there anyone else in the house?"

"My kids," she says, barely able to get the words out. She isn't breathing very well.

"Where are they?"

"Baby, behind this wall. My son, at the end—" She goes into another fit of coughing.

"Don't worry, ma'am. We'll find them." I grab my radio. "Neal is on the way out with a woman. Two kids inside. A baby and an older one."

The captain radios that he's on his way up.

I open the door to the room the woman pointed to and quickly locate the crib. The child inside it is wearing only a diaper. And he's not moving. "Got the baby," I yell into my radio as flashes of Leo go through my head. I scoop the baby into my arms. He starts moving, and relief flows through me when I realize he was only sleeping. I put his blanket over his head and run back to the stairs.

As I make my way downstairs and outside, the fire is moving closer to the second floor.

I hand the baby off to Debbe and Ryan and run back in to look for the other kid. Before I make it into the house, Bass comes out with a kid over his shoulder. He puts him on the gurney just as he comes to.

The kid, who can't be more than fifteen, is disoriented and slurring his words, and the soot on his face makes his complexion appear a shade darker than his African-American skin.

The mother, who is watching over her baby, stops what she's doing, rips the oxygen mask off her face, and accosts the teen. "This is all your fault! What were you doing? Smoking crack? Huffing paint?"

"What do you care?" the boy yells and tries to sit up. "You don't give a shit what I do since Dad died."

The woman pushes him back down. "You could have killed us." She motions to the burning house. "Look what you did to our home."

"Let it burn," the kid says. "You hate that fucking house. We all do. Maybe his goddamn ghost will die with it, and we can all get on with our lives."

I can't help feeling sorry for the kid. He lost his father. I'm all too familiar with what it does to a child when they lose a parent.

I knew a lot of kids who lost a parent in 9/11. We all handled it differently. Fortunately, I was able to turn my grief into a career. Emma buried hers in boys. But more often than not, kids dealt with it by turning to drugs and alcohol.

We put the fire out quickly, and after a few hours of overhaul, we pack up our gear as the sun is rising. Before I get in the rig, I do something I rarely do—I talk to one of the neighbors who'd been watching from his front porch.

"Sir, do you happen to know the boy's name? The older one?"

"Jaylen Tiffin," the man says, shaking his head. "Seemed like a decent kid until his dad passed. Shame."

"Do you know how his father died?"

"He had himself a bad heart attack—you know the kind no one survives."

"They call them widow-makers," I say.

"Yeah, that kind. Poor guy was only forty-five." He pounds his chest. "I done been smokin' and drinkin' for sixty years, and mine's still ticking. Don't seem fair."

"And Jaylen's mother. What's her name?"

"Brandi, with an *I*."

"Thank you, sir."

"You're welcome, son. Thank you for your service. You boys did good today."

I tip my helmet at him and return to the truck.

Jaylen and Brandi Tiffin. I pull out my phone and add their names to my notes so I won't forget.

~ ~ ~

Back at the firehouse, fresh from a shower, Denver walks up behind me and whacks the back of my leg with a rolled-up towel.

"What'd you do that for?" I ask.

"I thought it might wipe that shit-eating grin off your face."

"The *what?"*

"You got something going on today?" he asks.

"No," I say innocently.

"I'm calling bullshit," Bass says, coming around the corner. "I know exactly why you're in a good mood, and it has nothing to do with baked goods."

I shake my head and smack my lips together, admitting nothing.

"You gotta keep that one around," Justin says, emerging from the shower. "The woman can *bake*."

"I'm not with her, guys. She's not mine to keep around."

"But you want some of that, right?" Justin asks.

I shoot him a scolding look.

"What? You gotta quit living like a monk one of these days, Lieutenant. Why not today?"

Yeah, why not today? a voice rings in my head.

"Lieutenant!" someone yells from down the hall. "Someone's here to see you."

I throw on clothes and a little extra cologne. When I pass the mirror and get a glimpse of myself, I realize Denver was right. I do have a shit-eating grin.

CHAPTER TWELVE

EMMA

Brett rubs his stomach as we leave the firehouse. "You're going to make me fat, Emma."

No way could he ever get fat. He's pure muscle. I can't tear my eyes away from him. I notice the tattoo on his left arm again. I really want to see how high up it goes. I have the strangest urge to reach out and trace it with my finger.

I try not to smile when I see him adjusting himself. God, that's sexy.

My attention is drawn to a girl running down the street with her father, and suddenly, I remember who I am, where I came from, and what Brett is.

When I turn back to him, he's eyeing me strangely. "What just happened?" he asks. "You seemed happy and then you were sad." He notices the girl and her father. "Are you still missing your daughter?"

"It's not that. She got back two days ago."

"I'll bet you're glad she's home. I'm not sure I could go two weeks without seeing Leo."

I want to ask him about his ex, but I don't.

"How'd the talk go?" he asks. "You told Evelyn what happened, right?"

I'm mildly impressed that he remembers her name. We start slowly toward the school and I'm grateful he's trying to distract me with conversation.

"I told her. I think it was harder on me than her, however. She's a kid. Don't all kids think they and their parents are invincible?"

He looks at me sadly. "Not when the kids are us."

"It's strange. Evelyn knows what happened to my father but since he was never a part of her life, it has no real effect on her."

"That's a good thing," he says. "Not that she never met him, but that she didn't have to experience losing him."

"I couldn't agree with you more. But don't you worry about Leo? About putting him through that?"

"Not really," he says.

"But what you do is so dangerous."

"Emma, what you and I are doing right now is dangerous. We're walking the streets of Brooklyn. We could step off the curb and get hit by a bus. We could—"

"Get abducted by a gunman?"

He shrugs. "It happens."

I slow my steps. "You're making me want to run back to my house and never leave."

He puts a hand on my elbow and nudges me forward. My eyes close at his touch. His large hand wraps around my arm, and I decide I like the feel of it. I like it way too much.

I wiggle free. "I'm fine. I was kidding. Kind of."

"Where is Evelyn now? She didn't want to come with you?"

"She goes to a day camp in the summer. All her friends go, too. It's good for her, and it keeps her busy and active and off her phone for the better part of the day."

"What keeps *you* busy and active in the summer?"

I try to think of something that makes my life sound more interesting than it is. But nothing can sugarcoat the boring existence I lead. "I teach an online English class for high school students. I hang out with other teachers. We work out and sometimes go to dinner. I play softball in a league for teachers. And I do some volunteer work."

He looks amused. "Volunteer? That's commendable."

"It's kind of a given when your mom runs the charity."

He spends the next few minutes asking me about her work and then, before I know it, we're back where we were on Friday, across the street from the school.

"Here we are." He motions to the bench we sat on the other day. "Want to sit for a minute?"

"No."

"Do you want to cross the street?"

"No. Yes. No."

"Well, would you look at that? A woman who can't make up her mind," he jokes.

I playfully punch his arm.

"Ouch," he says, rubbing it melodramatically. "You must work out a lot."

"Oh, shut up, Lieutenant."

He smirks. He likes it when I call him that.

He motions to the school. "You have to do it sometime. Why not now?"

"Are you saying you're going to *make* me cross the street?" I ask.

"Of course not," he says, looking appalled that I would make such an insinuation.

I stare him down. "Are you saying that if I don't move my legs, you'll drag me across the street like a child, so I have no choice but to walk with you or get hit by a bus?"

He smiles. He gets my game. "Yes, Emma. If you don't do this on your own, I will make you cross the street."

"Well then, I guess I don't have a choice."

"No, you don't, do you?" he says with a snarky rise of his brow.

I draw in a long breath and then blow it out. *I can do this.*

The hand on the crosswalk turns green, and Brett steps off the curb into the street. He looks back at me, waiting.

"I'm coming … maybe."

He reaches back and grabs my hand, gently pulling me into the street with him. The crosswalk hand flashes yellow.

"Remember what I said about us being more likely to get hit by a bus?" he says. "Come on, Emma. I was in that room with you. I know how strong you are."

His hand holding mine gives me the courage I need to cross the street. But then I stop dead on the other side. My feet are cemented to the pavement. I can't take another step. All I see when I look at the front steps of the school is Kenny Lutwig, pointing a gun at me and forcing me back through the doors.

My heart pounds when I think about that day. "I … I can't." I turn my back to the school.

The worst thing I can imagine happens. Tears roll down my cheeks. I will them to stop, but I have no control over myself at this moment. I don't want him to see me like this. I'm an emotional wreck. I look away, shielding my face from him as I turn into a blubbering fool.

"Emma?" he says, angling himself so he can see me.

The look in his eyes is one of horror, and I'm positive mascara is running down my cheeks. I frantically wipe my face. "I'm fine. I'm so sorry. I don't understand why, uh, … this isn't like me."

I'm lying to him. To myself. I'm anything but fine right now. I can't get the tears to stop flowing and my body is beginning to shake uncontrollably.

"*You're* sorry? Emma, I'm the one who's sorry. I pushed too hard. You weren't ready."

Why is he trying to take responsibility for my mental breakdown?

"Come on," he says. "Let's get you back across the street where you can sit down."

I nod, but when he tries to lead me, my feet won't move. I can't force myself to take even one small step. I'm frozen in place, shaking. I am in a full state of panic and feel as if I'm going to faint.

He grips my head in his hands and looks into my eyes, which I'm sure are glazed over. "Emma!"

He talks to me, but my head is spinning, my ears are ringing, and I can't hear anything he says.

When I don't respond, he just looks at me. Then, without any exchange of words, he picks me up, cradling me in his arms as he carries me across the street.

When we get to the other side, panic turns to pure mortification. This may be the most embarrassing moment of my life, being hauled across the street like a helpless woman. At the same time, the feeling of being in his arms is unlike anything I've experienced. I want him to hold onto me forever. I've never felt so protected in my entire life.

He stops walking and just stares at me. I just stare at him. Then I see some passersby looking at us and I think maybe this is getting a little weird.

"We're at the bench," I say.

He's still staring at me, but I'm not sure he hears me.

I nod my head at the sidewalk. "Brett, we're at the bench. You can put me down now."

The loud sound of a car horn in the street startles him and he finally breaks his stare. "Oh, yeah, sorry," he says, embarrassed that he's still holding me.

He sets me on my feet, and I sit, trying to process what the hell just happened—and I'm not talking about my panic attack.

He sits next to me. "It's no big deal," he says, like whatever just happened between us wasn't the most confusing thing of all time. "Next time I bet we'll make it all the way through the front doors."

I don't miss the way he says *we'll* make it, like he has something to work through too.

I look back at the school, ashamed that I couldn't make it all the way there today. Then I glance at the grocery store on the corner, wondering if the Shettlemans are as pathetic as I am, or if they've gone back to work. I've been stopping there for years for my morning coffee. All the teachers have. The lovely old couple know us all by name. They treat us like family. They must have a soft spot for teachers being that they're right next to the school.

I sometimes patronize another store closer to my house, but it almost feels like I'm cheating on the Shettlemans. Most days I go out of my way to visit their place.

"Actually, I think I'd like to go *there.*" I point to the corner grocery.

He stands, putting himself between me and the school. *How does he always manage to do the exact thing I need him to do?* He holds out a hand as if he knows I need it to cross the street. "Come on, then."

I don't find it hard to walk into the store. My eyes immediately go to the counter, where I see Mr. Shettleman selling a Coke to a teenager. Then I notice Mrs. Shettleman perched in her regular spot, on a chair behind the counter, working the usual crossword puzzle.

It's like nothing happened. Like they weren't held at gunpoint and robbed by that maniac.

Mrs. Shettleman looks up from her crossword, drops her newspaper, and comes toward me with her arms out. "My dear Emma." She wraps me in a hug from which there is no escaping until she decides it's over. "I was hoping you'd come in. I'm so, so sorry to hear what that man put you through."

"I could say the same for you."

"Pish. It's not the first time we've been robbed, and it won't be the last. It goes with the territory. We've learned to cooperate so no one gets hurt."

"But someone did get hurt, Mrs. Shettleman. A man lost his leg."

Her head bobs up and down, empathy bleeding from her wrinkled face. "I know. And I heard what you did while being locked in that dreadful closet with him for hours on end. You're a hero, my girl."

"I'm not the hero," I say, motioning to Brett. "He is. Mr. and Mrs. Shettleman, meet Lt. Brett Cash. He's the firefighter who saved Carter's life and got the rest of us out of there unscathed."

Mrs. Shettleman's eyebrows shoot up and then she looks back and forth between Brett and me like she's watching a tennis match.

"Is that so?" she says, taking Brett's strong hand into her old, weathered one.

"You were right, Mrs. Shettleman. Emma was the hero."

"Why don't we just call you both heroes?" she says.

Her husband comes over to shake Brett's hand. "Thank you for your service, son."

"Just doing my job, sir."

"How is that feisty daughter of yours?" Mrs. Shettleman asks me.

"Still feisty."

"You'll bring her by this summer, won't you?"

"Of course. We'd better go. It was nice seeing you. I'm glad you're both okay."

"And you, dear," she says, giving me another hug.

Outside, I take one more look at the school and then walk in the opposite direction.

"They're a nice old couple," Brett says.

"They are. They didn't deserve to be robbed."

"*Nobody* deserves bad things to happen to them."

"Except maybe Kenny Lutwig," I say.

"Maybe not even him. You don't know his story. Could be he lost a parent too, and never learned how to cope."

Suddenly, Brett stops walking and turns around, staring blankly down another street.

"What is it?"

"Nothing. I was just thinking about someone I met who lives over that way."

He looks torn between wanting to stay with me or walk away. Is he thinking of a woman? If he is, why would I even care? Except that after the way he held me in his arms, I do care.

"Emma, I want to walk you home, but there is something I need to do."

I wave him off. "I'm not a child, Brett," I say curtly. "I don't need an escort."

"I know you don't. But I was going to walk with you anyway. Maybe next time?"

"Yeah, maybe."

"So, Friday?" he asks. "Same time, same bench?"

I consider turning him down. But I realize seeing him every three days has been the highlight of my summer, even if nothing can ever come of it. I don't seem to have any control over myself around him. It's something I haven't felt around a guy in over twelve years. Heck, if I'm being honest—*ever*. So I don't turn him down, even though I should. But I don't, because I tell myself I'm the one in control. And because, apparently, I'm a stupid, stupid girl.

CHAPTER THIRTEEN

BRETT

I don't turn around to see if she's watching me walk away. I'll pretend she is. Because I can't seem to get a solid vibe from her. Sometimes, like when she was in my arms and it felt so right to be holding her, I think I want to ask her out. But then she gets all cold on me, like a few minutes ago when she snapped at me about not needing an escort. She's fighting something, and it's more than her struggle to get through what happened at the school.

I've never felt the need to protect anyone as much as I want to protect Emma. When I was holding her, I realized I didn't ever want to see her cry again. I wanted to do everything in my power to make things all right for her. I couldn't tear my eyes away. I'm sure she thought I was a grade-A idiot.

I try to put it out of my mind when I get to my destination a few blocks over. An FDNY car is parked in the street. I climb the front steps, the smell of an old fire wafting in the air. A familiar face appears.

"Lt. Cash," Kellan Brown says, slinging his kit over a shoulder. Kellan is one of the investigators who figures out how fires are started.

"Hey, Captain. You have a cause for this one?"

"Faulty wiring in the kitchen."

I'm surprised. "You sure?"

"Are you questioning me, Cash? You do understand that I outrank you, and I've been doing this job longer than you've been a firefighter."

"I'm sorry. It's just that the woman who lives here was so sure it was her son's drug habit that started the blaze."

"I did find paraphernalia in a back room, but I can say with certainty that wasn't the cause. You were in on this one?"

"Yes. Everyone got out okay. But something about the boy—I just felt the need to check on things."

"They won't be living here for a while, if ever. The fire damage alone will likely get the house condemned, not to mention what the smoke did."

"That's going to be a hard blow. The woman lost her husband not too long ago."

He tosses his bag in the backseat of his car. "Tough break. I'll see you around, Lieutenant."

I lift my chin at him before I turn and stare at the house. I can't imagine what the boy must be going through. He loses his dad and then his home. Was what he said true? Was he glad his place burned? He said something about hating the house and wanting the ghost of his father to die. Then again, people often say things they don't mean in stressful situations.

"Hello?" a woman says behind me.

It's the owner of the house. She's wearing clothes now instead of pajamas. Her face looks worn and tired, and she's obviously been crying. Her teenage son is standing behind her, staring at their house. I look around for the toddler, but he's not with them.

"Hi. I'm Lt. Cash. I was here during the fire."

"I don't remember you," she says.

"It's okay. There was a lot going on."

"I saw you talking to that man in the fire department car. Is there an investigation?" She scowls at her kid. "As if we need one."

"The cause of the fire was determined to be faulty wiring."

"Really?"

"I told you it wasn't me," Jaylen says. "You never believe anything I say."

"That's because you never tell me the truth." It looks like she's about to start yelling at him, but then she turns to me. "I'm sorry to be so rude, Lieutenant. I'm Brandi Tiffin, and this is Jaylen."

I shake her hand and then his. "Call me Brett. Your other son, is he okay?"

"He's fine. We're staying a few blocks over at my sister's, until we can figure something out."

"Do you have insurance?"

"We do. My husband was always good about that."

"I heard you lost him not too long ago. My condolences."

Jaylen kicks a rock on the sidewalk.

"Thank you," Brandi says. "Is it okay if we go inside and get a few things?"

"Someone from the Department of Buildings should show up today and make a determination about its safety, but I doubt the place will collapse if we head inside and let you look around."

I follow her up the front steps, then I turn around to see Jaylen still planted on the sidewalk. "You coming, Jaylen?"

"Jay. She's the only one who calls me Jaylen."

"Okay, Jay. How about we see what we can salvage out of this mess?"

He looks at the ground and nods sadly.

Brandi opens a closet under the stairs and pulls out suitcases. She hands one to Jay when he comes through the door. "Pack some clothes for you and Anthony. I'll be up in a second."

Brandi follows him with her eyes as he goes up the stairs, banging the suitcase against each tread. When he reaches the top, she shakes her head. "I don't know what to do with him. He's always been somewhat difficult, but it got so much worse after Andre died."

"Losing a parent can be hard on a kid."

Brandi studies me. "You say that like you know from experience."

"I lost my mom when I was eleven."

"Oh, dear. I'm sorry."

I look at the ceiling. "How old is he?"

"He just turned fifteen."

"Tough age. I'd like to help if I can. With Jay."

"How do you mean?"

"I'm not sure yet. Maybe he needs to talk to another guy who's been through something similar."

"I'd be grateful for whatever you could do, Brett."

"Do you mind if I go upstairs and check on him?"

"Please."

"Don't go into the kitchen or family room. I don't know how stable they are."

"I won't."

Upstairs, I find Jay sitting on the floor holding a model car.

"You like cars?" I ask.

He drops it like he's embarrassed. "I'm not two," he says defiantly.

"You don't have to be two to like cars. I've always liked them." There are more models in the room. "You have a lot of these. What's your favorite?"

He shrugs.

"That's okay. You don't have to tell me."

"They're stupid. I don't build them anymore." He gets up and goes to the closet.

It dawns on me that he must have built the models with his father. I peruse his collection. "If they're so stupid, you won't mind if I take one then." I pick up a 1968 Ford Mustang. "This one is a beauty."

He walks over and grabs it out of my hands and throws it in his suitcase.

"You like Mustangs, huh? I have one, you know."

"You drive a 1968 Mustang?" he asks curiously.

"I don't *drive* one. It's in my backyard under a tarp. I'm restoring it. It doesn't even run though, so I've got a long way to go." I look at him thoughtfully, thinking about how the car has been sitting in my yard for a long time without any attention. "Hey, I have an idea. Why don't you help me?"

"Why would you want me to do that?"

"Because you like Mustangs. And I could use the company."

He stares at the model car sitting on top of his clothes. He looks conflicted. "I'm going to be a mechanic. My uncle owns a shop in Harlem. So I know a lot about cars."

"Looks like I'm in luck. What do you say, maybe once a week on one of my days off? I'll even spring for pizza."

He's doing his best to look uninterested, but I can clearly see he is.

"Pepperoni?" he asks.

"Whatever you'd like. We'll have to clear it with your mom."

"She won't care. She doesn't care what I do."

"I'm sure that's not true."

He snorts. "You don't know her."

"No, I don't. But I'm going to ask her permission anyway."

"Suit yourself."

An hour later, after the three of us roll their suitcases over to Brandi's sister's house, I give Jay and his mother my address and phone number. "How about we get started tomorrow?"

"Tomorrow?" Jay says, like he doesn't believe I'm serious about him helping me.

"Why not? Unless you have something better to do."

He's going to bail on the whole thing. I can see it in his eyes.

"Tomorrow will be perfect," Brandi says. "What time do you want him there?"

"How about I come get you at eleven?" I ask him.

He clenches his jaw. "I'm fifteen. I can get there by myself."

"Of course you can. See you then."

Brandi follows me. "I appreciate what you're doing, but don't be surprised if he doesn't show up. Jaylen lies about everything lately."

"I've got his number. I'll see that he gets there."

She smiles. "Even if it doesn't work out, thank you for trying. It's been so hard."

I briefly touch her arm. "It'll take time, but things will get better."

"I hope you're right," she says as I walk away.

I hope I'm right, too.

CHAPTER FOURTEEN

EMMA

Evelyn is lying on her bed with her earbuds in. I lie down next to her and pull her into a hug for the umpteenth time since she returned a few days ago.

"What's that for?" she asks.

"It's just nice to have you home."

"I was only gone for two weeks."

"But it felt like forever. I don't know what I'm going to do when you go off to college."

She looks at me with crazy eyes. "I'm twelve. We have plenty of time to get used to that idea."

"I know. It just seems like only yesterday I was bringing you home from the hospital."

She nudges me. "You always say that."

"It's always true. Wait until you have a child of your own." I lean on an elbow and give her a hard look. "Which should be in no less than fifteen or twenty years."

Evelyn laughs. "Don't worry. I'm not going to repeat your mistakes."

I brush a stray hair behind her ear. "I have never once thought of you as a mistake. You are the best thing that ever happened to me."

Her smile becomes a frown.

"What is it, sweetie?"

She looks over at her dresser. On it is the only picture she has of her father. Actually, it's a series of pictures of the two of us from one of those photo booths at the mall. My God, we were so young. I was only a few years older than Evelyn is now.

She shrugs.

I sigh, knowing what's on her mind. Every so often she brings up the idea of finding Stefan. She's even suggested going to Germany. I understand the urge. I've tried to put myself in her shoes, and I guess I'd want the same thing. But he's too far away, and I wouldn't even know where to start. What keeps me from putting more effort into it—other than the fact that I don't fly—is that I don't want her to be disappointed. What if we found him and he rejected her? I don't see it turning out any other way. If he'd wanted to be part of her life, he would have contacted me a long time ago.

She says, "Hey, aren't you going to be late for Taco Tuesday?"

"I can skip it and stay home."

"Grandma's here."

"Yes, but I can skip it if you want me to."

She shakes her head. "It's important for you be with your friends. You don't want to disappoint them."

I study her, thinking, not for the first time, how she is like a grown woman in a child's body. My feisty daughter is wise beyond her years. Sometimes I wonder who is parenting whom in this relationship. "I don't want to disappoint *you*."

"You could never. You're the best mom I've ever had."

We both laugh.

"Besides, Grandma said she'd make popcorn and watch *Divergent* with me again."

"Aren't you getting tired of that movie?"

"It's a cinematic masterpiece, Mom. Don't diss my favorite movie of all time."

"I wouldn't dream of it, sweetie." I kiss her and hop off the bed. "Don't wait up."

"Be safe," she says. "Make wise choices."

I laugh. "Yes, *Mom*."

~ ~ ~

Becca and her boyfriend—fellow teacher, Jordan—are already sitting at a large table when Lisa, Kelly, Rachel, Michelle and I walk in and join them. Jordan is the only man who comes to Taco Tuesday. He's only one of a handful of male teachers at our school. We've asked others to come, and some have tried over the years, but none of them stuck with the group as the seven of us have.

"What's up with Becca?" Lisa asks. "She's practically bouncing out of her chair."

"She's probably happy that Emma is back," Kelly says. "We missed you last week."

Becca is almost bursting at the seams with giddiness. "That's not it," I say. "Something's up."

Before we can take our seats, Becca holds out her left hand so we can all see the brand-new ring on her finger. "We're engaged!" she shouts.

After we all scream, and fawn over the ring, we settle into the booth.

Jordan takes Becca's hand and looks into her eyes. "After what happened … well, you just never know how much time you're going to have with someone, so why wait?"

"When's the wedding?" Kelly asks.

"End of the summer," Becca says. "We'll take our honeymoon the week before we return to school."

"Seven weeks?" I ask. "That's not a lot of time to plan a wedding."

"We don't need a huge fancy affair. We're going to get married at Jordan's parents' church just outside the city."

"We'll help you plan it," I say. "It will be spectacular."

"Thanks, guys. That means a lot to us."

"How have you two been doing?" Michelle asks, motioning to Becca and me. "You know, since the incident."

Becca and I look at each other. We both know she got over it a lot quicker than I did.

"We're good," Becca says.

Kelly stares at me. "Have you been back to the school yet?"

"Not exactly."

"What does that mean?" she asks.

"I made it to the corner this morning, but I couldn't go in. I did check on the Shettlemans though."

"I could go with you," Kelly says. "Maybe we all could. We'll meet up and give you support."

I think of Brett and all the support he's given me over the past week. "Thanks, but I've got it covered."

Lisa's eyes sparkle. "What aren't you telling us, Emma?"

"What do you mean?"

"You got all dreamy-eyed."

"Huh?"

"You know what I'm talking about," she says. "Who is he?"

My cheeks pink.

Becca pounces. "You're blushing. I don't think I've ever seen you blush." She straightens as realization dawns. "Oh my God, it's the fireman, isn't it? The way you talked about him at the police station that night, I knew you wanted him."

"The fireman?" Rachel asks.

"He helped us," Becca says. "He's the one who saved us. It's him, isn't it? Come on, Emma, spill."

"First off, I wasn't all dreamy-eyed. The firefighter from the incident is the one helping me get back to the school. I get a little farther every day. He's been great and not pushy." I see the way they're all looking at me, like they're waiting to find out how he swept me off my feet. "Quit looking at me like that. It's not what you're thinking."

"Oh, really?" Kelly asks. "How did it come about that the two of you met up? Did he call to check on you?"

"I took muffins to the firehouse."

Lisa muffles a squeal. "You *like* him!"

"I don't *like* him. I wanted to thank all of them, and he was there."

"Oh, he just happened to be there," Becca says suspiciously.

"Yes," I say, not offering that I'd called ahead to make sure.

"And how many times have you seen him?" Lisa asks.

"Three."

"Holy shit," Becca says. "When should we plan the wedding?"

My jaw goes slack. "Stop it. We aren't dating. We aren't doing anything."

"But you want to," Michelle says.

"No, I don't," I force myself to say. "He's a fireman."

"Uh, yeah," Rachel says. "Why the hell wouldn't you want to date a hot, hunky fireman who's a hero?"

Everyone else at the table stares Rachel down until she gets it.

"Oh, God. I'm sorry, Emma. I forgot about your dad. I didn't mean to be so insensitive."

"You're not. It's fine."

"Are all firemen off limits?" Rachel asks. "As in you won't date *any* of them?"

"Pretty much. It's not worth the risk."

"Does that mean you wouldn't date a cop, a marine"—Jordan bites his lip in thought—"a lion tamer?"

"I hadn't really thought about it, but I guess not."

He looks at me in disappointment. "You're really narrowing your chances, there, Emma. Why would you let someone's occupation get in the way of true love?"

"There are plenty of guys out there with safe jobs," I say. "You, for instance. Being a teacher is safe."

He snorts. "Unless you count what happened to you and Becca."

"Okay, fine. You've got me there, but that was a one-in-a-million thing."

"How come I've never seen you get all dreamy-eyed over a teacher?" Lisa asks. "For that matter, how come you don't date teachers? Or *anyone*?"

"Would you quit it with the dreamy eyes? And I date."

Six pairs of eyes look at me like I'm full of shit.

"What?" I ask.

"You don't date," Kelly says. "You fuck."

My chin hits the table for the second time tonight. "Do you have to be so crude?"

"Well, what would *you* call it when you have random men over and then kick them out before they can so much as cuddle?"

"I'd call it being responsible by not giving my daughter the wrong idea."

"That is so ass-backwards, I don't even know where to start dissecting it," Jordan says.

"Huh?"

"Sleeping with random men is not responsible."

"That's not what I meant. I don't want Evelyn seeing me with a man and thinking I'm going to have some happily-ever-after relationship."

"Well, why the hell not?" he asks.

"Because despite how much two people love each other, not every relationship ends up that way."

"I think you're using what happened to your dad as an excuse not to have a mature adult relationship," he says.

Becca hits him in the arm.

"What?" he says. "You know we're all thinking it."

"Do you mind if we talk about something else?" I ask.

"You mean something other than the hot, hunky fireman?" Michelle says. "What was his name, anyway?"

"Brett Cash," Becca says. "*Lieutenant* Brett Cash."

Michelle snickers. "God, Emma. Even his name is sexy."

I know it is. "Whatever. Come on, guys, let's order a few pitchers of margaritas and plan an epic wedding."

CHAPTER FIFTEEN

BRETT

"You're the first person I wanted to call," Brianna excitedly screams into the phone. "Can you believe it? I might be the next backup singer for White Poison. Oh my God, Brett. I'm going to meet Adam Stuart and go on tour with him. Well, if I make it that far. I mean they told me there's like a hundred girls up for the gig. But still, there's a chance, right? Do you really think I can do it? Eeeek!"

I laugh. "Of course you can do it, Bria. What a sensational opportunity for you."

"This could be epic. Can you imagine the kind of exposure I'd get, being on stage with White Poison? It's the break I've been waiting for."

"I'm so proud of you," I say.

"Don't be proud yet. I might not make it."

"It doesn't matter if you make it or not, I'm still proud of you."

There is a long pause. "Do you think Mom would be proud of me?"

"Hell yes I do. You're going after your dreams, Bria. Not many people have the courage to do that."

"But I've done so many things that would have disappointed her."

"All bumps in the road, little sister. What doesn't break us makes us stronger and all that."

"Do you really think so?"

"I know so."

I look out the window. Emma is walking around the corner. It's not as if I've been waiting for her or anything. Except that I totally have. Just like an adolescent in heat. "Bria, I have to go."

"Wait, is she there? I almost forgot she was coming. Are you so excited? Are you going to ask her out?"

"Slow down. I don't know yet. Once she makes it inside the school, she might not want me around anymore. I have zero idea where this is going, if anywhere at all."

"She'd be crazy not to want to date you. You're the whole package. And if she says she doesn't want to, introduce her to Leo. That kid is a chick magnet."

Emma comes inside. I watch her from the common area. "I'll call you tomorrow, okay?"

"Okay. I'm going to want details. Good luck."

I laugh. "I'm not the one auditioning to join a famous band."

"Eeeek!" she screams again. "Bye."

"Oh, hell yeah," Justin says when Emma appears with a tray of goodies. He hops off the couch and gives her a kiss on the cheek. "What's for breakfast?"

She peels back the corner of the tin foil. "Individual coffee cakes. I wasn't sure what you'd like, so I made cherry, cream cheese, and apple."

"We all want to marry you," he says. "I hope you know that. Even the ones with wives."

She blushes and looks in my direction.

"Good morning." I take the tray from her. "You don't have to keep doing this, but it sure is appreciated."

"I like doing it, especially in the summer when I have more time on my hands."

I put the tray on the table and pick up a cherry coffee cake, eating it in two bites. "Dang, Emma. These are heavenly."

Dispatch comes over the loudspeaker, and my heart sinks. Damn, there's only ten minutes left on shift.

"I'm really sorry," I say, turning and running to the rig. "I'm not sure how long I'll be. If you don't want to wait, I'll understand."

She shrugs. "I'll wait a while."

"You can stay here if you want, hang out in the common room."

She follows me into the garage. "Nah. It's really nice outside. I think I'll go wait on—"

"Our bench," we say at the same time and then smile.

"See you soon, Emma."

"Okay, Lieutenant."

Fuuuuck me. The way she says it almost gets me hard, even when I'm racing out the door to a fire.

I watch her as she walks out of the garage after the trucks pull out. I can't tear my eyes away from her. And apparently, she can't tear her eyes away from me either.

Twenty minutes later, the call having been a false alarm, we're pulling back into the garage. I hop down and wave to Emma, holding up the fingers on my right hand, indicating I'll be five minutes.

She flashes me the okay sign.

"What's up with you and the brunette who always sits on the bench?" Kent Hayes, from the next shift, asks.

"I'm still trying to figure that out."

He smirks. "If you can't figure it out, I'm sure *I* can."

"Don't even think about it, Hayes."

He raises a brow. "Territorial, are we?"

"Just. Don't."

I go to the locker room to change clothes, and realize that for the past week, I haven't stopped thinking about her. Even when I was working on the car the other day with Jay, all I wanted to do was tell her how great it was. Jay really got into it and was excited about fixing it up with me. His mom called me later that night and told me she already saw some changes in him. He even asked her to buy him a model car kit—something he hadn't done since before his father died.

I felt such a sense of accomplishment, and all I wanted to do was tell Emma.

Five minutes later, I'm crossing the street. Emma stays seated on the bench, so I join her.

She's quiet and contemplative. "What are you thinking?"

"Isn't that what women say after sex?" she says with a giggle. Then she turns a deep shade of red. "I mean, not that I wanted, or we were … oh, God, you know what I meant, right?"

I laugh. "I know a joke when I hear one. I only asked because you looked deep in thought, and I wondered if you were having second thoughts about this whole thing."

She looks confused.

"You know, about going into the school."

"Oh, right." She shakes her head and rolls her eyes, making me wonder just what *thing* she was thinking of. "I feel like such a wimp. Everyone else has been back to the school, even Becca. Everyone but me."

"You're not a wimp."

"I have nightmares about it," she says sadly.

"I've had a few myself. But that's nothing new. In this job, it goes with the territory."

I don't tell her that one of those nightmares was about her. About Kenny Lutwig shooting her because I was stupid and riled him up. I watched her die at my feet, unable to save her because the blood was used up. I woke up sweating so badly, I had to change the sheets.

"I haven't had nightmares like this since my dad died," she says.

"I had a lot after my mom died, too."

"Did you dream about her dying in the south tower?" she asks.

"Actually, no. I dreamed of her coming into my room the morning she left. Then I dreamt of her getting hit by a car or drowning. It was always something different. My dad never shied away from letting me watch the 9/11 footage, so I knew exactly how she died, but I never saw that in my dreams."

"We watched it on TV, too," she says. "But after the first tower collapsed, my mom made someone take me out of the room. I never saw another minute of coverage. To this day I turn off the TV if they start talking about it. Unlike you, I always had the same dream. He tells me everything happens for a reason and then walks into the south tower right before it collapses."

"Wow, that's prophetic."

"Yeah, well, I'm still waiting to find out the reason."

I take this opportunity to tell Emma about Jay and the old Mustang. "I thought I'd fix it up and give it to Leo one day, but now I have the feeling that maybe the reason I've had the car all along is for Jay."

She looks at me pointedly. "Talk about prophetic."

"I don't know. It's just been on my mind a lot lately."

"You want to give the car you'd been saving for your own son to a stranger?"

"He's not such a stranger anymore. I feel a sort of bond with him. And somehow I sense he needs that old car more than Leo ever could."

She studies me for a second. "You're really something else, Lieutenant."

"I'm just trying to help a kid who went through what we did. It's no big deal."

"You're wrong, Brett. It's a very big deal."

I stand and offer her my hand. "What do you say, Emma Lockhart. Want to go kill this bitch?"

She laughs briefly, but then her face turns serious as she looks in the direction of the school. She puts her hand in mine and I pull her to her feet. She looks at our hands. Does she feel the same spark I do?

"Yes," she says. "I do."

For a second I wonder if she's answering my spoken question or my silent one.

Our hands part as we stroll to the school. I tell her about Jay, but I'm not sure she's listening. A bead of sweat trickles down her temple, despite the morning's coolness. When the school comes into view, she slows considerably. Her breathing accelerates, but she crosses the street. When we get to the same spot as the other day, between the school and the grocery, she stops.

I don't say anything, I simply stand by her side and wait.

"I just need a minute," she says.

"I know."

She turns. "You do, don't you?"

I nod, and we share a moment of clarity about the unfortunate bond we share. "You've got this, Emma."

"You really think so?"

"I do."

She shuffles her feet slowly until she's standing in front of the school. She looks at the steps, and I know she's thinking about the moment she was taken hostage.

I'm positive she's about to turn and leave, so I trot up the steps and try the door. It's locked, so I press the call button. I keep my eye on Emma to see if she's going to bolt. She doesn't. She just watches me.

A minute later someone comes to the door. The woman takes in my FDNY shirt and then notices Emma on the sidewalk. Her expression becomes compassionate. She obviously knows who Emma is and unlocks the door.

"Thanks," I say. "Can you give us a minute?"

The woman backs away. "Take all the time you need. I'll be in the office if you need anything."

I stand in the doorway, holding one of the heavy glass doors open as I wait patiently to see what Emma will do. "It's only a few more steps. I'll wait here all day if that's what it takes."

"I'm being ridiculous," she finally says.

"You're being human."

Her feet inch forward, and she climbs the first step.

"Look at me," I tell her. "You're just going to work, same thing you've done for years. Think of all the students you've taught here. You are shaping the lives of those who will run the country one day. I can't think of a more important job than the one you do."

"I can," she says, looking at my T-shirt.

"Eyes on me," I say.

She locks eyes with me and ascends the last few steps. I nod encouragingly and my smile grows bigger as the gap between us closes. She makes it all the way to the doorway.

I step aside. "All you have to do is walk through."

She holds my stare as she steps across the threshold. She's done it. She's conquered her fear. I'm about to throw a fist pump when Emma starts to panic.

Her eyes glaze over and she starts shaking. I consider rushing her outside the door, but that will only make it twice as hard for her to come back next time.

Think, Brett.

I impulsively pull her into my arms. I cup her face. I kiss her.

At first, she resists, and I think this was a horrible idea, but then she kisses me back. She kisses me hard and grabs onto my sides, locking me to her. She kisses me like a drowning woman who has come up for air. It's desperate. Deliberate. Passionate.

It's the first kiss I've shared with a woman other than Amanda in almost a decade. And I could be wrong, but I'll bet it's the best damn first kiss anyone has ever had.

I'm not sure how long we stand here and kiss, but eventually she pulls away. "Why did you do that?"

"I thought you needed a new memory of this place to replace the old one."

She wipes her bottom lip, and I see the hint of a smile.

She turns to the administration office. "I need to do it all. Get it over with."

I gesture to the inner doorway. "Lead the way."

She carefully walks through the door, taking us behind the glass wall that separates the office from the reception area. She gazes at the corner where the gunman kept most of the hostages. She keeps moving until she's in front of the storage room door. Her hand shakes.

"Do I need to kiss you again?" I joke.

She looks at me, her eyes focusing on my lips as if she's about to take me up on my offer. "I'm … I'm fine." She looks at the door again. "Do you think you could …?"

I step up to the storage room door and open it.

She slowly follows my path and pokes her head in cautiously, as if she thinks something will jump out and attack her. "Don't let the door close."

"No way," I tell her. I'm not too happy being back here either.

She glances around the storage room from the doorway, looking at the tables and boxes. "Everything is back in its place. There's not even a trace of blood on the floor. Isn't that strange? I mean, I figured they'd clean it up, but it's like nothing ever happened."

I smile. "You did it, Emma."

"I'd like to go to my classroom, if that's okay with you."

"Sure thing. Let's go."

She backs out of the room and watches the door as it closes, shaking her head like she can't believe what once happened behind it.

She leads me through a door to a back hall, where we pass dozens of classrooms. "Here's mine," she says, pointing to one.

"It doesn't even look like a classroom," I say.

"That's because they move almost everything out for the summer. It's much nicer during the school year. Here, let me show you."

She pulls out her phone and scrolls through some pictures, then stops and hands it to me. "Here's what it normally looks like."

She is with her students, standing in front of a white board that has her name written in large block letters: **MISS LOCKHART**. Around the edges of the white board are colorful drawings, presumably made by her students. I notice how happy she looks. Happier than I've ever seen her.

"You love teaching, don't you?" I ask.

A smile brightens her face as she looks at the picture over my shoulder. "I do. I've been so worried that I'd never be able to do it again. But now ..."—she looks around her classroom—"I feel like nothing could ever keep me from it. Not even Kenny Lutwig."

A huge sigh escapes her, and I can see the tension draining from her body. "Thank you, Brett. I don't know that I could have done this without you."

"You'd have done it. Because anyone who loves teaching as much as you would do anything to keep doing it."

She studies me thoughtfully. "Is that how firefighters feel about their jobs?"

She's not talking about me. She's asking about her dad. "Every single one I've ever known."

Someone walks into the room. "Sorry," the man says when he sees us. "I didn't know anyone was here. I'm supposed to set up for the CPR class."

"We were just leaving," Emma says.

As we walk down the hallway, she looks longingly back at her classroom. That makes me smile. She's going to be just fine.

She barely glances at the storage closet as we pass it, and back on the front steps, she looks relaxed and calm.

"Congratulations, Miss Lockhart. You climbed the mountain. It feels good, doesn't it?"

She smiles.

"It took me a long time to feel comfortable going into tall buildings," I admit. "Here you are, just two weeks after, already conquering your fears."

She laughs ruefully. "I wouldn't say that. I still don't go into tall buildings. And I never fly."

My eyes widen. "Never?"

She shakes her head.

"We'll have to see what we can do about that."

"One step at a time, Lieutenant."

We make small talk on the way back. She stops as we pass the firehouse. "Isn't this where you get off?"

"I figured I'd walk you home today. Besides, my house is this way."

"Okay."

We get to the end of the block and turn the corner. She looks at me. "You live down here?"

I point in the direction of my townhouse. "At the end of the block, then one street that way."

She seems surprised. "You're kidding. That's where I live, too."

"Wow. That's unreal. I can't believe we haven't run into each other."

"Brooklyn has 2.5 million people." She smirks. "Yeah, what a surprise."

We turn another corner, and she starts to cross the street. "I'm just down here." She stops in front of a townhouse, and my jaw drops. "What is it?" she asks.

I point to the townhouse directly across the street from hers. "See the blue curtains in that second-floor window? That's Leo's room."

"You must be joking."

"Small world, huh?"

The street is lined with cars on either side. It's busy enough that one generally crosses at the corner. But now I know why she looked familiar to me when I first saw her. I've probably seen her hundreds of times and paid no attention. When you live in New York City, with its millions of people, everybody blends together.

"How long have you lived there?" she asks.

"A little more than two years. We moved in just before Leo was born. You?"

"My whole life," she says. "It's the house I grew up in. Mom couldn't bear to leave it after Dad died and then when I had Evelyn at such a young age, I couldn't leave. Even though I could now, it works for us. I love living with them." She starts to climb the steps. "Thanks for helping me, Brett. I really appreciate it."

Disappointment rises from the pit of my stomach. She's saying goodbye. I'm not sure what I was hoping for. An offer for a cup of coffee maybe? I know this isn't the last time I'll see her, now that I know she lives so close. But could it be the last time she wants to see me?

"Dinner?" I blurt out.

She turns around and draws her brows at me.

"I mean, would you go to dinner with me? Tomorrow night."

I see the answer in her eyes before the words leave her mouth. "I don't date firefighters, Brett."

"Oh." I stand here and once again try to figure out the woman in front of me. "You don't date them as a general rule, or you don't want to date me specifically."

"I'm sorry. I can't."

The sad look on her face tells me it's not me. It's her dad.

"So there are three things you're afraid of then: tall buildings, airplanes, and firefighters."

She doesn't answer me. She reaches the door and waves. "Thanks again."

"Anytime."

After she goes inside, I try to think of things I should have said to get her to change her mind. I'm no good at this anymore. I'm sure Bass or Denver, or hell … *anybody*, would have come up with something.

I'm about to walk away in defeat when I hear a bloodcurdling scream from her townhouse. I rush up the stairs only to find the door is locked. "Emma!" I shout. When she doesn't answer, I kick in the door, breaking the frame in the process. "Emma!"

CHAPTER SIXTEEN

EMMA

"In here," I yell, thankful to hear Brett's voice.

He runs into the kitchen to see me perched on a chair. I point to the corner. "Snake. There."

Brett lets out a huge sigh as he looks up to the ceiling in relief. "Jesus Christ, Emma. I thought you were being murdered."

"I was about to be," I say, peering at the snake.

He takes a look. "It's a garter snake, Emma. Small. Non-venomous. Mostly docile."

"Well how was I supposed to know that?"

He puts a hand on the chair to stabilize it. "You can come down now."

"Not on your life."

"So tall buildings, planes, firefighters, and snakes," he says.

"Apparently."

He picks up the snake as if it were a kitten. He nods to the back door. "I'll just put him out there."

I am aghast. "Not there!"

"Do you know how many of these are already living in your backyard?"

I shudder. "I don't want to know. Just get rid of it please."

I watch as he opens the sliding door to the back, crosses the small deck, goes down the stairs, and then carries the snake all the way to the back corner of our tiny yard.

"Thank you. Again," I say when he returns.

He goes into the kitchen and washes his hands at the sink. "No problem. But don't thank me yet. I busted down your front door when I heard you scream."

I run to the foyer and see the door off kilter and the door frame splintered. I groan. "Oh gosh."

"Do you have a hammer and some nails?" he asks.

"Of course."

"I'll nail your frame back into place so you can lock the door. Then I'll come by tomorrow to replace the wood, paint it, and get it back to normal."

"You can do all that?" I ask, impressed.

"I have skills, Emma."

"Right. Firefighter. Mechanic. And apparently, carpenter."

"Maybe even a few more you don't know about," he says with a wink.

I'm blushing again—when did this become a thing with me?—and I quickly fetch the tools he wants. I don't need to be thinking about his other *skills*. I can only imagine. There's a twinge in my belly when I turn around and he's standing so close I almost run into him. I hold up the hammer and nails. "Here you go."

He chuckles and works on the door. Men who can *do* things always impress me.

"Could you come back for the other stuff on Monday instead of tomorrow?" I ask.

"I suppose," he says. "You don't want me to come back tomorrow?"

Tomorrow is Saturday. I don't want Evelyn and my mother getting the wrong idea. My mom always blows everything out of proportion. And Evelyn, well, I know how her mind works. It's just safer if he returns when they aren't here.

"Will the door hold until then?" I ask.

"It should, but it won't look pretty." He hands me the hammer. "There. Done for now." He closes the gap between us. "Emma, why don't you really want me to fix it tomorrow? Are you afraid your mom or daughter will get the wrong idea?"

How does he seem to know everything I'm thinking? "Of course not," I lie. "I just don't want to take away from your weekend. I'm sure you'd like to spend it with your son."

"Whatever you say, Miss Lockhart."

He inches closer and lifts a lock of my hair, rubbing it between two fingers. I swear, even though I know it's not possible to feel his touch on the ends of my hair, I feel it all the way to my toes.

I step back. He steps forward. I take another step back. We continue this dance until my back hits the wall, and I have no place else to go.

My heart is beating wildly. My mind races back to the kiss we shared at the school. The incredible kiss that made it possible for me to be in a place that gave me one of the worst memories of my life.

His face is mere inches from mine. "What are you afraid of, Emma?"

"Everything," I manage to get out before his lips collide with mine.

He presses me against the wall as he kisses me. His lips are strong and demanding. Mine betray me as they open for his tongue. He frames my face before moving his hands down my arms and around my waist.

I will my arms to stay at my side, feigning no interest in what's happening. But the heat rising in me wins the battle and my arms snake around his neck. He moans into my mouth when my fingers thread through his hair.

He leans into me, and I feel his erection. My hips involuntarily press against his, increasing the friction between us.

"Jesus, Emma," he murmurs when his lips pull away from mine to find my neck.

I stretch my head back and let him explore the area. "Oh, God," escapes me when he sucks on a sensitive place under my ear.

I feel his smile against my skin as he doubles his efforts.

His hand finds its way under my shirt, and his strong fingers tease my side as they travel upward. He wastes no time fumbling with my bra but simply pushes it up and cups my breast in his palm. His other hand follows a similar path until he's holding both breasts.

I remove my hands from him just long enough to hurriedly pull my shirt and bra over my head. He's instantly back, kissing my neck and fondling my breasts and grinding his erection into me all at the same time. Just when I think I can't take it anymore, his fingers lightly pinch my nipples and I find myself exhaling his name.

"Where's your bedroom, Emma?" he whispers into my ear.

"Up," is all I can manage to say.

He lifts me off the ground, and I wrap my legs around his waist, not losing contact between me and his erection. He only stops kissing me to make sure we don't fall as he carries me up the stairs.

"On the left," I say, hoping I didn't leave any dirty clothes on the floor this morning. Not that I really care at this point. And not that he'd notice.

He lays me down on the bed and crawls on top of me, maintaining contact with my skin. It's almost as if he knows if he gives me time to think about this, I'll stop. *I should stop.*

But before I can push him away, his mouth is on my breast. Then his tongue is on my nipple. Wet heat floods through me, and I buck my hips into him.

He sucks and licks and teases my nipple as his finger traces a line under the waistband of my jeans. I play with his hair again, pressing his head to my chest. Then my hands travel down the back of his shirt. Needing to feel his skin, I lift his shirt and explore the taut muscles of his back.

He breaks the seal on my breast, sitting up and straddling me as he removes his shirt. We're both naked from the waist up. And we stare at each other unabashedly.

He's gorgeous. His tattoos travel all the way up his arm and over the top part of his left shoulder and chest. *Oh my.*

"You're beautiful, Emma," he says, grinding into me. He grasps the button of my pants. "I'd very much like to see the rest of you."

I close my eyes and bite my lower lip. *I should stop.*

His weight shifts off me and I feel his breath on my ear. "Don't overthink this," he whispers as he unbuttons my pants and slips a hand beneath my panties. He groans when his finger glides through my wetness. "Christ, I want you."

His words bounce around in my head. *He wants me.* It's not like I haven't been with men before. I have. As recently as a month ago. But no one has made me feel like this. And none of them have said those words to me. Is it the words, I wonder, or is it Brett?

I rub his erection through his jeans as he slips a finger inside me. As we manipulate each other, I feel the coils tightening in my belly.

The sense of loss I feel when he pulls his hand away is almost laughable. I think a whine may have escaped my mouth, and he chuckles as he quickly removes our shoes and the rest of our clothing.

The sun shines through the window as we lie gloriously naked next to each other. He caresses the curve of my hip as his eyes drink me in. He only utters a single word after his visual assault of my body.

"Wow."

His penis stands at full attention. I reach out and run my fingers along the shaft, teasing him before wrapping my hand around him. He inhales sharply. He's trying to control his breathing, and I wonder if he's trying not to come. I've only had my hand on him for ten seconds, but I feel as though he might. How long has it been since he was with a woman?

He bites his lip and makes a noise. "Not yet," he says, pushing my hand away before crawling down my body until his mouth is between my legs.

Now *I'm* the one biting my lip and making noises. *Oh my God.*

His tongue is on my clit, circling it before sucking it into his mouth. His fingers work inside me until they find that one spot that has me moaning in pleasure.

He lifts his head briefly. "That's it, Emma. I'm going to make you come. Jesus, you taste good."

Nobody's ever told me they are going to make me come. He's watching me. I'm watching him. Right here in the daylight, naked in my bed, I'm watching him go down on me. I've never seen anything so erotic.

When it gets so intense that I can't watch anymore, my head falls back against the pillow and I grab the sheets, fisting them as he takes me higher and higher.

He moves one of my legs to the side, holding it there. I can't tighten my thighs around him, and it heightens the pleasure. I'm wound so tightly, I'm going to explode. And then I do.

"Oh, Brett!" I shout as my orgasm crashes down around me. I spasm as he works to draw out every last quiver.

I blow out a few deep breaths and then open my eyes. He's smiling at me with shimmering lips.

"Top drawer," I say breathily.

He reaches over and grabs a condom. He quickly sheathes himself, and before I have time to recover from my climax, he's pushing inside me.

"Damn, this feels good," he says, starting out slowly, then increasing his pace.

He pulls out, teasing my entrance with the head of his penis before pushing back in. He does this over and over until I find myself building back up.

"I'm going to make you come again, Emma," he whispers into my ear. "If you could have seen the look on your face when you came, you'd know why. You're incredible."

He pushes in and out again, removing himself completely until I reach around and grab his ass and push him back in.

"That's it," he says, picking up the pace. "You feel so good. Your walls are so tight around me. You're going to make me come, too."

He reaches between us and rubs my clit. His words, his thrusts, his manipulation—they all come together, and my insides tighten again before I detonate around him.

"Emma!" he shouts, his climax gripping him.

He collapses on me, both of us breathing heavily. He rolls off to one side, gazing at me with his alluring green eyes. We stay like this for a long time, just looking at each other. Maybe we're trying to wrap our heads around what just happened. Maybe we're not sure what to say now that it's over.

"That was …" He tries to find the words but can't. "You *have* to go to dinner with me now."

"I told you I don't date firemen."

"Even after—"

My heart races when I look at the clock. "Oh my God! Is that the time?" I shoot up in bed. "Shit, Brett. You have to go." I hop out and get my robe off the hook on the door. I gather his clothes and throw them on the bed. He looks at me like I've gone mad.

"I'm serious. You have to go now," I say, pulling a fresh pair of panties out of my dresser. "It's Friday. Evelyn only has a half-day, and my mother volunteered to bring her home so we could all have lunch together."

He glances at the time. It's eleven-thirty. He sits on the edge of the bed, removing the condom before pulling on his boxer briefs.

"Faster," I say, pacing the room, worried they could be home at any second.

"Slow down, Emma. It's okay."

"It's *not* okay. I'll never be able to explain this," I say, thinking of Mom's reaction to my having a man over in the middle of the day. "I'll never hear the end of it. Please, Brett, can you hurry?"

He laughs as he finishes putting on his shoes. "I suppose you want me to go out the back and sneak through the yard, too."

"If you wouldn't mind." I look at the clock again.

He shakes his head and chuckles. "I was kidding."

"Please?" I beg and give him a push toward the stairs.

"Fine. But just so you know, I was seventeen the last time I had to sneak out of a girl's house."

"I'm sorry," I say, hurrying him down.

As we pass the front door, I glance out the sidelight to make sure they aren't walking up. I'm about to breathe a sigh of relief when Evelyn hops up on the first step.

Panic rises within me. "They're here." I pick up my shirt and bra from the floor and point to the back door. "Go now. Fast. Let yourself out."

He starts toward the back door but turns around briefly. "See you Monday, Miss Lockhart."

"Brett, please."

He laughs, runs to the back door, and gives me a wink before ducking through it.

I barely make it back up the stairs before Mom and Evelyn come in. I throw my clothes on and check my makeup in the mirror. Then I go down to greet them.

Mom stands at the door, staring at the damage. "What happened here?" She looks at me and her eyebrows shoot up. "More importantly, what happened to *you?*"

Damn it. How does she always do that? It's like she has a sixth sense or something.

In my experience honesty is usually the best way to go. I tell them the story. Some of it anyway.

"There was a snake," I say, going into the kitchen for a much-needed glass of water.

As I pass the back door, I think of the man who just went through it. Tingles shoot through me as I think of his whispered words in my ear.

CHAPTER SEVENTEEN

BRETT

Through the baby monitor, I hear Leo stirring. I throw on sweatpants and cross the hall to his room. "Morning, buddy."

He stops playing with the stuffed animals in his crib and stands, waiting for me to pick him up.

I pull him into my arms and give him a hug before putting him on the changing table to get him in a fresh diaper. Leo's window is next to the table. I peek out, hoping to see her.

"Binky," Leo says, reaching toward the crib.

He calls the pacifier his binky. He never goes anywhere without it. I pick him up and fly him around like an airplane, swooping him down so he can snag the binky. He squeals in delight.

I stop mid-flight when we pass the window. I stand in front of it and pull the curtains back, checking the view. I know exactly which window is hers. I've been in her room. In her bed. In *her*.

My cock twitches thinking of it.

Her curtains are still drawn. It's early, and the sun isn't fully up yet. Still, I stare at them, willing them to open. Did she think about me after I left yesterday? She wouldn't go to dinner with me, not even after what happened. Is she that scared of dating a firefighter?

I think of her other fears. Tall buildings. Airplanes.

I used to be afraid of going into tall buildings for the same reason she is. But if I wanted to be a firefighter, I had to get past it. And just like how she went back into the school, the only way to get over fears is to confront them.

I feel a gnawing in my gut, knowing I want to be the one who helps her do it. But the way she kicked me out yesterday, as comical as it was, I still got the feeling that what happened was a one-time thing.

As I'm staring at her window, her curtains flutter open and suddenly she's standing there in a nightgown. She can look anywhere—the street, the sidewalk, the sky—but she looks right at me. I wave, knowing she can see me. She's obviously surprised to see me standing here looking at her. She pulls her robe around her and backs away. She backs away without acknowledging my wave.

Does she regret yesterday?

"Daddy fly," Leo says, patting my face to get my attention on him.

"Okay, buddy."

I take one last look out the window to see her curtains drawn again. Then I look at my son. "How about we make pancakes today?"

"Paycakes," he says in excitement as I fly him into the hall.

In the kitchen, Bria is sitting at the table drinking coffee with Bonnie.

"Bia! Bia! Bia!" Leo screams, wiggling out of my arms to run over to his aunt.

She scoops him into her arms and plants kisses all over his face.

I love the relationship they have. She's definitely the "cool" aunt. The one who lets him eat more chocolate than I allow. The one who takes risks and has fun.

"What are you doing here so early?" I ask.

"Couldn't sleep," she says. "Too excited."

"Right. The audition." I pour myself a cup of coffee and join them at the table. "Tell me how it works."

"White Poison is based out of New York. They're all Brits, but they live here, which is great for me. But unless I make it to the final cut, I won't even meet them."

"How long will the whole process take?"

"Probably a month or more. They need someone before they go on tour this fall, and I assume they want a month or so of practice. I'd guess they'll make a decision by the end of August."

"When is your first audition?"

"Next Friday. Will you go with me?" Her eyes are full of hope.

I run through my schedule in my head. "I'm not on shift, so yes. I'm really happy for you."

"I'm not worried about those other ninety-nine singers," Bonnie says. "You'll be the best one. I'm sure of it."

Bria leans over and gives her a kiss on the cheek. "You're my biggest fan, Bonnie."

"I think I'm your second biggest," she says, looking at me.

"Paycakes," Leo says.

Bonnie starts to get up from the table, but I put a hand on her arm to stop her. "I'm making breakfast today. You enjoy your coffee."

Bria puts Leo into his highchair and then helps me with the pancakes. "So," she says quietly, looking at Leo out of the corner of her eye, "heard from Momzilla lately?"

I laugh at her nickname for my ex. "Not since Leo's birthday."

She shakes her head. "I can't believe she's okay with missing so much."

"At this point I'm surprised he even knows she's his mother."

"The only reason he does is because of you. I've seen you show him pictures of her and talk about her like she's not the bitch who abandoned you both. You're a saint, big brother."

"I'm no saint, Bria. I just hope that one day—"

She grabs my arm, almost making me spill the pancake batter. "You're not still thinking she could come back and be a part of your life, are you?" She whispers so Leo can't hear. "Tell me you wouldn't take her back."

I look over at Leo, saddened that he has to grow up without a mother. I've often thought about what I would do if Amanda came back, wanting a second chance. What if she really was suffering from post-partum depression, and that's what made her pull away from us? Then I think of the two years of hell she put us through. Leo and I are better off without her.

"I wouldn't take her back. But I do want her to be a part of Leo's life. She was a good person once. I think she could be a good mother if she put some effort into it."

"You're a better man than anyone I know," she says. "If it were me, I wouldn't even let her see him."

I flip the pancakes. "She's the only mother he'll ever have."

"That's not true," she says. "If you get married again, he'll have a new mom. Hey, speaking of that, how'd your date with the hot teacher go?"

"You're getting way ahead of yourself, Bria. It wasn't a date."

"But you wanted it to be."

"It doesn't matter. She doesn't date firefighters."

She looks at me like what I said was crazy. "Who doesn't date firefighters?"

"Someone who's dad was a firefighter."

"Was?" she asks tentatively.

"She lost him on 9/11."

Bria backs up and slumps against the counter. "Oh, Brett."

My sister was only three years old when Mom died. She has no recollection of that day, or the bad times after. She was raised by a single father and her older brother, having little memory of what it was like to have a mother.

I glance at Leo who is banging his toddler-sized fork on his tray. "Okay, buddy."

I put two pancakes on a plate and cut up a third into small pieces. Then I serve Bonnie and Leo. Bonnie is busy having a conversation with him about the different phases of the moon. I love that she talks to him like an adult.

Bria is pouring the second batch of pancakes when I return to the stove. "Maybe that's your connection," she says, thoughtfully watching the pancakes until they start to bubble.

"What are you talking about?"

"You know, the thing that ties you and Emma together. You both lost a parent in the same disaster. Not to mention that you're both single parents. And you went through the hostage thing together. You have a lot in common."

"None of that matters if she won't go out with me."

"That's a shame," she says. "I was hoping she'd be the one to pop your post-divorce cherry."

Until yesterday with Emma, it had been almost a year since I'd been with anyone and well over two years since I'd been with a woman who wanted me. Amanda and I had sex sometimes after Leo was born. But every time, I felt like it was just a chore for her.

Something she needed to check off her list as a weekly or monthly obligation like picking up toothpaste or making a dental appointment.

But yesterday, with Emma—Jesus, I never remember it being like that. Not even when Amanda and I first got together.

Bria is staring at me with her mouth open. She flips the pancakes onto a plate and pulls me into the hall. "Oh, my God. You slept with her."

I sigh and lean against the wall.

"Don't try and look all innocent with me, Brett. You had sex with the teacher, didn't you?"

"It's not a big deal. It was a one-time thing. She kicked me out right after."

"She kicked you out? Were you *that* bad?" she jokes.

"Very funny. Her daughter was coming home, and she didn't want her to see me there."

"Ooo, a clandestine affair. How exciting."

"Like I said, it won't happen again."

"So, you're just going to give up? Roll over and die because she claims she won't date a firefighter? That doesn't sound like the big brother who raised me to go after everything I wanted. Do you know why I'm auditioning to be the backup singer for White Poison? Because of you. You taught me never to give up on my dreams."

I'm full of pride for my little sister. The things she had to overcome to get where she is today. I swallow the lump in my throat. I blinked and she became this amazing woman. "I'm so damn proud of you," I choke out.

"We both deserve to do incredible things with our lives. We deserve to be happy. Go after what makes you happy, Brett. Don't let her silly little rules get in the way. Show her you're good for her."

"I'm not sure I know how. It's been almost a decade since I've dated."

She hooks an arm through mine and drags me back to the kitchen. "I'm practically an expert on dating. I'll give you some tips over breakfast."

CHAPTER EIGHTEEN

EMMA

I wonder if he'll show up today. I know it was bad, the way I kicked him out on Friday. But what choice did I have?

Anxious and on edge, I roll over in bed and pull a pillow over my head.

He'll show up. Somehow, I know that Lt. Brett Cash is a man who always shows up.

The thought of seeing him again makes my insides burn.

I made excuses to look out the window at least a dozen times over the weekend. Seeing him standing there, bare-chested and holding his son, was … awe-inspiring. But I took great care after that first time, not to be seen doing it. I don't want to give him the wrong idea. He's a nice guy. A hero even. But the last thing I want or need is another hero in my life.

Still, I feel bad about how I pushed him out. I hop out of bed, bypassing the window altogether because it's too dark outside to see anything anyway. Besides, he's at work. I go downstairs and page through my recipes until I find the perfect one.

Two hours later, I take my peace offering to the firehouse.

"Yes!" someone shouts when I'm seen with my bounty. "We weren't sure you were coming back."

I have an urge to turn around and run away. Did Brett tell them what happened between us?

Brett steps forward, sensing my unease. "He means since you went back into the school." He looks at me guiltily. "I hope you don't mind that I told them about our going there. They saw you sitting on the bench."

"Great job, Emma," one of the guys says, offering me a fist bump. "Way to kick fear's ass."

I try to gauge the sincerity on his face, and I could be wrong, but I really do think that he's just talking about the school. I bump my fist to his. "Thanks, uh …"

"Denver," he says. "Denver Andrews. I know a little something about conquering fears, so I understand it's not an easy feat. We're all happy for you."

"Thanks, Denver."

Brett watches as some of the guys congratulate me. I wonder what he thinks about my showing up here today. I need to make sure he understands it's an apology, not an invitation.

"Wait here," Brett says when his shift comes to an end. "You can come to the hardware store with me to pick up the supplies to fix your door."

"I'm buying," I say.

He gives me a scolding look. "It was my fault, Emma. I'm paying for the repairs."

"You were saving me, Brett."

"It's not up for negotiation."

I roll my eyes at him. "Okay then. I'll meet you out front."

"I know where to find you," he says with a wink.

I walk to our bench, thinking he shouldn't be winking at me. And further, I shouldn't be getting that feeling in the pit of my stomach when he does. I don't know what I was thinking coming here. I should stay far away from Brett Cash and his winking, and his inviting green eyes, and his heroic tendencies.

"Ready?" he asks, walking up with a duffle bag over his shoulder.

I stand. "Before we go, there's something I want to tell you. I, uh, wanted to say I was sorry about how we left things on Friday. I … I hope we can still be friends."

"Friends?" he says with a raised brow. "Haven't we crossed that threshold, Emma?"

I flush, recalling just how far across that threshold we went. "About that. I really think it's best we just be friends."

He studies me for a second. I'd give anything to know what he's thinking. "And *I* think it's best we get your door fixed. Let's go."

And just like that, it's as if Friday never happened. I'm glad he's not going to harp on it and think that because we had sex once, it makes me his girlfriend.

My breath hitches. *Girlfriend.* It's not a title I've possessed in over twelve years. It's not one I've wanted. So why, when I think of the word, do I have flashbacks of him on top of me?

An hour later, I'm making a pot of coffee as Brett hammers away at my front door. I try to keep myself busy so I don't notice the way his arm muscles bulge as he works. Or the way the back of his shirt is damp with sweat. When did sweat become so sexy?

He puts the last coat of paint on the door jam and sits on the bottom step. "This will need a few hours to dry. Don't close the door fully, or it'll get stuck and you'll rip the paint off."

"Got it."

"I could stay if you want, since you can't close and lock it."

"I'm a big girl, Brett. I think I'll be okay."

He stands up and puts his tools away. "Is there anything else that needs fixing while I've got my tools here?"

"I don't think so, not unless plumbing is one of your hidden talents, too."

"What's the issue?"

"You really want to know?"

"I dabble in a lot of things, Emma. Show me what you need."

He follows me into the kitchen, and I show him the problem with the faucet. We clear out the cabinet under the sink, and he lies on his back and takes a look. As he's messing with the pipes, his shirt rides up and I see a strip of his abs. *Oh, God. Why did I bring this up?*

"Emma?" He scoots out a little and looks at me.

I've been caught gawking and turn beet red. "What?"

"Can you hand me the wrench?" he says, trying to hide a smile.

I fish around in his toolbox until I find one, then hand it to him. "I'll be right back," I tell him.

I leave but I don't go far. I stand in the hallway and sink against the wall, needing a break from all the sexiness.

When I hear the faucet running, I go back in.

"All done," he says.

"Wow. I don't know what to say. You really are a Jack of all trades, aren't you?"

"Say you'll go to dinner with me."

I shake my head. "I'm not going on a date with you."

"Not a date. An exercise."

I cock my head. "Exercise?"

"Have you ever been to Seasons Twenty-one?"

"The restaurant across the bridge on the twenty-first floor?"

"That's the one."

"I told you I don't go into tall buildings."

"Thus, the exercise."

It finally dawns on me what he's doing. "You don't need to save me from *everything*, you know. I'm perfectly fine living my life on the ground floor. I suppose after that you'll want to take me up in a plane. Oh, God, you're not a pilot, are you?"

He laughs. "No. Come on. It's just dinner. And it's a great restaurant. You know you can do it. You went into the school. It's only twenty-one floors. It's not even a high-rise." I'm about to say no when he hits me with, "Consider it payment for fixing your sink."

Well, shit. I exhale deeply. "You are not kissing me when we get to the top."

"Deal. Pick you up at seven?"

"No. I'll meet you there."

"How about we meet at the corner and catch a cab together?"

"Meet me in the lobby, or no deal," I say, not wanting to give him the wrong idea.

Toolbox swinging from one hand, he moves to the front of the house. "You drive a hard bargain, Miss Lockhart."

My stomach does a flip when he calls me that. I hold the door open for him. "See you at seven."

"Remember, don't close it yet. Put a shoe in it to remind you. And don't go upstairs until you can lock it." He nods to Evelyn's bedroom door near the bottom of the stairs. "Is that your study? Maybe you could hang out in there while the paint dries."

"That's my daughter's room."

His feet shift uncomfortably. It's amusing how he's worrying about me. "I really hate the idea of you leaving the door open for a few hours. Why don't you find me a hair dryer so I can—"

"Brett, it's fine. Go."

"Are you kicking me out again?" he jokes.

"See you at seven," I say.

I watch him walk down the front steps before I retreat into the foyer. On the sidewalk, he turns back. I take off my shoe and melodramatically put it against the frame. He laughs and runs across the busy street, dodging cars along the way.

I duck into Evelyn's room and peek out the window, wondering how he's lived there for two years, and I haven't noticed him.

Then again, it's easy to miss things when you aren't paying attention.

~ ~ ~

I look up at the tall building. Well, it's tall to me. To everyone else, it's nothing. Barely a blip on their radar. I get dizzy thinking about going to the top. This was a bad idea—for more than one reason.

"You look nice," he says behind me.

I turn around and see Brett wearing khakis and a dress shirt with the top two buttons undone. My heart may skip a beat. I've seen him in his uniform. I've seen him in jeans. Heck, I've seen him naked. But Brett Cash dressed for dinner might be my favorite look of all.

I smooth my sundress. "So do you."

"Are you nervous?"

I hold out my hand to show him it's shaking. "Not at all."

"It's okay to be nervous, Emma, but don't let it stop you." He gestures to the sign for a first-floor lounge. "We're early. Our reservation isn't until seven-thirty. How about we stop here for a drink?"

"You think I need to get drunk to go up there?" I ask, craning my neck to look up twenty-one floors.

"I didn't say let's get drunk. I said let's have a drink. As in *one*. It can help relax you."

I give him a hard stare. "I'm not sleeping with you again."

He raises his hands in surrender. "I'm not trying to get you into bed. I'm just trying to get you to the twenty-first floor. I hear they serve a mean filet mignon."

"What if I'm vegan?"

He looks a little green. "Are you?"

I chuckle. "No."

He opens the door for me. "Shall we?"

I glance up at the top floor again, and my heart races.

"We're going into the lobby," he says, seeing my reaction. "Baby steps, remember?"

I raise an index finger. "One drink."

Inside he pulls out a barstool for me. It's nice to know chivalry isn't dead even though this isn't a date.

I think of the four outfits and three pairs of shoes I tried on before settling on the sundress. I've never put so much thought into what I'm wearing. Not even for *actual* dates I've gone on.

"What'll you have?" the bartender asks.

I order the house chardonnay, and Brett asks for a Crown and Coke. "Have you ever been to Seasons Twenty-One?" I ask.

"No. But my friend, Bass, and his wife go there a lot. He's the one who recommended it."

"Do you go out much?"

"Some. A night out with the guys here and there. Sometimes we go to a baseball game."

"But not to dinner?"

He takes a sip of his drink, eyeing me over the rim of the glass. "Are you asking if I go on a lot of dates?"

"Of course not," I say, taking a drink of my wine. "But now that you brought it up, do you?"

A smile spreads across his face. "I just got my final divorce papers a few weeks ago, so no, I don't date a lot. How about you?"

I shrug. "A little."

"When is the last time you went on a date?"

"About a month ago I guess."

"Didn't work out? Did he have bad breath? A third nipple? A hairy back maybe?"

I laugh. "No, no, and no. I just rarely go on second dates."

"Oh." He looks at me sideways. "Well I know *you* don't have bad breath or a hairy back. And I definitely would have found a third nipple. So I doubt the issue is with you. They must all be duds. Are they teachers?"

"Some."

"Some? Just how many dates do you go on?"

The conversation is getting too personal, but I can't think of anything to say, so I blurt, "Are you hungry? Should we go eat?"

"You're ready? You've barely touched your wine."

I bring the glass to my lips and gulp the rest. Then I leave a twenty for the bartender. "There. Ready."

Brett gazes at the money I left on the counter. I can almost see the battle going on in his mind. "Fine. But I'm paying for dinner."

"I thought dinner was payment for you fixing my sink."

"*Going* to dinner was payment, not *paying* for it."

"You can't buy my dinner, Brett. This isn't a date."

"I get that I haven't done this in almost ten years, and maybe times have changed, but date or not, I'm a guy and you're a girl, and I'm not letting you pay for dinner. If you think that's somehow sexist of me, then I'm sorry, but that's how I roll."

I have a hard time not smiling. He's pretty handsome when he's demanding. "Fine. Pay for dinner. Jeez. Did you always get your way when you were married?"

As we step inside the elevator, I think that maybe Brett was right. Having a drink before going up does help.

"Amanda," he says angrily and moves to the back wall.

"Yeah, did you always get your way with Amanda?"

He nods to the person walking up to the elevator. "No, *that's* Amanda."

Oh, God. His ex is about to get on the elevator with us.

Two beautiful women, one blonde, one brunette, get in the elevator, both of them oblivious to Brett and me. They are chatting away about a "spring line" when Brett interrupts them.

"What the fuck, Amanda?"

They stop talking and the blonde turns around and looks at Brett and then at me. She looks at me the way someone might look at a piece of gum on the bottom of a shoe.

"Brett," she says in a high-pitched voice that can't possibly be real. "How nice to see you."

"You're kidding, right?" he barks. "I haven't heard from you since Leo's birthday and you just step in this elevator like you live here and not three thousand miles away. Were you even going to tell me you were in town? Were you going to take two fucking minutes out of your day to come and see your son?"

"I literally just got into town," she says.

"Yet you had plenty of time to get all gussied up for a night out," he says.

"I was going to call you tomorrow."

"It's good to know you have your priorities in line."

"This is my job, Brett."

The woman Amanda is with is wearing a flashy skirt and low-cut top. He sticks out a hand. "Brett Cash. You're obviously someone very important. President of the company perhaps? Is this a business meeting to save the fashion industry from imminent demise? It must be if it keeps her from picking up the goddamn phone and calling her son, who she hasn't seen in months."

The woman has no clue what to do. She shakes his hand. "Uh … hi. I'm Victoria."

"Brett, quit it," Amanda scolds. "It's not that big a deal. He's two. It's not like one day will make a difference. I was going to call tomorrow. I promise I was."

He laughs. "As if your promises mean anything." He's fuming inside.

Amanda apologizes to Victoria and then gives me the once-over, as if I'm her competition or something. "Aren't you going to introduce me to your little friend?"

Little friend? I'm not sure if it's her condescending tone, the complacency she expresses when it comes to her child, or the mere fact that she seems like a cold-hearted bitch, but I make a split-second decision to stick it to her.

I scoot over next to Brett and take his hand. "Actually, we crossed that threshold long ago. Didn't we, babe?"

He's taken aback to see me looking into his eyes, batting my eyelashes, but he recovers quickly and tries to suppress a smile. "This is Emma," he says, lifting my hand to his mouth and kissing it.

"Emma," Amanda says flatly, sizing me up like a predator considering its prey. "How long have you been fucking my husband?"

I smile and push a stray hair lovingly off Brett's forehead. "Don't you mean *ex*-husband?"

She huffs as the elevator doors open. They walk out ahead of us and Brett beams. "That was awesome," he whispers.

"Oh, you thought we were done?" I ask.

He looks sideways at me.

We patiently wait for Amanda and Victoria to check in with the hostess and then, while they are waiting for someone to escort them to their table, I walk up to the hostess stand and say loudly, "Please don't forget about the romantic table for two my boyfriend requested for our very special occasion."

"Uh, of course not," the hostess says, clearly confused as she scrambles to find the nonexistent notes on our reservation.

Amanda's back is stiff as a board when they are led to their table. I fight a grin. I'm having so much fun.

I whisper to the poor hostess caught up in our dramatics, "I was just messing with that woman. We didn't really request that."

She sighs. "Oh, good. I thought I messed up. Between you and me, feel free to let me know how I can help. That woman is awful."

"Really? What did she say to you?" I ask.

"Nothing tonight, but she comes in a lot. The waitstaff hate her."

Brett joins our quiet conversation. "She comes in a lot? Which one, the blonde or the brunette?"

"The blonde."

Brett looks like he's about to blow a gasket. "Do you recall the last time she was here?"

"I can tell you exactly when it was because she got my boyfriend fired. It was last Saturday. She sent her food back three times. He got fed up and read her the riot act."

"Last Saturday," Brett says, gazing at Amanda across the room as if he's going to kill her. He takes a step in her direction, but I hold him back.

"Nothing you say to her will make a bit of difference. But I know for a fact that what you *do* might just drive her crazy."

"What do you mean?"

"She's his ex-wife," I say to the hostess. "If you really want to help, seat us where she can have a clear view, then give us the VIP treatment. We'll give her an Oscar-worthy show that will have her throwing a temper tantrum for sure."

The hostess laughs. "Gladly. Give me a few minutes to set it up."

Brett looks at me thoughtfully. "Emma, not to freak you out or anything, but we're on the twenty-first floor."

My stomach rolls for a moment as his words sink in. I'd forgotten why we're even here. I cross to the windows and look at the street below, then locate all the exits in the room. I look at Brett and know he'll protect me at all costs. After all, he already has.

An hour and a half later, while we're killing the last of the expensive bottle of champagne the hostess sent over, I find myself getting too much into the part I'm playing. For the last ninety minutes, Brett and I have been flirting incessantly to make his ex jealous. And he's *very* good at it.

He touches me when he talks. Sometimes it's my hand or my arm. He leans across the table and caresses my face. He removes a dab of sauce from my lips—licking his finger after.

I find myself squirming in my chair. We're doing this for Amanda's benefit, but I've never been so turned on.

After our dessert comes, he moves his chair closer to mine so we can share the chocolate delight. He goes all out, spooning bites into my mouth. I go all out, exclaiming at the decadence before I kiss him.

I kiss him right here in the middle of the restaurant. When I accidentally brush his lap, I feel what this night is doing to him. He's as turned on as I am.

"Is she looking?" I ask, when I pull my lips away from his.

"Who cares?" he says, gazing into my eyes.

"Brett," I say with a sigh. I pull back, realizing what a bad idea this was.

"Emma, don't push me away. Not because she's watching, but because you know we are great together."

"That doesn't matter," I say, with less conviction than I meant.

His hand finds its way under the hem of my dress, and he caresses my thigh. I don't push him away because I'm still playing a part. Or am I?

He leans close. "I want to make you come," he whispers. "I've seen your face when you do. When my tongue circles your clit, you claw at my hair because you love it so much. When I suck on your nipples, you arch your back into me because you want me. When you hold my cock in your hands, it takes everything I have not to explode. And when I'm inside you, Jesus, it's perfection."

He's still ten inches away from touching me *there*, but I'm ready to detonate from his words alone. I close my eyes in defeat. "Not to sound cliché or anything, but … *check please.*"

He laughs, his hot breath flowing over my ear.

And for the rest of the evening, I'm pretty sure neither of us can even recall his ex's name.

CHAPTER NINETEEN

BRETT

Emma nudges me when I start to fall asleep. "You have to go."

I look at the clock. It's just after midnight. "You're not a cuddler, are you?"

"No, so if that's what you want, you're looking in the wrong place."

"I'm not sure what I want," I say. "It's been a long time since I did this."

She rises on an elbow. "Are you telling me I was your first since Amanda?"

I nod. "How long has it been for you?" I quickly put my finger to her lips to stop her from speaking. "Wait—I'm not sure I want you to answer that. I think I'd like to remain blissfully unaware."

"Shh," she says when I get too loud.

I sit up and pull my pants on. That's when I notice the pile of clothes draped across the chair in the corner. Nice stuff, like the sundress she wore tonight. It makes me smile to think she couldn't decide what to wear for our *non*-date.

She gets out of bed, puts on a robe, and eases open the door. She listens for a moment, then goes into the hall and looks down the stairs. "The coast is clear. Please be quiet. And lock the door on your way out."

"You're not walking me to the door?" I whisper.

"I'm pretty sure you don't need an escort, Brett."

"When can I see you again?"

"When you look out your window," she whispers. "Now go. They'll hear us."

I hesitate, wanting to get a better read on the situation, but now is not the time for that conversation. I lean in and give her a peck on the cheek. "Bye, Emma. Thanks for tonight."

She smiles, but it doesn't touch her eyes. Once again I wonder if she regrets sleeping with me. After she sees me descending the stairs, she shuts her bedroom door.

I don't get it. One minute she's telling me she can't date a firefighter, and the next we're in bed together. Maybe she doesn't want to date. Maybe she just wants to fuck. If so, am I okay with that?

As I'm pondering my question, I reach for the front door. But then I catch movement to my left and look over to find a girl staring at me from a doorway. *Shit, Evelyn.*

She knows I've seen her. I can hardly walk out without acknowledging her. "Hey there," I say quietly.

She opens her door fully and steps into the moonlit foyer. "Are you my mom's boyfriend?"

I nod to the stairs. "I don't think you were supposed to see me."

"So, you're not her boyfriend?"

Something about this girl is familiar. "Do I know you?"

She flicks on the light, and I look apprehensively up the stairs.

"Don't worry. She's in the shower," the girl says. "She doesn't ever come down after."

I try to ignore the implication of that statement when I recognize this is the girl I saw with the Pop-Tarts and coffee at the store a few weeks ago. It dawns on me that's also why Emma looked familiar. She was the one staring at Leo. *"You're* Evelyn?" I ask, keeping my voice low.

She steps forward and offers me her hand. "Evie. My mom's the only one who calls me Evelyn."

"Evie. Right." I shake her hand. "We met before. At the corner store."

"You're Leo's dad," she says. Then she motions up the stairs. "I'm going to assume he doesn't have a mom or you'd be a pretty terrible human."

I laugh. "Leo's mom and I are divorced. Shouldn't you be in bed?"

Evie takes a seat on the bottom step. "It's the stairs. They creak when someone comes down, and my bedroom is right under them."

"Ah, so you're *not* a heavy sleeper."

"Is that what my mom told you?" she says, laughing quietly. "She thinks I don't know things, but I do. Please don't tell her we ran into each other."

"You don't want her to know?"

She shakes her head adamantly. "First off, she'd be mad at you. And I don't want her to be mad at you. I like you. Secondly, she'd think I was disappointed in her, and I wouldn't want her thinking that."

"Are you?" I ask. "Disappointed in her?"

"Of course not. I just want her to be happy."

I look up the stairs to make sure Emma isn't standing in the hallway. I can't believe I'm having this conversation with her daughter. "Do you think she is?"

Evie shrugs. "I think she's … content."

"Are you sure you're only twelve?"

"Twelve going on thirty," she says. "At least that's what Grandma always says."

I chuckle.

"You're the only one who's ever stopped to talk to me," she says.

I try not to think of the others who may have snuck down these stairs before me. "I am?"

"Yup. They look at me and then go right out the door. They completely ignore me, like I'm not even here. Why do you think they do that?"

"May I?" I ask, gesturing to the step.

She scoots over and makes room for me.

"First off," I say, using her words, "they probably have no idea what to say to you. They're trying to sneak out of your house undetected. Secondly, you're pretty intimidating for a kid."

She giggles. "But *you* talked to me. Are you a teacher?"

"I'm a firefighter."

"Shut up," she says in disbelief. "*You're* a firefighter? Wait—are you the one who was at the school with my mom and that guy who got shot? Is that how you met?"

"Guilty," I say.

She bounces. "I like you even more now. You're like my mom's hero."

"I'm not so sure about that, but either way, I don't think she wants another one of those in her life."

"You mean because of my grandpa?"

"Yeah."

"Can I give you a piece of advice?" she asks.

I try not to laugh at this twelve-year-old girl trying to impart her wisdom to me. "Sure."

"Mom doesn't know what she wants. She thinks she does. But she's wrong. For as long as I can remember, it's been just the three of us—Grandma, Mom and me. I totally get why Grandma doesn't want another man. But I think Mom doesn't want one because she's afraid she'll become my grandma, and I'll become her. Which is why I'm surprised that you're here. She doesn't date firefighters. Or policemen. Or anyone with a dangerous job. For the most part, she doesn't even date at all."

"I'm confused," I say. "Exactly what was the advice?"

"Not to give up on her."

"And how exactly do I go about doing that?"

"I'm twelve," she says. "I don't know. Tell her she's pretty. Send her flowers. Do whatever guys do to woo girls."

"Woo?" I say with a raised brow.

"Whatevs. You're the one for her, so you should try really hard to be her boyfriend."

"You only think that because I stopped to talk to you."

"Or maybe you stopped to talk to me because you're the one."

This twelve-year-old is messing with my head. "Evie, it was really nice talking with you. I hope to see you again sometime." I stand.

"Me too. And Leo. That kid is gorgeous," she says.

"He is. All the ladies like him."

"All?" Evie asks, looking worried.

"From afar," I add. "They like him from afar."

"Okay. Good. Because I don't think you should date anyone else."

"If you ask your mom, I'm not even dating *her*."

"Like I said, she doesn't know what she wants."

I open the door, but before I can make my escape, I see movement at the top of the stairs. My heart sinks, thinking Emma has caught me talking with her daughter. Surely there will be repercussions. But when I look closely, it's not Emma but an older version of her.

The woman smiles at me and nods.

I give her a wave. Then I wink at Evie and walk through the door.

CHAPTER TWENTY

EMMA

I bake when I'm happy. I bake when I'm sad. I bake when I'm stressed out.

I'm trying to figure out which of those I am at the moment.

I look in the pantry. *Damn.* I'm out of flour.

"Ready?" Evelyn asks from behind me.

I pick up the lunch I packed for her. "Yup. Just give me a second to write down my grocery list, so I can make a stop on the way back."

She sees the mixing bowls and measuring spoons on the counter. "What are you baking today?"

"I thought I'd make your favorite."

"Peanut butter chocolate chip cookies?" she asks with a smile. "Will you save me some batter?"

"You know I don't like you eating the batter."

"I'm twelve years old, Mom. I've been sneaking batter for how many years, and I've never gotten sick?"

"Fine. *One* spoonful."

She hugs me from behind. "You're the best."

As we leave the house, I try not to look across the street, but my eyes betray me and I can't stop myself from glancing in that direction. I don't see any activity at Brett's. The curtains are still closed. Maybe he's sleeping in. We did stay up late last night.

"Mom?"

"Yeah, sweetie?"

"I know I talk a lot about wanting to go to Germany to find my father. But just so you know, I wouldn't be upset if I ever had a stepdad."

I stop walking and look at her. "What brought this on?"

She shrugs. "I don't know. I'm going to be a teenager soon. And Mrs. Garrison says teenagers need strong female *and* male role models in their lives."

"Who's Mrs. Garrison?"

"You know, Karoline's mom."

I start walking again so Evelyn doesn't see how irritated I am.

"Well, Karoline's mom needs to mind her own business. We're doing just fine."

She slips an arm around my elbow. "Even if we did find my father, he wouldn't really be my dad. I don't have any fantasies about you getting back together with him and us living happily ever after."

"Then why do you want to find him?"

"General curiosity, I guess," she says. "Do I have his nose? Is he left-handed? Is his second toe longer than his first? Things like that."

We arrive at the building where her summer camp is located. I hand her the lunchbox. "You don't have his nose, you have *my* nose. I'm pretty sure you already know that from the pictures you have of him. I don't recall him being left-handed. And I'm pretty sure I never looked at his feet."

"See? You don't know much about him. All the more reason to find him."

"You want to go all the way to Germany to find out if your father's second toe is longer than his first?"

She rolls her eyes. "Among other things."

I brush her long hair behind her ear. "Evelyn, I'm afraid you'll be disappointed. If he wanted to be in our lives, he would be. He knows exactly where we are. I've lived in our house my entire life."

"I know. I just wish you'd think about it," she says.

"Sweetheart, I don't fly."

She's disappointed. I hate when she looks like that. "There's a first time for everything, right?"

I nudge her toward the door. "You'd better get going."

She turns around and gives me a kiss before going in. "Love you, Mom."

"Love you back," I say.

On the walk home, I think of how many times she's asked to find her father. Even if I could get on a plane, I'm not sure I would. So far I've been able to protect her from everything bad. Evelyn has had an ideal childhood. Right now, Stefan is just a fictional character in her head, someone who she might even believe will see her and instantly fall in love with her, like I did on the day she was born. It's not going to happen.

I stop by the store down the street from my house and pull out my shopping list. I don't need a basket, I can carry it all in my hands. I'm lining up at the register when someone barrels around a corner and smashes into me, breaking open the bag of flour. It explodes into the air and all over me.

"Why don't you watch where you're going?" the woman says, brushing off what little flour landed on her arm.

"I'm so sorry," I say, even though the collision wasn't my fault.

I look up, surprised to see who it is. Brett's ex-wife. And she's carrying a stuffed animal and a big bag of M&M's.

"Oh, it's *you*," she says. "I hoped I'd seen the last of you and your pathetic display last night."

"I don't know what you're talking about," I say, inching toward the register as I brush flour off my shirt and jeans.

"Let me get you another bag," the proprietor says and takes the busted one, leaving Amanda and me together at the checkout counter.

I look at what she's holding. "You're going to see Leo, I presume?"

"I said I would, didn't I?"

"M&M's are a choking hazard for two-year-olds," I say.

"Who are you, Mary Poppins?"

"Here you go, ma'am," the man says, putting a new bag of flour on the counter before he rings up my purchase.

"Thank you." I pick up the bag. "Enjoy your visit, Amanda."

"Oh, I plan to."

As the guy behind the counter rings her up, I notice what I didn't before. That she's wearing a short skirt and a tight blouse. Not exactly clothing for playing with a toddler. I wonder if she's got an ulterior motive. She was clearly jealous last night. Brett and I did put on an impressive display. But she left him. I get it, though. She might not want him, but she doesn't want anyone else to have him either.

I take in her sleek blonde hair, long legs, and impressive cleavage. *Yes, I get it all too well.*

I hurry down the street, hoping to avoid any more confrontations with the ex-Mrs. Cash.

"Where do you think *you're* going?" she says behind me, the clacking of her high-heeled shoes echoing off the sidewalk.

"Home," I say without stopping.

"You *live* with Brett?" she asks. "Are you kidding me?"

I stop and turn around. "You're a pretty poor excuse for a mother if you don't even know who's living in the same house as your son."

"How dare you," she says. "You don't know anything about me."

She's right. I don't know anything about her. Or Brett either.

I wait at the corner. She eyes me suspiciously until the light changes and I make my way to the other side of the street. At my place, I glance back to see her still watching me. I give her a curt wave before ducking inside.

I'd love to know what she's thinking at this very moment. Is she relieved that Brett isn't living with another woman, or pissed that I live right across the street?

I drop my bag of groceries on the kitchen counter and then go into Evelyn's room, hiding behind her curtain as I peek out. I watch Amanda climb the steps of Brett's townhouse. *Her* old townhouse. She tries the knob but the door is locked. She pulls out a set of keys and tries to open it. I laugh out loud when I see her stomp her high heel on the ground like a kid throwing a tantrum. Her key doesn't work. Score one for Brett for changing the locks.

"What are you doing?" my mother asks. "And what's so funny?"

I turn around in surprise. "I thought you'd be gone by now."

"I'm running a little late this morning. What's so interesting outside?"

"Nothing," I say, dropping the curtain. "I thought I saw someone I knew."

She looks at me like she knows I'm full of shit. "Oh, yes," she says. "I can see how that would be funny." She slings her purse over her shoulder. "I'll see you tonight."

"Bye, Mom," I say, heading back to the kitchen.

As soon as she's out the door, I race up to my room to stare out the window again. Amanda is already inside. I gaze in each of his windows. I know one of the upstairs windows is Leo's. I surmise the other is Leo's nanny's room, as I've never seen Brett look out of that one. And the large window to the right of the front door must be the living room. I can't see inside it very well, but I've seen flashes of light from a TV over the past few days.

I try to ignore the fact that I'm approaching creepy-stalker territory here.

To prove that I don't care about what's happening across the street, I busy myself making cookies for Evelyn for the next few hours. Then I grade some online papers. After lunch, despite my efforts to keep my mind occupied, the urge to look overpowers my sense of decency and I return to the upstairs window.

Looking over at Brett's, I'm not sure what I expected to see, but it wasn't this.

Amanda is holding Leo in full view of his window. It looks like he's fallen asleep on her shoulder. I don't miss the fact that she's standing right there, looking out as if taunting me.

I know she can't see me, but I hide even more, watching only through a small slit between my curtain and the window frame. She stands there for a few more minutes before walking out of view. Then Brett appears at the window. *He's there.* I wasn't sure he would be. But it makes sense, it's his day off. That he's there, *with her*, as a family, doesn't sit well with me, and I feel something I haven't felt in my entire life. Pure unadulterated jealousy.

I think maybe Brett is looking for me, too. I've caught him doing it before. Just as I know he's caught me. Suddenly, hands cover Brett's eyes from behind. He turns around and bumps into Amanda, who pulls him into a kiss.

My heart sinks. *She's kissing him?*

But it's not exactly her kissing him that saddens me. It's that he's not pulling away.

I hang my head and go over to my bed, landing on my mattress with a thump.

He hates her. How could he have kissed her? Especially after last night.

Then again, she's Leo's mother. If she wants to give it another go with Brett, maybe he's thinking of his son and what's best for him.

Sometimes I wonder what I would do if Stefan showed up on my doorstep. What if he said he was sorry? That he'd been young and immature, and now that he's older, he wants another chance. Would I do that for Evelyn?

I pick up the pillow Brett dozed off on last night. I pull it close and hug it. Never before have I wanted something so passionately, yet at the same time, *not* wanted it with the exact same passion and fervor.

CHAPTER TWENTY-ONE

BRETT

Bass nudges me across the bar, pulling my attention away from the baseball game on the TV. "Hey, isn't that what's-her-name who bakes like an angel?"

I look over to where he nodded and see Emma sitting at a corner table with several other women and one man. I smile. We come here a lot to watch baseball games. I wonder how often she comes here with her friends. Maybe we've been here at the same time in the past and never knew it. Like how we've lived across the street from each other for years, yet we had to be held at gunpoint to meet.

"Emma," I tell him. "Yeah, that's her."

"You ask her out yet?" Denver asks.

"She doesn't date firefighters."

I don't tell them we've slept together. *Twice.* But we're not dating. I have no idea what we're doing. Other than having great sex.

"She get burned by one?" Justin asks, chuckling. "Get it? *Burned* by one." He laughs a little too hard at his own joke, and the three of us throw the limes from our beers at him.

"No. That's not it."

One of Emma's friends catches me staring and elbows her, nodding in my direction. She looks shocked to see me here. Not surprised. Not happy. *Shocked.* She barely acknowledges me before returning to her conversation.

"Wow," Justin says, shivering. "I can feel the chill all the way over here. She totally just froze you out."

I put down my beer and make my way to her table. "Hi," I say to her. "Emma, right?"

"Yeah. Brent, was it?"

"Brett," I say with a smirk.

I notice a familiar face and hold out my hand. "Becca, I presume?"

She shakes my hand. "It's nice to meet you. Especially under better circumstances."

The man sitting next to her stands up and reaches across the table to shake my hand. "Jordan Kincaid," he says. "I owe you a huge debt of gratitude for saving my fiancée."

"Just doing my job."

"Can I buy you a drink?" Jordan asks. "It's the least I can do."

"I'm all set, but thanks for the offer. Emma, can I talk to you for a second?" I motion to the hallway by the bathrooms.

The waitress comes over with their food.

"Sorry," Emma says. "Our food is here, and I'm starving. Maybe some other time."

Jeez, Justin was right. She's giving me the cold shoulder. Maybe she doesn't want her friends to know we've seen each other. But why? "I guess I'll see you around then."

I overhear some of her friends scolding her as I return to the bar.

"Didn't go so well, huh?" Denver asks, handing me a fresh beer.

"I don't get it. She acted like we hadn't spent time together walking to the school." *Not to mention the time we spent in her bed.*

"Maybe that's her boyfriend," Bass says.

"It's not. He's engaged to one of the other women at the table."

"Forget her, man," Justin says. "Let's just watch the rest of the game."

I can't forget her. And I can't help looking her way every chance I get. She doesn't glance back, however. Not one single time.

~ ~ ~

I can't fall asleep. I roll over and look at the clock. It's eleven-thirty. I still don't get it. Why did Emma treat me like that at the restaurant?

I get out of bed and go to the dark living room. Looking out the window, I see a dim glow coming from Emma's room that tells me she hasn't gone to sleep yet. I get out my phone and text her for the first time.

Me: Emma, this is Brett. Can we talk?

Emma: I wasn't aware I'd given you my number.

No hello. No apology for blowing me off. What the hell did I do to her?

Me: I may have called myself from your phone when you excused yourself to use the bathroom at dinner last night.

Emma: How resourceful.

Me: Did I do something wrong?

Emma: Maybe you should ask your wife.

Amanda? What does she have to do with this?

Me: Ex-wife. And what does Amanda have to do with this?

Emma: I'm tired. I'm going to bed.

Me: Can you just talk to me? Come to the window please. I'm downstairs.

Emma: I've done enough looking out of windows lately. Goodbye, Brett.

Me: Emma, come on. What's the problem?

When I don't get a response, I sit on the couch and re-read our texts. She's done enough looking out of windows lately. What does that mean? I run through the day in my mind. *Shit.* My head falls back as I realize what happened.

Me: You saw me and Amanda in the window this morning. Is that what this is about?

No response.

Me: Will you let me explain please?

Nothing.

Me: Emma? Are you there?

Five minutes go by. I return to the window. Her light has gone out. I go back up to my room, knowing I won't be able to sleep. I throw on some clothes and pick up the phone.

Me: I'm coming over in two minutes. I suggest you meet me at your front door unless you want me ringing your doorbell and waking up your family.

Emma: Do not come over here. I mean it.

Me: Ninety seconds…

Emma: Brett, no.

As I'm crossing the street, I see her light come on. She opens her curtains and looks out. I wave as I pass under the streetlight. She shakes her head and disappears.

At her door I don't ring the bell, and I don't knock. I don't really want to wake up Evie and her mom. I just want to make Emma think that I will.

She opens the door and pulls me inside, then puts a finger to her lips. We go upstairs. When the floorboards creak, I turn around and look at Evie's closed door, wondering if she hears it.

Once we're safely in her room, she pulls her robe tightly around herself. "Why are you here?" she whispers.

"You blew me off at the restaurant and then you wouldn't text. You left me no choice."

"Won't your *wife* be upset that you're here?"

Even though she's whispering, I can hear the animosity in her voice. "Would you quit calling her that? She's my ex-wife."

"That's not what it looked like when you were kissing her," she says, nodding to her window.

I'm upset she saw that. But now I understand why Amanda did it. "I wasn't kissing her. She kissed me."

"That's not what it looked like from here," she says.

"We were in my son's room. He was asleep in his crib. I could hardly cause a scene. But you better believe I had words with her once we were out of Leo's earshot."

She sits on her bed, looking confused.

I sit next to her. "I'm not sure what you saw from the window, but she took me by surprise. It took me a moment to realize what was happening and then to figure out what to do about it with my son five feet away."

She sighs. "You were married. And she obviously wants you back. Maybe you should—"

"You know why she's doing this, right? It's because we made her jealous last night. She doesn't want me. She was just being a bitch."

"It sure looked like she wanted you," she pouts.

I almost smile. The woman who won't date me is jealous.

"You should have seen how mad she was when I ran into her at the store this morning," she says.

"Wait. You saw Amanda today?"

"And when she followed me out and saw me walking in the direction of your townhouse, she accused me of living with you."

I laugh out loud and then cover my mouth, not wanting to wake anyone up. "Oh, how I would have loved to see that. Did you tell her where you live?"

"No, but she watched me walk all the way home."

"Well that explains it then. She hoped the woman she thought I was dating might look out the window and see something going on."

She falls back against the bed and covers her face with her hands. "I fell right into her trap, didn't I?"

I quickly straddle her and pin her arms to the bed.

She looks at her closed door. "Brett, we can't."

I lower my head until my lips are next to her ear. "I'm not with her, Emma. I'll never be with her. *You're* the woman I want."

I trace her neck with my tongue, drawing a line from ear to ear as she writhes beneath me.

"We shouldn't," she says with no conviction whatsoever.

"Why shouldn't we? We already have, and we're explosive together. I can't stop thinking about you. How you look when you come. How you taste when I go down on you. How you stroke my cock exactly the right way."

Her hips buck under me, making me harder.

"You want me, too," I say. "See how your body reacts to mine? I'll bet your pussy is already wet. I'm going to stick my fingers inside you and find out." A moan escapes her as I push her panties aside and finger her slick folds. "Jesus, I knew it."

She arches into my hand as I stroke inside her. Her mouth falls open and her head pushes back into the bed when I touch her clit.

"You like it when I do that, don't you?"

She doesn't answer so I pull away until she opens her pouty eyes to look at me. When she does, I lick my fingers. "Tell me you like it when I do that."

She clutches my dick through my sweatpants. "Do you like it when I do this?"

I close my eyes at the feel of her touch. "You have no fucking idea."

I open her robe and push up her nightgown, finding her breasts with my hands and then my mouth. I manipulate each nipple with my tongue, flicking and sucking them until she squeezes me so hard, I can't take it.

"You want me inside you. Say it, Emma."

"Yes," she says, yanking my sweatpants to my knees.

I push a finger inside her and circle her clit with my thumb. "Say it."

"Yes, okay?" she loud whispers. "I want you inside me."

I smile as I reach into her nightstand and pull out a condom.

I lean down and whisper in her ear as I rub her clit. "I'm so hard I can't wait another second to have you. I'm going to make you come like you've never come before. I'm going to make you shout my name so loud, you'll have to muffle your screams with a pillow. I'm going to touch every part of you. Even the forbidden parts."

I'm about to come just thinking about what I'm going to do to her. I'm not sure why being with her makes me talk like this. I've never been much for dirty talk. But she makes me want things I've never wanted before.

I kick off my shoes and socks and get rid of my clothes. Then I pull her to the edge of the bed, realizing it's the perfect height for me to stand and enter her. I put her calves on my shoulders and push inside her, watching her face.

"You're so tight. God, you feel good. I could do this all day if it weren't for the fact that I'm almost coming."

Her lips form a smile as she reaches up to run her hands across my pecs.

I rub her clit with one hand and with my other, reach under my cock and run a finger along the pucker of her ass. "Has anyone ever touched you here?"

"No," she says breathily.

I slip the tip of my pinky into her ass. She resists at first, but then she relaxes, and my finger goes farther inside. It's soft and smooth and tight and not anything like how I thought it would feel. My balls tighten as she moans loudly and pushes herself onto my cock even more. I have to bite the inside of my cheek to keep from coming. *Not yet. Not fucking yet.*

"Brett, oh, God!"

She pulls a pillow to her mouth and I hear her muffled screams as her insides squeeze my cock and my finger at the same time. She pulsates around me so explosively that I come harder than I've ever come before.

"Unnnnnngh!" I bite my bottom lip to keep myself from screaming.

I pull my finger out of her and brace myself against the mattress, riding out the last of my orgasm. I stand here, breathing heavily as I go soft inside her.

She glances at the door. "I hope we weren't too loud."

"Well, *I* wasn't," I joke.

She rises onto her elbows and looks at the place where we're still joined. "Are you going to stay there all day?"

I look at the clock. It's 11:59. "The day is over in about one minute, so yeah, that's the plan."

She pulls her nightgown down to cover her C-section scar.

"You don't have to cover up," I say. "I've seen and felt *every* part of you. And it's all beautiful."

Her cheeks flush.

It turns midnight, and I pull out of her and remove the condom before lying down at her side. "How come you had to have a C-section?"

"I'm not one for pillow talk, Brett."

I lean on an elbow. "Are you seriously kicking me out again?"

She gets up and tightens her robe.

I sit on the edge of the mattress. "Can I at least use your bathroom first?"

"Of course."

After I wash up, I leave a message for her on the mirror using her makeup, knowing this is her private bathroom.

"Are you almost done?" she says quietly but impatiently on the other side of the door.

I open it. "You know I've made it my life's mission to stay in your bed for longer than ten minutes after we have sex."

"What makes you think we're having sex again?" she says.

"You're kidding right?" I motion to the bed. "After what just happened? We *have* to have more sex. We owe it to sex to keep having it. Sex would be disappointed if we stopped."

She tries to hold in a laugh. "Goodnight, Lieutenant." She steps into the hall, looks at her mom's door and then down the stairs. "Lock—"

"The door on my way out," I whisper, pulling her into my arms. "I know the drill." I kiss her. I kiss her long and hard. "Kissing would be disappointed too."

She offers me an uneven smile and retreats into her bedroom.

I quietly make my way downstairs, cringing when I hit the squeaky step. I make it all the way to the bottom, across the foyer, and I'm about to open the door when Evie says, "Peanut butter chocolate chip cookie?"

She holds out a cookie. In the background, the kitchen light illuminates the hallway.

I look back up the stairs.

"She's in the shower, remember? You can hear the water down here. You've got a good ten minutes."

"I get the feeling you know a lot more about your mom than she'd like you to."

"Do you want the cookie or not?" she asks. "We have milk, too."

"We?" I ask, then I look back down the kitchen hallway to see Evie's grandmother saluting me from the kitchen.

This is horrifying in so many ways. And Emma would be beside herself if she knew her mom and Evie had caught me leaving.

Evie's grandmother waves me into the kitchen. I follow Evie down the hall. Mostly because I'm curious about Emma's family.

"Hot or cold?" Evie's grandmother asks.

"Ma'am?"

"Do you like your milk hot or cold?"

"Uh, cold, thank you."

She pours me a glass and then sits at the table. She extends a hand. "Enid Lockhart. It's a pleasure to meet you, Lieutenant."

"How do you ...?"

"A mother knows things." She winks at Evie.

"Please call me Brett."

"Well, Brett, this has been an exciting few weeks for our little block, now hasn't it?"

I raise my eyebrows. She knows I live across the street?

"Don't be surprised," she says, handing me a napkin. "I'm a woman who knows everyone and everything. Bonnie, she's your nanny. We play euchre together every Thursday—when you're not on shift, that is. It's amazing what you can learn at euchre." She puts a finger under my jaw, closing my gaping mouth. "Now go on, eat your cookie. Everyone needs a midnight snack now and again."

I do what she tells me. I get the feeling this woman always gets what she wants. "Wow, this is good." I turn to Evie. "Did you make these?"

She shakes her head. "Mom did. She's a really good baker."

"I know. I've tasted a lot of her creations."

Enid smiles as if she already knew.

A strip of pictures is on the table. I pick it up and study the face of a beautiful girl who looks a bit older than Evie. "Is this Emma?"

She nods. "That's her and my father."

I look at the young man in the picture. "This is Stefan?"

"She told you his name?" Enid asks.

"Yeah, why?"

She smiles and wipes up some cookie crumbs off the table. "No reason."

"Grandma and I are planning a trip to Germany to find him," Evie says.

"You don't say?"

"Mom won't fly, so don't tell her. She would flip out. I mean, we'll have to tell her sooner or later because she's my mom and all, but we'll cross that bridge when we come to it."

Enid smiles and says to me, "Twelve going on thirty."

I laugh. "You're not afraid to fly, Enid?"

"No," she says. "If we let fear rule our lives, we'll never really live, now will we?"

"But you never remarried."

"That's not because of fear," she says. "It's because I had my one true love. Evie's grandfather was the love of my life and it's enough to last me a lifetime." She puts her hand on mine. "I'm sorry, I heard you also lost someone that day."

I look at her sideways, confused.

"Bonnie told me," she says.

"Oh, right."

Enid taps on the picture. "I just wish we could narrow it down. Do you know how many men in Germany have the name Stefan Schmidt?"

"Maybe I could help. I know someone. We're not close friends, but I've been to a few gatherings with him." I think hard to pinpoint exactly how I know him. "Ethan Stone is his name. My buddy Denver's twin sister is married to a man whose best friend's sister is married to Ethan's brother."

Enid laughs. "That's a lot of degrees of separation. Who is this Ethan?"

"He owns a private investigation business. I'm sure he could help you." I look at the ceiling. "I'm just not comfortable asking him without Emma's permission though."

Evie elbows her grandmother. "See? I told you he was the one."

The shower turns off upstairs, and I stand, handing Enid my empty glass. "Thanks for the milk and cookie. I'd better leave now."

"I suppose you'd better," Enid says. "You can go out the *front* door. It's works even better now than it did before."

I eye her curiously. Does she know Emma pushed me out the back door last week?

"Go," she urges. "This will be our little secret."

"It was nice meeting you, Enid."

"Same here." She takes Evie's glass and hands her the strip of pictures. "Now off to bed with you. And be quiet about it."

Evie walks me out. "I like you better than any of the others," she whispers.

"I thought you never met any of the others."

"I didn't. I guess that's why I like you the best."

I laugh quietly. "Goodnight, Evie."

"Night, Brett."

I really like Emma's daughter. I like her mother, too. I guess the only one I really have to win over at this point is Emma.

CHAPTER TWENTY-TWO

EMMA

"Daddy!" I yell as I run into his arms.

He scoops me up and carries me effortlessly even though I'm eight years old now and far too big to be carried by my father.

"Hey, sweet pea," he says, brushing my cheek with a finger covered with soot.

He marks both my cheeks, making me look like a fireman too. Then he puts his helmet on my head, but it covers my eyes, so I have to push it up. It falls off. Daddy laughs as he picks it up and puts it back on.

"Fits me better, huh? I guess you'll have to wait until you get older to wear your own."

"Daddy, girls aren't firemen. Girls are teachers."

He puts me down and gets on a knee in front of me. "That's not true, Emma. Girls can be whatever they want to be. We have a girl in our firehouse. She works a different shift, but she's tough. Just like me." He play-punches me in the arm. "Are you going to be tough when you grow up?"

"No, Daddy. I'm going to be soft. I don't want big muscles like yours."

A boisterous laugh comes all the way from his belly. "You're my little princess, aren't you?"

There's an explosion behind us. I turn around and see a tall building in flames. I scream.

"Daddy has to go to work now," he says without even taking pause.

"Daddy, no," I beg, holding onto his waist as he tries to walk away from me.

"It's okay, sweet pea. Everything happens for a reason."

I let go, and he runs to the building. Before he goes inside, he turns around. Only it's not him now. It's Brett. "Goodnight, Miss Lockhart," he says and runs into the building.

"Brett! No!" I yell.

I watch in horror as the building collapses, each floor pancaking down onto the next until there's nothing left.

I fall to my knees. "No!"

"Emma! Wake up, Emma."

I open my eyes to see my mother sitting on the bed next to me. I look around the room and get my bearings. My head falls back against the pillow. Another bad dream. I've been having a lot of them lately.

"Sorry," I say to my mom.

"It's okay, sweetie. I still have them too sometimes."

"I haven't had that kind of dream in years. Only since…" I almost say since meeting Brett. "… the robbery."

"It's understandable that what happened to you would bring them back."

I sit up on the edge of the bed. "I'm fine now. You can go back to sleep."

"You sure?"

"I'm a big girl, Mom."

She leans down and plants a kiss on my forehead. "Even big girls need their mothers from time to time."

"Love you," I say as she leaves my room, blowing me a kiss.

I put my head in my hands. I've lost count of how many bad dreams I've had over the past several weeks. But this is the first time Brett made an appearance in one. I go to my bathroom. I flick on the light and see the words he wrote on the mirror a few days ago.

GOODNIGHT, MISS LOCKHART

I can still hear those words in my nightmare.

I wad up a bunch of toilet paper, wet it down, and wipe off the red lipstick. It smears horribly, and I have to use almost an entire roll to get it clean.

I'm not sure why I kept the words there for so long. For some reason, I couldn't get myself to remove them. Not until the nightmare.

I close the toilet lid and sit on it, confused by my thoughts. I'm getting too close to him. I should date other people. Not that Brett and I are dating—but what we're doing is dangerously close. My friends are always telling me about men they could set me up with. I used to let them. Before the robbery. Before Brett. Maybe it's time I let them again.

"You can do this," I tell myself. I stand and look in the mirror. "Guys do it all the time. They have sex. They play the field. They date multiple women. Or not date them. Whatever. It's all good. You are a modern woman."

Before I leave the room, however, I touch the mirror, regretting that I erased his words.

I walk over to the window. Leo's room is dark, as is Bonnie's. But the television is on in Brett's living room. I can see the flickering of light. I wonder what he's thinking right now. Is he thinking about the other night? Because I am.

Which is exactly why I need to let Becca set me up with one of Jordan's friends.

I make a mental note to call her tomorrow.

There is movement in Brett's window and against the flickering light of the TV, I see him, bare-chested, swaying back and forth with Leo in his arms. It looks like Leo's crying, and Brett is … *singing?*

My insides get all warm and gooey, seeing him sing to his crying son in the middle of the night.

He stops at the window and looks over at my house. I know he can't see me. All my lights are off. But it's almost as if he knows I'm watching because he just stands and stares, rocking his son.

Leo eventually falls asleep and Brett moves out of sight. The TV goes off, and then there's a soft glow from Leo's room. A minute later, Brett draws the curtains.

I climb back into bed as my phone vibrates with a text message.

Brett: Goodnight, Miss Lockhart

CHAPTER TWENTY-THREE

BRETT

The past few weeks have been confusing at best. Sex with Emma is incredible. But I can tell she's fighting her feelings. She never lets me stay in her bed after, which oddly, I've become okay with because it means I get to talk with Evie.

At first it was strange, having a twelve-year-old waiting for me to get done having sex with her mother. And maybe it should *still* be strange. I mean, she's twelve. But for some reason it's not.

Evie waits for me in the kitchen. It's become our thing: cookies and milk. Sometimes Enid joins us. But never Emma. She remains unaware that I visit with her family.

While part of me feels guilty for that, the other part, the part that enjoys finding out who Emma is and where she came from, looks forward to our chats.

While eating breakfast, I check if Emma sent me a text. She never does unless I send her one first. And sometimes not even then.

I'm still upset by what I saw through Leo's window last night. A man walked Emma to her door and then kissed her on the cheek. *Is she dating?* He didn't go inside, but it definitely looked like a date. They talked for a minute, him with his hands in his pockets like he wasn't sure what to do with them. It's exactly what I did the time I walked Emma home from the school.

Have other men been in her bed? Do they leave lipstick messages on her mirror like me?

She must wipe them off after I leave. I've never seen one of my messages on the mirror. Not even when we hooked up two nights in a row last week. Does she erase them so Enid and Evie don't see them? Or is it because of other guys?

Maybe I'm overthinking this. Maybe she erases them because they're stupid and juvenile. I haven't done this in years. I guess I thought it was romantic or something. But as far as I can tell, romance is not what Emma is looking for. From me, at least. Maybe that's where the man from last night comes in.

"You okay?" Bonnie asks, bringing Leo into the kitchen. "You're stabbing at your eggs like they aren't already dead."

I push my plate aside. "I'm fine." I nod to the stove. "I made breakfast if you're hungry."

She puts Leo in his highchair and spoons eggs on a plate for him. Then she pours a cup of coffee and sits at the table. "You are obviously not fine, Brett."

I shrug.

"Does it have anything to do with the woman across the street?"

I look up in surprise, then remember Enid telling me they play euchre together.

"I don't want to talk about it," I say, getting up from the table. "I'm going to take Leo to Central Park, so we'll be gone most of the day. Are you still good with watching him tonight?"

"Of course," she says, ruffling his hair.

"How's the tooth coming in, buddy? Did you sleep well last night?"

Leo forks some eggs into his mouth and says, "Toof."

That tooth has been coming in for what seems like weeks. It's a big one. He often wakes up at night. Sometimes when I'm up with him, I look out the window. Occasionally someone is looking back.

Tonight, Emma and I are supposed to go to a rooftop party that's fifty floors up. *It's not a date*, she says in my head. *It's an exercise*. Funny, however, that after all our *exercises*, we end up in bed. I'm not sure how I feel about that now, knowing she's been dating someone else.

Thinking about her going to dinner with another man makes my skin crawl. Thinking about her doing what we do together in bed makes me insane. So I try not to. Except that I spent the better part of last night doing just that.

I gaze lovingly at Leo. "You want to go to Central Park today? Denver said he'd meet us there with Joey."

He claps his hands. He knows exactly who Joey is. Sometimes it amazes me they get along so well. Most toddlers play side-by-side but not necessarily together. Leo and Joey are different. They play *with* each other. Even more surprising, they *share*.

"We'll leave after I get a shower." I spoon some eggs onto a plate for Bonnie and place them in front of her. Then I give Leo and Bonnie a kiss on the head before going up to get ready.

~ ~ ~

"You're acting strange," Emma says in the cab on our way to the cocktail party.

If I've had any minor victories when it comes to Emma, it's that she now rides with me to our destinations.

"I'm just tired," I tell her. "Leo's been teething."

"Oh, I remember that. Evelyn would keep me up for hours, even when I put that nasty gel on her gums."

"Leo hates that stuff. I think it makes him cry harder than the actual tooth breaking through. The baby Tylenol helps, but it takes a while to kick in."

"Do you think you'll have more kids?" she asks.

I shrug. "I don't know. Maybe, if the right woman came along." Guilt immediately consumes me given the company I'm with. "I mean not that you aren't … But we aren't … well, you know what I mean."

She smiles sadly. "Yeah, I know what you mean."

"What about you? Do you want more kids?"

"I don't know. I was so young when I had Evelyn, I feel like we kind of grew up together. I suppose it would be different having a child in my twenties or thirties. Evelyn wants a sibling. She's even hinted lately about being okay with having a stepfather someday."

I have to bite my tongue. Evie and I get along great, but could she want me as more than her friend? In all honesty, I can't imagine a finer girl to have as a stepchild. Then again, with her mom dating other men, the odds of that happening are getting slimmer by the day.

"Are you sure you're okay?" Emma asks. "You seem off tonight."

"I'm the one who should be asking you that. We're about to go up fifty stories."

"Thanks for reminding me," she says.

The cab pulls up to the building, and I swipe my debit card before getting out. "It's my goal to get you to the top of the Empire State Building before the end of the month."

"Ha! Good luck with that. There's not enough chardonnay in New York City to make that happen."

"There's really not that much difference between fifty floors and one hundred."

"You mean, if the building collapses, we're still toast."

I shoot her a scolding look.

"Sorry," she says. "I don't mean to be disrespectful to the dead."

"What I mean is you've already gone up in buildings that have thirty to forty floors, and we're about to go to one with fifty. Once you've done those, it should be no big deal."

She stares me down. "Are you really not scared of anything?"

I don't tell her that I wasn't. That after conquering my fear of tall buildings, I wasn't afraid of *anything* until meeting her. But now, my biggest fear is being without her. How, in only a month's time, have I grown attached to a woman who's incapable of attachments?

"I'm scared of a lot of things," I tell her. "Projectile vomiting, gum on the underside of tables, loogies falling on me from above."

She laughs. "Who knew you were such a germaphobe?"

I nod to the bar next door. "Want to get a drink first?"

"Nope. I need to do this without the help of alcohol."

"Okay then, let's do this." I hold the door for her.

Her steps get slower as we approach the elevator. The doors open, but she moves aside, allowing the people behind us to enter.

"You comin'?" the woman operating the elevator asks.

Emma doesn't move.

"You go on ahead," I say. "We'll catch the next one."

Emma backs up against the wall. "I'm sorry. I'm being ridiculous. I'll be okay. We'll take the next one."

The second elevator door opens. Emma looks behind us as if to allow others to pass again, but there's nobody else waiting.

"You going all the way up?" the operator asks. "This one's the express."

"Are we going up?" I ask Emma.

She nods but doesn't move. I take her hand in mine and lead her inside.

"Evenin'," the man says, pushing the rooftop button before sitting on his chair.

I've often wondered why buildings have elevator attendants, let alone those with only one stop. "Good evening."

The doors close and Emma steps forward in a panic, trying to get them to open again. "No," she cries softly. "I changed my mind."

I squeeze her hand harder.

"I'm sorry, miss," the attendant says, "It's the express. If you don't want to get off up top, I can take you back down as soon as we get there."

Her eyes go wide in terror. "You don't understand."

"Emma," I say, pulling her back into the corner. "It's going to be all right. I'm not going to let anything happen to you."

She belts out a painful laugh. "As if you can keep a building from collapsing. Or a plane from … oh, God, why did I do this?"

She starts to shake and her breathing accelerates. I see on the illuminated display that there are thirty floors to go. I'm afraid she's close to hyperventilating.

"Breathe, Emma. Remember your breathing?"

She doesn't seem to hear me as she watches the numbers count up.

The attendant appears completely helpless as Emma has a panic attack.

"Excuse us," I say to him, right before I push Emma against the wall and kiss her.

I try to ignore the fact that we have an audience as I shove my tongue in her mouth in hopes of distracting her. She resists at first, squirming against me, but as I slide my hands up and down her sides and then up the back of her neck, she starts to relax. I know she's going to survive the trip when she threads her fingers through my hair and kisses me back.

The attendant clears his throat and the elevator stops. "Rooftop," he says loudly.

I pull away from Emma, wiping her smeared lipstick with my thumb. "We're here." I turn to the operator. "Sorry about that."

He shrugs. "I've seen worse. Do you want to go back down, miss?"

She looks at me, unsure of herself.

"We're already here," I say. "Might as well stay a minute. We can always catch the next one."

She lets out a breath. "Where's the bar?"

I move aside so she can exit in front of me.

"Seriously," she says, looking back at the elevator as the doors close. "Chardonnay. Now."

A waiter approaches us with glasses of champagne on a tray. I take two of them and hand one to Emma. "Will this do?"

She drinks it in three swallows.

"I guess that's a yes."

"I can't believe you did that," she says, motioning to the elevator.

"It worked, didn't it? You were having a panic attack. I didn't know what else to do." I wipe the lipstick off my thumb with a napkin and show it to her. "I got most of it, but you might want to hit the restroom to freshen up. It's right over there. Do you want me to walk you?"

She shakes her head and hands me the empty glass. "I'm fine. But if you can wrangle up another one of these, I'd be grateful."

"You got it."

She's much calmer than when we were on the elevator. We're fifty stories up; why isn't she afraid to be here? Surely the alcohol didn't take effect that quickly. While she's in the bathroom, I flag down a waiter for more champagne.

He looks at me curiously. "Brett Cash?"

"Yes. Have we met?"

"I'm Andrew Neal. You work with my cousin, Justin. We had drinks together last year at a Nighthawks game."

I hold out my hand before I realize he can't shake it because he's carrying a tray. I chuckle. "Sorry. Nice to see you again. You work here?"

"I moonlight here during the summers," he says. "I'm a teacher. Eighth-grade history."

"What a coincidence. I'm here with a teacher."

"Emma," he says looking over my shoulder.

"That's right. Do you know her?"

Before he can answer, Emma joins us. "Andrew, hi," she says, looking uncomfortable.

"Hey," he says. "I called, but you didn't …" He looks at me and then back at her. "I'd better get back to work."

He walks away before I can get a glass from him.

"That became awkward quickly," I say. "Did you two used to date or something?" When she doesn't respond, it dawns on me. "Did you go out with him recently? As in the last month?"

She snatches a glass of champagne from a waitress going by and sips, avoiding my eyes. "I may have."

Shit. He wasn't the man who walked her home last night either. "How many guys have you gone out with while we've been…"

She still doesn't look at me.

"Shit." I flag down a waitress, pick up a glass, and chug it.

"I'm not going out with *anyone*. Not really," she says. "And you shouldn't be surprised. I told you from the beginning that I couldn't date you."

"You're not going out with them," I repeat woodenly, anger rising from the pit of my stomach. "You're just *fucking* them?" Her jaw drops, and I can tell she's about to lay into me. "Don't answer that. We're nothing to each other, so why shouldn't you date?" I look at my empty glass. "Ready for another?"

"Brett, you're being unreasonable. We made it all the way here. Can't we be civil and have a little fun?"

Andrew is crossing the room. I scowl. "Sure, let's have some fun."

I yank her against me and give her a kiss. With tongue. She doesn't fight it, like I thought she would. We break apart just as Andrew goes by, staring at us.

I lift my chin at him. "Andy. How's it hangin'?"

Emma has a hard time not laughing. "You're terrible."

I smile, knowing she's okay with what I just did. "So, you never called him back, huh?"

She shakes her head.

"And the guy who walked you home last night, will you call *him* back?"

She looks surprised.

"What, like you don't do the same damn thing? Remember that time you thought I was kissing Amanda?"

"You *were* kissing Amanda."

"Do we need to go over this again?"

"I didn't kiss Monty like you kissed Amanda."

"I *didn't* kiss Amanda," I say, irritated. "And Monty? What the hell kind of name is that? Is he a teacher, too?"

"Banker."

"Andy the teacher and Monty the banker. Is that it?"

She chews on her lip.

"There's more?"

She takes another drink. "Antonio."

Three of them? "So what does good ol' Tony do?"

"He sells insurance."

"Jesus, Emma. Could you have found three guys more boring than that?" I sound like an insecure asshole, but I don't care.

"Being a teacher is not boring," she says defensively.

Andrew is glancing at us from across the room, so I slip an arm around her waist and lean close enough to whisper in her ear. "Do any of them kiss you the way I do? Do you like their tongues as much as you like mine?"

I kiss the tender spot just under her ear.

"You're not playing fair," she says when I pull away.

I take a fresh drink from a passing waitress and raise my glass. "All's fair in love and war."

She raises a brow at me. "Which do you think this is, love or war?"

I lean into her and say, "You tell me."

I watch the movement of her throat as she swallows.

I spend the next hour teasing and toying with her. And taunting Andrew. Who knew this night would turn out to be so much fun?

The elevator attendant smiles at us when we step into the car. He remembers us from earlier. But this car is full. We won't be putting on a show this time.

We back into the far corner, making room for the others. As we start our descent and the others talk about their evening, she becomes uncomfortable again. Not as bad as on the way up, but there is a lot of tension on her face.

I run my hand sensually down the back of her dress, starting at her shoulders and ending between her legs. I can feel her body heat through the thin material of her dress.

"Brett," she whispers in warning.

Knowing nobody can see, I squeeze one of the globes of her ass and then run a finger between her ass cheeks. I lean close so only she can hear. "Do the others touch you here? Do they make you squirm like I do? I know how you like it. I know every inch of you, and I'm going to make you come so hard, you won't ever want to scream anyone's name but mine."

She blows out a long, controlled breath and shifts her weight from foot to foot.

When we reach the lobby, I lead her to the street and hail a cab. After we get in, I ask, "Am I getting off on your side of the street or mine?" I lay a finger across her mouth to silence her before she can answer. "Because either way, I'm getting off."

She nibbles her lip and smiles.

~ ~ ~

Forty-five minutes and two Emma orgasms later, I'm once again being kicked out of her bed.

Before I put my clothes on, I use her bathroom. I leave a lipstick message that I know she'll erase as soon as I leave.

BRETT – 2

ANDY / MONTY / TONY – 0

I look at what I wrote, knowing it's tonight's score, but what about every other night? The nights I'm at work—who is she inviting into her bed then?

I stand naked in the bathroom doorway. "I don't think you should go out with anyone else."

She pulls her robe on. "Are you having fun with me?"

"Of course."

"Then why rock the boat? We don't need to put a label on anything, do we? I'm not dating anyone. I go out to dinner sometimes. Sometimes I go up in tall buildings. Can we just leave it at that?"

"I don't want to leave it at that. We're obviously into each other. The sex is off-the-charts fantastic. Do you plan to use me until you find the guy you want to marry?"

"Whoa, who said anything about getting married? I'm not looking for that."

"I didn't say I was either, but I'm also not wild about dipping my stick in the community pot, if you get my drift."

"Are you calling me a slut?"

"If the fuck-me heels fit."

I half expect her to slap me. But she doesn't. She doesn't even yell at me.

"Get out, Brett. Just go."

"Gladly."

I put my clothes on in brooding silence while she makes sure the coast is clear. I almost tell her it doesn't matter. That Evie is most likely in the kitchen waiting for me.

But tonight is not one of those times I want to stay for cookies and milk. I just want to go home and be pissed at Emma and angry at myself for being such a goddamn doormat.

"Bye," she whispers as I walk past her.

I don't bother replying.

When I get to the bottom of the stairs, I don't even look around to see if Evie is awake. I go straight to the door.

"You're mad at her," Evie says behind me. "I can tell by the way you stomped down the stairs."

"Go back to bed," I say, opening the door.

"She doesn't have other guys over, you know. You're the only one who's snuck out of here in months."

She has my full attention. I turn around. "*Months?* Are you sure?"

She nods. "She really likes you. I'm just not so sure she *wants* to like you. You know, because of my grandpa and all."

"Yeah."

"I like you. Grandma likes you. That has to count for something."

"I think you're pretty cool, too."

"Stay for milk and cookies?"

"Not tonight," I say. "I really need to go."

"Promise me you'll come back. Don't give up on her."

"Evie …" I run my hands through my hair and sigh. "It's complicated."

She sits on the bottom step, pouting. "Well, it shouldn't be. When two people like each other, they should be together. It's stupid if they aren't."

I laugh silently. That might be the most twelve-year-old thing she's ever said.

But that doesn't mean she's not one hundred percent right.

CHAPTER TWENTY-FOUR

EMMA

It's been a week since I've seen Brett.

Well, that's not entirely true. I've seen him plenty of times in the window. But never when he's been able to see me back.

Since the night of the cocktail party, it's been complete radio silence. And despite my continued nightmares I have to admit I miss him.

If you miss him so much, why did you go on two more dates this week? my inner voice asks.

I put down my coffee. Brett's right. I *am* using him until I can find someone else who can make me feel like I do when I'm with him.

The problem is—no one has even come close.

But I'm not giving up. There has to be someone out there. Just *one* man who's not a firefighter, who can make me feel like he does. I've kissed some of them. I even let one put his hands on me, thinking that was what I needed to get over this thing with Brett. If there even is a thing anymore.

I refuse to buy into the belief that there is only one person out there for everyone. I look up at the ceiling, thinking of my mother.

No—it was her choice not to date. She could find someone if she really wanted to.

I check my phone again as if he would have magically sent me a text in the last ninety seconds. Silly, because I know he's at work.

I roll my eyes at myself thinking how I know Brett's schedule a little too well for a woman who isn't interested in dating him.

I look at all the baked goods I've made this week. It's way more than usual. I've been trying to keep busy. But the problem is baking keeps the hands busy, not the mind. What am I going to do with all these cookies, muffins, and buns?

I know what I want to do with them. But that would be giving him the wrong idea.

Maybe if I go with a purpose. An excuse to be there other than to get him into bed. Because that's not what I want.

It's not.

"That's a lot of stuff, Mom," Evelyn says, coming in the kitchen to collect her sack lunch.

"The three of us will never eat it all. I was thinking I'd drop it by the local fire station."

Her face breaks into a bright smile. I eye her suspiciously, wondering why that would make her happy.

"I think it's a great idea," she says, reining in her overeager smile. "Grandpa would be happy. Did you know Grandma used to take cookies to him when he was at work?"

"I did know that. That's why I started baking in the first place."

"Really?"

I nod. "As soon as I was old enough to stir the batter, she let me help, and then once a week, we'd walk over a mile to take them to him. He didn't work at the fire station around the corner; his was farther away."

Would I have been able to walk into Brett's firehouse if it had been the same one as my dad's? I haven't been back there since he died. The memory of Mom and me taking him cookies has always been too painful for me to consider going back.

"Maybe one day I can help you bake stuff for the firehouse," she says.

My mind plays a trick on me, and I see flashes of Evelyn and me taking cookies to Brett, just as Mom and I took them to Dad.

"We'll see," I say, gathering up the excess baked goods and putting them in a bag. "Come on. Time to get to camp."

Evelyn asks me some strange questions on the way, like did I enjoy dinner last night with Jake, a fellow teacher from my school? And do I like him? And what kind of qualities do I like in a man?

"What's up with you and the questions?" I ask, horrified that maybe I haven't been as discreet as I should have been with the men in my life.

She shrugs. "I don't know. Just curious about boys, I guess."

I breathe a sigh of relief, but at the same time, my insides twist when I think about her growing up. "Oh, no. Don't even think about it. You are not allowed to date until you're sixteen."

"That's actually pretty progressive," she says. "Kendra and Allie's moms say they have to be seventeen."

"Progressive?" I say with a raise of my brow. "Kind of a big word, Evelyn."

"In case you haven't noticed, I'm kind of a big girl."

I stop and give her a hug. "I guess you are."

"Big enough to go to Germany?"

"That again?"

"I really, really, really want to go, Mom. I never ask you for much."

"I know, baby. But this is different. I don't want you to be—"

"Disappointed," she says, finishing my thought. "I know. And I won't be, I promise. I'm just curious."

We arrive at camp and I nod to the door. "We're here. We'll continue this conversation another time."

"That's what you always say."

I give her a kiss. "Have a nice day, Evelyn."

She sighs in frustration. "Bye, Mom."

On my way down the block, I wonder about my real motives for not taking her overseas. Yes, it's true, I believe she'll be disappointed if we go. But is that the real reason I won't take her? Or is it strictly my fear of flying? In all honesty, it's possible she could have grandparents who don't know about her and would love to have her in their lives. Am I selfish for keeping her from that?

Squad 13 is pulling into the station when I arrive. Brett sees me but doesn't have any reaction. No wave. No smile. Not even a cordial nod. When he jumps off his truck, I notice he's covered with soot. My heart sinks. He's not the one for me. If I think Evelyn will be disappointed when she meets the biological father who doesn't want her, I can't even imagine how she'd feel if she got attached to someone like Brett and then lost him.

He strolls over to me, raising his eyebrows as if to ask why I'm here.

I shove the bag at him. "I had extra, so I thought I'd bring them."

"Okay, thanks." He takes the bag and starts to walk away.

I panic. "I think I'm ready," I blurt out.

He spins around. "Ready for what?"

I'm so stupid. He probably thinks I'm saying I'm ready to date. "To go up in the Empire State Building. You said you'd take me by the end of the month. Well, it's almost the end of the month, and I think I'm ready."

"Maybe Andy could take you," he says spitefully.

"Brett, please. You started this."

He takes a step forward. "Are you going to let me finish it?"

My insides turn over. "Are we still talking about tall buildings?"

"I don't know. Are we?"

We stare at each other until Denver comes over and snatches the bag from him. "I was hoping you'd be back. We've missed your baking, Emma."

"Enjoy," I say.

"We sure will."

"So …?" I say, chewing a fingernail.

He looks over toward Manhattan and then back at me. He pinches the bridge of his nose and I wonder if he's having second thoughts about it. "When?" he asks, after what seems like a million agonizing seconds.

"How about now?"

"Now?"

I shrug. "No time like the present. Unless you need to get home to Leo, that is."

"Bonnie's with him. Give me ten minutes to change." He looks at the dirt and soot caked on his hands. "Better make it twenty."

For twenty minutes I think of all the horrible situations that could have put him in that state. What if one day his truck didn't pull back into the fire house? What if he was trapped without a way out? What if—I think of Dad—what if the hero one day became the victim?

I pull out my phone and text Jake, accepting his invitation for a second date. Maybe there isn't anyone who can make me feel like Brett does, but it's not worth the risk. Maybe finding someone *almost* as good is good enough.

~ ~ ~

"How come you've never mentioned going to the top of One World Trade Center?" I ask at the entrance to the Empire State Building. "It's taller than this one, you know."

He looks in that direction. "I know. But I figured the Empire State Building wouldn't evoke as many memories."

"You'd be right. I'm not sure I could go there. Have you ever?"

"Yeah."

"Have you been to the memorial?"

"Dozens of times." He looks at me sideways. "You have too, right?"

"Once," I say.

"You've only been there *one* time?"

I nod sadly. "My mom made me go when it opened back in 2011."

"She *made* you go? You didn't want to?"

I shake my head.

"Oh, right," he says. "This is all about you not forgiving your father, isn't it?"

I shrug.

"Surely you've been to his grave."

I look at the ground. "He doesn't have a grave. He was buried in the south tower."

He runs a hand through his hair. "Emma, you need to let this go. He did not leave you on purpose. Maybe if you could accept that, you'd be willing to accept other things in your life."

"Don't try and shrink me, Brett. I'm long past that."

He laughs disingenuously. *"Clearly* you're past that," he says sarcastically. He motions to the building. "Are we going to do this or what?"

"Of course. That's why we're here."

"Well, let's get on with it."

He's more than a little irritated at me. I'm just not sure I can pick the reason why. Kicking him out of my bed? Dating other guys? Not forgiving my dad? Maybe it's a combination of all of them.

At the ticket counter, he pulls out his wallet. I step in front of him. "You are not paying."

He puts his wallet away without the slightest hesitation. Although I really do want to pay, him not protesting makes me sad. He *always* protests.

He looks at the tickets. "Eighty-sixth floor observatory. I've always thought that's the better one. The higher one is encased in glass."

"Someone once told me there's not that much difference between fifty floors and a hundred, so I figured this'll do."

He smiles. "Listen, Emma. I may not be in a good place right now, but I don't want that to take away from what you're doing here. I'm really proud of you."

I look over at the line for the elevators to the observatory. "Don't be proud of me quite yet."

He holds out his elbow for me to take. "Let's kill this bitch."

Standing in line gives me too much time to second-guess myself. I almost walk away five times, but each time Brett convinces me to stay. I don't miss the crazy looks I'm getting from strangers. Neither does Brett.

"Ignore them," he says, as we inch closer to the elevators. "They have no idea what your story is, and that gives them no right to judge."

The doors open, and it's our turn to pile in. I start to sweat. Around us are families of tourists, two businessmen, and a single lady checking out Brett.

"No kissing," I say to him before the doors close.

"Wasn't planning on it."

Disappointment courses through me at his curtness.

When the elevator ascends, it feels like my heart is going to stop. I can't catch my breath.

"Emma, eyes on me," he says. "Don't think about it. Think about something else. Tell me about a good memory. The day Evelyn was born. Tell me about that."

"I … I can't," I say shakily.

"Is she going to faint?" the woman next to me asks. "Oh, Lord, she's not going to be sick, is she?" She pushes her child farther away from me. "People shouldn't do this unless they can handle it."

Brett gives her a quelling look. "She's fine. I'd appreciate it if you'd mind your own business."

I feel the stares of all the people in the elevator. They look at me and whisper amongst themselves. My stomach rolls. Maybe the woman is right. Maybe I *am* going to be sick.

Brett looks at a loss. We don't have alcohol. He can't kiss me. My knees get weak.

Brett fusses with his phone. I hear music, and a few seconds later, Brett breaks into song.

He's singing Elton John.

He turns the volume on his phone as high as it will go and sings along loudly. I'm shocked and maybe a little embarrassed, because he's so off-key.

"B-B-B-Bennie and the Jets," he sings, belting out the chorus.

Everyone in the elevator looks at him, but he doesn't seem to care.

After the first verse, a man in the corner sings along. Some of the kids laugh. Then a woman joins in. A minute later, almost all the adults, including the rude woman, are singing the explosive chorus of my happy-place song.

Before I know it, I'm smiling. I don't sing along. I'm too shocked to speak. But I do spend the rest of the elevator ride completely floored over what this man will do to distract me.

The doors open to the observatory and people exit, still singing or humming.

I pull Brett aside once we've cleared the doors. "You're crazy," I say, laughing.

"And *you're* laughing," he says, taking a bow. "Mission accomplished. We're here."

I look around and blow out a deep breath, realizing I'm not as scared as I thought I'd be when I got up here. "I thought you didn't like Elton John."

"I never said I didn't like him. I said I didn't know the words to his songs."

I stare. "You learned the words? For … me?"

"Come on," he says. "Let's check things out."

We stroll the perimeter, admiring the picturesque skyline. I even look through one of the binocular thingies.

I catch Brett staring at me. "What is it?"

"You're having a good time, aren't you?"

I look around, enjoying the open-air deck. "I guess so."

"And when we went to the other tall buildings, you had fun as well, once we got to the top."

"I suppose."

"Emma, you don't have a problem with tall buildings. You have a problem with elevators."

"That's crazy," I say.

"Do you ever take elevators?"

"Of course I do." But then I think back over the past six weeks and I realize I haven't gotten into any elevators in a while. Not even when I go to Lisa's apartment on the sixth floor. I told myself I needed to get in my steps, but maybe he's onto something. "Or I did until recently. I'm not sure why I stopped."

"After the incident at the school, I was a bit claustrophobic," he says. "I'm guessing you're experiencing some sort of PTSD from being held in the storage closet at gunpoint."

"Do you really think so?"

"I'm almost positive. Just look what you've been doing the past twenty minutes. If you were afraid of tall buildings, you'd be having a panic attack up here, but you're totally fine. Just like the other times."

I look at my hands. Steady as a rock. "Oh, my God, you're right. So the buildings? You don't think that was a real fear? But all this time I thought …" I shake my head in amazement.

"It was as real as you thought it was. You never tried to go up in a tall building in all these years. If you had, maybe you would have figured it out long before now."

"Back then I wasn't afraid of small spaces, so I would have been fine in elevators." I look around again, amazed I'm actually here, and I'm okay with it. "I can't believe it." I move to the edge. "I can even look over the side. This is incredible."

I try to take in everything: the buildings below us, the maze of streets, the sky. I see airplane trails crisscrossing the horizon and turn to Brett in excitement. "I think I'm ready."

He looks at me, confused. "Ready for what exactly?"

Damn. I did it again. "I'm ready to fly. If I'm not scared of tall buildings, maybe I'm not scared of airplanes either. I want to do it. I want to go in an airplane." I'm struck by a specific idea. "I want to take Evelyn to Germany."

"Whoa," Brett says. "One thing at a time. Germany is a long plane ride. There's no getting off once you get on."

"So go with me," I blurt.

He laughs. "Now you're just talking crazy."

Do I want to take it back? It takes me two seconds to realize I don't. "I'm serious. Look what I've accomplished with your encouragement. You know all about the breathing and the song. You're a paramedic, for Pete's sake. You can help if I freak out or go into shock or something. Come on, it'll be an adventure."

"What about your daughter?" he says, raising a brow at me as if to challenge my request.

Oh, right. There's that. "You're my friend. Evelyn has male friends. There's nothing wrong with friends taking a trip together."

I could swear he gives it some serious thought, but then he looks sad. "Friends. That's what we are." He stares off into the distance. "I'm not sure Germany is a good idea."

"Please, Brett. This is something I need to do for Evelyn *and* for me."

"Emma, you realize how fucking twisted this is, right? You kick me out of your bed repeatedly. You brush me off. You ignore me for a week. And then you ask me to go on vacation with you?"

"It's not a vacation. Far from it. Plus, I've never been overseas, and it would be nice to have somebody to protect us—you know, two single ladies all alone."

"Jesus." He rubs his jaw in contemplation.

I bite my lip in anticipation, like a kid waiting for a Christmas present.

He laughs at my impatience. "I'm not promising anything, but I'm sure as hell not going on an eight-hour flight with you until we figure out if you're okay flying."

"What did you have in mind?" I ask. "A test flight to a nearby airport?"

"Too many other people. You saw what can happen in the elevator. People can be dicks." The wheels in his head spin. "I have to make a call. A buddy at FDNY moonlights as a pilot for a small airport outside the city. The planes he flies are small charters, the kind that only have ten or twenty seats. People rent them for parties."

"People rent planes for parties?"

"It's kind of like renting a limo, only a lot more luxurious."

I shake my head. "That sounds expensive. I'm going to need every bit of my savings for our trip to Germany."

"Like I said, let me make a call. He owes me a favor or two."

"As in you think he'll take us up in a private plane for free? Must be one hell of a favor he owes you."

"It is. But Emma, these are small planes. If you can't be in an elevator …"

"Just how small are we talking?"

"I don't know. Maybe as long as your townhouse from front to back, but narrow."

"So, bigger than an elevator?"

He laughs. "Yes, bigger than an elevator."

"Sold," I say. "Make the call."

"When I get home," he says. "Ready to go?"

I nod.

"Oh, shit," he says, looking toward the elevator. "What goes up must go down. How do you feel about walking down eighty-six flights of stairs?"

"Uh, no."

"Well, there's always kissing or whispering naughty things in your ear. That worked before."

My insides quiver at the thought of him whispering naughty things. But we both know where that will lead us—right to bed. And that's not what I want. Well, I do, but I don't. But I can't. So I won't.

"How about you sing to me instead?" I say, half joking.

"That was a one-time performance." He pulls earbuds out of his pocket as we step on the elevator. He studies them in his hand and then he laughs. "This would have made the ride up much less humiliating." He hands one earbud to me and puts the other in his ear.

He plays my happy-place song all the way down. He doesn't sing out loud this time, but he does mouth the words. The whole ride I watch him "serenade" me. And damn if he's not just serenading me with his silent words. He's serenading me with his eyes. With his body.

During our cab ride home, I make a mental list of all the reasons he's perfect for me.

Then we pass by my Dad's old firehouse and I remember the one reason he *isn't.*

"Enjoy your day with Leo," I say when we exit the cab and go our separate ways.

At my door I turn and watch him go into his townhouse. *Because you never know what can happen.*

CHAPTER TWENTY-FIVE

BRETT

"Hand me that ratchet and socket," I say from under the Mustang. Jay puts them in my hands, and I finish attaching the oil pan. "I'm ready. Pull me out."

He yanks me out from under the car. It's kind of become our thing, pulling each other out from under it.

Bonnie appears, carrying the pizza that just got delivered. "Mind if I steal a slice for Leo? He's worked up a good appetite, running around the car while you boys tinker with it."

"Peeza, Daddy! Peeza!" he screams, wielding his toy screwdriver as if it was a sword.

I take a slice from the box and put his pepperoni on my slice. "Here you go." I set him up at the picnic table.

Bonnie chastises me. "You could at least wash your hands," she says, tearing Leo's slice into bite-sized pieces.

I look at the grease and grime coating my hands and laugh. "True mechanics don't wash their hands. Right, Jay?"

Jay shrugs and picks up a slice.

We sit next to Leo, the three of us eating grimy pizza. Bonnie rolls her eyes and goes back inside.

I say to Jay, "She's going in to make a salad or some other girl food."

He laughs. He's been doing more of that lately. At first it was hard to get him to laugh. But in the past few weeks, he's taken on the carefree attitude his mom said had died along with his father.

I gaze fondly at the car. "It's really coming along, isn't it?"

"Yeah," he says. "Have you decided what color to paint it yet?"

"I was thinking I'd let you choose." He has no idea I'm going to give him the car. I cleared it with his mother last week. They have a shed out back where he can park it when he turns sixteen.

"Me?"

"What do you think? Blue? Green? Silver?"

He looks at the Mustang. "I'll have to give it some thought. It's a big decision."

"It is, but we have time."

Bonnie comes out to collect Leo when he's done eating. "I think this one's ready for his afternoon nap."

"Sleep tight, little man," I say, ruffling his hair. "Later today we're going to a baseball game with Joey and Uncle Denver."

"Yay!" Leo claps his hands as Bonnie whisks him inside.

"You want to come, too?" I ask Jay

"Me? Why would you want me to come?"

"Because we're friends? And friends do things together."

"How come you're always so nice to me?"

"I like to think I'm nice to everyone," I say.

He picks at his pizza. "Not many white guys are nice to me," he says. "All they see when they look at me is a poor black kid."

Hearing him say that makes me fume. "I guess you've been hanging around the wrong white guys then. Come on, what do you say? It'll be fun. We usually only stay for half of the game. It's all Leo and Joey have the patience for. You'll be home by eight."

"Okay."

"Great," I say giving my hands a clap. "Then we'd better finish before Leo wakes up. I'd say we have about ninety minutes."

My phone vibrates in my pocket. I pull it out and see who's calling. It's Amanda. I point at the car. "Get that belt on. I have to take this." I move a few yards away. "What's up?"

Amanda's been calling more lately. She even came for another visit a few weeks ago. I suspect seeing me with Emma made her realize what she's been missing. It doesn't matter, though. I see through all her bullshit.

"Hey, babe," she says cheerfully.

I shake my head. For two years, she didn't use that endearment for me. And now that we're divorced, she thinks it's okay to start using it again? "What do you want, Amanda? I'm a little busy right now."

"I just wanted you to know that I've scheduled my summer vacation. I'll be spending it in New York."

"I'll alert the press," I say dryly.

"Come on, Brett. It'll be fun. I'll be there for an entire week. Leo and I can spend so much time together. And maybe you and I—"

I cut her off right there. "When are you arriving?"

"Two weeks from Saturday."

"I'm sure Leo will be happy to see you."

"What about you, Brett? Will *you* be happy to see me?"

I ignore her question. "I assume you'll be staying at your sister's house?"

"Actually, no. Jamie is having some renovations done. I thought I'd stay at the house with Leo and you."

"You want to stay *here?*"

"Sure. It'll be a blast. You're always saying I should spend more time with our son."

"There are plenty of hotels close by that would be more comfortable. There's no place for you to sleep here."

She blows a sigh into the phone. What the hell does she think? That I'll let her back into my bed when it's convenient for her?

"I can sleep on the day bed in Leo's room," she says.

"It's not a good idea."

"Why not? Is it because of that woman across the street? You think she'll get jealous? She'd better get used to me being in Leo's life. In *your* life. We'll always be connected, you and me."

I wasn't even thinking about Emma and how she'd view it. I was thinking that I didn't want to have to see Amanda morning, noon, and night. "It would be better if you stayed somewhere else. I don't want to give Leo the wrong idea."

"He's two, Brett. What ideas could I possibly put in his head? I'm his mother. Don't I deserve to rock him to sleep sometimes? And comfort him when he has a nightmare? And make his favorite breakfast?"

"What is his favorite breakfast?" I ask.

She huffs. "That's not fair."

"It *is* fair, Amanda. You don't know Leo, and now, suddenly, you want to play Mother of the Year? I'm not buying it."

"I've had a lot of time to think, Brett. I want to be a better mother to him. I need this. Leo needs this. Do you really want to keep me from him? Make me stay in a hotel? I never thought you were that kind of person."

I pace around the car, watching Jay expertly assemble the alternator.

I don't want her staying in my house. But maybe she's right. Leo has the right to get to know his mother. Her staying with him for a week would do that. "Fine, but you're sleeping in Leo's room. I mean it, Amanda. We're divorced. You can't kiss me and shit."

"I'll see you in seventeen days." She disconnects.

I slip my phone into my pocket and growl.

"Trouble in paradise?" Jay asks, looking up from the car.

"I'd hardly call my life paradise."

My phone vibrates again. "What?" I snap without checking who's calling.

"Is that any way to treat the guy who's about to do you an epic favor?"

"Christian?" I ask. "Were you able to arrange something?"

"That depends. You on a shift tomorrow night?"

"No."

"Then I'm about to make your day. We had a cancellation. Won't cost you a dime because they didn't make the window."

"Seriously? That's fantastic. I can't tell you how much I appreciate this."

"Yeah, well, I do owe you one, my friend."

"We can call it even now."

"We'll never be even, man. Not after what you did for me."

"I was just doing my job," I say.

He snorts into the phone. "It's more than that and you know it."

"So, can you text me the details?"

"As soon as we hang up. See you tomorrow night."

"Thanks."

I sit on the picnic table, waiting for his text. Then I text Emma.

Me: Clear your schedule tomorrow night.

Emma: I'm not going on a date with you.

Me: How about a date with a Cessna?

Emma: Does that mean what I think it does?

Me: Meet me out front at 5:30. Our flight is at 7:00.

Emma: I think my heart just fell into the pit of my stomach.

Me: Having second thoughts?

Emma: Of course I'm having second thoughts. And third. And fourth. But it's something I have to do. Thank you so much. I can't believe you made it happen.

Me: I have many skills.

Emma: Are we still talking about flying?

Me: I don't know, are we?

Emma: See you tomorrow.

I put my phone away and return to the car.

Jay looks at me. "Dude, did you just win the lottery or something?"

I might be smiling too much. But the thought of going on a sunset flight down the coast with Emma makes me feel like, yeah … I might have won the lottery.

CHAPTER TWENTY-SIX

EMMA

"Nervous?" Brett asks, as we're escorted onto the tarmac.

"As nervous as anyone else would be who's never been in an airplane."

"You've been on a roller coaster before, haven't you?" he asks.

"Sure. Evelyn loves them."

"Takeoff and landing are kind of like riding on a roller coaster. Everything in between is amazing, especially if you have a window seat."

"Window seat. Got it."

I look at the long, sleek plane, in awe that Brett was able to make this happen. "Are we really the only people going on the plane?"

"Us and the two pilots."

"And you really didn't have to pay anything for this?"

He laughs. "If you think I can afford thirty thousand dollars on my salary, you're crazy."

My jaw drops. "That's what it costs to do this? Oh my God. And this is a thing? People pay that?"

"They pay a lot more than that. That's just for a two-hour flight. It goes up from there."

I'm stunned. Do people really have nothing better to do with their money?

A man who looks like a pilot approaches us.

"I can't tell you how much I appreciate this," Brett says, giving him a hug.

"It's my pleasure."

"Christian Merric, meet Emma Lockhart."

Christian shakes my hand. "Nice to meet you. I hear we're going to pop your cherry."

"My, uh …" I feel my face turn beet red. What does he think is going to happen on this plane?

"You know, your first flight," Christian says. "I'm glad I get to be the one to take you up."

"Oh, right." I feel stupid for thinking anything else.

"Don't worry," he says. "The conditions look perfect. We'll take good care of you. My copilot is already onboard." He gestures to the stairway leading up to the plane. "Come on, I'll show you around."

I follow Christian and Brett onto the plane, amazed at what I'm seeing. I'm not sure what I thought it would look like, but it wasn't this. Brett was right. It is like the inside of a limousine. Only thirty-thousand times better.

Behind the cockpit are six rows of seats facing each other, one seat on either side of the aisle. Behind them is a couch that extends along one side of the plane. Opposite the couch is a bar and a flat-screen TV.

"Help yourself to drinks. Just make sure all the bottles are secure for takeoff and landing. In the back is a bathroom. It's small but nice. We'll be in the air two hours. We leave in about ten minutes. I'll announce over the intercom when you should prepare for takeoff and then a short safety video will play on the TV." He points to various places that have call buttons. "Use one of those if you need to talk to me. Otherwise we'll stay up front so you can enjoy your privacy."

"Did you just wink?" I ask him, irritated. I look at Brett. "What did you tell him? Does he think we're going to join the Mile-High Club or something?"

Both men try to contain their laughter.

"Of course not," Brett says. "I didn't tell him anything except this would be your first flight."

Christian backs away, looking embarrassed. "We always stay up front. I didn't mean to offend you. I hope you enjoy your flight, Emma. I'll see you after."

Now *I'm* the one who's embarrassed. Maybe he didn't wink at all. Maybe it was all in my mind. "Thank you, Christian. I apologize. I'm nervous."

He nods and retreats into the cockpit.

"See?" Brett says, motioning around the plane. "Much bigger than an elevator."

"It's huge. I didn't expect this. I don't feel claustrophobic at all."

He looks in the liquor cabinet, then pulls a bottle of wine out of the mini fridge. "You won't be needing any of this then?"

"I didn't say that," I tell him, going in search of glasses.

He chuckles as he opens the bottle and pours us each a glass. "Where do you want to sit? I'd recommend not right over the wing. You'll have a better view."

I look out each window, assessing which view might be the best. Then I take a seat, placing my wine in the cup holder next to me.

Brett sits in the seat facing me, our knees almost touching. It's hot today. I'm wearing a sundress, and he's in shorts. Our bare knees being inches apart gives me flashbacks of our lovemaking.

"You okay?" he asks. "You kind of zoned out for a second."

I shake it off and look out the window. "I'm fine."

Christian's voice comes over the intercom, telling us we're going to depart. I feel the plane move, and my heartbeat goes from zero to sixty. I bring the wine glass to my lips and drink until it's gone.

Brett must notice my growing anxiety. "Are you thinking about your dad?"

"No. Yes. I don't know. Maybe it's just the fact that we're in a tin can that's about to defy the laws of gravity or physics or whatever."

He puts a hand on my knee. "Just like a roller coaster ride, remember?"

I blow out a deep breath. "If the roller coaster went up ten thousand feet."

"More like thirty," he says.

My head falls back against the seat. "Gee, thanks."

"Sorry." He points to the TV. "The video is starting."

It does nothing to relieve my nerves. "In the event of a *water landing?"* I say in horror.

Brett reaches for my hand. "That never happens."

"What about that movie? You know, about the plane that landed in the Hudson."

"Okay, it *rarely* happens. But Emma, you're much more likely to get in an accident in a car than on a plane."

"I don't have a car," I blurt out.

"Okay, a cab then. Hell, even walking the streets of Brooklyn is more dangerous than this."

The video ends, and the plane moves faster and faster. My heartbeat quickens. I gaze out the window and it looks like we're going a hundred miles per hour. Probably because we are.

"Do you want me to have Christian turn around?" Brett asks.

I shake my head over and over. "No. I have to do this."

Brett pulls out his phone and turns on the music. But I can't hear it over the loud drone of the engines.

"Sorry," he says. "I forgot to bring my earbuds. I could kiss you, but …" He looks down at the seatbelt anchoring him to his seat.

"I don't want you to kiss me."

It's a lie. I'd give anything for him to be kissing me right now, and not just because it would take my mind off what's happening. I've thought about nothing else for the past few weeks. Nothing but his lips on mine. His hands on my body. Him inside me. But I look at the FDNY logo on the breast pocket of his T-shirt and remember why I can't let him kiss me anymore.

Suddenly, my stomach is in my throat. I glance out the window to see that we're leaving the ground. I grip the armrests and squeeze my eyes shut. "Oh, God. Oh, God. Oh, God."

When I feel like I'm about to throw up, Brett touches my knee. His hand runs up and down my thigh, caressing the skin between my legs in a soft, circular motion. I should push him away, but I can't get let go of the armrests.

Instead of pushing him away, my body defies me and my legs fall open, giving him easier access. Under my dress, he runs his fingers along a line from my knee to my hip, grazing my panties without touching me there.

Touch me there! I scream silently.

"You want me to touch you?" he asks as the plane shimmies violently back and forth.

I can't answer. But I'm not sure my silence is because of his question, or the plane.

He teases me relentlessly and my insides shift from fear to desire. I don't know how long he keeps this up, but him not touching me where I want to be touched is just this side of torture.

I look out the window and see wisps of clouds below us, then realize we're not rocking anymore. I turn to him, ashamed for letting him touch me when I shouldn't have.

"I'm good now," I say, brushing his hand off my leg.

"You're *good now?"* he asks, confused.

"Yeah, we're up. I guess we've leveled off. You were right about the roller coaster thing."

"What if *I'm* not good now?" he asks, glancing at his lap.

An erection tents his shorts. Warm heat floods my insides. I can't keep leading him on like this.

"I'm sorry," I say, focusing my attention back out the window.

"You don't want me to touch you?"

I shake my head.

"But I'm … Christ, Emma, I'm all worked up here."

I clamp my lips together.

He stares at my legs, my thighs still exposed from him moving my dress. I cover my legs as best as I can.

"God, you have no idea how much I want you," he says.

Me, too.

His hand grazes his erection as he looks at me. "I'm not going to touch you if you say I can't. But you can't keep me from touching myself."

"I … *what?"* Did I hear him correctly?

His lips form a snarky half-smile. "You heard me."

He unbuckles his seatbelt and then unbuttons his shorts. He pushes his boxer briefs down, exposing his stiff penis. He grips it and gives it a slow stroke up and down. *Oh, God.* As embarrassed as I am watching him do it, I can't look away.

"Does this turn you on?" he says, stroking himself faster. "Are your panties getting damp watching me?"

I don't answer him. I *can't* answer him.

"You resist me, but you want me, don't you? You wish you were touching me. I wish it was you, too, because I love it when you touch me. You stroke my cock just the way I like it."

His eyes close and his head falls back against the seat. I've never seen anything so erotic.

"You like it when I stroke your clit, don't you? I know exactly how you like to be touched. I know just where your G-spot is. I know you come harder when I put a finger inside your tight little ass."

I blow out a long, slow breath. I can't believe he's doing this. I can't believe I'm watching him. I can't believe how incredibly turned on I am right now.

"I want to claim that ass of yours," he says. "I want to put my cock in it and make you come harder than you've ever come before."

I squirm in my seat, barely able to contain myself. I want him to stop what he's doing and touch me. I want to reach out and touch him. But I can't. Because watching him is better than any fantasy I've ever had.

A bead of pre-come seeps from the tip of his penis. "I'm going to come. Do you know how many times I've come thinking about you? About what we've done together? About the things I want to do to you? Look how flushed you are. I'll bet you want to touch yourself. Jesus, I'd like to see that."

He's breathing hard and his hand moves faster.

"I'll bet you are soaked. I want to feel how wet you are. I want to taste you." His face contorts, and he bites his lip. "Christ, Emma!" he shouts. He grabs the napkin under his glass, spilling the wine, and spurts into it.

Watching him make himself come almost has *me* coming.

He smiles at me when it's all over. He doesn't even look embarrassed. That turns me on even more, baffling me.

He buttons his shorts and then uses my napkin to clean up the wine. He laughs. "Better to spill wine than jizz."

I want to laugh, but I can't. I'm still reeling.

He puts both napkins in the trash and sits back down. He studies me. "Have you never seen a man do that before?"

I shrug.

"It turned you on, didn't it?"

I shrug again.

"Emma?"

I'm still unable to speak.

"Do you want me to kiss you now?"

That's the stupidest question I've heard in all my twenty-seven years. Of course I want him to kiss me. I want him to do everything he just said he wanted to do. So, despite my resolve not to, I nod.

He slides off his seat and kneels between my legs, pulling me toward him until our lips meet. He kisses me hard, like he knows I need that right now after going almost two weeks without his lips on me. "Do you want me to touch you?"

I put his hand between my legs.

He moves it up my thigh and under my panties. "Jesus, Emma," he says when he feels how drenched I am.

He removes my panties and pulls me to the edge of the seat, making it clear he's about to put his mouth on me. "I'm going to make you come now, Miss Lockhart."

I feel his fingers inside me. A moan escapes me when his tongue lashes my clit. I look over at his empty seat and still see the image of him stroking himself.

My head falls back and my insides tighten. He pushes me over the edge when I feel the vibrations of him audibly humming against my clit.

Oh.

My.

God.

I grab onto his head, holding him to me as my orgasm crashes down around me. "Yes!" I scream over the engines as I buck myself into him, wanting to feel every last pulse as it washes through me.

"That was damn impressive," he says after I slump into my seat. He glances out the window. "And I'm not just talking about the sunset."

It feels good to laugh with him. It feels good to *be* with him.

He hands me my panties, and I put them on while he pours us more wine.

I drink as I gaze out the window. "Did we just join the Mile-High Club?"

"Technically, no, but we've got another hour up here to remedy that."

I have a hard time not smiling. But it fades when I have an unsettling thought. "Unless you're already a member."

He takes my hand in his. "I'm not."

Even though we can't end up together, the thought of having a first with him makes me happy. "As long as what happens in Vegas …" I shrug.

He sighs and shakes his head. He gets what I'm saying. But he doesn't push back.

An hour later, after we've joined the club *twice*, we're making our approach at the airport.

He holds my hand. "Did you ever stop to think about how we met? You told me your dad always said things happen for a reason. Maybe there was a reason you were taken hostage at the school. Maybe there was a reason I was the one who volunteered to help you."

"What are you saying?"

He points a finger between us. "You and me. Maybe this is the reason."

I look out the window and watch the houses get bigger and bigger. "My dad was wrong," I say. "Not everything happens for a reason, Brett. There was no reason for him dying. No bigger picture. No good that came from it." I put his hand back in his lap. "He was wrong."

CHAPTER TWENTY-SEVEN

BRETT

I put down my hamburger and look at my sister. "Do you have any idea how proud I am of you?"

Bria smiles. "I don't have the gig yet."

"But you made it to the final cut. And you're going to meet the band."

"Eeek!" she screams. "I can't believe it. If nothing else comes out of this, I'll get to say I know Adam Stuart and the rest of White Poison."

"Something will come out of this," I say. "I know it."

"Do you really think so? I mean, do you think I have what it takes to be their backup singer?"

"Bria, you have what it takes to be their *lead* singer."

"They are a *guy* band, Brett."

"I know that. What I'm saying is you're that good. You should be the lead singer of something. I predict someday you will be."

She puts her head on my shoulder. "You're always there for me, aren't you?"

"You just remember that when you get rich and famous. You remember who supported you along the way." I nudge her in the ribs. "And maybe get me some backstage passes?"

"You know it." She bounces in her seat. "Can you imagine if it really happened? This whole thing is kind of freaking me out." She shows me her hand. "See, I'm shaking. I'm so damn nervous. I don't even want to think about what a wreck I'll be when I actually have to sing in front of them." Her eyes get huge. "What if I throw up? It would be humiliating. What if I have an asthma attack? What if I'm sick that day, and my voice totally sucks?"

I grab her shaking hands. "Bria, you haven't had an asthma attack since you were ten. You're not going to throw up. You sing better when you're sick than most people do healthy, but if you're worried about it, double up on the vitamin C and maybe stay away from Leo for a week before your audition—that kid is cesspool of germs."

"That kid is freaking amazing," she says like a doting aunt.

"He is, but he sticks his fingers everywhere. Up his nose, in his ears, in his dirty di—"

She cups a hand over my mouth. "Will you shut up? I don't want to think about where his fingers have been the next time I see him. Just … gross."

Both of us are laughing when I see a group of women enter the restaurant. I become quiet and focused, thinking I see Emma. But when the woman turns around, I realize it's not her.

"What is it?" Bria asks.

"Nothing. I thought I saw someone I knew, that's all."

She looks at the women and back at me. "Speaking of women, how's the sexy single mom?"

"Still using me," I say bitterly.

"You mean because she only wants to sleep with you?" She laughs. "You do realize how many guys would kill for that kind of NSA relationship."

"NSA?"

"No strings attached."

I shake my head. "Maybe, but not me."

"Why not you?"

I've been asking myself that question for a long time. I've just never been honest enough with myself to give the answer. I run my hands through my hair. "Because I think I'm in love with her."

"No way. Really?" She can't wipe the smile off her face.

"Yes really. But it's nothing to smile about. She's dating other guys."

"I know. You told me. You also told me her daughter says she isn't sleeping with any of them."

I belt out an incredulous laugh. "You mean the twelve-year-old I have a secret relationship with? God, Bria, do you know how fucked up this is? And now Emma wants me to go to Germany with her and her daughter. The woman who doesn't want a relationship with me wants me to fly halfway around the world with her."

"She's full of shit, Brett. She totally wants a relationship with you. Girls don't ask men to fly to Germany unless they are into them."

"I never said she isn't into me. I said she doesn't want to date me."

"So she sleeps with you but doesn't date you, and she dates other guys she doesn't sleep with."

I nod at the absurdity of it all. "Like I said, fucked up."

She studies me intently. She takes a bite of her salad and then points her fork at me. "She's seeing if there's another you out there. One who isn't like her father. But deep down she's probably drawn to you *because* you're like her father, even if she can't admit it."

I narrow my eyes at my introspective little sister. "Maybe you're in the wrong profession."

She laughs. "It just so happens I know the inner workings of the female mind."

"You think I should just sit back and put up with her kicking me out of bed and dating other men?"

"As long as she's not sleeping with them—yes. Let her keep searching, big brother. She'll never find another Brett Cash. You're one of a kind. She'll come to her senses sooner or later."

"I hope you're right. So, you think I should go to Germany with her?"

"Hell yes. Maybe Germany is where she comes to her senses."

"We'll be there with her kid. That's hardly the setting for some kind of romantic epiphany."

"Mark my words. You go to Germany with her, and she'll cave." She looks at her watch and puts down her fork. "I've gotta bolt. I have a jam session with some friends."

"You're ditching me for a jam session?"

She looks guilty. "I have to practice, Brett."

"I'm just kidding, Bria, go. I've got this."

She kisses my cheek. "Thank you for dinner. You're the best."

"No, *you're* the best," I say. "Just remember that when you're singing for Adam Stuart."

She blows me another kiss on her way out.

I finish the rest of my burger and go home, wondering if Bonnie and Leo are back yet. She takes him to a "Grandma and me" class twice a month.

I think of leaving Leo to go to Germany. I hate to do that. It kills me to be away from him when I work twenty-four-hour shifts. But there is no way he could come along. Taking a two-year-old on a plane for that long a flight would be pure torture for him and everyone else. And I wouldn't want to do anything to take away from the real reason for the trip—to find Evie's father.

I shake my head in disbelief once again. The woman I'm … *fucking,* for lack of a better term, wants me to go with her and the daughter whom she thinks I haven't even met to find her ex-lover from high school.

"Brett!"

It's Emma. She's is running to catch up with me. "Hey."

"Hi," I say, continuing to walk.

When I become silent, she asks, "Are you mad at me?"

"I'm not really sure what I am, Emma. Do *you* know what I am?"

It looks as though she's having an internal battle in her head. "Listen, I didn't want to get into a deep conversation right now. I just wanted to find out if you've given it any more thought."

"About going to Germany?"

"Yes. Have you? Will you?"

I stop walking. "It's complicated. And then there's the planning."

"There's no planning," she says. "It turns out Evelyn and my mom have been looking into going for a while now. They have all the flight schedules and have scoped out the best moderately-priced hotels. They've done all the legwork. Which is good since I have to go soon. Becca is getting married on the twenty-second, and I'm one of her bridesmaids, so I have to be back at least a week before that and then I have to report to work a week after her wedding. So, I'd pretty much have to leave two weeks from tomorrow." Her face falls. "Oh, gosh. Can you even get time off on such short notice? I didn't think this through. Do you have a passport? Oh, please say you have a passport. Go with me, Brett. I'm begging you."

"What did you just say?"

She laughs. "Which part? I was kind of rambling."

"About when you'd have to go. Two weeks?"

"Yes. Tomorrow is Saturday, we'd have to go no later than two weeks from then. I'm not sure we could leave any sooner than that."

"Two weeks from Saturday," I muse aloud, remembering my phone call with Amanda a few days ago. "I think I can make that work."

"Really?" she says brightly. "You'll go?"

"As long as it's two weeks from Saturday, yes."

She looks at me strangely. "Why that day?"

"Because Amanda just informed me she's coming to town that week, and she thought staying at the house with Leo would be beneficial."

"She wants to stay at *your* house?" She puts her hands on her hips, a sure sign of jealousy. Then it dawns on her, and she laughs. "You want to leave town while your ex stays at your house? She'll be livid."

"That's kind of the idea."

When she stops giggling, she studies me, and her face instantly sobers. "You'll go to Germany, but only to get away from Amanda."

I look her dead in the eye. "You'll sleep with me, but you won't date me."

She kicks a rock off the sidewalk. "I guess we both have issues, don't we?"

"I guess so."

She glances at her place. "Do you have a minute to come in?"

I look at my watch. "It's only eight o'clock. Won't your family be home?"

"That's the whole point. You have to meet Evelyn if we're taking her to Germany together."

"And you want to do that *right now?"*

My house is still dark; Bonnie and Leo aren't home yet. I scramble to come up with an excuse. How awkward might it get, pretending we've never met? Will we 'fess up and risk Emma being pissed at us? I wish I had time to talk to Enid first.

"Why not? It doesn't look like anyone is home at your place. Come on." She tugs on my arm. "I promise they won't bite."

"Emma, I'm just not sure this is going to turn out the way you had hoped."

"What does that mean?"

"Nothing. Let's go."

As we cross the street, I try and come up with explanations as to why I know Evie. Emma would be mortified to know that her daughter is aware of her nocturnal activities.

She opens the door and we go inside. "Mom! Evelyn! I have someone I'd like you to meet."

"Back here!" Enid shouts.

Emma leads me into the kitchen, where Enid is standing over Evie's shoulder as Evie works on a laptop.

"This is Brett Cash," Emma says. "Brett, meet my mom, Enid, and my daughter, Evelyn."

They look at me in shock. I gaze at them in dread that soon becomes something else. All at once, the three of us laugh uncontrollably.

Emma joins in for a minute, then stops. "Wait, what's so funny?"

I try to stop laughing, but every time I look at Evie, she sets me off again.

"You guys! Tell me." She looks annoyed at being left out, and we laugh even harder. "What the hell is going on here?"

"Honey," Enid says. "We've already met."

"You met?" she asks, confused. "What, at the store or something?"

Evie and I stop laughing because this is about to get real. I nod at Enid, letting her know I want to be the one to tell Emma.

"Emma," I say apprehensively, hoping she isn't about to take a swing at me. "I bumped into Evie the first night I, uh …" I look up at the ceiling where Emma's room is. "The first night I left."

Emma slumps into a chair, horrified. "You *what?"* She looks at her daughter and then back at me. "And you call her *Evie?* Just how many times did you 'bump' into her?"

"The first time was at the corner store," I say. "So technically, we did meet there. But I didn't know she was your daughter then. She thought Leo was cute. Then I saw her here and, well, we had milk and cookies and—"

"You had milk and cookies?" she says loudly. "With my *daughter?* After we …?"

"Not just with Evie," I say quickly, so I don't sound like a pervert. "Your mom, too." I'm not sure that makes it any better.

Emma looks like she doesn't know if she's going to laugh, cry, or scream.

"The stairs are squeaky, Mom," Evie says. "It's not his fault. My room is right under them, so I pretty much hear it every time someone comes down."

"Every time?" Emma asks in horror.

Evie nods. "It's okay, Mom. You're a single woman in the modern world. I'm not a baby. I know how things are."

Emma lowers her head until her forehead meets the table and then knocks it against the surface over and over.

"It's not that bad, honey," Enid says.

"What's not that bad?" Emma asks. "That my twelve-year-old daughter knows I have men upstairs? Or that my mother and daughter have been sharing secret midnight snacks with him? Or, and here's the real kicker—that everyone has been lying to me about it."

I feel guilty when she looks at me after saying that.

"Come on, Evie," Enid says, holding out a hand to her granddaughter. "Let's you and I go for ice cream."

Emma and I remain silent until the front door shuts. Then Emma gets up from the table and stomps around the kitchen. "How could you do this to me?"

"What was I supposed to do when Evie caught me coming down the stairs, just ignore her like all the others?"

She puts her face in her hands. "Oh my God, this is not happening."

"It's okay, Emma."

"It's *not* okay. Putting my daughter aside for a minute, you lied to me, Brett. Why didn't you tell me you had met her?"

"I suppose because she asked me not to."

She looks surprised. "Why would she do that?"

"Because she doesn't want you to think she thinks less of you for having men in your bedroom. Which she doesn't, by the way. You've got one hell of a kid there, Emma. She's smart. And she might know you better than you know yourself."

"What's that supposed to mean? Just what do you two talk about?"

"Lots of stuff. Her friends. My job. Germany."

"She discussed finding her dad?"

"She's told me how much she wants to go, but that you think she'll be disappointed when he doesn't want anything to do with her."

"She will be."

"Of course she will, but that doesn't mean you shouldn't try. There might be grandparents who want to be in her life."

"I've thought of that." She sits back down. "I'm still mad at you for not telling me."

I take the seat next to her. "I was trying to keep the peace between you. But if I'm being honest, I might have been a little selfish about not saying anything."

"How so?"

"If you'd found out, you would have stopped having me over." I grab her hand. "I don't want you to stop having me over, Emma."

She studies our entwined fingers. Then she looks up at me with a sullen face. "Even if it can't go anywhere?"

I think of what Bria said earlier—that Emma just needs time to figure out that she wants this, too. Because I have to believe that she does. I force a smile. "Yeah, even if it can't."

"No more lies," she says.

"No more lies. Although I think of it as more of an omission."

"I'm not sure I can do it anymore, Brett. I mean us, upstairs, when I know Evelyn is waiting for you to come down."

"So you'll come to my place."

She thinks about it. "You have a child, too. And a nanny."

"Leo's two. And Bonnie's discreet. And hard of hearing."

"She is?" She almost looks excited about it.

"No. That was a lie. I just didn't want you to feel self-conscious about coming over."

She laughs. "So, what now?"

"I don't know. I guess we have a trip to plan. That is if you still want me to go. Everything else can wait until we get back."

"We're getting separate hotel rooms," she says.

"That's a given."

"And I'm not leaving Evelyn alone in mine in a strange country to sneak into yours."

"I never thought you would."

"Fine," she says, relaxing into her chair. "Then it looks like we've got a lot of planning to do."

CHAPTER TWENTY-EIGHT

EMMA

Evelyn is teeming with excitement as we board the airplane.

"I get the window seat," she says.

I laugh. "You've only told us that a thousand times."

"Not if I get it first," Brett says, pretending to try and pass us.

"Brett!" she squeals.

I find it fascinating that she calls him Brett and not Mr. Cash. Miss Manners would certainly not approve. But their relationship—it does seem to be more of a friendship than anything else.

Brett has come for dinner a few times over the past two weeks so we could plan our trip.

Dinner. Nothing else.

Neither one of us has talked about how uncomfortable I am at the thought of him in my bedroom again. And he hasn't asked me to join him in his. It's been a frustrating two weeks to say the least.

"Wow," Evelyn says as we go through first class. "I wish we could have *those* seats."

"We could have," I say. "But it was either that or your college education."

"We have great seats," Brett says. "We got the ones with extra legroom so we can stretch out and try to get some sleep."

"You think I'm going to be able to sleep?" Evelyn asks as we get to our row and she looks out the window to see luggage being loaded into the cargo hold.

"Believe me," Brett says. "After an hour of seeing nothing but water, you'll be so bored, you won't be able to keep your eyes open."

Water. Him saying that reminds me of the video we watched on our last flight. We're going to be flying over water for many hours with no place to land. Anxiety starts to take hold.

"You okay?" Brett asks.

I nod and try to think of something else to keep my mind off what we're about to do.

Brett loads our carry-ons in the overhead bin, and I stuff my backpack under the seat. Then I sit and put my seatbelt on. *Tight.*

Evelyn laughs. "Mom, we don't even leave for another twenty minutes."

"Oh, right." I loosen the belt.

He pulls earbuds out of his pocket. "I came prepared this time."

"Elton John?"

"Nothing but."

"I brought mine, too," Evelyn says. "Brett told me it can get loud in here."

"So loud you might not be able to hear someone scream," he says with a wink in my direction.

"Who's going to scream?" Evelyn asks.

"Nobody, honey." *Stop it,* I mouth to Brett.

"Oh, come on. You know you have to be thinking about it a little bit." He leans in close so Evelyn can't hear. "And I did make you scream. More than once if I recall."

He has no idea just how much I *am* thinking about it. Remembering what he did to me—what he did to himself—might be the one thing that keeps me from embarrassing myself with a panic attack. Well, that and some Elton John.

"I think I see our luggage," Evelyn says.

I lean over her and look out the window. "There's no way you can tell from here. They all look alike."

"No they don't. My suitcase has stickers all over it."

"Well, good. At least we know it made it on the plane."

Brett looks irritated when his phone rings. "Sorry," he says, showing me the screen. "I have to take this."

It's Amanda. What if she says there's a problem with Leo? Will Brett ask to be let off the plane? Would she go so far as to lie to get him to stay? I saw her brooding on the front porch when we left, calling after him and telling him what a horrible father he is for leaving his son.

"I told you earlier that Bonnie knows this," he says into the phone. "She *lives* there, in case you forgot. She knows where the sewing kit is, which, by the way is *not* an emergency, even if it is Leo's favorite stuffed toy."

He doesn't talk for at least thirty seconds, and I can tell he's getting frustrated with her. She must be giving him another earful.

"Amanda, we've been over this." Another pause. "I'm not changing my mind. In fact, I'm already on the plane and the flight attendant is staring at me. I have to turn my phone off now." He looks impatient as he listens some more. "Would you stop with the fake crying and save it for someone who cares? I have to go. I hope you and Leo enjoy your time together. I'll text you from Germany. I'm hanging up now. Bye."

He promptly puts the phone in airplane mode, even though we haven't been told to yet. "The woman never gives up."

"Why do you think she went so long without being interested in the two of you and now she acts like she can't live without you?"

"Because I drove off with two beautiful girls today, that's why. It's human nature to want what you can't have."

"Are we still talking about Amanda?" I ask.

"I don't know. Are we?"

I laugh at the little game we always seem to play.

"Still, hasn't she been a bit over-dramatic today? I mean it's not like she just showed up on your doorstep and you walked out."

He looks guilty.

"Oh, my God. That's exactly what happened, isn't it?"

He laughs. "It wasn't quite as thrilling as that. But I didn't tell her I was leaving until she arrived this morning."

"Why not?"

"Because more than likely, she would have changed her plans and come a different week. I did not want to spend a week with her up in my business. I love my son more than anything in the world, and I want him to have a great relationship with his mother, but that does not involve us playing house for seven days."

I try not to smile but fail.

"You're enjoying this, aren't you? You like the fact that I can't stand my ex."

"It's"—I try to think of the right word, one that won't give him the wrong idea—"entertaining."

He looks at me like he knows I'm full of shit.

My mouth goes dry when the flight attendants go down the aisle, closing the overhead bins, making me remember where we are. I pull out a bottle of water and chug it. When we taxi away from the gate, I tighten my seatbelt again.

Evelyn puts a hand on my arm. "Hundreds of thousands of people fly every day. It's safer than driving."

"So I've been told," I say.

"You can hold my hand if you want to." She leans closer. "But I really think you should be holding Brett's instead."

I give her a scolding stare.

"Oh, come on," she whispers. "I know you like him. And I know you haven't had him over lately even though you want to. Probably because of me. You should let him hold your hand, Mom. He has strong hands, I can tell."

She goes back to looking out the window. Me—I can't stop staring at Brett's hands.

I try not to listen when the flight attendants give their spiel. I don't need to hear any more about cushions under the seat and water landings. I close my eyes, take a deep breath, and grip the armrests.

"Here we go!" Evelyn squeals.

I feel hot breath on my ear. "Do you know how much I'd like to *distract* you right now? Oh, the things I could do to you."

"Don't even think about it," I say, not opening my eyes. "You'd get arrested for sure."

A short while later, Evelyn keeps poking me, so I open my eyes. "We're up. Look at the ocean. Isn't it fabulous?"

I stretch my neck as far as I can. "It's great, honey."

Evelyn breaks into a huge smile, and I quickly see why. I hadn't even realized that Brett and I are holding hands. I try to pull away, but he won't let me.

Evelyn pulls her earbuds out. "I'll be listening to music, so I won't be able to hear you talk. You know, in case you and Brett want to say mushy love stuff."

Brett chuckles and squeezes my hand.

"Don't get any ideas," I tell him. "I don't speak mushy love."

He nods to the small video screens embedded in the seats in front of us. "Want to watch a movie?"

"Actually, I'd like to see what you found out about Stefan."

Brett had a private investigator look into his whereabouts. He was just emailed this morning, and he hasn't had time to go over it with me yet.

"There is a possibility we may not find him. None of the leads Ethan gave me could be him."

"We know."

He taps on his phone. "He's narrowed it down to four men, all similar in age and who have grown up in or around Munich. He said if he'd had more time, he could have gotten pictures and more detailed information."

"That's fine. Four men shouldn't be too hard to track down."

He looks at Evelyn, making sure she's not listening. "Emma, one of the four died five years ago in an industrial accident."

Would her father being dead be easier than him being alive and rejecting her? Then again maybe I've been wrong all along. Maybe after all this time, he'll be mature enough to want a relationship with his daughter.

"We should go to that one first," I say. "To rule him out. Was he married? Does he have relatives?"

He scrolls through the email. "Not married, but it lists his next of kin as a sister. I have an address. It shouldn't be too hard to find her. Some of the profiles have phone numbers, if you wanted to try and call."

"I don't want to call. I think it's best to confront him in person."

Brett brushes a stray hair out of my eyes.

"What?" I ask.

"I'm glad I'm here. I hate to think of you and Evie going to the houses of strange men without protection."

I glance at Evelyn. "We're glad you're here, too."

"We?" he asks, rubbing his thumb across the back my hand. "You need me, Emma. You need me for more than just getting you back into school, going up in elevators, and riding on planes. When are you going to admit it?"

I pull my hand away. "We should get some sleep. I have a feeling we're going to have a long day tomorrow."

CHAPTER TWENTY-NINE

BRETT

Evie gets in the backseat of the rental car. She leans over the headrest. "Isn't the steering wheel supposed to be on the right?"

"That's in Britain, sweetie," Emma says.

I pull out onto the street and head towards the hotel.

"Aren't you driving on the wrong side of the road?" Evie asks.

"That's in Britain, too," I say. "Driving here is like driving back home."

She pouts and leans back in her seat. "What's the fun in that?"

"You want fun?" I ask. "Wait until we get on the autobahn. There's no speed limit on parts of it."

Emma hits me on the arm. "I didn't come all the way here to get in a car accident."

"Well, from what I've read, you're more likely to get in an accident if you drive too slowly."

"From what you've read?"

"I may have done some research."

"What kind of research?" Emma asks.

I shrug. "I thought if we had time, we might check out some sights."

"We're only here for five days," she says. "There may not be time."

"I like to be optimistic," I tell her. "And prepared."

"What kind of sights?" Evie asks from the back.

"Well, there's Neuschwanstein Castle. It's the one Disney modeled Cinderella's castle after."

"I've never been to Disney World," Evie says.

"But your mom says you love roller coasters."

"Yeah, but she doesn't fly, remember? And it's a really long drive from New York to Florida."

"Well, she flies now," I say.

I see Evie's face light up in the rearview mirror. "Mom, will you take me to Disney World?"

Emma laughs. "One thing at a time, Evelyn. Let's get through this first, okay?"

"Have you taken Leo there?" Evie asks.

"I have. It was our first guys-only trip. We went in the spring."

"Did he love it?"

"He may have been just a bit too young to get the most out of it, but I think he enjoyed it. I, on the other hand, got really tired of going on that Dumbo ride that just goes around in circles. I think once he's three, he'll really get into it."

"We should all plan a trip together," Evie says. "Next summer when Leo is three."

"Evelyn, that's enough," Emma scolds her.

"Fine," Evie pouts. "So, what other sights do you think we should see?"

I look apprehensively at Emma. "Well, I'd love to go to the top of Zugspitze."

"Zugspitze—what's that?" Evie asks.

"It's the tallest mountain in Germany. But I'm not sure your mom would be up for it."

"Why wouldn't I be up for it?" Emma asks.

"Because you have to go up by cable car, the last hundred yards anyway. You can take a train up most of the way."

"What's a cable car?" Evie asks.

"It's kind of like a really big elevator."

"Okaaaaaay," Emma says. "Let's move on."

Evie and I laugh.

I nod to my phone in the cup holder. "Emma, can you check Google maps on my phone and see how far we are from the hotel?"

"The hotel?" Evie asks. "Can't we try to find him first?"

"Sweetie," Emma says. "You barely slept on the plane. We have days to find him."

"Mo-om," she whines. "It's why we're here. Why do we have to wait? What good is lying around the hotel going to do us? They say you should stay awake so you can acclimate to the time change easier. Plus, the sooner we find him, the more other stuff we can do. Right, Brett?"

"She has a point," I say.

"Fine," Emma says. "But we're going to the hotel first. We can drop off our luggage and freshen up. I haven't peed in anything but a teeny-tiny bathroom since yesterday, and I'd really like a quick shower and some real food."

"Your mom's right," I say. "Let's check in, change our clothes, and get a quick bite. Then we can go find your dad."

"My father," she mumbles from the back seat.

"What was that?" I ask.

"I said he's my father, not my dad. There's a difference."

I lock eyes with Evie in the rearview mirror. I can't put my finger on it, but I could swear her motives for being here are not exactly the motives Emma believes to be true. Maybe Evie wants to find out where she came from. Maybe meet her grandparents. Emma thinks Evie has delusions of grandeur. She thinks Evie has a fantasy about Stefan seeing her and them becoming one big happy family. I think Emma is wrong. In fact, I'd bet on it.

We pull into the hotel parking lot.

"The Hilton?" Evie says. "Seriously, guys, are we going to do *anything* here that doesn't reek of America?"

I drop the girls and luggage off and find a place to park. When I return, Emma's at the front desk, checking in. I'm helped by another woman behind the counter. I'm amazed by how many people speak English here. The airport workers, the guy at the rental car place, everyone at the hotel.

"What floor are we on, Mom?" Evie asks when we reach the elevator.

"Fourteen."

Evie turns to me. "What floor are you on?"

"Same."

Emma gives me a look. "Is that so?"

I shrug.

Emma spends the ride up eyeing me suspiciously. It keeps her mind off where she is.

We get off the elevator and I follow them to their room. "Where's yours?" Emma asks.

"Oh, look." I gesture to the door adjacent to theirs. "I'm right next door."

"How convenient," she says dryly.

I disappear into my room. Ten seconds later, I knock on the connecting door. Emma opens the door a little too abruptly. "Connecting rooms, Brett? Really?"

"I thought you'd be happy about it. Remember how you went on and on about two girls being here alone and needing protection?"

She shakes her head, clearly unable to rebuff my comment.

"Be careful what you wish for, Emma," I say and close the door.

~ ~ ~

We pull up to an old house in a village outside Munich.

Emma takes off her seatbelt and looks into the back seat. "Evelyn, this house belongs to a woman who is the sister of one of the Stefan Schmidts we found." Emma looks at me warily. "She's his next of kin. Do you know what that means?"

Evie looks down. "It means he's dead." She glances at the house. "It's not going to be him, I know it."

Emma lets out a deep sigh. "Please don't get your hopes up."

"I'm not," she says. "I just know it's not him."

We walk up the cobblestone sidewalk. Emma goes to knock on the door, but Evie pulls her hand away. "I want to do it."

Emma steps aside and Evie knocks. Then she knocks again. She is disappointed someone doesn't answer the door.

"We can always come back tomorrow," Emma says.

"One more time," Evie says, knocking louder this time.

The door opens, and a woman about our age talks to us in German.

"Do you speak English?" Evie asks.

"Why yes I do," she says, smiling at Evie. "How can I help you?"

Evie pulls the strip of pictures of Emma and Stefan out of her pocket. She holds it out to the woman. "The man in this picture is my father. His name is Stefan Schmidt. I'm trying to find him."

The woman shakes her head without bothering to look at the photos. "My brother passed away several years ago."

"We know," Emma says. "Please accept our condolences."

"It could be him, though," Evie says. "Can you take a look?"

She gives us a skeptical look before gazing at the pictures. "That man is not my brother."

"Are you sure, ma'am?" I ask. "Maybe you should take another look."

"Wait here," she says, leaving the door open as she retrieves a framed photo off the wall. She hands it to Evie. "This is Stefan. He doesn't look anything like the photos you have."

Evie compares the two and nods. "You're right. It's not him."

"We're very sorry to have bothered you," I say.

"It's not a problem. I hope you find him, young lady."

"Thank you," Evie says over her shoulder as we return to the car. There is a big smile on her face. "I told you guys it wasn't him."

"I'm glad it wasn't," Emma says. "But that doesn't mean he'll be one of the other three."

"He will," Evie says.

"Evelyn," her mom warns.

"What? Aren't you always telling me to be optimistic and have faith?"

I raise my eyebrows at Emma. "*You* tell her that?"

"You don't think I can be optimistic?" she asks.

I laugh. "You're not serious, are you?"

"I'm optimistic," she pouts.

"Name one thing you're optimistic about, Emma."

She stares at me as she tries to think of one. "I … well …"

"When you guys are done bickering, do you mind if we go find the next one?" Evie says.

Emma gets out the notes she made from the email I got from Ethan Stone. "There's only one more we can try today. The others are too far away." She holds up a piece of paper. "If *this* Stefan isn't the one, we'll try this guy in Nuremberg tomorrow and then the one from Stuttgart."

"We can't go to both tomorrow?" Evie asks.

Emma shakes her head. "Nuremberg is almost two hours away and Stuttgart is the other direction. We'll only be able to do one each day."

"Maybe we won't have to," I say. "Maybe the other Stefan in Munich is the one."

Evie smiles in the rearview mirror. "See, Mom. Brett can be optimistic, too. How far away is he?"

Emma programs the address into Google maps. "Not that far. Go back to that main road, and we should be there in twenty minutes."

In the rearview mirror, I catch a glimpse of Evie jotting in a notebook.

"Writing your memoirs?" I ask.

"Kind of. Every year when we go back to school, our teachers make us write a stupid essay on what we did over the summer. I'm getting a jump on it."

"Essays aren't stupid," Emma says.

"Are you looking forward to going back to school?" I ask.

I'm asking Evie, but I'm watching Emma out of the corner of my eye to see if there's any reaction. Nope. She seems relaxed, considering we're on the hunt for her ex.

"I'm going into middle school, which means I'll be ignored, teased, pushed around, and basically miserable for a year."

"Is someone bullying you?" I ask.

She laughs. "No. It's pretty much a rite of passage for all sixth-graders. Don't worry, things like that don't bother me."

I shake my head. "Sometimes I forget how young you are, Evie. Especially when you say things like 'rite of passage.'" I turn to Emma. "Did you know about this?"

"Who do you think told her? Wasn't it like that for you when you went to middle school?"

"It wasn't. You know, considering what had just happened."

Emma covers her mouth. "I'm so sorry. I forgot you were almost exactly Evelyn's age when …" She glances at Evie.

"I know all about Brett's mom. He told me."

"You told her?" Emma asks, surprised.

"We talked a lot over milk and cookies."

"You know," Evie says. "You guys have a lot in common. Way more than just living on the same street. Coincidence? I don't think so."

"Look," Emma says, pointing to a street sign. "Here we are."

I wink at Evie in the mirror. I know what she's doing. And I can't say I don't appreciate it.

We pull up in front of a mailbox with large block letters on it: **SCHMIDT**

The car in the driveway has the same ridiculous window clings as in America. But I don't point it out. Because these particular clings indicate the person who drives the car has two children. I can't imagine what Evie would feel, knowing her father went on to have other kids while he ignored her very existence.

"Here we go again," I say, getting out of the car.

Evie knocks on the door, like last time. It opens almost immediately, and we look down at a boy of five or six.

"Is your father here?" Emma asks.

He runs away, and a woman comes in his place. "Ja?"

"Do you speak English?" I ask.

She shakes her head.

I get out my phone and type into Google translate while Evie blurts out something in German. "Ich suche meinen leiblichen vater."

Emma's eyes widen, as I'm sure mine do. "You learned German?" she asks Evie.

"Just that one sentence."

"What did you say?"

"I said 'I'm looking for my birth father'."

The woman narrows her eyes at Evie and then studies the three of us, rambling on in words none of us can decipher.

I quickly type into Google translate: *This girl is looking for her birth father. We have a picture. Do you know the man in the photos? His name is Stefan Schmidt.*

While the woman is reading the translation, a man appears behind her. "Wer ist das, Maus?"

She shows him what I typed. After he reads it, he says with a heavy accent, "I'm Stefan. Vat is this about?"

Evie shows him the photo strip. "I'm looking for my father."

Emma puts a hand on her arm. "It's not him, honey."

"Are you sure?" Evie asks, disappointed.

Emma nods and turns to the couple. "I'm sorry we bothered you. We'll be on our way."

As we walk back down the driveway, the woman yells at the man in German. I hope we didn't start something. I never thought about the fact that we're showing up and accusing someone of having an illegitimate child.

"Maybe he just looks different," Evie says when we reach the car.

"It's only been twelve years, Evelyn. He wouldn't look *that* different. This man has different colored hair, is shorter than I remember, and he doesn't have a birthmark on his cheek."

Evie studies the photos. "That's a birthmark? I always thought it was a piece of dirt or something on the camera lens."

"Nope," Emma says. "Birthmark."

Evie's head falls against the headrest. "Darn it."

"I'm sorry, honey. We have two more chances. But we're tired and jet lagged. Let's return to the hotel, eat, and turn in early. We have a bit of a drive tomorrow."

Evie puts in her earbuds.

I lean across the console and whisper to Emma, "Turn in early?"

She pushes me away. "Don't even think about it, Lieutenant."

I laugh. When she calls me that, she most definitely does *not* want to turn in early.

~ ~ ~

I open my part of the connecting door and listen to see if I hear voices. I do, but it could just be the television. Damn doors are thick. Evie looked tired earlier. Surely she's in bed by now. Then again, maybe Emma is too. She could have fallen asleep with the TV on.

I knock quietly and wait.

I knock again. A little louder this time.

The door opens a crack, enough so I can see that Emma is in her pajamas.

"Is she asleep?" I ask.

Emma looks over her shoulder. "She crashed an hour ago. I'm surprised she made it that long. Why?"

I raise my eyebrows.

She whispers, "I told you no funny stuff."

"Just come in for a minute."

"Brett." She gives me a scolding look.

"Emma," I say in return, staring her down. Staring her all the way up and down.

"Just for a sec." She leaves the door ajar. "What is it?"

I push her against the wall and kiss her. It's been weeks. I'm instantly hard.

She lets me kiss her, then pulls away. "What are you doing?"

"What do you mean, what am I doing. You called me lieutenant."

"You've lost me."

"Earlier in the car, you called me lieutenant. You do that when you want to hook up. You know, like how I call you Miss Lockhart. It's our thing."

"Our thing?" she says. "I do *not* do that."

"Oh, but you do. Tell me you haven't missed this. Look at me," I say. "I just touch you, and I'm hard." I brush her hair aside so I can speak softly in her ear. "All I have to do is think about you, and I get hard. Do you have any idea how fucking blue my balls are right now?"

She tries to suppress a smile. "I'm not having sex with you when Evelyn is in the next room."

"You realize how ludicrous that is, right? The population of the Earth would cease to exist if adults didn't have sex with their kids in the next room."

"Married adults. I don't want to give her the wrong idea."

"Sweetheart, that ship sailed long ago."

"You shouldn't call me that," she says. "And, I'm only trying to repair the damage that's already been done."

"You haven't damaged her, or your relationship, by acting like a normal healthy single woman."

"Listen, I can't think about sex or anything else right now. I've been lying in bed for hours, wondering what we're doing here. I'm not sure I really thought this through. What if we find him and everything changes?"

"What do you think would change?"

"What if he *does* want her, Brett? What if he wants to take her from me?"

She's making herself crazy, thinking about things that most likely would never happen. I pull out the chair by the desk. "Sit."

She hesitates.

"It's a chair, Emma, not a bed."

She sits. I stand behind her and rub her shoulders. "You're holding onto a lot of tension. Try and relax. You know as well as I do that if Stefan wanted her, he'd have contacted you long before now."

"But what if—"

"What if nothing. You're over-tired and your mind is racing with what-ifs. So just stop it and relax."

"But—"

"Shh. No talking."

Touching her does nothing to get rid of my erection. Her smooth skin feels incredible. Her moans remind me of other times

I've elicited the same noises from her. But I don't let my hands stray from her shoulders. She needs this more than I need a release.

I lose track of time but eventually realize she's gone still. The back of her head is resting against my stomach. She's fallen asleep. I carefully pick her up and carry her back to her room, laying her on the empty bed next to Evie's.

I half expect the girl to wake up. It seems like she's always awake when her mother and I get into a compromising position. And me carrying Emma to bed in her nightgown is most definitely a compromising position. But she doesn't. I gaze at her for a while, noticing how much she looks like Emma. The curve of their noses is identical. Their hair color is a dead match. Even the way they sleep is similar.

For the first time, I think of how jealous I'd be if Stefan wanted a relationship with Evie.

I want to be the only man in her life. Just like I want to be the only man in Emma's.

CHAPTER THIRTY

EMMA

I look at the time. It feels like we've been driving forever. "Are we almost there yet?" As soon as the words leave my mouth, it occurs to me how childlike I sounded.

Brett laughs. "We'll be there soon."

I am particularly anxious today, maybe because I know we're running out of options. Two down, two to go. What if neither of them is Evelyn's father? What then? My daughter, however, is cool as a cucumber.

Brett turns one last corner and pulls into a parking lot.

"*This* is it?" I ask, looking at the old, rundown apartment building that looks like it belongs in some not-so-desirable parts of New York City.

"If the address is correct, yes," Brett says.

As he finds a place to park, I look at our surroundings. "Is it safe?"

"That's why you brought me, right?" he says with a wink.

He's trying to lighten the mood, but I feel myself becoming consumed with grief and regret. I see little hope of this ending up the happy reunion Evelyn has been dreaming of for years. Am I a terrible parent for allowing her to get in this situation?

Kids run around a small grassy area nearby, which makes me feel marginally better. That is, until one of them picks something up off the ground and shows his friend.

"Jesus," Brett says before running over to them. He takes what looks like a syringe away from the young boy and has a few words with them before going to a trash bin, finding something inside to wrap around the needle, and tucking it into a bag.

I dig around in my purse for my small bottle of hand sanitizer. I hold it out to him when he rejoins us. "Use it all. That was horrible."

He douses his hands and says to Evelyn, "Don't touch anything."

"What did you say to those kids?" she asks.

"I told them to never pick up a needle or it could make them very sick. But I'm not sure they understood me." He continues to the building. "Let's get this over with."

I shake my head, disgusted. What if this is where Stefan lives?

"What's the apartment number?" Brett asks when we're inside.

"Two-eleven."

Evelyn walks ahead of us, eager to get there, but Brett forces her behind him and takes the lead. I'm amazed she doesn't have a problem with his protectiveness. Every time *I* try to do anything to keep her safe, she calls me on it.

"This is it," Brett says, standing in front of the door.

It's dilapidated and missing two numbers. The remaining one is askew. And the only reason we know it's the correct door is because 210 is on one side and 212 is on the other.

Evelyn knocks on the door.

Loud music plays inside, so there is no way anyone heard her. Part of me wants to suggest that we just walk away now because I have a bad feeling about this.

She knocks again, much louder this time.

Still no one comes to the door.

Brett pounds on it with the side of his fist.

Finally, the door opens, and a tall blonde woman, haphazardly wrapped in a sheet, stares at us.

"Is Stefan Schmidt here?" Brett asks.

The woman looks us over and then closes the door.

Evelyn says, "Maybe she doesn't speak English."

Brett pounds on the door again. It opens with a jerk. "Vat ze fuck do you vant?" a man holding a cigarette asks.

My heart officially breaks. The emaciated half-naked man standing in the doorway has blond hair and is exactly the same height as I remember. And despite the fact that he looks much older than he should, there's no mistaking the birthmark on his right cheek. It's him.

Nobody says anything. I think Brett and Evelyn know it's him as well.

Stefan looks at me as if he's eyeing a piece of meat. But it quickly becomes obvious he remembers who I am. Other than my hair being a few inches longer and my waist a few inches thicker, I look very much like I did in high school.

He looks at Evelyn. I can practically see him make the connection.

"Vy are you here?" he says with a heavy German accent. It's the same voice I remember, except a little deeper and rougher.

"Why do you think, Stefan?" I say.

He takes a drag from his cigarette and exhales, not bothering to blow the smoke in the other direction. "If you're looking for an invitation to Sunday dinner, you von't get one," he says. "You're vasting your time."

Evelyn pulls out the strip of photos. "You're my father."

He drops his cigarette on the floor, grinds it into the floorboard with his bare foot, and takes the photos from her. He looks at them, then rips them to shreds. "I'm no one's father," he says and tries to close the door.

My first inclination is to lunge at him, hurt him for his deplorable behavior, but Evelyn stops me the same protective way Brett stopped her earlier. She shoves me behind her and sticks her shoe in the doorway, preventing it from closing.

Stefan looks down at her foot. "You came a long vay for nothing, kid."

"I came a long way to find you. The least you can do is talk to me."

Stefan looks at Brett, who has a hand on my and Evelyn's shoulder. "There's nothing to say," he says, pulling another cigarette from his jeans pocket and lighting it. "Go back to verever the fuck you came from."

Brett squeezes my shoulder, fingers tense. I wait for Evelyn's tears. She's been completely rejected by the man she wanted to find for so long.

Instead of crying, however, she does something that utterly shocks me. She steps forward, rips the cigarette from Stefan's fingers, and throws it down the hallway. "You have no idea how grateful I am that you're such a deadbeat, because if you weren't, my life wouldn't be nearly as amazing." She touches my arm. "My mom is the strongest person I know. That's probably thanks to you leaving her when she was fifteen and pregnant. You bailed on her and made her figure this out by herself. She's the best mom anyone could ask for. She made it so I didn't need a father. And she raised me to be just like her.

"So thank you for being an asshole who can never measure up to my fantasy about what a dad should be." She glances at Brett and then back at Stefan. She picks up the torn picture and throws it at him. "Crawl back inside your hole and enjoy your pathetic little life, *Stefan*, because nobody needs you."

After a stunned moment, he slams the door in her face. That's when I realize we had an audience. An old lady in the apartment across the hall is looking at us through her cracked-open door.

Evelyn strides down the hall, not a single tear in her eye.

I reach out to her. "Sweetie?"

She turns. "What? You think I wanted to find him and have some kind of happy reunion?"

I scrunch my brow. "Well … yes."

Brett and I look at her and then each other, both completely bowled over by what just happened.

"Your daughter is kind of a badass," Brett says with a huge smile on his face.

Evelyn shakes her head. "A reunion was never what I wanted. But you wouldn't have let me come here if I'd told you the real reason."

I'm confused. "You planned all along to tell him off?"

She nods.

Brett offers her a fist bump, which she reciprocates. "You're pretty damn awesome, kid," he says.

The old lady across the hall opens her door wider and steps out. I offer her an apology. "I'm sorry if we bothered you," I say, not even knowing if she understands English.

She pulls her housecoat around her and approaches Evelyn. "That nasty man is your father, little one?"

Evelyn nods.

The woman shakes her head. "All he be is trouble, that one. Wait here for a minute, child." She retreats into her apartment.

"What's going on?" Evelyn asks.

"I'm not sure," I say.

She returns and hands Evelyn a piece of paper with two names and an address on it.

"What's that?" I ask.

She points to the second name. "That's your sister."

The three of us gasp.

"That's right. Nasty man has another gorgeous girl he don't pay mind to. She and her mother used to come around. They don't anymore. He stopped answering the door when they knocked." She points to the peephole in her door. "He could see them through that. They left their information with me in case he ever wanted to contact them." She looks sad. "He never asked." She puts a hand on Evelyn's arm. "Now I know why I kept this piece of paper all these years. Everything happens for a reason."

Brett and I look at each other. He smiles at me. Yeah, I guess she really did just say that.

"Thank you," I say. "You've been very helpful."

She goes inside her apartment and closes the door. Evelyn runs a finger across the second name on the paper. She looks up at me with more excitement on her face than I've ever seen. "Can we, Mom?"

"I googled the address," Brett says. "It's not too far from our hotel."

I had all kinds of thoughts about how this day would turn out. And not one of them took into account what an incredible, strong, larger-than-life daughter I have.

Evelyn takes my hand and then Brett's. His gaze is fixed on Evelyn, and his eyes are filled with love and pride.

"What are we waiting for?" I ask, swallowing hard to keep tears from falling. "Let's go find your sister."

~ ~ ~

Evelyn and Greta hit it off right away. Greta speaks perfect English. That comes from her stepfather being American. He sits with us while the girls get to know each other.

"I'm sorry you couldn't meet my wife. She would have loved to have met you. Perhaps another time, when she's not out of town."

I say, "I'd like that."

"We visit the States quite often," he says. "I have business in New York. We'll be sure to schedule some of those trips around Greta's school schedule so she can come along."

"That would be wonderful," I say. "Evelyn would love to see Greta again." I study the girl who is not even a year older than Evelyn. "I can't believe she's thirteen. When the lady at Stefan's told us about her, I pictured a little girl."

"Why do you think Stefan was sent to America?" Bill says. "His parents didn't approve of his relationship with my wife. When Pia got pregnant, they denounced their grandchild and sent him away."

I shake my head. "So they're as bad as Stefan? I suppose we shouldn't even try to contact them."

"It would be a waste of your time," he says. "We've tried to get them to have a relationship with Greta, but they'll have nothing to do with her."

I look at the girls. They are getting on like long-lost friends. "I can't believe it. I'm not sure what I expected when we came here, but it wasn't this."

Brett takes my hand under the table. "Looks like the old lady was right."

I narrow my eyes at him.

He squeezes. "Looks like your dad was, too."

CHAPTER THIRTY-ONE

BRETT

Evie gazes out the small window when we take off, and Emma doesn't seem nervous to be on the plane.

This week has been empowering for her. After Evie told off her father and bonded with her half-sister, Emma seemed to become stronger.

We even ended up at the top of Zugspitze. Emma said if Evelyn could do what she did, surely she could get over her own fears.

I've since wondered if that applies to *all* areas of her life. Because even though she's clearly changed, I'm not sure she's changed her stance when it comes to me. Although we had a few close encounters, Emma never let herself come into my bed the entire time we were in Germany.

When we're up in the air, Evie finally turns away from the window. She leans forward so she can see both of us. "I want to tell you how much I appreciate what you did for me this week. You guys are the best. I mean that. This has been the most awesome week of my life." She looks at her phone, where her background picture is a photo of her and Greta. "I don't know any other mom who would have done what you did or any other man who would have gone along with it." She takes Emma's hand. "You deserve to be happy. You two belong together. Everyone can see that. Grandma, Brett, even Greta said something. When are you going to realize it was no mistake meeting him? I'm stuck with a crappy biological father, but I got a sister out of it. You grew up without a father, but in some strange way, maybe that's why you ended up meeting Brett. You know, what goes around comes around."

I laugh. "I think you mean to say, 'everything happens for a reason'."

"Yeah, whatevs." She puts her earbuds in. "I'm going to listen to music now."

"You've got one heck of a kid," I say to Emma.

I flip through the pictures of Leo on my phone.

"You really miss him," Emma says.

"Like you wouldn't believe."

"Actually, I would." She glances at Evie. "She's the best thing that ever happened to me."

I put down my phone. "In case you haven't figured it out by now, *she's* the reason, Emma."

"What?"

"Your whole life you've been looking for a reason for what happened to your dad. The answer has been right in front of you. You said you became promiscuous because you were looking for acceptance from men. You said you never would have gotten pregnant if your dad had been around."

"I didn't say that, my therapist did."

"That doesn't make it any less true. Think about it, Emma. The paths our lives take sometimes lead us down roads we don't expect. I never expected to get divorced and hate my ex-wife. Would I change anything? No, because I have Leo, and he's the best thing about my life. I'm not saying losing your dad was a good thing, but just look at what came of it."

She nods over and over as tears well up in her eyes.

"Brett, uh … I'm not sure how to say this …"

"What is it?"

She blows out a long breath. "Well, I'm not scared of tall buildings anymore. And I'm not scared of airplanes. I'm not even sure I'm scared of elevators after going up in that cable car. So, maybe if I'm not scared of all those things …" She pauses and bites her lip. "Then maybe I'm not scared of—"

"Firefighters?" I say.

She shrugs. "I think I might be ready."

My heart thunders. But she's said those words several times before. "Ready for what, Emma?"

"Ready for us."

My smile is tremendous. "I really want to kiss you right now."

"Then maybe you should."

I give her the kiss that I've wanted to give her for two months. The kiss a man gives his girlfriend.

I hear a noise from Evie and open my eyes, still kissing her mom. Evie looks at me with a huge grin and puts up her hand for a high-five.

~ ~ ~

"What now?" Emma says during the cab ride home.

"Well, I'd like to take you to dinner."

"How about you take me to Becca's wedding next Saturday?" she says. "You did save her, after all. I know she'd be honored to have you there."

"I'll be happy to be your plus-one. But I'm not waiting a week to see you. I have to work tomorrow, so how about Monday?"

"That works for me. I bet you're excited to see Leo."

My face splits in two just thinking about it. "I am. This is the longest we've ever been apart."

Her face falls. "Is your ex-wife still there?"

I damn near forgot all about Amanda. "She's returning to California tomorrow."

"So she'll be there with you tonight," she says, looking out the window.

I put my finger under her chin and make her look at me again. "She'll be at my house. But she most definitely won't be *with* me."

It looks like she's pouting. It's immature of me, but I love that she's jealous. "It'll be okay."

"I know. I'm sorry. I'm just not used to this."

"Used to what?"

"You know, having a … a …"

"Boyfriend?" I say, laughing.

"Yeah, that. It's been a long time."

I lean in and whisper, "It's been a long time since I've had a girlfriend. And I'm really looking forward to it. Oh, the things I plan to do with you."

"We're home!" Evie announces. I'm sure she's eager to tell her grandmother everything.

I help them get their bags up to the house. But before I leave, I tell Emma, "If you're still awake, meet me in the window at eight o'clock."

"It's a date."

"I think I like the sound of that," I say. "Us dating."

"I like it, too."

"Can I kiss my girlfriend goodbye?"

She smiles her answer.

I'm pretty polite, considering the circumstances, but I still give her a kiss that reminds her she's mine.

~ ~ ~

"Daddy!" Leo says, running over to jump into my arms.

"You've gotten bigger, buddy. I missed you." After I finish showering him with kisses, I notice Bria in the corner.

"Did you miss me, too?" she asks.

I laugh. "Always."

She sits on the couch with us and says out of Leo's earshot, "Someone had to make sure Momzilla didn't corrupt you-know-who."

I look at her curiously. "You mean, this isn't the first time you've come over this week?"

Bonnie joins us. "Your lovely sister has stopped by almost every day."

"I didn't want the little guy to get lonely."

"How did it go?" I ask. "You know, with Amanda?"

"Did someone say my name?"

I look to the kitchen where Amanda is standing at the counter with a glass of red wine. I check the time. It's not even noon yet. "A bit early for happy hour, isn't it?"

"It's always happy hour when you're on vacation," she says. "Want to join me? It's probably after five where you came from."

"I'm good," I say. "I just want to hang with Leo." I slip off the couch onto the floor while Leo gets out his Legos. "What are we building today? A spaceship? A race car?"

Leo points to the box. "Fire twuck."

Bonnie ruffles his hair. "He's wanted to build it every day. He really missed you."

Amanda brings her wine into the living room and sits down. "What does he build when he misses *me?*"

Bria laughs. "Lego doesn't sell sets of stone-cold bit—"

"Bria!" I scold, nodding at Leo.

"Oh, right. Sometimes I forget he's always listening. What I meant to say is that Lego doesn't make sets of passive-aggressive, narcissistic, self-serving, evil female parental units."

Amanda huffs. "You really are a gem, aren't you, Brianna?"

"I try. When do you go back to California?"

"Tomorrow." She gives me a look. "I was hoping we could talk before I go."

I pull Leo onto my lap and help him fit Lego pieces together. "Later. I'm busy right now."

Amanda goes back into the kitchen, refilling her wine glass before going upstairs.

"She's done a lot of that this week," Bonnie says.

"A lot of what?" I ask.

She mimics drinking.

"Seriously?"

She nods.

Bria snaps a Lego into place. "She was slurring her words when I was here yesterday afternoon."

"Afternoon?" I look at her in surprise. Amanda was not a big drinker when we were together.

Bonnie says quietly, "I've found more than a few empty bottles buried in the trash. I'm afraid she might have a problem."

I look down at Leo, concerned that he's been with her all week. Was he alone with her when she was drunk?

As if reading my mind, Bonnie says, "Don't worry, I stayed close."

I put my hand on hers. "I don't know what I'd do without you."

"Hey, what am I? Chopped liver?" Bria asks.

"You, too," I say. "I don't know what I'd do without both of you."

An hour later, when I've completely worn Leo out, I take him up and put him down for a nap. I look out the window before drawing his curtains. I wonder what Emma is doing right now. It's only been a few hours, but I miss her already. I resist the urge to text her. I don't want to start our relationship by being overbearing and needy. But the truth is, I do need her. I glance at Evie's window. I need her, too.

I take my suitcase to my bedroom to unpack. When I walk through the doorway, I see Amanda reading a book in bed. In *my* bed. "What are you doing?"

She puts down the book and looks at me like I'm crazy. "I'm reading, Brett. What does it look like?"

"Yes, but why are you *here*?" I look around and see her things scattered about. "Did you sleep here this week? We said you were going to sleep in Leo's room."

"No, you said that. What's the big deal? You were traipsing halfway across the world with what's-her-name."

"Emma," I say through my teeth. "Her name is Emma."

Looking at Amanda, I realize what I hadn't before. She's dressed like she's going for a night out. Is she really going out, now that I'm home? Or is she wearing the enticing outfit just for me?

She sits up on the side of the bed and takes a drink of wine.

"Don't you think you should slow down?" I ask, nodding to the glass. "It's not even dinner time yet."

"Are you trying to tell me what to do?"

"I really don't care what you do, Amanda. Except when it affects my son."

"Don't you mean *our* son?"

"Have you been drinking around him?"

She puts down her glass. "Don't get all righteous on me. Like you don't drink around him."

"I don't drink by myself in the middle of the day," I say.

Her expression softens as she looks up at me. "I guess I was nervous about seeing you again."

"Why would you be nervous?"

She runs a finger from her neck to her cleavage. "Leo and I have bonded this week. I was hoping you and I could bond, too."

"Bond?" I shake my head. "You mean *fuck?"*

She gets up and comes over to me, placing a hand seductively on my chest. "We were good together once. We can be again."

I step back. "You pushed me so far away over the past two years, there is no turning back. Not to mention you've ignored Leo."

"I was depressed," she says, stepping forward and taking my hand. "I'm not anymore."

She tries to kiss me, but I move my head aside, avoiding her lips. I look over at the wine, thinking about what Bonnie and Bria said and pry my hand away from hers. "I think you're still depressed. You need to see someone. Work your shit out."

"I don't have any shit to work out," she says. "I just want my family back. I can transfer back to New York and we can be together."

"Funny how that never occurred to you until Emma came into my life."

She makes a rude noise. "Her again?"

"Yes, her. I'm with Emma now, and you and I will never be together again. I love her, Amanda. You'll always be Leo's mom, but we'll never be a family."

"You *love* her?" she says in disgust. "Are you kidding? We've only been divorced a few months."

"But you haven't been my wife for two years." I pick up some of her things and shove them into her arms. "Get out of my bedroom. I don't want you here."

She stomps her way to the door and then turns around. "You have no idea what you're missing. Plenty of men want me in their beds. They've wanted me for years."

"Years? Is that why you quit sleeping with me? So you could fuck other men?"

"Why do you think I moved to California?" she says smugly.

"Wow," I say with a shake of my head. I sit on the bed and laugh. "Thank you, Amanda. Up until today, I actually felt sorry for you. I thought that somehow becoming a mom had messed up your hormones or something. I even bought into the post-partum depression thing for a long time. But you've opened my eyes. The alcohol. The other men." I glance at a picture of Leo on my nightstand. "I'll never keep you from seeing him, but you are no longer welcome as an overnight guest in this house. I'm calling you a cab and making you a hotel reservation. You can come back tomorrow to say goodbye to Leo."

Her mouth hangs open in surprise. "You're kicking me out? But I live here."

I pick up another piece of her clothing and walk it over to her. "You *lived* here, Amanda. Past tense. The townhouse belongs to me now, or did you forget that part of our divorce agreement? Go back to California and whoever's bed you've been sleeping in."

Anger emanates from her and she shoves me. "You think you're so special. You think you're some kind of hero. You're not. You're just a public fucking servant who can't even make enough money to keep a woman happy. You want your pitiful little teacher? Fine. She can have you. I promise you there are men lined up to get into my bed. Men who like to buy me nice things."

"My ex—the whore. How proud you must be."

She pushes me aside and makes a beeline for the wine. "Fuck off, Brett," she says, throwing the wine in my face before getting her suitcase from the closet.

I dry off with my T-shirt as she packs her clothes and makeup.

She zips up her suitcase and heads for the door. "And tell your sister and the nanny to fuck off, too. You think you're so much better than everyone. You can all go to hell."

She storms down the stairs, and I hear the front door slam.

When I walk into the living room, Bonnie and Bria stare at my wine-soaked shirt and try not to laugh.

I smile wryly. "If I were a betting man, I'd say we won't be seeing much of her anymore."

"She wasn't here for Leo," Bonnie says. "She was here for you. That woman barely paid him any mind. She was on the phone half the time. And the other half she was drinking and watching television. She went out several nights, only to stumble home in the wee hours of the morning. One night she didn't tell me she was leaving. I found Leo playing by himself on the kitchen floor. It's like she forgot she was responsible for him."

I shake my head in disbelief. Bonnie was right. She doesn't want Leo. "Thank you for being here and watching over him."

"You know I love that boy like a grandson."

"I know, and I'm grateful."

Bonnie thumbs at Bria, who is practically bouncing up and down on the couch. "Your sister has been very patient, but she's about ready to burst out of her skin. Go on, honey. Tell him."

Bria smiles. She smiles big.

"Oh my God, you got it?"

She jumps off the couch and into my arms. "I got it!"

I hug her hard. "Why didn't you tell me earlier?"

"You needed time with Leo. I didn't want to interfere with that."

We sit on the barstools at the kitchen counter. "Tell me everything."

"I don't know much yet. I only got the offer last night. We'll practice in New York for two months and then in late October, we go on tour. Three months, forty cities."

I look at her, amazed at what she's accomplished. "My sister, the backup singer for White Poison. I'm so proud of you, Bria."

"We should celebrate," Bonnie says. "When you're over your jet lag."

"That's a date. But tonight, I need to go to bed and sleep for ten hours straight. Oh, that reminds me. Bonnie, can I borrow your bedroom window at eight o'clock?"

"Borrow my *what?"* she asks in confusion.

I laugh. "It's a long story, but it started in a storage closet."

CHAPTER THIRTY-TWO

EMMA

My alarm goes off. It takes me a minute to figure out where I am and what's going on. Then I look at the texts on my phone and smile.

> **Brett: I know we said eight, but I couldn't wait.**

> **Brett: Are you there? It's your boyfriend. Do you have any idea how good it feels to say that?**

> **Brett: You're probably asleep, which is what I should be doing. I wanted to see you one more time before bed. I won't be able to concentrate at work tomorrow, thinking about seeing you Monday night.**

I smile. I almost thought the whole thing was a dream, but he's my boyfriend now. That really happened. And I'm not freaking out about it.

Me: I'm here. Sorry. I fell asleep, but I set my alarm so I wouldn't miss our talk.

Brett: You set your alarm? Man, you must really dig me.

I laugh out loud.

Brett: Come to the window.

I do what he asks, but I don't see him in his living room window. I look at Leo's. He's not there either. Then I see him.

Me: What are you doing in Bonnie's room?

Brett: I wanted some privacy.

I remember who he needs privacy from. I strain to look into his living room to try and see his ex.

Me: How'd it go when you got home?

Brett: Pretty great. Leo was happy to see me. My sister was here.

Does he know that wasn't what I was asking?

Me: That's nice. How about Amanda?

Brett: She left.

Me: I thought she was staying until tomorrow.

Brett: She tried to seduce me. We got into a fight. I told her I was most definitely with you and she and I would never be together. I offered to get her a hotel for the night. She threw red wine on me, then she left with all her stuff. I don't think she's coming back anytime soon.

Once my brain gets around the part where she tried to seduce him, I'm deliriously happy that he rejected her and said he was with me.

Brett: Emma, are you smiling? I think I can see it from here.

I look over and could swear he winks at me.

Me: She threw wine at you? That's awful.

Brett: I miss you. Is that weird?

Me: Not so much.

Brett: You miss me too?

Me: Maybe.

Brett: I'll take maybe. Would you consider taking your shirt off?

My jaw drops when I read his text. I look up and see him laughing.

Me: I thought you were serious.

Brett: I was. Sort of. I mean I really really want to see you naked. But I'm not willing to risk every Joe Schmo on the street seeing you too.

Me: How about a rain check?

Brett: Now you're talking.

Me: Monday night?

Brett: I won't be able to think of anything else when I'm at work. Maybe you could send me a nudie picture to get me through.

I look up at him to see him laughing again. Who knew he had such a sense of humor? Suddenly I'm anxious to know everything about him.

Brett: You're so easy.

Me: Nobody's called me that since high school.

Brett: A joke? I knew you were funny.

I try to support my weight on the windowsill, wanting to continue texting, but I can barely keep my eyes open.

Brett: I don't want to keep you. We both need sleep. Put your hand on the window.

Me: Why?

Brett: Just do it.

I press my palm against the window. Then I see why he wanted me to do it. He presses his palm against his window. We may be fifty feet away, but I swear I can feel him.

We gaze at each other for a long time. I feel a sense of loss when he takes his hand away.

Brett: Goodnight, Emma.

Me: Goodnight.

We put our phones down, but neither of us walks away. Not until my eyelids grow so heavy, I have to sit down or risk falling. I've never wanted to stay awake more than I do right now. I touch the window one last time, then wave at him.

He blows me a kiss.

I've done nothing today but think about his kisses. His touches. His dirty talk.

I go to bed knowing this is going to be a long couple of days.

~ ~ ~

I stare at his front door. I don't know why I'm so nervous. I'm meeting a two-year-old, not the Pope.

Brett warned me Leo takes to men much easier than women. I don't want to think about how it will affect our relationship if his son hates me. It's been so long since I've had a toddler that I can't remember how to act around them.

Brett opens the door before I can ring the bell. His scent is the first thing I notice. For an entire week, I was surrounded by the heavenly smell that was a combination of rainforest and cinnamon. Oh, how I've missed that smell these past few days. It faded from my pillows even before I laundered them. And I realize just how long it's been since we've been together in my bed.

I take him in, perusing his crisp clean button-down shirt and gray linen pants. I tingle in anticipation of what will happen later tonight.

He chuckles at my obvious ogling. "Hello to you, too Miss Lockhart." He hugs me and whispers, "Just so you know, I'm going to spend the next few hours teasing you. By the time I get you into my bed, you'll be so wet, you'll be begging me to make you come."

Heat floods through me. I'm tempted to skip dinner and go straight for dessert. We part, and I look past him into the townhouse.

He must see my hesitation. "It'll be fine," he says. He takes my hand and leads me inside. "Come in."

"I hope he likes what I brought him," I say, second-guessing my choice. "It's actually pretty stupid."

Brett glances at the bag in my hand. "That's for Leo? I thought maybe you brought *me* a toy. You know, for later," he says with a wink.

"Stop it, Lieutenant." I elbow him in the ribs.

He laughs. "But it's so much fun teasing you. And if you keep calling me Lieutenant, we just might have to skip dinner and go straight for dessert."

I smile at his words that mimicked my exact thoughts.

The back door opens and someone small runs toward us. Leo stops in his tracks when he sees me. The smile on his face fades and he scurries behind Brett, holding onto his leg as he hides from me.

Leo is gorgeous. He has messy dark blond hair that he obviously got from his mother, but the rest of his features are all Brett: his adorable nose that turns up slightly at the tip, his large green eyes, his strong jaw. This one is going to be a lady killer—I look up at Brett—just like his father.

"It's okay, buddy," Brett tells him. "This is my friend, Emma."

Leo buries his head in Brett's pant leg.

A woman enters the room. She walks right over to me and I extend my hand. She ignores it and hugs me.

"It's wonderful to meet you, Emma," she says, squeezing me tightly.

"You too, Bonnie. I've heard great things about you. Brett says you're amazing with Leo."

Leo hears his name and peeks at me from behind Brett.

"They are the amazing ones. I don't know what I'd do without my two boys." She pulls back. "Can I get you anything? A bottle of water or a glass of wine?"

I look at Brett for direction. I'm not sure how long he plans to stay here. He checks the time. "We have reservations at eight, so we have twenty minutes."

"Water would be wonderful, Bonnie. Thank you."

When she goes to the kitchen, the rest of us make our way to the couch. Or more precisely, I walk to the couch and Brett drags his son behind him.

"Leo, can you say hello to Emma?" he asks.

He shakes his head and climbs up on the couch to hide behind Brett.

"Hello, Leo," I say. "Your daddy told me all about you." I put the gift bag on the coffee table. "I brought you something."

He doesn't look interested.

"Don't you want to see what Emma brought you?" Brett asks.

He shakes his head, still refusing to speak or look at me.

"I'll open it then," Brett says. "But if it's candy, I get to eat it."

Not even that veiled threat gets him to budge; he holds his ground at the far end of the couch.

Brett opens the bag and pulls out the plastic donkey, turning it over and examining it in his hands.

I could kick myself over my poor choice. I let Evelyn talk me into buying it as she thought it was hilarious.

"It's a … donkey?" Brett asks with a raise of an eyebrow.

I'm suddenly very embarrassed to have brought him this cheap piece of plastic. But there's not much I can do about it now, so I take it from him. "This isn't just any donkey. He eats. And he … well, I'll just have to show you." Then I realize I forgot the most important part. "Oh, gosh. Please tell me you have Cheerios. Do you like Cheerios, Leo?"

He hides again.

"Leo loves Cheerios. Don't you, bud?" Brett calls to the kitchen. "Bonnie, could you please bring a box of Cheerios with you?"

She returns with a bottle of water and the cereal.

"Thank you," I say. I open the box and reach in for a handful. I turn to Leo. "Do you want to feed him?"

He shakes his head and sinks into the couch.

"Okay, I'll do it." I put Cheerios in the donkey's mouth. It makes a burping noise.

Brett laughs. "Isn't that funny, Leo?"

He isn't amused.

"What happens when he gets full?" Brett asks.

"Well, you uh …" I'm sure my face is bright red. "You turn his tail around."

Brett looks at me in surprise.

"I told you it was stupid."

He grabs the donkey's tail, turns it, and the donkey lets out a "hee-haw" when a Cheerio comes out his ass.

Brett laughs uncontrollably and turns the tail a few more times.

Leo crawls out from behind him and tries it, but all the Cheerios must be gone because nothing comes out. I hold out my hand with some cereal in it. "You have to feed him first."

He looks at Brett, who gives him an encouraging nod, then takes Cheerios from my hand and puts them in the donkey's mouth. He turns the tail and giggles when a Cheerio comes out, along with a "hee-haw."

"Poopy donkey," he says as he fills and empties the toy over and over, eating the Cheerios as they emerge.

Brett whispers, "My kid is eating donkey crap. Thanks, teach."

I smile every time Leo giggles. Then something amazing happens. Leo takes a piece of donkey crap and hands it to me. "Why, thank you. It's so nice of you to share." I pop the Cheerio into my mouth. I make a mental note to thank Evelyn.

"And now my girlfriend is eating crap," Brett says.

"I think your daddy needs some," I say to Leo.

Leo gives the tail a few more turns. "Here, Daddy. Donkey poopy."

Then Leo gives some to Bonnie. And the four of us sit around the coffee table eating donkey poop until it's time for us to go.

On our way out, Leo hugs my leg, and I have to hold back a tear. I don't want to do anything to scare him, like try and pick him up, so I ruffle his hair. "Bye, Leo. See you soon."

~ ~ ~

Everything about tonight has been amazing. I'm twenty-seven years old, yet I feel like this is the first date I've ever actually wanted to be on. Yes, I've been out lots of times with lots of guys. But only because that's what adults do. They go on dates in search of the person they hope to end up with.

Me—I didn't have to do that. I had to get taken hostage in a storage closet.

I shake my head thinking of all the time spent on needless dating rituals.

I pick at my potatoes. "I'm glad Leo finally warmed up to me. I thought it was going to take a lot longer."

"You bought my kid a toy that craps Cheerios," he says, laughing. "I think that makes you the coolest girlfriend ever."

"You have Evelyn to thank for that. She picked it out."

"Leo doesn't know that. To him, you'll always be the woman who gave him the pooping donkey. I bet we'll still be talking about this when we're old and gray."

I make a face.

"What? You never thought of us in the long term?"

"Brett, I just accepted the fact that you're my boyfriend. You'll have to give me a while to work up to old and gray."

"That's bullshit," he says. "When you know, you know." He gestures between us. "This is happening, so you'd better get used to it."

"Can we at least *pretend* to go through the motions?" I ask, knowing that on some level, I've always felt the same way.

He winks. "Oh, I plan on going through a lot of motions with you."

My heart skips a few beats when I think of being with him again. It's been so long.

I put down my fork and push my plate away.

"You're not done, are you?" Brett asks. "You still have half a steak left, and you haven't touched the bread. Is everything okay?"

I smooth the front of my dress knowing that I'm not necessarily stopping eating because I'm full. I just don't want to feel stuffed and uncomfortable later when we're together. And I might just be a little nervous, which is ridiculous considering we've had sex on numerous occasions. "The food is fabulous. I just don't want to eat too much."

He gives me a scolding stare. "You mean you think you'll look fat when we get naked later."

"I didn't say that."

"You didn't have to." He laughs through his nose. "You forget I saw how much you can eat when we were in Germany. I know you can put away a lot more than this. Plus, I've seen you naked lots of times. You look amazing."

I smile and bite my lip.

He leans over the table as much as he can without his shirt dipping into his peppercorn sauce. "I like that you're thinking about us getting naked later. You have no idea how much I've been thinking about that."

I shrug. "I don't know, maybe I do."

His eyebrows shoot up. "Really? Now just how often do you think about it? All the time? Or only at night when you're alone in bed?" He looks around to make sure no waiter is standing behind him. "Do you lie in bed and touch yourself when you think of me?"

"I, uh …" I feel my cheeks flush.

"The thought of you touching yourself is getting me hard. Shit, I have to get the check. You didn't want dessert, did you?"

I shake my head and think about the kind of dessert I really want. Heat courses through me and I reach out and wrap my hand around my glass of ice water. His eyes follow the movement of my hand and he smiles.

He motions for the check and then stares me down. "How many orgasms do you want tonight, Emma?"

I take a drink of wine, contemplating his question.

"Give me a number," he asks.

"Two, I guess."

He looks disappointed with my answer. "I think we can do better than that."

"Okay, three."

"At the very least," he says. He grabs my hand and runs his finger across my thumb. "How do you want them?"

"How do I …" I can't believe we're having this conversation in the middle of a restaurant. "I don't know, the normal way, I guess."

"The *normal* way? Maybe that's good for the first one, but we need to think outside the box, Emma. What are your fantasies?"

The waiter puts the check in front of Brett and looks at me with a smirk on his face. I think he must have heard Brett talking.

I'm too worked up to even protest the fact that he's paying the bill.

The whole way home, he teases me. He whispers dirty words in my ear. He tells me what he wants to do with me. To me. By the time we get to his townhouse, I'm putty in his hands. I tingle with anticipation. I can feel the wetness between my legs.

When he leads me inside and up the stairs, I realize Bonnie and Leo have gone to bed. I'm grateful I don't have to walk past them, looking like a sappy, love-sick girl.

The door to his bedroom barely closes when I jump him. He catches me, and we both laugh as I kiss him.

"I could get used to this girlfriend thing," he says, walking us to the bed.

He puts me down, and I go right for his belt, unbuckling it before I almost rip the button off his pants.

"What did they put in your steak?" he asks. "Because I need to bottle and sell it."

"Oh, come on. You can't stand there and tell me you aren't totally turned on after that dinner."

He chuckles, removing his shirt before pulling my sundress over my head. He grabs my breasts. "Sweetheart, there hasn't been a single time I've been with you that I haven't been turned on."

I drop his pants to the floor. "Think about what you just said."

"What?" he asks innocently. "So I was turned on by you even in the storage room. I told you, when you know, you know."

"You're crazy," I say, lowering his boxer briefs.

"Crazy about you."

He draws in a sharp breath when I grab his penis. I run my hand along his hard shaft in long, slow strokes, then I dip my head and take him in my mouth.

"Jesus," he exclaims as I work my tongue around him.

His hips do a lot of the work for me as he pushes himself in and out of my mouth. His grip on my breasts becomes firmer. More barbaric.

"God, Emma," he says, pulling out of my mouth before he lays me back on the bed and crawls up my body, taking my panties off along the way. "I want that, but right now, I need to be inside you."

We lock eyes as he glides inside me. Oh, the feeling. Was it always this good with him, or does being a couple somehow make it better?

"You feel incredible," he says in my ear. "I'm going to make you come like this. Then later, I'm going to lick you exactly how you like it. I know every part of your body like the back of my hand. I know you love me to suck on your clit and run my tongue around it in little circles." He reaches between us and pinches one of my nipples. "I know you like it when I do this. You squeeze my cock with your tight little pussy when I do it."

Just when I think I can't take anymore, he grabs one of my legs and puts it on his shoulder. Then he reaches beneath me and touches the pucker of my ass. "I know you love it when I sink my finger inside you right here." He pushes his finger in, and I moan in pleasure. "I want every part of you, Emma. And tonight, I'm going to have it."

The feel of his finger inside me, and the promise of what else he has in store, has me biting my lip so I don't yell when I come harder than he's ever made me come. I can't even think about the fact that this is just round one.

He lets himself go right after I do, bracing himself on the bed while he rides out his orgasm. He collapses on me, sweaty and satiated.

"Holy shit," he says, pulling out and rolling to my side.

"You can say that again." I lean my head into the pillow enjoying the post-coital bliss.

"Emma?" he says, his voice laced with concern.

I open my eyes and look at him. "What is it?"

"I, uh … Shit, I didn't use a condom. I'm so sorry. I never expected to get so caught up that I'd forget. I—"

I put my finger to his lips. "It's okay, Brett. I'm on the pill. And I've never gone without using a condom. Not since I was fifteen anyway."

"Me either," he says, relieved. "I mean, I didn't with Amanda, but like I told you, I haven't been with anyone but you since her." He sits up. "You really aren't mad?"

"I'm really not mad."

A broad smile crosses his face. "Well, then, give me a few minutes to recharge, and we'll go again."

I don't need a few minutes, I'm ready to go again now. But I don't tell him that, because lying next to him is almost as good as having him inside me.

I look at the mirror on his wall. "I'm going to miss you leaving messages on my mirror."

"You are?"

I nod.

"Do you have any lipstick with you?"

"In my purse," I say, pointing to where I dropped it by his bedroom door.

He gets out of bed and retrieves it, giving it to me so I can find the lipstick. I hold it out to him. "You're going to leave yourself a message?" I say laughing.

"Not exactly." He straddles me and removes the top of the lipstick, then writes something on my chest as I squirm beneath him.

I can't see what he wrote. "What does it say?"

He sits me up so I can see myself in his mirror. My heart grows when I read it.

MINE

CHAPTER THIRTY-THREE

BRETT

Evie: Who was that woman leaving your house?

I go to the living room window and look across the street. Evie is sitting in her bedroom bay window.

Me: That was my sister, Brianna. I told you about her.

Evie: Okay.

Me: You're not spying on me, are you, squirt?

Evie: No. It's just that Mom is so happy. I've never seen her like this. I don't want anything to ruin that.

I lean against the window frame and re-read her text a few times, glad to hear that Evie sees a difference in Emma. This past week has been everything I've hoped for. We introduced our kids to each other. Leo is enamored with Evie, and she fell right into the role of big sister. Every day I haven't worked, Emma and I have been together. She even came over yesterday afternoon when Jay was here, working on the Mustang. It's like we've been trying to make up for lost time or something. Maybe we're both thinking about how, when she goes back to work, our time will be limited.

I love that Evie and I have fallen into this easy friendship that was only made stronger by our trip to Germany. While we haven't had many late-night conversations lately—mostly because I no longer sneak out of Emma's room—we do text frequently.

Me: I don't want anything to ruin it either.

Evie: Can your sister hook me up with concert tickets? And when can I meet her? I've never met anyone famous before.

I laugh at the notion, but then it strikes me that Bria *is* about to become famous. I doubt she'll be a household name or anything, but she may get recognized. Suddenly, I feel protective of my little sister. I make a note to talk to her about safety and responsibility.

Me: She'd be happy to meet you anytime. I'll set up a dinner next week. But I'm not sure your mom would approve of you going to a concert. It's White Poison. They aren't exactly a kid band.

Evie: Mom lets me listen to whatever music I like. So they have cuss words in their songs. Who doesn't? She'd let me go. OMG, can Bria get us backstage passes?

Me: The tour doesn't start for months, and they don't play here in the city until the very end. I'll talk to your mom about it, okay?

Evie: Okay.

Me: Is your mom nervous about tonight? Being a bridesmaid and all?

Evie: I don't think so. Wait until you see her dress. She's beautiful.

Me: Of course she is. I'd better get ready. I'll talk to you later.

Evie: TTYL

She waves to me from her window.

Leo tugs on my leg, and I pick him up, pointing across the street. "Can you wave to Evie?"

I'm not sure he sees her, but he waves frantically, and she waves back, blowing him a kiss before she disappears.

"You like Evie, don't you?" I put him down and get on my knees. "Leo, do you like Emma?"

He runs to the table and brings back the donkey. I think that's his way of telling me he does, or at least he likes the gift she brought him.

"I really want you to like Emma. Daddy loves her, you know. She doesn't know it yet. I'm not sure if I'm afraid to tell her or if I'm afraid she won't say it back."

While Emma and I have had a great week together, I can tell she's holding back emotionally. Then again, we've only officially been a couple for seven days—maybe that's just too soon to be throwing around words like love and commitment.

"She does love you, Brett," Bonnie says, entering the room. "I can tell by the way she looks at you."

"I hope so. I think this is the real deal." I stand up and look at Leo. "Do you think he will be okay with it?"

She sits on the couch, and he climbs up next to her and pages through a picture book. "I think he'd love it. He deserves to have a real family. So do you."

She looks sad, and I guess what must be going through her head. "You're his family, too. I want you to know you'll always have a place with us. No matter what."

She waves my comment off and wipes her eyes. "I'm not a fool. I know things will change one day, and that's okay."

"We'll still need you. Leo is still so young, and who knows? There may be more."

"More?" Her face lights up.

"Sure. Why not? I think Leo would make a great big brother someday."

"That he would," she says, placing a kiss on his head.

"I have to go get ready for this thing."

"Ah, the wedding." She smiles. "Watching two people declare their love for each other sometimes brings out our own feelings."

"We've only been together a week, Bonnie."

"Yeah, but when you know, you know," she says.

I cock my head thinking how those are the exact words I said to Emma.

~ ~ ~

Emma looks incredible in her light green bridesmaid's dress, despite running around the church, making sure everything gets done.

"I'm sorry," she says as she races past, then comes back and stops. "I don't mean to ignore you, but no one has a safety pin. Can you believe that? I have to find one."

"Go. You don't have to babysit me. I'll see you after."

She kisses my cheek. "Thank you for not being mad."

She jogs down the hall in bare feet. She took off the five-inch heels she was wearing when I picked her up an hour ago. I'm glad she did. She'd break a leg otherwise.

A man comes over and offers me his hand. "You must be Emma's plus-one."

"What gave it away?" I shake. "Brett Cash."

"Brian Kaling. Lisa, my wife, is also in the wedding party. She works with Emma and Becca."

"Right. I think I met her at a Mexican restaurant a while back."

His eyebrows shoot up. "*You're* the firefighter from the school hostage thing?"

"That's me."

"I've heard a lot about you," he says. "And you went to Germany with Emma and her daughter?"

"Yup."

"Lisa and I traveled overseas quite a bit this summer."

"What do you do, Brian?"

"I'm in banking."

Banking. It makes me think of Tony or Monty or whoever it was that Emma dated last month. Emma liked that he was a banker. She thought it was safe. I wonder if Brian was the one who introduced him to Emma.

Brian laughs. "I know banking isn't as exciting as firefighting, but I didn't mean to bore you into silence."

"Sorry," I say. "Hearing you say that made me think of a guy Emma went out with before."

"Ouch. I didn't mean to bring up bad memories. Want to give me his name so I can ruin his credit?"

I narrow my eyes.

"I'm kidding." He motions to the sanctuary. "They are letting people in now. You want to sit together since we're both going solo?"

"Lead the way."

We get seated six rows back from the altar. Brian and I talk about our summer trips overseas as the organist plays softly. After about ten minutes, the music gets louder, signaling the ceremony is about to start.

Everyone stops talking when the preacher, groom, and groomsmen come in through a doorway in the front. The family of the bride and groom are escorted to their seats, then all heads turn to watch the flower girl and ring bearer traipse down the aisle.

The ring bearer can't be more than four years old. He gets distracted a few times before making it all the way to the front of the church. He earns a few laughs when he takes a bow.

Brian's face lights up when his wife appears. I'm sure my expression mimics his when I see Emma. She spots me and smiles. I give her a wink and then watch her make her way to the altar.

We all rise as the bride appears with her father. Everyone looks at Becca, but I look at Emma. The happiness radiating from her as her friend walks down the aisle is almost palpable. She takes my breath away.

I glance at Jordan, the groom, wondering if I'll ever be lucky enough to be standing at the altar like he is, waiting for the woman I love.

Amanda and I didn't have a big wedding. We barely had a wedding at all. We each brought a friend with us and got hitched in a municipal building in the city. We didn't have much money, and she wanted a big honeymoon rather than a big wedding. Judging by the look on Emma's face, she would want the wedding.

When Jordan and Becca recite their vows to one another, Emma and I lock eyes. We stare at each other as the bride and groom pledge their love to one another. It's almost as if we are pledging our love as well. I don't think either of us does so much as blink. It's the most intense conversation I've ever had, yet no words are spoken.

The preacher pronounces them husband and wife, and that's when the spell is broken. Emma goes back to being a bridesmaid, and me, a spectator.

Brian stares at me curiously. "Just how long have you and Emma been dating?"

"Officially? About a week."

He laughs. "Shit, man, you're toast. I saw the way she was looking at you. She wants this. She wants it bad."

I can't help my smile, because *I* want this. I want this, too. Bonnie was right. All the mushy love stuff makes me want to tell Emma how I feel.

As soon as I make my way out to the vestibule, I find Emma and pull her off to the side. I don't say anything, I just look at her.

She puts a finger to my lips to keep me from speaking. "Can we wait?"

I kiss her finger and then push it aside. "Wait for what?"

"To say what I think we're about to say."

I shake my head. "I'm not sure I can."

"Please, Brett? Because I'm pretty sure I know what you're going to say. I want to say it, too. I really do. But this isn't the time."

I lean back against the wall. "I suppose we can wait, as long as you promise to dance with me."

She smiles. "Oh, I'll dance with you alright." She leans her body into me and gives it a shimmy. "And if you play your cards right, I might even go home with you."

I push her hair behind her ear and blow a hot breath across her neck. I whisper, "You want to go for the record, Miss Lockhart?"

Her breath hitches and she inhales deeply. She takes my hand and puts it on her hip, running it up and down. My dick starts to swell when I realize what she's doing. She's showing me she doesn't have any panties on. Then she turns her head and faces me so our lips are only inches apart. "Game on, Lieutenant. Game on."

CHAPTER THIRTY-FOUR

EMMA

"Your daughter is gorgeous," I say to Ivy. I'm looking at a picture on her phone. Then I look at Sara's phone. "Joey is super cute, too."

I pull out my phone so they can see a picture of Evelyn. Sara looks at the picture and then back at me. "Emma, she could be your sister."

I laugh. "I was a teenager when I had her."

I look across the table and catch Brett's eye. He winks at me before going back to his conversation with Denver and Bass.

Brett wanted me to meet his friends. Technically I met them at the firehouse, but this is different. We're out to dinner with them and their wives. We all have kids so there is no shortage of conversation.

"Brett tells me your family owns a chain of flower shops, Ivy. That sounds heavenly."

"My parents have three shops. My sister Holly and I run the one here in Brooklyn."

"Is that how you and Bass met?" I ask. "Did he go into your shop to buy flowers?"

She shakes her head. "We met in Hawaii."

"You met in Hawaii and you both live in Brooklyn?"

"Nice little coincidence, huh?"

Almost as odd as Brett and I living across the street from each other for years before meeting.

"Have you been to Hawaii?" Ivy asks. "It's amazing."

"No. I don't fly. Well, I didn't until very recently."

"How come you didn't fly?" Sara asks.

"I was afraid to. I lost my dad on 9/11."

"I'm so sorry," they both say.

"He was a firefighter. A lieutenant like Brett."

Ivy and Sara take a moment to absorb that. It makes me wonder if they've ever really thought about what Bass and Denver do on a daily basis. Do they know that one day they could run into a building and never come out? My heart begins the descent into my stomach.

Sara puts a hand on mine. "It takes time to get used to it. You never really get over that feeling when they leave for work, but it does get easier."

"I'll have to trust you on that one," I say. "I can't imagine ever getting used to it. Not when I've experienced firsthand what can happen."

"I know this doesn't help much, considering what happened to your dad, but statistically, you have more of a chance of getting into a car accident than he has of getting seriously injured in the line of duty," Sara says.

"Believe her," Ivy says. "She knows."

"You were in an accident, Sara?"

She bows her head and parts her hair, revealing a long scar on her scalp. "It's how Denver and I met. He saved me."

I look at Brett. He lifts his chin and gives me a smile. He seems to sense every time I look at him. It's like he's having a conversation with his friends but at the same time, he's making sure I'm okay.

"Brett saved *me*," I say. "In fact, he saved me and the four other people I was with."

"We know," Ivy says. "Our husbands told us. How scary that must have been for you, being held hostage."

"It was, but I'm not mad it happened, because if it hadn't, I'd never have met him." I remember Carter. "I'm not sure if you know this, but in a few weeks, there is going to be a benefit for the kid Brett saved. They're raising money for Carter's prosthetic leg. Evelyn and I will be selling baked goods there."

"We'll be there," Sara says. "I've been working on a collection of paintings, and Ivy's family is donating a ton of floral arrangements."

"I hope it raises a lot of money. Carter is so young. He deserves every chance he can get. Brett says if they get enough, Carter might even be able to get several prosthetics, like one for everyday wear and another for playing sports."

"I'm sure they'll raise enough," Ivy says. "You'd be amazed how generous the people in the fire department are. If the benefit doesn't cover all of Carter's expenses, I'm sure they'll pass the boot."

I have a flashback to when I was little. My dad kept a small, ceramic firemen's boot in the kitchen. He asked my mom to put her change in it every day. Occasionally, I'd see him open his wallet and put in a few dollars. I thought he was saving for our summer vacation or something, but one day he emptied the boot into a bag and took it with him. Right after, I overheard Mom talking to someone on the phone about a fireman who was sick or hurt. I put two and two together and figured out the boot wasn't for us at all. The money was used to help people in need. That was when I set up my lemonade stand. I remember being so happy when I put twelve dollars and change into the boot. But the best part of that day was when Dad came home from work and tucked me into bed. He said he heard what I'd done, and he'd never been prouder.

"We should exchange phone numbers," Sara says. "Maybe we could all get together and go to lunch. Or have a girls' night."

"I'd like that."

We spend the rest of dinner getting to know each other better, and by the time we leave, I feel I've made two new friends.

Brett pulls me close in the cab on the way home. "It looked like you enjoyed yourself."

"I did. Ivy and Sara are really nice, and I like that they have kids. A lot of my friends at school don't yet."

He squeezes my hand. "How are you feeling about going back next week?"

"I'm good," I say. "I took some supplies to my classroom yesterday."

His eyebrows shoot up. "You did? You didn't tell me that."

"Because it wasn't a big deal."

"It's a huge deal, Emma. How was it?"

I think about all the six-year-olds I'll get to mold this year. "It was pretty great, actually. I'm excited to meet my new students."

"You've conquered all your fears," Brett says with a look of pride. "You even took the elevator like a real pro tonight." He kisses my cheek. "My girlfriend is made of steel. Nothing scares her. Maybe we'll just call you Superwoman."

I smile even though he's wrong. There *is* one thing that still scares me. It scares me to death.

~ ~ ~

Becca walks into my classroom, dragging her cart behind her. I drop what I'm doing and give her a hug. "How was the honeymoon?"

"Tiring, and I don't mean from all the snorkeling." She glances over her shoulder to make sure nobody is listening. "I have a raging UTI from all the sex we had."

I laugh. "Sounds like a good time."

"You have no idea," she says, smiling.

"Being married looks good on you, Mrs. Kincaid."

"I think so too. I never thought I could be so happy. You look pretty radiant yourself. We're two lucky ladies, aren't we?"

"We are."

She looks around my classroom. "So, you're okay being back here?"

"I'm more than okay. I can't wait for the kids to show up next week."

"I swear you are the only teacher I know who'd rather be teaching than summering."

"What can I say? I love it here."

"I'm glad that bastard didn't ruin it for you."

A few more familiar faces appear.

"Hey, guys," Lisa says, with Kelly and Rachel not far behind her. "You want to go to lunch?"

Becca looks at the time. "But I just got here."

Rachel laughs. "We can't help it if that husband of yours keeps you up so late that you don't make it here until noon. Go drop your stuff in your classroom. You can start organizing after lunch."

"Better yet," I say. "Leave it here and get it after. Come on. It's been three weeks since we've all been together for Taco Tuesday."

"But it's Thursday," Becca says.

"Whatever. We can hit the Mexican place across the street."

Lisa looks down the hallway. "Is your husband here?" Then she laughs. "I think it's going to take me a while to get used to calling Jordan that."

"You and me both," Becca says. "I left him home in bed. He says he doesn't need much time to get his classroom in order."

"Men," Rachel says.

"Yeah, he'll probably do it the day the students come back," Becca says. "Teaching fifth grade is *so* much easier than first and second."

"But not as rewarding," I say.

I lock up my room and we head out of the building and cross the street.

"Anyone for margaritas?" Lisa asks. "It will be a long time until we can drink at lunch again."

We all nod.

We're finishing lunch and working on our second pitcher when something on the television draws my attention. I get up and go over to it.

A building is on fire. A *tall* building. In Brooklyn. My heart races and my eyes are glued to the screen. I read the closed captioning, trying to pick out information as it scrolls across the bottom of the screen. *What building? Where in Brooklyn?*

I feel like I'm going to be sick when I finally recognize where it is. And I don't just feel sick because of flashbacks or irrational fears. I feel sick because Brett is on duty today.

The news camera is showing dozens of fire trucks and police cars. They pan by them too fast for me to see if Squad 13 is there. But I know it is. Even if Brett is out on another call, he'll eventually show up at this one. That's how it works when they have a three-alarm fire.

"Turn it up," I say to a passing waitress. "Can you please turn up the volume?"

"I'm sorry. We aren't allowed to do that."

"That's ridiculous!" I say, hearing the panic in my voice.

Someone comes up behind me, putting an arm around my shoulders. "I'm sure everything is under control."

"Under control? Fire is spewing out of the windows twenty stories up. Look at it, Lisa. Does that look like it's under control?"

"Maybe he's not even there," she says.

Tears well up in my eyes. "He's there. He and every other firefighter in Brooklyn." I head for the door. "I have to go over there."

"You can't," Becca says. "You know you won't get close. It looks like they've got the entire block cordoned off."

I look at my shaking hands. "I'll go home then. I can't go back to work."

My friends look at each other like they don't know what to do. "We'll go with you," Lisa says.

"No. You guys get your classrooms ready. I'll call Ivy or Sara. They're married to men at the firehouse."

"I'm not letting you go home alone," Becca says. She turns to the others. "You guys go ahead. I'll make sure she's okay."

I practically run down the block, with Becca not far behind. I slow when I pass the firehouse, hoping I'll see Squad 13 parked in the garage, but it's not there. I knew it wouldn't be.

At my house I can't even fit the key in the lock.

Becca takes it from me. "Let me do it. Your hands are shaking a mile a minute."

The door opens to an empty house. I'm glad Evelyn is at camp. She'd be devastated to know Brett was involved.

I turn on the television. The coverage is on all the major news networks. I sink down on the couch. "This isn't a routine fire. They wouldn't give this much attention to it."

"You still don't know if he's inside," Becca says. "He could very well be outside the building trying to put out the fire."

I shake my head. "That's not what he does. Brett is the one who runs *into* the burning building, Becca. He's on Squad. They rescue people when no one else can." A camera in a helicopter shows people frantically waving on the roof. "Oh my God, look, people are trapped up there. That means they can't get below the fire."

I pick up my phone and call Ivy. It rolls to voicemail. Then I try Sara, only to have the same thing happen. I try Ivy again and leave a message. "It's Emma Lockhart. What's going on? Do you know anything? Please call me." I leave the same message on Sara's phone.

My head slumps. "Why isn't anyone answering?"

Becca gently touches my arm. "I'm sure everyone is calling them. Friends. Family. They are probably trying to make calls to get information too. They'll call you as soon as they can."

I can't just sit here and wait. I can barely hold still. I continue to call them over and over.

News coverage shows people being carried out of the building and put on gurneys. But the cameras are so far away, there's no way to tell who they are. Not that I'd be able to recognize Brett in his helmet and turnout gear anyway.

I sit and watch the TV, hot tears rolling down my cheeks, hoping for any indication that he's okay.

It's stupid and futile, but I send him a text anyway.

Me: Are you okay? Just send me a text. One word even. I need to know.

It's ridiculous to think he would have time to send me a text. Does he consider how worried I am about him? Does he care? I put my head in my hands. I can't do this.

Becca puts a cup of tea on the table in front of me. "Drink this. It will help calm you."

"Calm me?" I say, sounding like a crazy woman. "An entire bottle of Xanax couldn't calm me right now. He's in there, Becca. I know he is."

My phone rings. It's Ivy.

"Please tell me they aren't inside," I say.

"I don't know much," she says. "Their entire house is on the scene, along with just about every other company in Brooklyn."

"Oh, God."

"Emma, this is their job. I promise you they are doing what they can to stay safe and help people at the same time. And I'm sure it looks worse on TV than it really is."

"Are you there? On the scene?"

"No. The last thing they need is more people getting in the way."

"Will they tell you anything?" I ask. "Is there anyone we can call?"

"We're trying. I promise to let you know as soon as I know anything."

"I … I …"

"Emma. I know what must be going through your head right now. But listen to me. Hear my voice. I'm not panicking. And neither should you."

"Why aren't you? How can you not worry about them?"

"Because I've been through this before. Of course I'm worried, but I'm not going to panic until I have a reason to."

I look at the TV, thinking that is reason enough. "You've been through this? Bass has been in fires this bad before?"

"Maybe not *exactly* like this, but he's been in some precarious situations. Is there anyone with you right now? Maybe you shouldn't be alone. Can I come over?"

The truth is I want her here. I want both Ivy and Sara. But they have families. Kids whose fathers are in danger. *Oh, no. Leo.* I run to the front window and look out, wondering if Bonnie is aware of what's happening.

"I can't ask you to do that," I say. "You have your daughter to think about. I'm fine. There is a friend here with me."

"Okay, good. I'll call you as soon as I hear anything."

"Thank you."

"It's going to be okay, Emma."

"You don't know that. Not for sure."

"I suppose I don't, but we need to hope for the best. I'll talk to you soon."

I put down the phone and turn to Becca. "She doesn't know anything except that they are there."

Becca nods to the tea. "Do you want something stronger?"

I shake my head and change the channel to see if another network has newer information. A reporter is interviewing a man covered in soot.

"I'm on the scene with Lane Folson," she says. "Lane, you were in the building. You were on the floor where the fire started, is that correct? Can you tell us what it's like in there?"

"It's mayhem," he cries. "It's like 9/11."

My eyes widen, as do the eyes of the reporter. She quickly tries to control the situation. "Folks, there have been zero reports that terrorism is associated with this fire." She walks away from the guy, the interview clearly over. "Mr. Folson is worried about his coworkers and is obviously under a great deal of stress, but I'd like to reiterate that this is not a terrorist attack. Early reports from multiple building workers indicate it may be related to a gas leak. FDNY and NYPD are working closely with the utility company to locate and shut down any gas leaks that could affect neighboring buildings."

"She looks pissed," Becca says. "I can't believe that man said that. Does he know he just freaked out half of New York City?"

"This can't be happening," I say.

I look at the time. Four hours until Evelyn comes home. What if the fire isn't out by then? What if I still haven't heard from Brett? What will I tell her?

I scroll through pictures on my phone of Brett and Evelyn and me in Germany. *Why did I let her get close to him?* I study the way she looks at him. It's the way a girl might look at her father.

Thirty minutes later, I scream at the television. "Doesn't anyone know anything? Where is he?"

"Emma!" Becca yells. "Someone's at the door."

I run to open it, hoping Brett will be standing there. But it's Ivy and Sara. "Hi."

They are alone. They don't have their kids with them or their family or friends. Why would they leave everyone to come see me? I back up and sit on the bottom step of the stairs.

"You know something," I say. "You wouldn't be here otherwise. Is he dead?"

They come in and close the door behind them. "Maybe we'd be more comfortable in the living room," Sara says.

"I'm comfortable *here*. What is it?"

It's bad. I know it's bad. I know this because Ivy and Sara sit on the floor in front of me. People don't sit on the floor unless they are about to tell you something terrible.

"Denver called," Sara says. "He told me"—she looks at Ivy, and Ivy nods at her—"he told me Squad 13 is trapped above the fire."

My mouth goes dry, all moisture diverted to my eyes, which are crying an endless river of tears. I put my head between my knees, feeling faint. "He's trapped?" I sob through my words.

"They're airlifting people off the roof," Ivy says. "But the winds are high, so the helicopters can't land. They have to take people one at a time."

"I have to get back to the TV," I say, standing.

I look at the family pictures on the foyer wall, focusing on the photo taken of my parents the day they got married. They look so happy. I catch a glimpse of myself in the mirror and have a hard time catching my breath. *Oh, God. I'm my mother.* Did she feel like this that fateful morning when we watched the twin towers burn? I remember her trying so hard to keep it together. For me. She couldn't let me think she was scared. But I know she was. How could she not have been?

I hope my mother doesn't know about this. I would hate for her to think about that horrible day. But she's at the Connecticut office today, so maybe news hasn't traveled that far.

"What about Bass?" I ask Ivy when I'm back on the couch. "He must be okay if you're here."

"Everyone from Engine 319 is below the fire," she says. "Squad 13 are the only ones still up there. I think he said there are firefighters from neighboring firehouses up there too."

"Are they communicating with Brett? They must be, right?"

"I'm sure they are, but that's all we know right now," Sara says. "Denver said he or Bass would try to give us an update the next time they break for a drink."

I laugh maniacally. *"Break for a drink?* Brett and the others could be dying, and they are going to *break for a drink?"*

Ivy puts an arm around me. "They are forced to, Emma. They have to hydrate every time they come out of the building. They can't risk collapsing in that heat wearing the heavy turnout gear."

"I know. I'm sorry. Of course they need to drink. It's just … what if he can't? What if Brett gets dehydrated and falls down because he doesn't have any water and it's too hot? What if he runs out of air and it's too smoky? What if …" —I look at the TV and am nauseated— "What if the building collapses?"

I run to the bathroom, barely making it to the toilet before I retch up tacos and margaritas.

Sara follows me. She holds back my hair and offers me a hand towel when I'm done.

I sit on the cold tile floor and lean against the wall. "This is what it's like, isn't it? Dating a firefighter. I knew I shouldn't get involved. I was crazy to think it would work out."

Sara sits next to me. "This is *not* what it's like. Things like this almost never happen."

"Well, it's happening now."

Ivy comes to the door, holding out my phone. "It's your mom."

She never calls me from work. She knows something.

"Hello?" I ask, trying not to sound like I've been crying for the past two hours.

"Hey, sweetie. How are you doing?" She sounds cheery but guarded.

"You know about the fire, don't you?"

"Yes, but I didn't know if you did, and if you didn't, I didn't want to alarm you."

"Well, I'm alarmed," I say, crying. "He's inside, Mom. He's trapped above the fire floor."

There is a pregnant pause and she sighs deeply. She's no doubt thinking of my dad. "What about the helicopters? I've seen them airlifting people."

"He's a firefighter. You know as well as I do Brett will be among the last to be rescued. But what if there isn't time?" My last words come out in a sob.

"Sweetie, there will be time."

"But what if there's not?"

She doesn't know what to say, because what *is* there to say? "I'm on my way home."

I get off the floor and return to the living room. "You shouldn't have to watch this."

"That's not your decision to make, sweetie. I'll be there in an hour."

"Evelyn will be home at four," I say. "I can't let this happen to her, Mom."

"*You* aren't doing anything to her. Nobody is."

I look at the television again, sickened by the images of a forty-story building being engulfed by flames. The entire thing is going up in smoke, like a chimney.

"I knew this would happen."

"Stop it, Emma. You don't know anything."

"I have to go. I'll see you when you get here."

Ivy and Sara flank my sides as Becca keeps a close eye on me from across the room. Just this morning we were talking about how lucky we were. How happy we were. But *she's* the lucky one. Becca doesn't have to worry about this happening every time Jordan walks out the door.

Sara's phone rings. I hear bits and pieces of her conversation. "Denver, she's freaking out. Isn't there anything you can tell us?" She holds the phone out to me. "He wants to talk to you."

I take it. My hand is shaking. "Hello?"

"I only have a minute. We're in contact with Brett, but personal conversations aren't allowed over the radio. I wanted to tell you what he would say if he could talk to you right now. He'd say that if you or Evie or Bria or Leo were ever in a situation like this, he hopes someone like him would do everything they could to help you without thinking twice about it. That's what he's doing right now, Emma. He's saving people so they can go home to their husbands and wives and children. Those people being airlifted off the roof? They're alive because of him." Someone shouts in the background. "I have to go. Just know he's not him, Emma. Brett is not your father."

"He t-told you?" I ask, shaking with sobs.

"Yeah. He did. Listen, Brett is the most skilled firefighter I've ever known. Have faith in that."

I can only nod.

"Bye, Emma."

The line goes dead.

I feel like *I'm* going to die when I see part of the building explode. Audible gasps come from the three women in the room with me when glass is blown sideways, along with concrete and other debris.

For the next thirty minutes they try to comfort me, but I'm not sure I hear any of their words. My ears ring and my head is spinning. My thoughts go to Leo. I wonder if he'll ever forgive his dad. Then I go numb. I shut down, waiting for the fateful call.

"Emma! Emma!"

Ivy is shaking me, trying to get my attention. I look up at her.

"He got out. Brett is out. He's okay."

I'm not sure I heard her correctly. "What?"

"The explosion somehow created a pathway for them to evacuate down through the building. He's being taken to the hospital for smoke inhalation, but Bass said it's just a formality. He's fine." She puts her hands on my shoulders and looks me in the eye. "Did you hear me? Brett's going to be fine."

Sara hands me my purse. "Let's go. You can see for yourself."

We leave for the hospital, and all I think the entire time is that I don't want to be here. I don't want to be doing this. I don't want this to be my life.

I have to protect my daughter.

CHAPTER THIRTY-FIVE

BRETT

My body aches badly. My throat is sore. I'm covered with sweat, soot, and dust. But I smile anyway.

Being in that building was as bad as it gets. I've never been so worried about getting out before. We were trapped. Literally trapped more than twenty floors up with no way down. The fire was eating more and more, burning faster and hotter, and there were still over a hundred people to evacuate. None of us said it, but we were all thinking that maybe there wouldn't be enough time.

My eyes close and I rest against the pillow, breathing through the oxygen mask they put on me as a precaution. As hard as it was, these are the days firefighters live for. I beat it. I beat the fire. It didn't get me. It didn't get *anyone*. Zero casualties. It's almost unbelievable, considering what a disaster it was.

I can't wait to go out with the guys and celebrate our victory. It feels like we just won the goddamn Super Bowl.

I hear a noise and look over at the door. Emma is leaning in the doorway, staring at me.

"Aren't you a sight for sore eyes," I say. I take off the oxygen mask. "Come here."

She moves slowly across the room, her face red and puffy, all her makeup having been cried away. *Damn.* I was hoping she wouldn't be aware of what had happened until it was over. Denver told me he spoke to her earlier, and she was really worried. I can't imagine what she must have been thinking.

Fresh tears pour out of her eyes when she reaches me.

"It's fine," I tell her. "I'm okay."

She throws herself on top of me, holding me tightly. I let her hug me as long and as hard as she needs to. She shakes as she cries on my chest.

"It's okay, sweetheart."

She straightens. "It's not okay." Then she stands. "Nothing about this is okay." She steps away from the bed. "I can't do this, Brett. It's too hard. I should have stood my ground."

"But nothing happened, Emma. I'm here. The mask and IV are just a precaution. They're giving me fluids because I got dehydrated. I don't have a scratch on me."

"This time," she says, taking another step back. "But there will always be a next time. And I'm not going to put my daughter through what I went through."

"What are you saying?"

"I'm saying that Evelyn will be upset not having you around. She'll be sad for a while. But that will be a whole lot easier than her falling in love with you and treating you like a father and you treating her like a daughter and then you leaving her like my dad left me."

I reach out for her, but she moves farther away. "I'm not going to leave you."

"Can you promise that?" she cries. "Can you promise you won't leave us?"

"You know I can't. But you can't make that promise either. How can you stand there and realistically say you'll never be in an accident or get cancer? Nobody can predict the future."

"But the risks you take," she says.

"I'm good at what I do. Great, in fact. I don't take unnecessary risks. I play it safe more often than not. Hell, I'm more likely to get hurt in a pickup game of football with my friends on Thanksgiving."

She wipes her eyes. "Are you saying my dad wasn't a good firefighter?"

"Jesus, I can't win here, can I? Of course I'm not saying that."

"I'm sorry, Brett. I can't put Evelyn through this."

I sit on the edge of the bed, unable to get up because I'm tethered to the IV bag. "I wish you would quit hiding behind your daughter, Emma. At least own up to it and tell me the truth—that you don't want to be with me because *you're* the one who's scared. Because you don't care enough about me to understand how important my job is. Because you'd rather give this up than try to have something incredible."

"My parents had something incredible, and now they don't."

"And you think your mom would take it all back if she could? You think she would choose to have never met him?"

She shakes her head. "I don't know. All I know is how I feel. I'm glad you're okay, I really am. But I have to do what I think is best for Evelyn and me. Goodbye, Brett."

She moves to the door. I'm stunned. I can't believe it's going to end like this. "Emma!" I shout, making her turn around before she leaves.

She is sadder than I've ever seen her. More devastated even than when she was a hostage in the storage closet.

"I love you," I say.

A tear escapes her eye and rolls down her cheek. "I know," she says. Then she walks out the door.

~ ~ ~

As if today weren't bad enough, I have to add insult to injury by sitting in the front window, drinking a beer, hoping to catch a glimpse of Emma. If I'm being honest, drinking *several* beers. I figure I'm entitled. Today has been a shitty day by most standards.

Before Leo went to bed, he just *had* to make me play with the donkey. He loves that stupid thing. It's become his favorite toy. And damn it, every time I hear the audible burp or the "hee-haw," it reminds me of her. I'd step on the cheap piece of plastic and grind it to bits if I didn't think Leo would hate me for it.

"That's a lonely sight," Bonnie says, coming into the room and flipping on the light. "A man sitting in the dark, drinking a beer while spying on his ex."

I take a drink. "Turn off the light, Bonnie, and let me wallow in my patheticness."

"Patheticness? Is that even a word?"

"It is today."

She turns off the light. "I'll give you today," she says. "But I'm not about to stand around and watch you self-destruct. There are plenty of other fish in the sea."

"G'night, Bonnie," I say, turning away from her.

"Goodnight, Brett."

I look out the window again. Her room is dark. I wonder what she's doing. Is she even thinking about me? How can someone just turn off their feelings like that?

My phone pings with a text.

Evie: Hey.

Me: Hey, yourself.

Evie: I saw that building on the news tonight. Mom and Grandma said you were there but you're okay. I was just checking.

Me: They're right. I'm okay.

Evie: Good. The fire looked bad. Mom's been hiding in her room all day. She must have been really worried about you.

It dawns on me that maybe Emma hasn't told Evie she tossed me to the curb.

Me: I'm sure she was. That's perfectly normal. But everything is fine.

Evie: You're not lying to me, are you? You really are okay? Are we still going to the benefit on Saturday?

Me: There isn't a scratch on me. About the benefit, I'll be there for sure, but you'll have to ask your mom if she still plans on going.

Evie: Why wouldn't she be going?

I don't even know how to answer that. So I don't.

Evie: Brett, why wouldn't Mom be going? We've been planning this for weeks. We have a ton of flour and sugar in our kitchen.

Damn it, Emma.

Evie: Did something happen? What aren't you telling me?

Me: I'm not sure this is a conversation you and I should be having.

Evie: OMG. She broke up with you, didn't she?

Me: Today was very hard on her. She was feeling all kinds of emotions she hadn't felt since your grandpa died.

Evie: How could she do that?

Me: I don't know. Listen, if you want to talk, let's talk about something else. Are you ready to go back to school next week?

Evie: School? I can't talk about school at a time like this. We have to figure out a way to get you and Mom back together. I can do recon on this end. I'm sure I can get Grandma in on it too. But you have to do your part. When my best friend, Karoline, got dumped by her boyfriend last month, she made him jealous by kissing Kyle Young. Maybe you could make her jealous. You know, not for real, but maybe you have a friend who could pretend to be your date, and I can make sure Mom looks out the window and sees you.

Me: Slow down, Nancy Drew.

Evie: Who's that? Is she a woman you can use to make Mom jealous?

Me: I'm not going to use anyone to make your mom jealous.

Evie: But it can work. Don't you even want to try?

Of course I want to try, I just don't think there is anything I can say or do to change her mind.

Evie: Can I tell you something?

Me: Always.

Evie: Back in Germany when I told Stefan I was happy with the way things were, and I didn't need a father, I meant it. I've always meant it. Until I met you, I never knew what I was missing in my life. Now I know.

I close my eyes and nod. God, I love that kid. Who knew this precocious twelve-year-old could work her way into my heart the way she has.

Me: I feel the same way about you, Evie. About both of you. In some ways I feel like the two of you complete my family. I wish things could be different.

Evie: Me too.

Leo is making a lot of noise through the baby monitor.

Me: I have to go. Leo needs me. We'll talk soon. Maybe I'll see you Saturday. I'll be at the dunking booth if you want to find me.

Evie: We'll be there, I promise.

Me: Goodnight.

I go upstairs to Leo's room and find him standing up in his crib. "What's up, buddy? Bad dream?"

As I walk over, I get a whiff of his diaper and realize what the problem is. I laugh. "Poopy diaper." I pick him up and flick on the light before taking him to the changing table.

"Poopy donkey," he says while I change him.

"Thankfully, donkey's poops aren't as messy as yours." I give him a meaningful stare. "Never eat your poop, Leo. Yuck."

He giggles. I pick him up.

"Kiss, Daddy," he says.

He puckers up, and I give him a smooch.

Returning to his crib, I can't help looking out the window. It's become more a habit than anything. But I'm surprised at what I see.

I didn't expect Emma to be standing at her window. *Does she see me? Is she having second thoughts?*

I walk up to the window with Leo still in my arms. She sees me and starts to back away. I put my palm against the glass.

She hesitates, then draws the curtains.

I look at Leo. "I really thought she was the one."

He yawns and puts his head on my shoulder.

"Yeah, I'm tired too," I say, turning off his light. "Come on, you can sleep with me tonight."

CHAPTER THIRTY-SIX

EMMA

"I can't believe we've already sold half of everything, Grandma," Evelyn says, reaching under the table to get more bags of cookies. "Carter is going to get an awesome leg."

"And it's only been an hour," Mom says. "There's two more hours to go. If we're lucky, we'll sell out."

I look in the fanny pack I've been using to collect money. Looks like there's over five hundred bucks in there. It's amazing what people will pay for things when they know all the proceeds are being donated to a good cause.

The event organizer called me earlier this week and went over what prices I should charge for my baked goods. I thought she was crazy. But she told me to trust her. She does these charity functions all the time. And she was right.

I couldn't be happier for Carter.

I check out booths selling crafts and specialty foods; they seem to be doing well too. There are also several carnival games across the lawn and a silent auction for some higher-priced items.

"Why don't you and Evie play some of the games," Mom says. "The initial rush is over. I can handle it myself for a while."

I don't want to. If I walk around, I'm more likely to run into Brett. I've done everything I can to avoid doing that over the past week. I've stopped going to the corner market. I make sure I'm not walking to work the same time he's getting off a shift. I don't look at his townhouse.

Complete and total avoidance. That's what's become of my life. But tonight is the night I take the first step toward a new me. I let Becca's husband set me up with one of his friends. Dan Daughtry is the guy's name. He teaches at a school in Manhattan. And he's exactly the kind of man I should be dating.

I won't tell Evelyn, however. She's been giving me the cold shoulder since I broke things off with Brett.

"Oh, yes, please?" Evelyn asks, suddenly okay with speaking to me. "I saw some fun things I really want to do."

"Okay," I say reluctantly and hand my mother the fanny pack. "We'll be back in twenty minutes."

"Take all the time you need. I'll be fine here."

Evelyn claps her hands. "I know right where I want to go." She pulls me across the lawn to the dunking booth.

I look at her sideways. "Wouldn't you rather do the ring toss or something?"

"I want to do *this*."

"Evelyn, I've never seen you throw a ball in your life. You do realize you have to hit a fairly small target."

"Come on. It's only five dollars for three tries," she says. "It's for Carter's leg. We'll do the ring toss next."

I dig in my pocket and hand her the money. There are a lot of people standing in line. This seems to be the most popular game.

When we get closer and I read the sign, I see why: **DUNK A FIREFIGHTER**

I don't want to look, but I force myself to. When I see who's sitting on the platform above the water, I know exactly why Evelyn was so eager to come over here. "Did you know Brett was going to be doing this?"

She shrugs.

"You're still talking to him, aren't you?"

"Mom, he's my friend."

"Evelyn, he's thirty years old. You're twelve. It's not right."

She puts her hands on her hips and gives me a stern look. "You want to talk about what's *not right?* How about two people who are crazy about each other but can't be together because one of them is being ridiculously stupid about it?"

"I'm not going over this again," I say, trying to pull her out of line.

"Mom, I'm doing this. You'll have to throw me over your shoulder and carry me out of here. But I'm pretty sure you don't want to cause a scene."

I huff my displeasure. "We'll talk about this later."

I watch the booth out of the corner of my eye. Maybe he'll go on a break before we make it up there.

He gets dunked one time before it's Evelyn's turn. His FDNY T-shirt is plastered to his skin, outlining his tight torso and sculpted abs. I try to look anywhere but at him, then mentally kick myself when I do it anyway.

"My turn!" Evelyn says excitedly.

She waves to Brett and steps up to the line marked on the ground. He waves back. He sees me and lifts his chin as if to say hello. I dip my chin in response to be polite.

"Hi, Ms. Lockhart," says the boy holding the softballs.

"Hello, Jay."

I was so focused on Brett that I didn't notice Jay until he said my name. "This is my daughter, Evelyn."

"You mean the famous Evie?" He hands her a ball. "It's nice to meet you. Brett has told me a lot about you."

Evelyn scowls at me. "Did he tell you my mother broke up with him?"

Jay looks surprised. "Uh, no. He didn't tell me that. That sucks."

"It sucks bad," she says. "Did you hear that, Mom? Everyone thinks it sucks."

"Just throw the ball, Evelyn."

She winds up and makes her throw, missing the target by ten feet.

On her second attempt, she hits the front of the tank; closer to her goal but still laughably far off. Wow, she really is bad at this.

The last ball goes up and over the glass and right into the tank, where Brett snatches it. He smugly tosses it into the air and catches it.

"You should try, Mom. You're on that softball team for teachers."

"That's okay. I'll pass."

"It's for charity, you know," Jay says.

Crap. I'm being bullied into this by my daughter and Brett's little protégé.

I pull out another five-dollar bill and hand it to Jay. He tries to give me three balls. I push two away. "I only need one."

I shake my head, not quite believing this whole situation. I wind up and zero in on the target. Then I release the ball and watch it slice through the air, hitting the bullseye only slightly off center. The seat falls, dropping Brett in the water.

"You did it!" Evelyn screams as spectators clap behind us.

"What's next?" I ask, needing to get away from here as quickly as possible.

"Emma?" a man calls. "Emma Lockhart!"

A young man on crutches approaches us. He's missing a leg. My heart melts and I break into a smile when I see Carter. I immediately walk over and pull him into a hug, careful not to throw him off balance.

"Carter, it's so nice to see you." His face is full of color, like he's been out in the sun. "You look fantastic."

"Thank you. It's probably because I lost twenty pounds."

I look at him, confused. He doesn't seem any thinner.

"Amputee joke," he says, laughing.

"Oh." I laugh with him. "I'm glad to see you're in such good spirits."

He sweeps his crutch around, motioning at our surroundings. "Can you believe all of this? It's unreal that people are here just for me."

"Believe it," I say. "You're a survivor, Carter."

"Thanks to you," he says.

I shake my head. "No. Not thanks to me."

"You kept me alive until Brett got there," he says. "You guys are my heroes. Both of you." He looks over my shoulder. "Hey, speak of the devil."

My heart jumps. *Oh, God.*

"Carter, great to see you," Brett says, offering him a hand. He looks at me. "Emma."

I nod hello.

A woman joins us, looking like she's about to cry. "This is my mom, Grace," Carter says.

"What you did for my Carter—I'll never be able to thank you. Oh, heavens, I need a picture of the three of you. Is that okay?"

"Give me a second," Brett says. "I'm soaking wet. Let me get some of the water out of this shirt. It'll make for a better picture."

Then, right here in the middle of everyone, he takes off his wet FDNY shirt, wrings it out several times, and then puts it back on. I try to get myself to look away.

Look. Away.

Brett catches me staring but strangely enough, he doesn't so much as smirk.

"Okay," he says. "Where do you want us?"

"On either side of Carter," Grace says. "Put your arms around him."

I put my arm around Carter and freeze when I realize I'm touching Brett's hand. I want to pull away, but I don't want my awkward moment to ruin the picture, so I stay where I am and pray it's over soon.

After Grace is satisfied she got a good picture, I pull my arm back. But not before Brett grabs my hand ever so briefly and gives it a squeeze.

My heart beats out of control at his touch. I will myself to ignore the feelings coursing through my body. "We better get back to our booth."

"But you said I could play some more games," Evelyn whines.

I give her a hard stare. "Evelyn."

"Why don't you let me take her around?" Brett says. "I'm on a break. We can go find Leo. He and Bonnie are around here somewhere."

"Please, Mom? I really want to see Leo. He's the cutest kid I've ever seen. Isn't he cute? And remember, every game I play is more money that goes to Carter and his bionic leg."

"She makes a good point," Brett says.

Man, am I tired of being manipulated today. But Carter and his mother are standing right here. What am I going to do, tell Evelyn she can't participate?

"Fine." I pull a twenty out of my pocket. "Be back at our booth in half an hour."

"Not a second later," Brett says, leading her away without taking the money.

I stare after them for a minute, watching them joke around with each other. Then Leo comes running out of nowhere. He goes right up to Evelyn. She picks him up and spins him around. The three of them look so happy together.

Grace stands next to me. "They all seem to get along well. You'd almost think they were family."

I look away. A family she can never be a part of.

"It's been wonderful to meet you, Grace. Please come by our booth, and I'll give you one of my famous cinnamon rolls."

"I think I'll do just that, Emma. Thank you."

~ ~ ~

"Jordan tells me you've taught first grade for six years."

"I have," Dan says.

"It's pretty unusual for a man to teach first grade," I say.

"I guess so, but I like it. The kids respond to me well. I didn't go into it intending to teach six-year-olds, but it was the only job I could get that first year. It kind of grew on me, so I stayed."

It's nice that he likes kids. Points for that.

The waitress brings our food.

"Do you have any children of your own?" I ask.

He chokes on his sip of beer. "God, no. Teaching first grade is the best form of birth control."

Becca and Jordan stare him down from across the table, and he backtracks. "Uh, but I do like them, though. Do you have any?"

"I have a twelve-year-old daughter," I say, shooting Jordan a punishing glance. "I'm surprised Jordan didn't tell you."

"That's cool," Dan says. "I'll bet she's a handful at that age, all those hormones going wild." He studies me. "Twelve? Exactly how old are you, Emma?"

"I'm twenty-seven."

He does the math in his head.

"Evelyn is anything but a handful," I add. "She's a godsend."

"Okay, well, that's … brave of you, I guess."

I guess? Who the hell is this guy? I give Becca a disapproving stare over my glass of wine. She just shrugs at me.

"What do you like to do in your spare time?" he asks.

"I don't know. Lots of things. Go into tall buildings. Fly. Hang out in storage closets."

Becca spits out her drink, and Jordan offers her a napkin. She kicks me under the table.

"Those sound like … uh, interesting hobbies," he says. "Do you like music?"

"I listen to it from time to time."

"Who do you like?"

"Elton John."

"Isn't he dead?"

I wonder how soon I can dump this guy and go home.

"Dan," Jordan says, trying to ease the insurmountable tension. "Why don't you tell Emma about your collection?"

"You're a collector?" I ask. "Of what?"

"Coins." He pulls one out of his pocket. "Look at this. It was minted in error. See how the head is off to the side and there is the bit of another head showing along the edge?"

I take it into my hand and study it. "Interesting. Is it worth a lot?"

"Do you think I'd be carrying it around in my pocket if it were?"

"I guess not. So why *do* you carry it around?"

"It's my lucky quarter."

"You think you're going to get lucky tonight?" I joke.

He tosses it in the air and catches it. "I don't sleep with women on the first date," he says in total seriousness. "I request a clean bill of health before going down that road."

Did he really just say that? I could be home playing scrabble with Evelyn and Mom or soaking in a hot tub with a book. Both ideas appeal to me greatly at the moment.

"My best coins are locked in a safe deposit box. I have quite the collection of mules."

"Mules?" I ask, wishing this torture would end.

"Coins with designs not normally seen on the same piece."

"You've lost me."

"You know, like the front side of one coin with the back side of a totally different coin. They are very rare."

"Why are they called mules?"

"They're named after the animal. The mule is a hybrid offspring of a horse and a donkey. Just like the coins are a hybrid of two different coins not meant to be together."

Donkey.

Now I'm thinking about Leo. Does he still play with the gift I gave him? Did Brett smash it to smithereens when I broke things off?

Dan goes on and nauseatingly on about some Sacagawea dollar he got out of a Cheerios box nineteen years ago that made him want to start collecting coins.

I share a *get-me-out-of-here* look with Becca.

"Oh, gosh," I say, faking getting a text. "My daughter is having a little emergency. Girl problems. I have to run to the store and get a few things for her."

Becca tries not to let the guys see her smile.

"See? That's why I don't have kids," Dan says. "They suck up all your time. They're time-suckers. You are tied to them for eighteen long years. Maybe more. No thank you. I'll stick with my dog. At least with dogs, you can take them to the pound when you get tired of them."

My jaw drops, and I have to bite my tongue to keep myself from going off on him.

"Why don't we call it a night?" Becca says, thwarting my impending attack. "We didn't need dessert anyway. I'm still trying to lose the five pounds I gained on our honeymoon."

"I'll get the check," Jordan says.

"Separate checks please," Dan says. "For all of us." He turns to me. "I make it a point not to pay for women until the fifth date. I hope you brought money with you."

This time I can't hold back. "Sure, because by then you'll know if she's diseased or not, but I'm willing to bet you don't get to that fifth date very often, do you? Not even with that lucky mule thing in your pocket."

"It's not a mule in my pocket. It's just a misprint." He seems confused by my outburst. "Did I say something to offend you?"

"No, Dan. You've been the perfect gentleman. In fact, let's do this again. I've been looking for someone to become my kid's new father. You interested?"

He stumbles over his words. "Uh, well, Jordan just said we were going to have some fun. I wasn't … I'm not …"

"Your checks," the waitress says.

Thank God.

After we leave the restaurant, Dan quickly excuses himself, barely even saying goodbye to me.

Becca laughs as she watches him run away. "That was—"

"A disaster?" I say.

"I was going to say awkward, but yeah."

I turn to Jordan. "Would you mind screening your friends next time?"

"What exactly are your requirements?"

"Tall, dark and covered with soot?" Becca says, laughing.

"You know that's not what I mean," I say. "That guy doesn't even like kids. I pity his students. And he's soooooo boring. I mean, coins. Really?"

"I thought boring was what you wanted," Jordan says.

"Safe and boring are not the same thing, Jordan," I tell him as we start the walk home.

"I'll keep that in mind for next time. But maybe you could get me a list of acceptable occupations, hobbies, and interests."

I hit him in the arm when he starts laughing. "Shut up."

"So there wasn't really a *girl problem* emergency?" he asks.

"No. Evelyn's not there yet."

We get to my townhouse, and I give them both a hug. "Thanks for walking me home. And thanks for trying."

"Anytime," Jordan says.

"Look." Becca motions across the street.

I look before thinking about it. I see Brett standing near his living room window, holding Leo.

"Now, there's a guy who loves kids," Becca says. "And he's most definitely not boring."

I quickly look away before he catches me staring. "Et tu, Brute?" I say sharply. "I get enough of that at home, Becca. Can you please back off?"

She holds up her hands in surrender. "You're right. I'm sorry." She looks at Jordan. "I just want everyone to be as deliriously happy as we are."

Jordan kisses her temple.

"Deliriously happy doesn't last," I say. "Safety and security do."

I say goodbye and go up my steps. I'm not sure why I feel compelled to turn around and look across the street once more before I go inside. But I stupidly do. And I see that he's noticed me. He smiles and puts a hand on the glass.

Me—I do the only thing I can.

I turn and walk away.

CHAPTER THIRTY-SEVEN

BRETT

Bria and I make our way through thousands of people. I used to think people would stop coming to the memorial after so much time has passed, but today I feel the opposite is true.

I never bring Leo with me, especially not on the actual anniversary. I take him to Mom's grave sometimes, but I'll wait until he's much older to bring him here. All the names engraved on the parapets. The distraught people. It can be confusing for a child.

After the ceremony, Bria and I make our usual trip to the south memorial and find Mom's name. Her name is listed with her coworkers, who also ran inside to help. We see the familiar faces of the friends and family of those coworkers, who come every year to pay their respects.

"Where are you going?" Bria asks, when I start to walk in the opposite direction.

"I want to find another name this year."

She nods and follows me in silence.

I know exactly where to look. Like my mom, Emma's dad died in the south tower. I researched where his name was engraved.

It's around the corner from Mom's. I find his name and run my hand across it.

William Abernathy Lockhart, Jr.

Bria puts a hand on my shoulder. "How long has it been since you've seen her?"

"Since I've seen her or since she dumped me?"

Her face fills with compassion. "Maybe she just needs time."

"You didn't see her face when she walked out on me, Bria. She's done with me. Look around. We're surrounded by people who've lost a loved one. She's tired of being one of these people. Maybe I can't blame her."

"Well, *I* blame her," she says. "She broke your heart. You weren't even this sad when Amanda left you, and you guys were together for almost a decade."

She's right. I think with Amanda, I was angry more than I was sad. Angry at her for not loving Leo. Angry at her for putting her job before her family. But sad? I guess I must have been, but it was nothing like this. Nothing like my heart actually hurting like it has a hole in it and is missing a piece. Two pieces actually. Sometimes I find myself missing Evie almost as much as I miss Emma.

Evie and I still text each other, but it's not the same. It's nowhere near the same.

After Bria leaves to go to rehearsal, I attend the annual 9/11 FDNY luncheon and wonder if Emma is here. I'm not holding out much hope, however. If she won't go to the memorial, she probably won't come here.

I don't see her, but I do see two other familiar faces. Evie runs over and gives me a hug.

"Hey, squirt. Long time no see."

"Too long," she says.

I nod to her grandmother. "Hi, Enid."

I know Emma's not here, but I look behind the two of them just in case.

As if reading my mind, Enid says, "She never comes to these things."

"I know. I was just hoping …" I run a hand through my hair. "How is she?"

"Immersed in work."

"But she misses you," Evie says with a sad smile. "I know she does."

This is nothing new. Evie tells me similar things when we text.

"I've always taken pride in how smart my daughter is," Enid says. "I'm sorry to say this is not one of those times."

I'm surrounded by people who have lost someone. Even all these years later, the memory of that day is still raw. "I didn't really get it until today," I say. "Being here, and earlier, at the ceremony, I'm beginning to understand how she wants to distance herself from the possibility of history repeating itself."

Enid shakes her head. "Fear is no reason to forgo happiness."

"I agree, but fear is often irrational."

"It's a strong emotion," she says. "Maybe even stronger than love, I'm afraid."

"It's not," Evie says. "There isn't an emotion stronger than love. Love always wins in the end."

I ruffle her hair. "You watch too many Disney movies."

"Stop it," she says, irritated that I messed up her hair. "And maybe I do watch them, but it's how I know you will end up together, no matter how many other guys she dates."

Evie immediately looks guilty about what she said. Enid scolds her. "Evie, you need to learn when to be discreet."

"She's *dating?"*

"She's trying to get over you," Evie says. "It won't work, you know."

She's dating. After only two weeks. But when I think about it, I realize Emma and I were really only together for a couple of weeks ourselves.

"Evie," Enid says. "Will you be a dear and get me some more iced tea?"

"Sure, Grandma."

Enid watches Evie walk away. When she's out of earshot, Enid turns to me. "My daughter loves you. I don't say that lightly, having only loved one man in my life, so believe me when I tell you she's only ever loved one in hers."

I raise an eyebrow. "She told you this?"

"A mother knows." She glances after her granddaughter. "We all know how smart Evie is. She thinks she understands love, but she doesn't. Her mother is strong-willed. Always has been. That's why a big part of me thinks that even though she loves you, she's going to let fear and stubbornness stand in her way. It pains me to say this, but I think you need to find a way to move on."

I stand here, confused as hell. "Enid, why would you tell me she loves me and in the next breath encourage me to find someone else?"

"Maybe because I don't want to give you false hope. At the same time, however, I want to believe that love conquers all. What's that saying? If you love someone, let them go and if they come back to you it was meant to be?"

I snort.

"All I'm saying is you can't sit around and wait for her, because it might be in vain. Go live your life. Have fun. Date. You deserve happiness too, you know."

"Here, Grandma," Evie says. "Are you finished talking about all the love stuff you don't think I'm old enough to hear?"

Enid and I laugh.

"I've got to get this one to school," Enid says. "I promised Emma she'd only take half a day off."

Evie gives me another hug. "Bye, Brett. See you in the window."

~ ~ ~

Bonnie catches me holding a beer, pacing in front of the window after Leo goes to bed. She raises a scolding brow. "Again?"

"Stop judging me," I say. "I can't help it, knowing she's right across the street."

"Maybe you should think about finding another place to live."

"I'm not going to let a woman drive me out of my house, Bonnie."

"No, you're just going to let her drive you crazy."

"I'll get over it sooner or later."

She looks at me with gentle eyes. "So you're just going to fall out of love with her?"

"Yes. No. I don't know. But it's only been a few weeks."

"Maybe it's time to put yourself out there, Brett. There's no better way to get over a love than finding someone new."

"You mean *sleep* with someone new."

"You said it, not me."

I sit on the couch and lean back against the cushion. "The funny part is I've actually thought about it. Guys at the station have a list of women they want to set me up with."

"You're not a kid anymore," she says. "You're a responsible adult. There's nothing wrong with having a little fun."

"Every time I think about taking one of them up on it, I feel guilty."

"You shouldn't."

"I know, but I do. Why is that? She dumped me, but I feel guilty about dating another woman. Hell, I'm pretty sure *she's* out there dating, so why shouldn't I be?"

Bonnie sits next to me and takes my hand. "Because you are one of those men who loves with your whole heart. I knew that about you when you hired me. What Amanda did was horrible. Inexcusable. But you stuck by her side. You stuck by her side, even when I thought you shouldn't."

"Can I tell you something?" I ask.

"Of course."

"I know it seems impossible, but I think I love Emma more than I loved Amanda. Isn't that crazy? I've only known her for four months and I love her more than the mother of my child."

"It's not crazy. But that's why it hurts so much." She moves to the kitchen for a bottle of water. "This too shall pass." She flips off the light, leaving me in darkness, and goes upstairs.

I get up and obsessively look out the window, knowing it's stupid to do it, but I do it anyway.

I watch all the people pass on the street. Couples. Families. Single people heading out for a late night on the town. People living their lives. Yet here I sit stuck in some limbo I can't get out of.

Then I see her. Emma appears with a man. They walk up her steps. He looks like a goddamn banker in his tailored suit. She's being escorted home by Richie Rich.

I stand up and almost yell when she opens the front door, and they both go inside. *What the fuck?*

Evie's light is on. She's still awake for cryin' out loud. So now Emma is introducing men to her daughter?

I chug the rest of my beer and go to the kitchen for another when my phone pings with a text.

Evie: She's not taking him upstairs.

Me: What are you talking about?

Evie: Oh, come on. I saw you standing in the window watching my mother. You saw them go inside. I just wanted to tell you she's not taking him upstairs.

Me: We really shouldn't be discussing this.

Evie: You don't want to know what they're doing right now?

Me: Of course not.

I return to the window. Evie's in her room, looking at her phone. How pathetic am I? A twelve-year-old is spying for me. I've truly hit rock fucking bottom. The fact that I'm thinking that while texting her does not escape my attention.

Me: What are they doing?

Evie: She asked for his jacket. He spilled something on it at dinner, and she's going to try and get the stain out.

Typical. The old *spill something on your clothes so you have an excuse to take them off* trick. I try to think of anything but what might be going on in her kitchen.

Me: Tell me about Greta. How is she?

Evie: She's amazing. So much better than I imagined. She's not stuck up, like a lot of my friends' big sisters. We text all the time and call once a week. She even called me her BFF yesterday.

Me: I'm so happy for you.

Evie: She's teaching me German. Oh, and she's coming to visit next month with her mom and stepdad. We're going to have two whole days together. I wish you could be here for it.

Me: I wish I could, too.

Evie: Just so you know, I don't think my mom likes this guy at all.

Me: How can you tell? You're in your bedroom.

Evie: And I'm staying here until he leaves. I don't want to meet him. I know she doesn't like him because I can hear her fake laughing. Like how you do when something's not funny, but you laugh anyway.

I move away from the window and sit on a barstool as we text for several more minutes, her telling me about how cool sixth grade is, and me telling her about some of the strange calls I've gone on in the past week.

It's odd, yet at the same time not, being friends with her.

Evie: I think he's getting ready to leave.

I race to the window, watching Richie Rich step onto her front porch. He leans in and tries to kiss her. She backs away at first, and I could swear she glances in my direction, but then she lets him kiss her.

It's not a long kiss. Not a deep one either. It's more like a peck on the lips. Anger crawls up my spine as someone else kisses the woman I love.

Evie texts me again, but it's evident she didn't see what just happened.

Evie: He's gone now. I told you there was nothing to worry about.

Me: Yup. Nothing to worry about. I'll talk to you later, squirt.

Evie: Goodnight, Brett.

Richie Rich bops happily down the street, and I decide I'm tired of being the guy who's sitting at home, feeling sorry for myself. I pick my phone up and text Bass.

Me: The girl you told me about? Ivy's sister? Go ahead and set it up.

CHAPTER THIRTY-EIGHT

EMMA

I finish cleaning up my centers and sit at my desk to prepare tomorrow's lesson plan. I look around my classroom, happy to be in a place I love. But I can't help feeling like something is missing. Maybe I'll never feel the same here after what happened last May.

As if I've been dropped back in that very nightmare, I hear a bloodcurdling scream and then people running in the hall. Kenny Lutwig's face clouds my vision. Is he back? Did he get released from jail and wants revenge on me for calling 911 from the storage closet?

I drop what I'm doing and hide under my desk. *Damn it.* My phone is in my purse in a drawer on the other side of the room.

Oh, God, my name is outside the door. And my door is unlocked. But I can't get myself to move. I'm frozen.

Someone opens my door and I tense as bile rises in my throat. "Emma?" a woman calls out.

I peek around my desk and see Lisa standing there. Then I hear faint sirens in the background.

"What's happening?" I ask, still shielding myself behind my heavy metal cover.

"Come quickly. It's Jordan. He's hurt."

"Is he shot?" I ask in confusion, wondering why she's standing in my doorway and not taking cover. "Where's the gunman?"

"Gunman? No, he fell down the stairs. He's bleeding badly. Becca was screaming for me to get you. She said you could help."

I finally come out from behind my desk, conflicting emotions of relief and alarm coursing through me. "Where is he?"

"In C hallway. Come on."

As we run over there, I ask, "Why did she think I could help?"

"Maybe because you helped that Carter kid when he was bleeding."

"I'm not the one who helped him, Lisa."

We turn the corner and I stop in my tracks, sickened by what I see. Jordan is lying on the floor at the bottom of the stairs. There's a pool of blood around his head, and he's convulsing.

"Somebody help him!" Becca screams.

I have no idea what to do, and neither does anyone else. I drop to the floor and try to stabilize his head so he doesn't get injured any further. The door at the end of the hall flies open and firefighters come through, one wheeling a gurney.

Brett won't be with them. I know his schedule, and he isn't working today.

"Move aside," one of them says.

"Can someone tell me what happened?" another asks.

Becca is sitting against the wall sobbing, her hands covered in Jordan's blood. "He f-fell. There were s-some papers on the floor at the top of the stairs. He slipped on them and tried to steady himself, but he was c-carrying all my stuff." She looks at her hands and screams. "Help him!"

"We're doing everything we can, ma'am."

The firefighters push everyone back, creating a perimeter in which the paramedics can work. They pull a bunch of medical equipment out of their bags.

Lisa stays on the floor with Becca while I try to see what's happening. They put a collar around his neck and open his eyelids.

"His left pupil is blown," one says.

"I'm losing his pulse," says another.

A paramedic puts his hands on Jordan's chest. "Starting CPR."

"What's happening?" Becca cries.

"I don't know," I lie. "They're trying to help him."

Jordan is lying lifeless, his blood all over the paramedics and floor. He bounces up and down with every chest compression. They have a bag over his mouth to force air into his lungs.

"I have a weak pulse," someone says. "Let's get him on the gurney."

They put him on a backboard and then lift him onto the gurney.

"Where are you taking him?" I ask.

"He needs a level-one trauma unit. We'll take him to Med across the bridge."

I motion to Becca. "She's his wife. Can she go with him?"

"I lost his pulse," someone says.

A woman climbs on top of the gurney and does CPR again.

Becca cries and gulps and looks sick. I take her in my arms.

One of the firefighters looks at Becca and then at me. "You'll have to get her there yourself," he says. "We need all hands on deck in the ambulance."

They wheel Jordan down the hall, leaving bloody footprints behind. I shield Becca from the scene, not wanting her to see the massive amount of blood on the hallway floor. "Come on," I say, walking her in the opposite direction. "We're going to the hospital."

~ ~ ~

Becca and I are in the waiting room. She doesn't want anyone to talk to her. She keeps looking at pictures of their honeymoon on her phone.

There are a dozen people here from work. The whole Taco Tuesday bunch. Our principal. Some of the school counselors.

I rub Becca's back, recalling how only a few weeks ago, she was doing the same for me.

An hour after we arrive, a doctor comes into the waiting room. "Mrs. Kincaid?"

Becca stands.

He motions to a door. "Can we speak in private?"

My heart sinks. That can't be good. If Jordan were okay, he'd just tell her right here, right now.

More tears roll down her face. She looks at me, terrified. "I can't."

I get up. "I'll go with you."

I realize she's about to get some bad news. I just don't know how bad. And none of her family is here. None of *his* family is here.

We're escorted into a small private room and asked to sit on a couch. The worst possible words come out of the doctor's mouth. Words like *brain death* and *organ donation*.

The doctor tries to comfort Becca, but she's hysterical. He calls in a nurse, who gives her a mild sedative. Then he leaves us with organ donation papers.

"I apologize," he says. "But there is only a small window of time. A decision has to be made soon."

Shortly after he exits the room, both sets of parents show up, and I have to watch them experience what Becca went through. It's the most devastating thing I've seen since the day my father died.

Becca leaves all decisions to Jordan's parents. She's practically a zombie after the sedative kicks in.

"We're going to take her home to White Plains," her mom says. "She needs to be with family."

"Is there anything I can do?" I ask, knowing full well there's not.

"You've done everything you can. Thank you for being here with her."

I give her my number. "I'll always be here for her," I say. "Day or night."

I find a bathroom and wash the blood off my hands, feeling sick all over again as I watch the water turn pink and swirl down the drain.

Lisa comes in behind me, mascara running down her face. "I can't believe it. One minute he's here, they're happy and married, and now she's walking out of here a widow. It's not fair."

I look at myself in the mirror. "I have to go home. I have to hug my daughter."

What if Evelyn fell down the stairs? What if my mother did? I make myself crazy thinking of everything that can go wrong in the world.

"Is there anything we can do for Becca?" Lisa asks.

I shake my head. "We can be here to offer her support. But it's going to take time. Lots and lots of time."

Maybe even more than nineteen years, I think.

When I arrive home, my mother sees me before Evelyn does. She's horror-struck when she sees the blood on my clothes. "Lord, what happened to you? You can't let Evie see you like this. Is that your blood? What happened? Do I need to call the police?" She drags me upstairs.

As soon as she shuts the bedroom door behind us, I break down in her arms, telling her everything that happened. When I finish crying, she takes me into my bathroom. "Get in the shower. I'll make you something hot."

Twenty minutes later, she's back with a cup of steaming chamomile tea.

"What did you tell Evelyn?" I ask.

"The truth. That one of your best friends lost her husband today, and you're very sad about it."

I sip the hot tea, then sit on the chair in the corner. "Oh, Mom. They were perfect together. And then he slipped and fell and now he's gone. Why did this happen?"

She sits on the arm of the chair and sighs. "Sweetie, you know better than anyone that there isn't an answer for that. Life happens. Death happens. And no matter how hard we try, we have no control over it. And it's useless to live our lives in a way that we think we can."

I know exactly what she's trying to say. I get up and go to the window, putting my palm against it. I look out into the street just as the streetlights come on. I gaze into Brett's house. Bonnie is playing with Leo.

"How can Brett survive a massive fire while Jordon dies walking down a hall?" I look at her. "Did I screw up?"

"No, sweetie, you didn't. You did what you thought was best for you and Evie. But it's nothing you can't fix. It's not too late. But one day, it will be." She crosses to my bedside table and touches the picture of my dad. "I wouldn't give up the time I had with your father for anything. Even if I had known what would happen to him, I still wouldn't change a thing. He was—is—the love of my life."

I go over to her and stare at his picture, and it's as if everything I ever thought or felt changes in an instant. Big tears escape my eyes. "I've been a terrible daughter."

"Nonsense. You're a wonderful daughter."

I shake my head. "Not to you. To Daddy. I've blamed him. All this time, I've blamed him for leaving me." I sit next to her on the bed. "I was so wrong, and I'm so, so sorry."

She wraps her arms around me. "Shh. It's okay. He knows you love him."

"How?" I say. "How can he know when I never go see him?"

"Oh honey, he knows. Believe me."

When I'm all cried out, I straighten and try to gain some resolve. "I was wrong about a lot of things," I say, looking over at my window.

She smiles at me. "I was wondering when you'd come to your senses."

I return to the window, then immediately hide behind the curtain when I see Brett on his front porch, talking with a woman. A woman who gives him flowers. *What kind of woman brings a man flowers?*

My forehead meets the wall as I curse myself.

"What's wrong, honey?"

"It looks like I may be too late."

She goes to the window and looks out.

"Mom!" I pull on her arm. "Don't stand there. He'll see you."

I run over and flip off the light, then look out the window again. Brett is dressed up in khakis and a button-down shirt, and the woman is wearing a pretty dress. Definitely a date. He stashes the flowers somewhere in his foyer and then waves to someone inside—Bonnie and Leo, I presume. Then he motions for the woman to lead the way down his front steps.

They stroll down the street, smiling and conversing comfortably. When she throws her head back in laughter, a spear goes through the center of my heart.

When they're out of sight, Mom grabs me by the shoulders. "You know what I would do in this situation?"

"Bake?"

She laughs. "Yes, but I was thinking more along the lines of a grand gesture."

"You don't think it's too late?" I ask.

She shakes her head. "No. I don't. Now, come downstairs and get a hug from your daughter. I think you need one after the day you've had."

I do what she says. And she was right. She was right about all of it.

So, for the rest of the night, I bake.

I bake for Evelyn.

I bake for Becca.

I bake for the grand gesture mom was talking about.

I just hope it's not too little, too late.

CHAPTER THIRTY-NINE

BRETT

"I forgot to ask you yesterday how your date with Holly went," Bass says.

I shrug. "Good, I guess. She's a lot of fun."

"Fun?" Justin wiggles his eyebrows. "I know what kind of fun can be had with Holly Greene."

I throw my breakfast bagel at him. "I didn't sleep with her, you tool."

"Why the hell not? You aren't still itching for that teacher who blew you off, are you?"

"Dude," Denver says, kicking Justin under the table. "Sometimes you need to know when to shut the hell up."

"Hey, speak of the devil," Bass says.

My eyes go wide when Bass nods his head to the door behind me. I turn around and see Emma standing there with two arms full of baskets. She looks at the floor and shuffles her feet. "I, uh, didn't know what to make, since you seemed to like it all, so I brought a little of everything."

I frown. "Are you talking to me?"

She nods.

"Hey, hey, hey," Justin says, going over to her. "Damn, girl, we sure have missed you around here."

"Justin, get over here," Denver chides. "Give them some space."

"What are you doing here?" I ask.

"Extending the olive branch. Or maybe the breadbasket."

"Emma, what does that mean? You want to be friends? Fine, we're friends." I take the baskets from her. "Thank you. I'll be sure to have the baskets returned to you."

"I just thought—"

"What did you think? That you could come around anytime you want a goddamn booty call? I'm not that guy. I never should have been that guy. Go back to Richie Rich in the Armani suit and sit around and have a safe fucking life together."

Captain Dickerson comes over the loudspeaker. "Squad 13, see me in my office before you leave today."

I nod to the back hallway. "I have to go. I'll make sure the guys get these."

I put the baskets on the table and walk away. A pin drop could be heard in the deafening silence. When I'm out of her sight, I lean against a wall, waiting to see what she'll do.

I hear the door to the garage open and close, and then the guys are talking about what just happened. Bass pokes his head around the corner. "Kind of harsh, wouldn't you say?"

"You mean harsh, as in finally accepting someone into your life, making them fall in love with you, and then dumping them?"

"Okay, I get your point. But she didn't leave. She's sitting on the bench across the street."

"It's a public bench," I say. "Now if you'll excuse me, I have to see the captain."

Turns out some paperwork was filed incorrectly about a call we went on last week, so me and the other guys from Squad have to clarify things. It takes longer than expected, which is fine by me. I'm not in any hurry to leave today.

I don't want to see her. I'm trying to move on. It's hard. Even with a girl as great as Holly Greene, who's pretty and funny and amazing by most standards. But no matter how hard I tried, I couldn't pull the trigger. Every time I looked at her, I wanted her to be Emma. Every time she touched me, I felt guilty, like I was cheating on Emma. Cheating on a woman I'm not even dating. But in my mind, the fact that I'm in love with her was enough to make me feel that way.

I take my time getting ready to leave. In fact, I'm the last one from my shift to go home. But when I exit the garages, I find I didn't take long enough. Emma is still sitting across the street.

I have two choices here. Ignore her or talk to her. I'm mad at her, but not mad enough to be a total douchebag. So I cross the street and stand in front of her.

"I deserved that," she says. "What you said to me in there. I deserved it."

I look at the ground. "Why are you here, Emma?"

"Did you hear about the call the other day? At my school?"

"Yes. Did you know him?"

She nods, looking like she's trying to hold back tears. "It was Jordan. Becca's husband."

"Oh, shit," I say, taking a seat on the bench next to her. "I'm sorry to hear that. They told me he pretty much died on the way to the hospital, but the doctors still tried for over an hour to revive him."

"It was horrible," she says, examining her hands. "There was so much blood."

"You were *there?*"

"Yes. And I felt completely helpless."

"There's nothing you could have done," I say. "There's nothing anyone could have done. Not even if a skilled physician were there when it happened. He was gone as soon as he hit the floor, Emma."

"I've done nothing but think about it for the last thirty-six hours," she says. "He wasn't doing anything dangerous. He was walking down a hallway and slipped and fell. How screwed up is that? One minute he and Becca were getting married and now she's planning his funeral. He was a *teacher*. He was supposed to be one of the safe ones. I can't help feeling I was wrong. That I've been wrong all along. About everything. I was so stupid. I just … I just …" She starts crying.

I want to take her hand so badly. I want to comfort her. But I don't. "It'll be okay."

"Can you let me finish?"

"Sorry. Go ahead."

"I …" She looks at me, tears streaking her mascara.

"You what?"

"I just … love you, that's all."

I'm not sure I heard her correctly. I narrow my eyes at her. "You what?"

"I … I love you, Brett."

I lean back. "That's what I thought you said."

"I tell you I love you, and that's all you're going to say?"

"What do you want me to say, Emma? As I recall, when I said the same thing to you, you walked out of my life."

"I was wrong to do that. This whole thing with Jordan was a wake-up call. I want to go back to how we were before any of that happened. Those were some of the happiest weeks of my life."

"But what about next time? Are you going to run out on me every time I have to go into a fire?"

Her eyes close, and she takes in a deep breath. "I'm not going to lie to you. It's going to be hard, but being without you was even harder."

"Yeah, I saw that, with all the dating you've been doing."

She looks guilty. "I don't know what to say. I was trying to get you out of my head. I didn't do anything with them, I swear. When I was with them, I wanted them to be you. I was a fool."

"I was trying to get you out of my head, too."

She nods. "I know. I saw you with that pretty woman with the flowers."

"I didn't do anything with her," I admit. "I couldn't."

"See? That proves it. We belong together."

Part of me is jumping up and down in joy. She's saying everything I've longed for her to say. But another part, the cautious part, is worried she's going to break my heart again. Break Leo's heart. Not to mention Evie's.

I get up, thinking it's just too easy for her to say she wants me back. I'm not convinced she means it. She's sad that Jordan died. She wants to feel better. That's all this is.

"I have a lot of thinking to do. I'm not about to jump into anything. I won't be your doormat again."

She sighs. "So that's it? Just like that you're tossing us aside?"

"About as easily as you did that day in the hospital."

"Don't do this, Brett. Please."

"How do I know you won't get spooked again? I can't take that chance."

"I won't get spooked, I promise."

"How can you make that promise after what you've already done?"

"I just know I can."

"How, Emma? How do you know?"

"Because I'm ready."

I run my hands through my hair in frustration. We've been through this before. "What are you ready for?"

She looks at me with tears in her eyes. "I'm ready to forgive my father."

Suddenly, everything changes. "You are? Are you sure?"

"I'm sure. I was wrong about him and about you. All of it."

I can't believe what I'm hearing. She wants to forgive her father. It's everything I've ever wanted for her. "Say it again."

She looks up at me, confused.

I take her hand and lean closer. "Say it again, Emma."

Her lips quiver. And then she says it. She says it, and my heart explodes. "I love you."

I pull her up and into my arms. "I love you, too."

I wipe away her tears, then I kiss her. I don't care who sees. I kiss her the way I love her—hard and with passion.

"Come home with me," she says. "I need you like I've never needed anyone."

We start walking, and everything looks different. The sun is higher in the sky. The people on the sidewalk are happier. The trees lining the street are greener. I may be six-foot-one and two hundred and ten pounds of pure muscle, but I feel like leaping in the air and clicking my damn heels together.

"Admit it," I say, wiggling my pinky finger. "What you really need is this."

She turns crimson.

I laugh. "Missed my dirty talk, did you?"

She pulls me along, walking faster. "I missed everything about you."

Neither of us can stop smiling. By the time we get to her bedroom, I'm so hard I can barely control myself. We rip each other's clothes off. I tell her all the things I want to do to her.

"I promise I'll never leave you again," she says when I climb on top of her.

"Move in with me," I say, wanting to get the most out of her promise.

"Wh-what?"

"You heard me."

"I can't do that, Brett. We just got back together."

"Are you going to leave me again?"

"No."

"Then what's the issue? If we're going to be together forever, you may as well move in with me."

"It's so sudden. I'm just not sure—"

"Not sure of what? How much you love me?"

She shakes her head. "No. I'm sure about that. It's just … it's a lot."

I stare her down and smile, wiggling my cock against her. "You know you want to."

"How would it work?" she asks. "I'm not saying yes, but there's my mom. And you have Bonnie."

"I've actually thought about this. I have a plan."

"You do?"

"Sure. What else did I have to do when I was sitting at my window, pining for you?"

She smiles smugly. "You were *pining* for me?"

I pinch her nipple, and she squeals. "You and Evie could move in with me and Leo, and Bonnie would move in with your mom. Evie could take Bonnie's room, and Enid could move into your old room, that way she'd just be a window away from Evie.

We'd still need a nanny, who'd be right across the street." I rub her belly. "You never know when we might need her for more than just Leo. We could all have dinner together twice a week. More if you want. But definitely on Sundays. Bonnie and Enid are already friends, and neither of them has a significant other, so it makes sense. We'd all live happily ever after as one big family. It would be perfect."

She rises on her elbows and stares at me with a slack jaw. "Wow. You really *have* thought this through. I'm not even sure I know what to say to all that."

"Say you'll think about it." I lean down and take her nipple into my mouth.

She arches into me. "I'll think about it."

"Good." I run my tongue down her body, across her stomach, and all the way to her warm, wet center. "Now don't mind me and my pinky as we do everything we can to convince you."

She moans as I get to work trying to convince her over and over and over again.

CHAPTER FORTY

EMMA

I'm nervous. I haven't been here in years. Even then, I wasn't here for *him*. My mom dragged me.

"I don't remember where it is," I say.

"That's okay. I know," Brett says, holding my hand.

"You do?"

He nods. "I might have said hi to your dad on a few occasions."

"Really?" I smile. "Thank you."

"He's right around the corner from my mom."

"Can we stop and see her too?"

"She's right up here."

We stand in front of the parapet that holds his mom's name, and I think of how much I would have liked to know her and how proud she would have been of her son.

I look around at all the people here, paying their respects. I know most of them are tourists. It makes me feel guilty that people who don't even know any of the fallen have come here to honor them when I haven't even made an effort.

"Are you ready?" he asks.

I thread my fingers through his. "Yes."

We walk along the wall, looking at the names. There are so many. Three hundred and forty-three firefighters lost their lives that day, but thousands more died as well. Thousands who, like Jordan did a few weeks ago, simply got up one morning and went to work like it was any other day. Thousands who had no idea it was the last morning with their husbands, wives, or children. Thousands who had jobs like bankers, lawyers, and insurance agents. Safe jobs, yet they died anyway. Just like Jordan. And I wonder if any of them had daughters like me who blamed them for leaving.

"Here we are," he says. He studies the single white rose wedged into my father's engraved name. "You didn't tell me today was his birthday."

Even though I haven't been here since the dedication, I'm aware of the white roses. Several years ago, a memorial worker started putting the flowers in the names of people who had birthdays that day. It was one more way to honor them.

"Why do you think I wanted to come today?" I ask.

"I was wondering why you wanted to wait a few weeks."

"I wanted to do it right. Give him a real birthday present."

"I have a feeling that getting your forgiveness is better than every Christmas and birthday present he'd ever gotten in his entire life."

I run my hand across his name, tracing every letter with my finger. "Do you think he knows I'm here?"

"I like to believe he does."

Tears flow down my face. "If he knows I'm here, he also knows I haven't been here for many years before now."

"I'm sure he understands, Emma." He drops my hand and backs away. "I'll sit on that bench and give you a minute."

I touch his name again. "I'm so sorry, Daddy. I thought I was coming here to forgive you for leaving me. But there is nothing to forgive. You didn't do anything wrong. I'm here because I need *you* to forgive *me*. Forgive me for blaming you all these years." I glance around at the vast memorial. "If it weren't for you, there would be a lot more names here. Because of you, a woman might be giving birth to her first child she never would have had, a couple might be celebrating an anniversary that never would have come, a father might be walking his daughter down the aisle at a wedding that never would have happened. Because of you, many people got to live. How can I be mad at you for that?"

I look over my shoulder at Brett, who gives me an encouraging smile. "I almost threw away one of the best things that ever happened to me. If you know everything, you know about Jordan. Becca told me last week that she wouldn't have given up a moment with him, even if she'd known what was going to happen. Mom says the same thing about you. I love him, Daddy. I'm scared, but I love him. If anything happens to him"—hot tears fall from my lower lashes—"maybe you could take care of him for me."

I stand here, letting the tears fall until I find my voice again. "Brett once told me that Evelyn is here because you're not. Do you think that's true? I wish you could meet her. She's just like you. Strong and feisty. You should have seen her in Germany. I've never been more proud."

I touch the soft petals of the rose. "Happy birthday, Daddy. I love you. And I hope you can forgive me. Do you forgive me?"

A gust of wind comes out of nowhere, blowing hair across my face. *Was that …?*

I turn around to see if Brett felt it, too. But he's no longer sitting on the bench. He's down on a knee looking up at me.

"What are you doing?"

He takes my hand in his. "I want to marry you."

I'm in shock. "We've only known each other for five months."

"You're going to let time dictate when we get our happily ever after? I knew Amanda for years before we got engaged. And now I understand why. It was because I didn't know. But with you, I swear I knew the first day we met. So why wait? Why waste another minute apart when we can be together? Life is short. We both know that. I want to leave lipstick messages for you every day. I want us to take Evie and Leo to Disney World. I want to cram as many memories as we can into whatever time we have left, whether that's fifty days or fifty years."

I try not to look, but it's hard not to notice the people gathering around. My hands shake. This is all happening so fast.

"I was here yesterday," Brett says, still down on his knee. "I stood right where you're standing and told your father I wanted to marry you."

I find it hard to control the flow of tears. "You asked my dad?"

He nods. "And then I asked your mom and Evie."

My eyes widen in surprise. "What did they say?"

He looks to my left. "You can ask them yourself."

I wipe my eyes to clear my vision. Mom and Evelyn are next to a tree, holding each other's hands. Evelyn looks about ready to jump out of her skin.

"Getting the two of them in this deal will be an amazing gift," he says. "I'll have a mom again. And Evie—I can't even begin to tell you how much I already love her. In fact, if you'll let me and she doesn't mind, I'd like to adopt her."

The waterworks start again when I realize he's going to give me everything I ever wanted.

He drops my hand to pull a ring out of his pocket. It's made of beautiful rose-gold with a perfectly round diamond. "Evie helped me pick it out. Sorry, this one doesn't crap Cheerios."

This man. I laugh through my tears.

"Emma Lockhart, will you marry me?" His eyes tear up. "You've already become my best friend. I'm asking you to up the game and become my life partner. The mother my child deserves. My happy ending. Maybe we can get married right here, so our parents can be there. I know you'll be sad that your dad can't walk you down the aisle, but maybe this is the next best thing. I have no idea if they will allow it, but I have a feeling if we put our heads together, there's nothing we can't accomplish." He holds the ring out to me. "I've always said when you know, you know. What do you say, Emma? Do you know?"

I can't help the smile that overtakes my face when I realize just how much I want this. I want everything he said. I want him to be the father of my child. My future children. I want to help him raise Leo. I want him to be my happy ending.

I turn and put my hand on my father's name. "I'm getting married, Daddy!"

Brett sweeps me into his arms and kisses me before slipping the ring on my finger. Bystanders clap and cheer as Evelyn runs over and hugs us both.

"Does this mean I get to call you Dad?" she asks.

Brett looks at me with raised brows, his eyes filled with hope.

"Yes," I tell her, my smile reaching all the way to my tear-blurred eyes. "That's exactly what it means."

EPILOGUE

BRETT

Twenty-five years later…

"Happy anniversary!" people shout as I walk my lovely bride onto the rooftop terrace.

Emma's hand covers her heart in surprise. "Brett, you didn't."

"I did, and this isn't the only surprise I have in store for you this evening."

We make our rounds, being sure to greet everyone. Bass and Denver are here with their wives. We've remained close friends over the years, even though we've all moved on to different firehouses. Leo is here with his wife and kids. Evie is here with her husband and daughter. Our son Billy and his fiancée showed up, despite the fact that they're getting married in just a few days. Even Jay is here, or should I say *Captain Tiffin* of Engine 58 in Lower Manhattan.

We are handed two glasses of champagne.

Billy grabs the microphone and takes center stage. "I'd like to make a toast to my parents. After twenty-five years of marriage, I can honestly say you are the best example of what love should be. I only hope Danielle and I are half as happy as the two of you. You've been through a lot, and it's only made you stronger. I know Evie and Leo will join me in thanking you for being the most amazing parents any kids could ever ask for. So, everyone raise a glass to Brett and Emma Cash."

"To Brett and Emma," the guests say, followed by "Speech! Speech!"

Billy hands me the microphone.

"I'll make this short and sweet. What can I say? Except that I ask myself every damn day what I ever did to deserve this woman. Here we are, on our silver anniversary, and I love her as much as the day we married."

I kiss Emma's temple. "Twenty-five years, sweetheart. Can you believe it?"

Tears pool in her eyes. "Yes, I can—because you always made me believe in us. And you better give me at least twenty-five more."

The guests cheer and music plays.

I pull Emma aside. "Would you change any of it?"

She runs a finger across the long jagged scar spanning my arm that put me in the hospital for a week shortly after Billy was born. "No way, you?"

I look at her breasts, thinking of the three enduring years she battled cancer. "Nope. Like our son said, everything we've been through together had made us stronger."

She leans in to kiss me. Even after twenty-five years, I still get hard every time her lips touch mine. She laughs when she feels the beginning of my erection.

"Are you ready to open your anniversary gift?" I ask.

"Here?"

"Why not?"

I pull an envelope out of my pocket and hand it to her. She eyes it curiously and then takes it from me. I watch as she opens the letter and reads, then looks at me in shock. "This is a letter of resignation. You're retiring?"

"Yup."

Her expressions zip through an emotional gamut, and I'm surprised when happiness is not one of them.

"Brett, you love working, and you're only fifty-five."

"Sweetheart, I thought you'd be pleased."

She takes my face in her hands. "Babe, we're not getting any younger. These twenty-five years have gone by in the blink of an eye. Retirement will come soon enough. I married Brett Cash, the man who would rather be out there fighting fires than doing anything else in the world. Every time you leave for work, you have a smile on your face. And every time you come home, the accomplishment and pride I see in you is palpable. You save people. You inspire them." I nod to our children. "And damn it if you weren't so inspiring that all three of our kids followed in your footsteps. So, no, I'm not happy about you retiring. You wouldn't be you if you weren't out there every day on the front lines, commanding your battalion." She rips the letter to shreds. "Someday we'll have to get used to a life without you doing that. But today is not that day."

"God, woman. Do you know how much I love you?"

She smiles. "Of course I do. I've known for over twenty-five years."

"Because when you know, you know," I say with a wink.

"That's right, Chief."

My eyebrows shoot up and I pull her close. "You know what it does to me when you call me that," I whisper.

I wonder how long we have to stay. Because I need my wife. I need to show her just how much I love her. In some ways, I've loved her all the way back to the storage closet where we first met.

I take a moment to appreciate what I have. I look at our three amazing kids and think about everything that had to happen to get us to where we are today. I gaze at my wife—my best friend, the love of my life—and think about what Emma's father said: *Everything happens for a reason.*

I spot Jay and know he is who he is today because of the loss of his father.

I am amazed at all the good that has come about from the sacrifices of others.

If my mom hadn't run inside that building to help, I never would have become a firefighter. If Kenny Lutwig hadn't shot Carter and held Emma at gunpoint, we'd have never met. If William Lockhart hadn't died that day, Evie wouldn't exist. Neither would Billy.

I close my eyes.

"What is it?" Emma asks.

"Nothing." I squeeze her hand. "It's just that there's so many people to thank for everything we have."

She gives me a little shove. "Well, go ahead. Thank them."

"I can't," I say, taking her into my arms. "Because the ones I really need to thank aren't here."

She looks into my eyes, understanding exactly what I mean.

Tears coat her lower lashes. "Thank you, Kenny Lutwig," she says.

I nod, swallowing my own tears. "Thanks, Mom."

Emma smiles and looks up at the sky. "Thank you, Daddy. You were right all along."

ACKNOWLEDGMENTS

Fifteen books.

Fifteen books!

I had to write it twice because I still can't believe it.

The past six years have been a wild ride to say the least. I never thought I'd be in a position to say I'd written fifteen books – there it is again!

They say it takes a village to write a book. Okay, they don't say that. But to me, my books are like my children and it *does* take a village to get them from conception to publication.

My village may be small, but it's mighty.

To my editors who have been with me since the beginning, Ann Peters and Jeannie Hinkle, thank you for your encouragement and endurance. Also, to my copy editor, LS at Murphy Rae Solutions—you've made me a better writer.

To my beta readers, Shauna Salley, Joelle Yates, Laura Conley, and Tammy Dixon—you ladies are so good at finding inconsistencies and misplaced quotation marks. And you're pretty good at inflating my ego as well.

And finally, thank you to Thomas Butler, former FDNY firefighter, who was a first responder on 9/11. I can only imagine what you and every other person there had to go through. I'm sure all my questions brought memories to the surface and yet you answered them without fail.

The anniversary of that horrific day is bittersweet for me. My son was born on September 11th. And 9/11 was the day he turned six. I'll never forget having to put on a happy face for my child, who remained blissfully unaware for years how cruel this world can be.

This book is dedicated to anyone touched by that day.

Which is everyone.

ABOUT THE AUTHOR

Samantha Christy's passion for writing started long before her first novel was published. Graduating from the University of Nebraska with a degree in Criminal Justice, she held the title of Computer Systems Analyst for The Supreme Court of Wisconsin and several major universities around the United States. Raised mainly in Indianapolis, she holds the Midwest and its homegrown values dear to her heart and upon the birth of her third child devoted herself to raising her family full time. While it took time to get from there to here, writing has remained her utmost passion and being a stay-at-home mom facilitated her ability to follow that dream. When she is not writing, she keeps busy cruising to every Caribbean island where ships sail. Samantha Christy currently resides in St. Augustine, Florida with her husband and four children.

You can reach Samantha Christy at any of these wonderful places:

Website: www.samanthachristy.com

Facebook: https://www.facebook.com/SamanthaChristyAuthor

Twitter: @SamLoves2Write

E-mail: samanthachristy@comcast.net

Made in the USA
Columbia, SC
12 December 2019